Helen M Cumberland

HELEN M CUMBERLAND
104 TALLOWAY COURT
SYKESVILLE, MD.
21784

D1564768

WARWYCK'S WOMAN

ROSALIND LAKER

Warwyck's Woman

78   216995

DOUBLEDAY & COMPANY, INC., GARDEN CITY, NEW YORK
1978

Library of Congress Cataloging in Publication Data

Øvstedal, Barbara.
Warwyck's woman.

I. Title.
PZ4.03War 1978   [PR6065.E9]   823'.9'14
ISBN: 0-385-13448-7
Library of Congress Catalog Card Number 77-82955

Chapter 1

In the midst of the bustle and the thronging crowd in the Brighton market place he did not see the arrival of the woman who was to be put up for auction. The wagonette flashed past at a spanking pace, the wheels careening on the cobbles as her husband drove her to the rear of the auctioneer's office to await the time of the sale. Daniel Warwyck, his tall hat at a rakish angle, had picked up and unfolded a map of Sussex from a stall and was holding it spread wide when the stall-holder at his side gave him a nudge.

"Look! There she goes! Farmer Farringdon's wife. She'll be sold to the highest bidder once all the cattle have gone under the hammer."

Daniel let one end of the map flap back onto the stall and with deliberation he brushed his sleeve where the man's elbow had jabbed him. He disliked being nudged. Had one of his opponents in the prize ring taken such a liberty he would have smashed his countenance to a pulp, but the stall-holder was half his size and twice his age, and for that alone had to be spared. Daniel himself was of a superb height and build with hair glossy and black, brows straight over shrewd gray eyes in a square face, a nose long and bold, and a jaw ruthless and unpredictable. Not a man to be trifled with under any circumstances. The stall-holder, excited by the unusual event that was shortly to take place and ignorant of his own lucky escape, snatched up the fallen corner of the map and prodded it with a bony finger.

"There's Farringdon Farm in Uckfield. That's where she's come from today. How's that for detail? You won't find a map better than this 'un to show you the woods and rivers and roads as well as every town and village and hamlet in the county."

Daniel needed no pressure to buy, having already decided to purchase the map, and he jerked it irritably from the fellow's hand. "I thought the old custom among country folk of a man selling his wife had died out long ago."

"It still happens sometimes. There's many what don't approve, but how else can a man rid himself of an unwanted spouse?"

Daniel gave a nod, threw a sixpence down onto the stall as payment for the map and moved away, folding it up and slotting it into his pocket. With coattails swinging and high boots gleaming he sauntered deeper into the market. The stalls were doing a lively trade, the vendors shouting out their wares. Fish were slapped onto scales, old clothes were raked over and held up for size, fruit and vegetables were tipped into shopping baskets, and nosegays of flowers changed hands at twopence a time. There were displays of bric-a-brac and china fairings, stacks of farming implements, arrays of new-baked loaves and gingerbread, pies and hams and pudding ready for the pot as well as every kind of locally made merchandise from trugs and chairs to shrimping nets. All around were ancient buildings, squat under low roofs of thatch or slate, the flint walls rimed with sea salt, the colors muted and dark. In a far corner where the auction of livestock was in full swing a grimy-windowed tavern was conveniently situated for those who found bidding or selling thirsty work.

Before long Daniel's good humor had returned. It was always satisfying to escape his trainer's watchful eye whenever the chance came along, and old Jem, who had had him jogging the length of the seashore that morning before the tide came in, would fume over his failure to appear on the dot for a sparring session in the ring, particularly when the use of it had to be paid for at exorbitant prices, the rooms having been opened for the benefit of gentlemen of quality who liked to spar for amusement and not for common pugilists with a mill in the immediate offing. It would be difficult to convince Jem that he had taken a wrong turning in a maze of lanes and ended up passing an hour or two innocently at a market; he would be accused of being up to much more, but for once he could deny both women and liquor with perfect truth. Not that opportunity was lacking, for apart from the open tavern he was receiving more than his fair share of flickering female glances as he strolled along, the more comely receiving a dancing glint in return. None of them realized who he was, but occasionally men in the crowd, members of The Fancy as any follower of the world of pugilism was called, whatever his station in life, would stare in puzzled recognition until enlightenment dawned or a swift glance at one of the recently posted bills on the walls displaying Daniel's likeness confirmed that he was the renowned pugilist who was shortly to meet a fighter of equal repute, Slash Higgens, in a bare-knuckle mill at Deane Dell, situated south of Brighton's race hill on the Downs at noon the following day.

Suddenly there was a commotion near at hand and again Daniel heard the name of Farringdon. He found himself caught up with those drawing back to make a path for a hefty, stout-bellied man with a high, choleric coloring in his mid-fifties, who came striding purposefully along, swinging the knobbled cane he held as if he would use it across the ankles of anyone who blocked his way. His untrimmed brows jutted like bushes over pouchy eyes that showed an arrogant displeasure at being the focus of so much attention, and he breathed heavily as he went past, the heat of the day and the inevitable strain of the proceedings making the sweat trickle profusely down his face. In his wake people crowded forward and they jostled after him as far as the tavern door where the landlord barred their way long enough for the farmer to take the stairs to an upper room.

Daniel, spurred by curiosity, turned with anticipation toward the sale ring, welcoming the unusual diversion it was about to provide. The crowd was dense around the sawdust-covered sale ring, but gradually as people came and went he was able to move forward and secure a place for himself at the rails.

Some furniture was being disposed of, the contents of a house seized by the bailiffs, and afterward a few horses were put up for sale, all the cattle having already gone under the hammer. Daniel had an eye for good horseflesh, having grown up in a house where fine horses had been his parsimonious uncle's one extravagance, and although a chestnut colt of considerable promise went for a low price he made no attempt to top the bidding, having no need of it. As the colt was led away the auctioneer signaled to one of his assistants, who ran to fetch out a wooden tub, which he rolled on its side into the middle of the sale ring and there set it upside down. Instantly a ripple of excitement passed through the crowd. The moment had come. The woman was about to be auctioned. Around Daniel the talk among the men became ribald, accompanied by coarse guffaws, and even the womenfolk showed little sympathy for the sale wife about to face the ignominy of being disposed of at the same level as the livestock. A terrible kind of carnival spirit began to prevail and Daniel in his present amiable mood felt at one with it and those who jeered.

"I wager she had the tongue of a shrew," was one of the less offensive remarks uttered phlegmatically by one man in his hearing to a companion. "I hear she's docile-looking, but those are the ones who can be the very devil."

"Aye," came the reply. "No man gets rid of a wife without good reason and it's always for something worse than burning the Sunday drip pudding." They both laughed.

"I ain't sighted her yet," complained a short, fat girl, who was standing on tiptoe and craning her neck to try to see around people.

"You'll see 'er soon enough when they set 'er up for selling," declared a woman with her, "and let's 'ope they ain't too longwinded about it. Old customs like this are frowned on by the beaks."

"Ain't it legal?"

The woman snorted impatiently. "Of course it is. Nobody's breaking the law by it, but there's always church folk and other interfering busybodies who take 'igh-'anded notions about what should and shouldn't be done nowadays."

Daniel knew that well enough. A complaint lodged with a magistrate could prevent a prize fight taking place or stop one in midstream, making the combatants, referee, umpires, and all the spectators pack up and move to another area, often a distance of many miles away to escape that particular jurisdiction. Damnation to all in authority who interfered with an Englishman's rights to put up his fists in a prize ring or to get rid of a cantankerous wife by a country method ancient as time!

There was a stir in the crowd. People jostled each other for a better view as word spread that the sale wife had reached the gate through which cattle were admitted into the sale ring. When it was seen that the same assistant who had dealt with the tub was going to fetch her into it the questions flew in all directions.

"Why is he doing it? Where's her husband? It ain't nobody's duty but the husband to lead her around, and it's real cowardly to get out of it. It don't matter a tinker's cuss if he isn't in the best of health—he should do it. Where *is* Farmer Farringdon?"

"Up there!" A single pointing finger shot upward in the direction of one of the latticed windows of the tavern, and in a wave of movement every head in the throng looked upward to observe the man who sat there, having secured a grandstand view for himself of the sale ring below. Becoming the object of so much combined notice pleased him no more than the earlier attention he had received, and he reached out sharply to jerk the window almost closed, the reflection on the panes throwing back the sunlight and acting like a screen to hide him. But already the spectators' interest was diverted.

"There she is!" The murmur went up from those nearest the cattle gate, reminding Daniel of the moment at a public hanging when the condemned wretch emerged to mount the scaffold before the masses who gathered on such occasions. Then he saw the sale wife for himself and hardened though he was to brutal sights he experienced a sense of shock at her degradation, which had nothing to do with her being much younger than he or the rest of the crowd had expected. She was being led by a halter round her neck, the end of the rope being held by the assistant, an uncouth, rough-haired fellow who grinned widely as he strutted around the ring a few feet ahead of her. The auctioneer was less happy about the task in hand, mopping his brow under his pushed-back hat and easing his neckerchief with a finger. The young Mrs. Farringdon showed no such embarrassment. Walking straight-backed with a proud carriage to her head, a languor in her light blue eyes, her expression detached and chilly.

"Ain't she sour-faced," remarked the fat girl contemptuously.

"Matching 'er nature, no doubt," sniggered her friend.

What the sale wife's figure was like it was impossible to judge, for she wore an outmoded, high-waisted dress of faded red check wool, which hung straight as a sack, her shoulders and bodice enveloped in a fringed black shawl folded thickly into a triangle and worn crossed over the chest. Her hair was equally well concealed, every strand tucked out of sight within a frilled white cap over which she wore a gray cotton sunbonnet, but that her tresses were fair-colored was indicated by the pale, winged brows and the silvery-light lashes. Her features were chiseled into cool, classic lines, the nose straight, the forehead and cheekbones wide, well balanced by the firm jawline with its pointed chin, and although the upper lip was deeply indented it presently lacked any curve due to the compression of her mouth. As the parading around the ring finished and she stepped up on the tub, the end of the rope dropped to hang from the halter to the sawdust-covered cobbles, Daniel saw clearly that it was not sourness that stamped her features, but complete contempt for the proceedings that were about to take place.

"Your attention, please," bellowed the auctioneer after clearing his throat twice. "We have come to the last item of sale today. On behalf of Mr. Jervis Farringdon I'm putting up for auction this twenty-three-year-old woman named Kate, his legal spouse of four years, who has expressed herself willing to go to the highest bidder. Now, gentlemen, let me have your bids."

"Tuppence!" bawled a self-styled wit from a far section of the crowd, causing a rise of amusement. "Or a pint of gin!"

"One chicken!" shouted some other yokel, taking up the joke. "Plucked for the oven!"

"A sack of flour!"

"A dozen eggs—bad 'uns!"

"One pair of me worn-out boots!"

The noise was getting out of hand, and the auctioneer, sweating profusely over what was to him a thoroughly unpleasant task, sought to restore the order and respect that he normally commanded at cattle auctions and other markets. Holding up both hands widespread he appealed for silence, but nobody was in the mood to listen, there being something about the young woman's poise and aloofness that had succeeded in rousing the crowd to the kind of mob vindictiveness that would come to the fore at a baiting or a whipping or when there was a helpless victim in the stocks. Without being aware of it the men present took her indifference and lack of humbleness as a personal affront to their rightful dominance, and the women, at least those with domestic burdens and problems of their own to weigh them down, knew envy of her self-assurance and dignity, and it brought out a kind of angry spite in them. Only a few folk felt compassion and showed it by moving away from the spectacle, shaking their heads. Daniel, sickened by the scene, turned to find himself hemmed in by many more people who had jammed the narrow spaces between the stalls. Even as he began to push a path through for himself a single serious bid for Kate Farringdon was shouted out, which reduced the clamor of the crowd to such an extent that even those on the outskirts fell silent to strain their ears and catch what was happening.

"Three guineas! I said three guineas!"

Daniel abandoned all thought of leaving the market place. He knew that voice! It was his own nineteen-year-old brother who had made that bid! The sentimental young fool had stepped in to put a stop to the taunting, but unless he withdrew it there was every chance of his being landed with the wench! Swiveling round in the crush Daniel began to shoulder his way determinedly in the direction from which Harry Warwyck had made himself heard.

The auctioneer had taken over in relief. "A good starter, sir," he acknowledged, with a grateful nod toward Harry somewhere near the tavern steps, and addressed the crowd once more. "I'm bid three guineas. Let me hear four, gentlemen."

"Four!" It was a butcher from one of the stalls, smelling of meat and blood, his straw hat as stained as his apron.

"Five!" Another man this time, a soberly dressed fellow with hard, calculating eyes.

"Six!" It was the butcher again.

"Eight!" An accented voice cut across any interceding sum and a new spurt of excited interest gripped the crowd. The latest bidder was a foreigner with a seafaring look about him, recognized as a Frenchie from one of the packets that plied between Brighton and Dieppe. Kate had not glanced in any bidder's direction and neither did she look toward him. She could have been a snow queen in a remote winter palace, looking out on the world unseeingly through its ice walls.

"Nine!" It was Harry again. Daniel, who had let some of his concern ebb from him at the higher bid, thinking his brother's danger was past, knew explosive exasperation at such folly. Didn't Harry realize there was no need to continue?

"Ten!" The Frenchman was not going to give up. But neither was Harry.

"El—" Before he could get his bid out Daniel had reached him, grabbing down the arm he was raising to signal the auctioneer, and twisting him about to thud his back against the tavern wall.

"Are you out of your mind? Let the bidding be! You don't want to find yourself liable for her!"

Harry's face was set in determination and showed his resentment at the interference. His jaw clenched. "That's exactly what I do want. Keep out of this business! It's my affair!" He jerked himself from Daniel's clasp and shouted to the auctioneer. "Eleven guineas!"

"You're crazy!" Daniel roared, giving him a shove in the shoulder with a clenched fist. "Keep your mouth shut, for God's sake! You're not dry behind the ears yet! It's madness to think of saddling yourself with a woman—let alone one older than yourself. You don't earn enough to keep her in food and you never will with your lack of ambition in life!"

Harry, usually slow to anger, showed its crescent rise in a whitening about the mouth and a gathering together of brows. In a crisp and deadly tone he answered with a phrase from Daniel's own sporting slang. "I fancy her."

"Huh!" Daniel exploded mirthlessly. "You are already out of your depth with the bidding. I happen to know you have no more than twenty guineas to your name and half of that you owe to Jem."

"I mean to have her," Harry answered through hard, tight lips. Then, the Frenchman having increased his figure by another guinea, he caught the auctioneer's eye and mouthed, "Thirteen."

Daniel, who felt keenly responsible for his brother, seized him by the arms as if to shake some sense into him. "Listen to me! Buying her doesn't make her yours!" He jerked his head in acknowledgment of an unspoken point. "Oh, I know if you were a farm laborer or some other Johnny Raw the country community of a hamlet or village would recognize her as your wife through this archaic procedure, and think none the worse of either of you for it. But it wouldn't hold water legally! This old custom today is being played out for the farce that it is! A way of getting rid of a difficult wife that has been handed down through the centuries, but can't be recognized as divorce. By the law of the land she is bound to her rightful husband until death does them part! She would never be anything to you but a liability—her status ever in limbo! Neither maid, wife, nor widow!"

"That's nothing to do with you."

"It's everything to do with me." Daniel, all patience gone, wrenched him forward and slammed him back against the tavern wall. "Even if you were not my brother you would still be in my employ and subject to my rules. I'll remind you it was your choice to run away from home to join me, and a fine sight you were when you arrived at my door with your shoes worn through and you half-starved. You didn't even have the wits to steal a loaf of bread to help you on your way."

"You left Warwyck Manor when you wanted to!" Bitterly. Old jealousies on Harry's part and resentments previously unspoken by Daniel were searing forth.

"I was set on the prize ring and black-listed for it anyway, but you were to be our uncle's heir instead of me. You threw that chance away and now you want to ruin any future of worth through a second folly."

With wild defiance Harry threw up his hands and broke Daniel's hold. "Why should I have stayed on at Warwyck Manor? I hated living there on sufferance with Uncle William as much as you ever did."

"You had no right to leave the way open for the family house and lands to be bequeathed to outsiders by a bigoted old man!"

"I had as much right as you!"

Brother glared at brother. The auctioneer's voice repeating the most recent bid broke through to them.

"Thirteen guineas I'm bid, gentlemen. Is this fine young woman to fetch so low a price? Come, come. Let me hear fourteen."

Daniel saw that he and Harry had become the full center of attention, all eyes in the crowd turned toward the place where they stood under the overhang of the tavern, and there was an atmosphere of expectancy in the air that was almost palpable. The auctioneer's hot, sweaty face from his place of vantage hung like a crimson moon, his eyebrows raised inquiringly as his gaze slowly swept all present. The Frenchman had made no further bid! Harry's thirteen guineas were hanging in the balance, either to be topped by some last-minute bidder, or to be sealed as the purchase price with a bang of the hammer.

Harry's face slowly became jubilant as the passing seconds brought no other offer. Kate Farringdon with her strange, cool aura of mystery was to be knocked down to him! With a single swing of his body he moved away from his brother, asserting his right to make independent decisions, and set his feet firmly apart, practically rocking in triumph on his heels, while at the same time he flicked with his thumbnail the brim of his tall hat to set it at a more rakish angle on his head.

"For the last time of asking," boomed the auctioneer, raising his hammer. "Any advance on thirteen guineas?"

Daniel, despairing at his younger brother's folly, looked again at Kate Farringdon, puzzled to know what it was about her that attracted the lad and could only conclude that she had aroused the strong protective streak that ran in his veins. She looked dull, respectable, and unexciting—just the sort of wife he himself should have on his arm on the trip home to Devonshire arranged for next week if he wanted a trump card to play in showing that he had settled down and the prize ring had not brought him to the ruination of his life and the damnation of his soul as Uncle William had predicted. The idea flickered and flared. What did a little deceit over a woman matter when there was so much at stake? Otherwise his own inability to give an inch in the matter of pride would lose him what he wanted desperately to save. Within his grasp he had the means to free Harry from his headstrong foolishness and secure his own ends.

The auctioneer raised his hammer high in readiness to crack it down. "At thirteen guineas. Going—"

"Twenty-one guineas!" Daniel called.

A gasp went up from the crowd and a groan from Harry. Even Kate moved her head for the first time and looked toward the new bidder, the mask of her face stirred by surprise and then settling into immobility again.

The auctioneer, his commission having taken an astonishing increase, looked hopefully at Harry, but one look at the agonized disappointment registered on the young man's features was enough to tell him the auction was at its end. He raised his hammer once more. "Twenty-one guineas for Kate Farringdon! Going, going—gone!"

As Daniel reached into a high inner pocket of his coat to take out the purse of money he carried there Harry, his eyes glittering with the abnormally strong rage of the self-controlled brought to flashpoint, grabbed him by a fistful of sleeve, straining the fine broadcloth.

"Why?" he demanded through clenched teeth. "When you knew I—knew I—" His voice suddenly cracked horribly, much as it had done when it had first broken, and he knew himself to be on the humiliating brink of tears, something he had not experienced since boyhood.

"She can be useful to me," Daniel answered evenly. He did not add the old platitude that one day Harry would thank him for his intervention, but he thought it. "Trust my judgment. I'll explain my reasons later."

It should have been some consolation to Harry that Daniel had not bought Kate out of lust, love, or desire; simply for some cold-blooded purpose of his own, but his disappointment was too intense, his anguish too savage for him to find any comfort in his brother's words. He had looked at Kate and fallen in love with the whole of his impulsive, vulnerable heart, seeing something in her that he was basically too inexperienced to recognize: a reserve that covered depths full of promise, impossible to divine upon the surface, but lying there to be explored and brought to light should any man discover a way to break through the barrier she had set up around herself.

Daniel, whose lack of personal interest in Kate had enabled him to see no further than the image of respectability she would present to his uncle, went back to the rails of the sale ring to climb over and jump down into it. Among the dispersing crowd some men, who had recognized him, stayed to give him a clap and a cheer, shouting out encouragement.

"Well done, Warwyck! May you win the mill tomorrow as you have won a wife for yourself today!"

Almost through force of habit he acknowledged their good wishes with a grin and the raised fist of victory, but he was preoccupied with the present business, hoping his purchase would prove a profitable investment and not merely a liability and a waste of money. He paid over the gold pieces to the auctioneer and only then, with the receipt in his pocket, did he turn to claim the young woman.

She had stepped down from the tub, but had made no other move, the halter rope still trailing from her neck, for by the old custom it was his right as purchaser to remove it. Her gaze on him was level and direct, her expression calm, and her lips, still composed and under control, had nevertheless relaxed from their thin white line into a firm and generous fullness.

"Allow me to present myself, ma'am," he said formally to her. "I am Daniel Warwyck."

"Sir." She inclined her head stiffly in acknowledgment and then, ignoring the fact that her name had been shouted out several times during the auction for all to hear, added in her low-timbred voice, "My name is Kate Farringdon."

"Your most obedient servant, ma'am. In such circumstances as we find ourselves I intend to address you by your Christian name from this time forward and you may adopt the surname of Warwyck." He reached out and with both hands lifted the halter from her to hurl it away in revulsion. She breathed an almost inaudible sigh of relief, but in no way did her expression change.

Formalities over, he became practical. "Have you any baggage?"

She nodded and would have picked up a carpetbag at the back of the auctioneer's desk, obviously expecting to carry things for herself, but Daniel forestalled her, taking hold of the handle and swinging it up easily. It was not heavy.

"Shall we go?" he said, indicating the route they should take to leave the market place.

Obediently but not meekly she fell into step beside him. As they went Daniel looked about for Harry, but there was no sign of him. Only a few people turned heads to watch the two of them depart. The auctioneer had already disappeared into the tavern, and the open window from which Farmer Farringdon had watched the proceedings had been closed tight again. Kate did not give it as much as a glance.

"I was told you are from Uckfield, Kate. Is that correct?" Daniel asked, looking sideways at her as they walked along. She was taller than he had realized, not matching his height, but above average for a woman, her eyes on a level with his shoulder. There was a freedom to her movements as though she walked unhampered by her thick dress and petticoats, but it was not ungainliness or with any tendency to stride, more a natural buoyancy of step.

"Since my marriage I have lived there, but I was born in the nearby village of Heathfield and that's where I grew up. Both my parents are dead."

Her speaking voice continued to surprise him. No country twang marred it and yet it held a certain local intonation that was not unattractive. With the Englishman's ability to pinpoint the social status of his fellow countrymen from the moment a mouth was opened, he judged her to be the moderately educated offspring of a gentlewoman reduced to genteel poverty, which must have been why she had to allow her daughter to marry an uncouth farmer.

"Have you any other family?" he inquired. "Brothers? Sisters?"

"Nobody closer than a cousin who lives many miles away." She shot him an incurious glance. "What of you?"

"It was my younger brother, Harry, who opened the serious bidding for you. We have a sister named Jasmine, whom we call Jassy. She lives in Devonshire with the only relative we have, Uncle William Warwyck. I'll be taking you there when we leave Brighton shortly."

"Oh?" She gave a calm little shrug that came close to resignation. "As long as I never have to see Uckfield or Farringdon Farm again I don't mind where I go." Her tone was firm but not embittered.

"I can promise you that."

Her lids with their edging of silver-gilt lashes closed together briefly as though inwardly she mocked all promises, relying on no one but herself, and she made no reply. He spoke again.

"Did you work hard at the farm?"

"No. If I had been able to toil in the fields it would have suited me. Physical tiredness can keep mental fatigue at bay. I was kept like a cat on a cushion." A flash of wry humor showed through. "But without the cream."

She was, he decided, an odd young woman. Curiously matter-of-fact on the surface, and at the same time wholly guarded and restrained, making him feel that the few scraps she had given him about herself could be all he would ever learn. And yet there was a wealth of untold information behind everything she said, whole stories in themselves, that had merged into a single path leading to the most degrading of all experiences: sale by public auction. But somehow it had not touched her. Her dignity had turned the sordidness back onto those who had watched the spectacle, not least of all her husband, and even upon those who had made the bidding for her.

Faintly uncomfortable with his purchase, he said, "In some ways but not in others our lives have been on a par. When not in the prize ring I'm pampered to a certain extent, my trainer's aim being to bring me to the peak of fitness, albeit his ideas for my well-being are not my choice, but I can let off steam when we spar and the physical tiredness that you have craved is all too familiar to me after a long bout."

"Is that how you received that new scar on your cheek?"

"Yes—in my most recent fight."

"Did you win?"

"I did."

She was silent for a few moments. "You were reckless in your bidding at the auction. Twenty-one guineas out of a prize purse was a wicked amount of money."

"I had to go above the highest figure my brother could proffer."

"Oh." A pause. "Is he a boxer too?"

"No, he's my second and bottle holder, as well as being a Jack-of-all-trades in the way of looking after my horses, running errands, and helping my trainer arrange bouts and in other matters. Yet he should aim higher than the fringe of the milling world. At the present time he is content to take life as it comes, frequently in debt and idle when it suits him. It is sheer laziness, because he has a brain above the average and a remarkable intelligence. What is more, people like him. He has what is known as charm." Daniel spoke the last word on an ironic note.

Whilst talking they had left the market place behind and followed a narrow twitten, which had brought them out into one of the narrow lanes with a distant glimpse of the sea. She halted, catching her breath at the sight of it, her whole face blooming, all the chilliness gone from it like snow before the sun.

"The sea!" she exclaimed on a warm, vibrating note of which he would previously have deemed her incapable. "There it is! Mercy! Is it not magnificent?"

He watched her. There was something childlike and innocent in her reaction. "Have you never seen the sea before?"

She shook her head, still lost in wonderment. "Until this day when Mr. Farringdon brought me to Brighton by way of a country road I've never traveled farther than a few miles from my birthplace and then the farm. Is it possible to see France from here?"

"One must go towards Dover to catch the French shores through a spyglass. Would you like to walk down onto the beach and take a closer look at the English Channel?"

She clasped her long-fingered hands together. "I would!"

It did not take them long to reach the parade where they took some steps down onto the shingle. There she kicked off her heavy country shoes and ran lightly down the sands in her stockinged feet, her skirts billowing, her shawl fringe dancing. She was making for the water's edge where the gently rippling waves were spreading out like fans before withdrawing again, leaving the surface wet and shiny. He sat down on a large piece of barnacled driftwood to wait, resting his arms on his knees, the carpetbag set down on the shingle beside him, and followed her with his eyes.

She reached the water's edge and was glad she was alone to savor this first experience of meeting the sea. It was said to have healing properties, and she could believe it, even if it only brought tranquillity to the mind and to the soul through contemplation of its living color and eternal movement. On this warm day it was predominantly turquoise with sun diamonds riding on the waves, which broke in curves with a plash of foam and sent in the wavelets to within an inch of her toes. Cautiously she gathered her hems up an inch or two and stepped forward into them, gasping a little at the unexpected coldness. But it was not unpleasant, she thought. Quite definitely the opposite. Hoisting her skirt hems still higher she waded forward until the water swirled over and around her ankles, dyeing her darned stockings to a darker hue, and with its ebb it drew away the grains of sand from about her feet with a little tickling sensation.

A laugh rose in her throat of its own accord. She, who thought she had forgotten mirth and happiness, gave herself up to a rich, deep peal of joyous laughter that was an exuberant acclamation of the beauty of the day and the sea and her own release from a dark and terrible period in her life that she longed to forget. That she was experiencing an illusory sense of freedom she knew well enough, but for the moment the real truth could be put aside. Later she must accept whatever the hard-eyed Daniel Warwyck had in store for her. Later she must doubtless come again to terms with another of fate's devious tricks. But for this brief, private spell of oneness with the sea and the clean, salty air she was like a bird in flight. Soaring, soaring, soaring!

He thought he had heard her laugh, but he could not be sure. The seagulls wheeling overhead had not ceased their endless, raucous cries, the sound mingling with the shouts of the fishermen on the beach close at hand, who were offering lobsters, crabs, mussels and winkles and other shellfish for sale to passers-by. But when she made her way back up the sands, her pace slower than when she had run down them, her face set as before in its serious, perfectly composed expression, full of locked secrets, he decided that his ears had deceived him. Standing up, he waited while she slipped her wet, stockinged feet into her shoes, and then started up the shingle, she coming along behind.

"Did the sea live up to your expectations?" he asked over his shoulder.

Her lips moved, but did not actually form a smile. "It did indeed. When we are in Devonshire shall we be on the coast?" Having formed that affinity with the sea she did not wish to lose it, but his answer brought disappointment and surprise.

"No. Warwyck Manor lies inland."

Her eyes had widened slightly. "Is that your home? It sounds grand. But how can you be gentry when you mill for a living?"

He looked amused. "A good question indeed. Actually Warwyck Manor sounds a deal grander than it is, but it is a handsome old house and has been in the family for a long time. Uncle William took my mother in after my father, a gaming man, had a pauper's funeral, and she died five months later giving birth to my sister Jassy. Being a bachelor set in his ways, he was less than pleased to have three children to bring up, but I was his heir and he had to see that I received an adequate education." He gave a reminiscent shrug as he led the way to a seaweed-covered flight of steps up from the beach. "I was always in trouble, up to some prank or another in constant defiance. He must have had little hope of my being suited to inherit from the start, because instead of sending me away to school he hired a tutor to make sure that Harry received the same amount of knowledge without involving further expense. Later Jassy had a place in the schoolroom with us."

"Was your uncle so miserly?"

"That troubled us less than his viciousness. He had never liked my father and he made us pay the price. When I was fourteen I almost killed him for keeping Jassy shut in a dark cupboard for two days. Things were better for her after that, but he never forgave me. It was the final straw when I left for the prize ring with Jem, my trainer."

"How did you meet Jem?" She was ascending the flight after him.

"He had retired from the prize ring after an opponent gouged out his right eye, and he came to work at Warwyck Manor about the time my mother died. He taught me to put up my fists and gave me a means of making my own way in the world."

He had reached the top of the flight and waited for her to draw level with him, but she halted on the third tread down from him, the breeze playing with the frill of her uncomely cap and flicking her bonnet strings.

"If your uncle finished with you when you left home, why are you returning?"

He reached out a hand and assisted her up the remaining steps onto the parade. "It is best you know at once the reason why I bid for you at the auction. I plan to reinstate myself as my uncle's heir. I cannot in all conscience let the property pass out of War-wyck hands. Believe me, I want none of it for myself, associating it with nothing but unhappiness, but Jassy has written that Uncle William is not long for this world. He was taken ill after Harry left home a year ago and a nurse installed in the house at the time has been there ever since, although he did recover his health for a short while. Now he has been failing fast and has asked to see me, a newly drawn up will awaiting his signature. I'm determined my name shall be on it and you are to make it appear that I have married suitably and settled down."

Her cheeks hollowed and her eyes shadowed, but she faced him squarely. "Your uncle will know I'm not a lady born."

He guessed her to be nervous at the prospect of being presented to someone she imagined to be more lordly than he was and in surroundings of a grandeur that would awe her.

"You have dignity and a quiet presence," he reassured her, "and that will please him. He distrusts and dislikes any flamboyancy in appearance, clothes, or manners. I'm sure you'll more than fulfill the purpose for which I purchased you."

Outwardly she did not quail before the sharp edge of cruelty in his words, which had not been entirely unintended, for he wanted her to accept without any illusions the role she was to play. Her chiseled features became inflexible and she spoke icily. "It shouldn't be difficult to deceive an ailing old man on his deathbed."

His forehead contracted and he clamped his lips together. She had cut him down to size! Much more of that and he'd turn her off to fend for herself without a penny! Any scruples he had had toward his treatment of others had been discarded long ago and there would be none to hamper him now. Perhaps he was catching a first glimpse of the vixenish side to her character that had driven Farmer Farringdon to rid himself of the millstone round his neck. "Come along," he said abruptly. "I'll take you to the hotel where I'm staying. You'll want to change those wet stockings."

He set off at a swift pace and she had to hurry to keep up with him.

Chapter 2

At The Old Ship Hotel, Daniel was able to secure a bedroom for her on the same floor as his own rooms. Priority was given to his request, for the place was packed out, as the town was crammed with those who had come from far afield for the prize fight on the morrow, swelling the normal number of visitors. When Kate saw the single bed she seemed enervated by a private relief, and momentarily some of the straightness of spine ebbed from her. Resolutely setting her shoulders again she crossed to the open window and looked out at the sea with drawn features as if she sought to take balm from it. Again he wondered about her relationship with her husband. As he had heard someone remark in the market place, it was for more than burning the Sunday drip pudding that a man got rid of his wife.

"I think you should be comfortable here," he said. "Ring for bath water or anything else you want."

"I've never stayed in an hotel before!" she cried in near panic, swinging round to him.

"You had some domestic staff at Farringdon Farm, didn't you?" he asked, surprised.

She nodded, clasping and unclasping her hands nervously. "Four houseservants, a cook, and a scullery boy."

"Then you'll find it no different telling those who wait upon you here what to do." He relented slightly. "If you would prefer it we can dine privately in my rooms with Jem and Harry, instead of going downstairs to the public dining room."

A quick look of gratitude showed in her eyes. "I would prefer it."

"Then I'll expect to see you at seven o'clock," he said. "That's the hour when the three of us usually gather if no other arrangements have been made." He turned to leave, opening the door, but before he could close it after him she took a few steps away from the window into the center of the room.

"Daniel!" It was the first time she had addressed him by name.

He tilted his head in a listening attitude. "Well?"

"I appreciate your thoughtfulness."

He was not sure whether she was referring to his allotting her a separate bedroom where she might sleep by herself or to the dinner that was to be partaken of out of the public eye. "You are more than welcome, ma'am," he replied a trifle distantly and closed the door after him.

On the landing he took his gold watch out of his waistcoat pocket and glanced at it. Jem would have given up waiting at the sparring rooms by now, but he would set out and meet him halfway.

Emerging from the hotel he aimed to keep to the main thoroughfares this time instead of attempting any short cuts through the lanes again, but his pace was no more than a stroll since the appointment was missed anyway and he saw no need for haste when there was so much to look at on all sides.

Everything about Brighton pleased him: the fine streets and squares and well-planned gardens, the bow-fronted emporia and the libraries, the chophouses, the coffee shops, the Assembly Rooms at The Castle Inn and countless other places of refreshment and entertainment, all set about that grand arena of elegant promenade, the Steine. He regretted that until this warm July of 1826 he had never visited the resort that had long basked in Royal patronage. As he turned to follow the Steine he looked across at

the exotic Marine Pavilion, the King's seaside palace, which had
been that Royal Gentleman's favorite residence during his days as
Prince of Wales and later as Prince Regent. With its opal-tinted
minarets and bulbous domes glinting with gold in the sun it had
the appearance of an enormous, many-faceted Arabian Nights'
jewel set down gloriously and incongruously within sight and
sound of the English Channel. Much had happened to Brighton
since the rich and the famous had made it the mode to summer at
the seaside and a once quiet fishing hamlet had become England's
most fashionable coastal resort.

He spotted Jem Pierce a short while before being sighted in
turn, which was as well, because it gave him time to change his
mind about disclosing the nature of his purchase at the market.
Better to let Jem see Kate for himself later or else he would only
draw the wrong conclusions, which would result in a waste of
breath and argument, for even at a distance Jem's purposeful
stride showed his exasperation at having been kept hanging about
to no purpose.

Although not particularly tall Jem was often described as a
giant of a man, having a chest and shoulders of immense breadth,
arms that bulged muscles under the fine broadcloth of his tail
coat, and strong thighs and calves that were shown to advantage
in the outmoded knee breeches and stockings that he preferred to
the more fashionable pantaloons. But where physically he had an
imposing appearance his face was a sorry sight, the lids of his right
eye closed and sunken deep, his nose broken and flattened, and
his brow disfigured by a scar where once it had been laid open to
the bone. He looked what he was, a pugilist of the days when almost anything had been permissible in the ring and he would bear
the marks of it both inwardly and outwardly until the end of his
days. Suddenly seeing Daniel in his path he threw up his head
wrathfully. Daniel, undisturbed, kept on at his leisurely pace and
when they were within earshot he held up a hand placatingly at
his trainer, his eyes narrowed and amused.

"I was at a market, I swear it. I lost my way in those confounded
lanes."

Jem snorted, uncertain what to believe, but full of his griev-
ance. "Ye kept me kicking my heels in that lah-de-dah place. Some
damn popinjays wanted to hire me to spar with them. Me! Jem
Pierce, who floored the great Tom Cribb in ten rounds!" His glare
became highly suspicious. "Ye've been up to something. I can tell.
I can always tell."

"Naught but a little shopping," Daniel replied glibly, signaling
to an approaching hackney carriage. "I apologize for being late,
but I foolishly attempted a short cut. We'll get to the sparring
rooms together without further delay and make up for lost time."

"Unnecessary extravagance," Jem grumbled censoriously as he
got into the carriage after Daniel and sat down beside him. "It
would have done yer muscles more good to have run there."

"In these fine clothes? Through the streets of Brighton?"
Daniel threw back his head and laughed.

In the sparring rooms Jem regained the good temper normal to
him, only anxiety ever making him irritable, and he had been concerned about Daniel's nonappearance, angry with himself for leaving him to Harry's charge, but somehow or other the brothers had
not met up. He blamed himself utterly. No trainer worth his salt
let his fighter out of his sight when a mill was imminent, because
youth was youth and abstinence before a bout did not sit lightly
on a virile young man like Daniel in the peak of condition. God
alone knew what had happened at the market, but whatever it
was it had not dimmed Daniel's brilliance as they sparred together, for he showed the fire and force that made him such a
deadly opponent to all who met him in combat.

The sparring session was rounded off with a swim in the sea,
Jem being a firm believer in its chilly stimulation of the blood
stream being good for a fighter and Daniel, who had learned to
swim as a boy in a Devon river, needed no encouragement to
strike out past the waves lapping up the warmth from the sands
to where it was colder and deeper. There were other well-tried
rules for pugilists that Jem made Daniel live by in training, seeing
that he rose at six and retired at nine, suffered doses of physick,

was purged, bled, and sweated for his health's sake, and kept to a rigorous diet of beefsteak, fatless mutton, and floury boiled potatoes with a daily half-pint ration of porter. No London bread was ever put in front of Daniel, but country loaves not less than two days old, and no soups or fish or poultry appeared on the table, no salads or fresh vegetables or puddings or pies, and no strong spices, not even as much salt as Daniel would have liked. How often Daniel broke these rules of drink and diet Jem could not tell and feared his orders on all things were disregarded more often than he suspected. Not for nothing did he bed down on a couch across Daniel's door when a mill was only a few days away.

When they returned to The Old Ship Hotel, Daniel went to his room to rest and not until Jem was sure he slept did he go out to a neighboring tavern. Shortly before seven o'clock he came back to find Daniel up and dressed, reading a newspaper as he lay stretched out on a sofa in the suite's sitting room, his legs crossed at the ankles at one end, his head deep in a cushion at the other.

"Slash Higgens has arrived and is staying at The Castle Inn," Jem announced, full of the news and rubbing his big hands. "I saw him. He looks in fine trim, but if ye'll remember all I've told ye there'll be nothing to worry about." His glance fell on the table laid for dinner and he noted the four places. "Who's the company?"

The newspaper rustled as Daniel turned a page. "I've invited the new Mrs. Warwyck to dine with us."

"The new Mrs.— ? What the devil are ye talking about?"

Another page crackled as it turned. "I acquired a wife today in the market place. I told you I did some shopping. I bid twenty-one guineas for her."

Jem tore the newspaper away and looked down into Daniel's sardonic face. "Are ye telling me the honest truth or have you been drinking?"

"I'm as sober as you are, Jem. Probably a deal more so, because your breath tells me you've passed the last half an hour away in a taproom somewhere." He swung his feet to the floor and sat up.

"If you'll calm down and take that charging-bull expression off your countenance I'll tell you the why and wherefore of the matter."

With one hand Jem wrenched a chair about and straddled it, resting his massive arms along its mahogany back, his visage grim. "I'm listening," he stated in uncompromising tones.

His expression did not lift throughout the full account that Daniel gave him, although he did allow himself to give a faintly acquiescent nod when it was impressed upon him the necessity of saving Harry from his folly. When Daniel had concluded, Jem sat back and splayed his hands on his knees.

"That's the measure of it then," he said weightily. "Ye truly have a wife."

"Not in the eyes of the law, thank God!"

"But morally, Dan. Morally." Jem looked grave. "Ye've taken on the responsibility of this young woman, and ye'll have to take care of her until she skips off or takes up with some other cove, which I don't doubt she's liable to do afore long."

Daniel's mouth twisted. "I'd like to look forward to that happy chance, but I'll not bank on it. She's not a flighty piece. Quite the reverse. A chill creature—stony and reserved. I'd say she could be stubborn and strong-willed, but I consider myself a match for her in that field."

"Ay," Jem agreed on a laconic sigh. "I'll not disagree with ye there. Ye don't think then that she'll let ye down in front of the squire?"

"I believe not. I explained the circumstances and she understood what was expected of her. Uncle William will approve of her." His tone implied it was no compliment he was paying her.

"Ain't she much to look at?"

Daniel contemplated Kate's looks seriously for the first time. "I suppose she is, in her own way. Her features are well formed and some might consider her eyes very fine—Harry obviously did. As for her complexion, that is creamy and smooth—not beaten by sun and wind as you would expect the skin of a farmer's wife to be."

"That's odd, ain't it?" Jem queried.

"I agree," Daniel said, frowningly. "She let fall a strange remark that suggested she was kept confined to the farmhouse, not as a prisoner, but in decorative idleness, forbidden to soil her hands. She and her husband also appeared to live in some style—she mentioned a surprising number of servants. Farmer Farringdon must have been a deal better off than the average tiller of the soil—" There came an interrupting tap on the door and he rose from the sofa. "That will be Kate now."

Jem swung himself up from the chair. "I'll let her in."

Daniel reached out to jerk the bell rope as a summons for dinner to be brought up from the kitchens, and when he looked again toward the door Jem had opened it. Kate stood back in the shadows.

"Mrs.—Warwyck." It did not go easy on Jem's tongue to address thus the young woman who had intruded into their lives, admittedly through no fault of her own, but she was entitled to the courtesy of a married name and he had to use it. "I'm Jem Pierce —at your service, ma'am."

"A pleasure, sir. Daniel has mentioned you to me."

Kate entered the room. She was the same Kate, contained and poised, but she had dressed up for the occasion in a neat, gray-and-white dress over petticoats, which fitted her where the garments she had worn in the market place had shrouded her shape completely. She was full-breasted and small-waisted, and her hair, without the cap and the bonnet, was revealed as being paler than fair, quite moon-colored, straight and parted in the middle, its silky heaviness too much for the current fashion of side ringlets, and worn looped over the ears up into a simple, plaited topknot. Daniel, studying her blatantly from head to toe and up again, realized why she had chosen—either by instinct or design—to cloak her female assets in the market place, or else there was no telling who might have made the bidding, and he thought how she could have ended up being palmed off at Mother Hoskins's in London's Drury Lane, or Mrs. Emerson's in the Haymarket, or any other of the many night houses frequented by titled swells and Corinthians of the day. She had an intensely sensual body, the swing of her hips unintentionally provocative, which warred with her cool, prim air, and so clean and shining and abundant were her tresses that he would not have been the man he was if he had not been able to picture them hanging long and loose about her white nakedness.

"Please sit down, ma'am." Jem was not playing the gentleman, but displaying the kindly good manners toward respectable women that were natural to him, and he pulled out a chair at the table for her. "There'll be food coming through that door any second, and if ye're as hungry as I am ye'll be more than ready for it."

"Thank you, Mr. Pierce," she said, seating herself.

"Call me Jem, ma'am," he insisted, taking a chair himself. "No need to stand on ceremony with me. I've known that young fellow ye've got yerself hitched up with since not long after he were breeched."

"Then you must call me Kate."

Jem shook his big head firmly. "That I will not! No offense meant, I assure ye. But ye're to be known as Daniel's lady-wife and it wouldn't be fitting for me to address ye in any other manner but by yer proper title."

"Come, come!" Daniel said dryly, joining them at the table. "Kate and I aren't legally tied, Jem, as you know from our discussion a few minutes ago. The trouble with you is that you're a damnable snob."

Jem fixed his one blue eye fiercely on Daniel. "I give respect where respect is due. And ye'll watch yer language when there's a lady present—ye ain't Champion of England yet, and I can teach ye a lesson with these fists of mine any time I like!"

Daniel's good humor was getting as thin as his narrowing smile. "Kate and I will work out our attitude toward each other without interference from you. Keep the place into which you have slotted yourself since it appears to fit you like a glove!"

At that moment the food arrived, which Kate considered with relief to be a most timely interruption, not yet knowing how often Jem and Daniel were at loggerheads. As the waiters set the dishes upon the table and sideboard she realized how desperately hungry she was, her appetite returning after a complete inability to face food over the past couple of days. Even before leaving the farmhouse that morning she had had nothing more than a glass of milk, fearful that in her state of nervous tension her stomach might reject anything more substantial at an inopportune moment. Facing the auction had been terrible enough, but to have cast up either on the journey or in a public place would have added horribly to the awful indignity of it all.

"Ain't we going to wait for Harry?" Jem queried when the door closed behind the waiters. He and Kate had been served soup first, but Daniel was about to start the beefsteak essential to his diet without further delay. Kate put down her spoon at once, but Daniel took his first mouthful.

"No. Why should we? It's up to him if he chooses to be late," he commented. Then he added on an edge: "He's not in my good books at the moment anyway. It matters not to me whether he appears or not."

"Well, he has a right to be told that the victuals are on the table." Angrily Jem snatched the napkin from about his neck and threw it down. "I'll go downstairs and see if he is there and has forgotten the time."

The two of them were left alone. She spoke hesitantly. "Was—was there trouble with your brother over your outbidding him at the auction?"

His eyes met hers cynically. "Nothing that he won't get over by tomorrow." He made a swoop with his fork toward her soup plate. "Eat up. Don't let it get cold."

Kate succumbed to her gnawing hunger and began her soup. Under his lashes he observed her. She had delicate table manners. There was nothing about her that Uncle William would be able to fault.

"Is that your best dress?" he inquired.

Unexpectedly she flushed, not an ugly crimson, but a soft rose color that swept along her cheekbones. "It is now. I had others, but I wanted to take away nothing that my husband had paid for.

I have thrown away the garment I wore earlier today, and this dress—and one other—are two left from those I sewed myself shortly before my marriage." She spread her bare left hand flat on the table beside her and contemplated it. "My wedding ring stayed behind with everything else."

"I had better get you a ring at the first opportunity. I had not thought of it, and it is as well I was reminded. You must have some new clothes, too—three or four dresses, a coat, a bonnet, and some undergarments, I suppose."

Her color deepened. "I can manage with the wardrobe I have."

"Not if you're to appear anywhere with me, you'll not," he retorted brusquely. "What would my uncle think if I turn up at the Manor with you dressed like a pauper's wife?"

Her gaze became frosty. "You have the most insulting manner! A pauper's wife! Is a pugilist's wife any higher up the social scale?"

His brows swept into a wrathful frown. "I imagined you had enough good sense to realize I was speaking figuratively. In no way was I referring to your present appearance, which is—very pleasing. A deal better than earlier today in those garments fit only for gleaning in the fields."

"That's what they were worn for—before my marriage."

His frown eased and he spoke on a gentler note. "You knew hard times then as a girl?"

Her expression did not change. "I was not a stranger to hunger —or to poverty."

"Is that why you married Farmer Farringdon?"

She hesitated. "Yes." Then her voice strengthened. "Yes, it was."

As before when they had talked he had the feeling that although she had answered truthfully there was much more behind her words, but the set of her mouth was a sign that nothing more would be forthcoming that evening. He reverted to the original topic of their conversation.

"We'll go to the shops when the mill is behind me and visit the dressmakers' and the milliners'—we'll see what we can find to suit you."

"I said—" she began defiantly.

He lost patience. "You'll wear whatever clothes I buy you! And you can damn well leave them behind when life in my company becomes unbearable for you!" She whitened, and he swung his head round as Jem came back into the room alone. "Won't Harry come?" he barked, still irritated. "I'm not surprised. Let him sulk on his own for a while."

"I couldn't see him anywhere," Jem replied, his voice betraying some unease as he took his place again at the table. "I made inquiries and it seems like he ain't been back since he went out this morning. I'd say ye were the last to have contact with him, Dan."

"Then it's no wonder he's lying low for a while. Kate—let me remove that empty soup plate and offer you one of these prawn pasties."

He was making an effort to get their acquaintanceship back on a more tolerable line and she met him halfway, allowing herself to be drawn into the general conversation, which was kept at an impersonal level. Although Harry's name was avoided he was in their minds, and at the end of the meal Jem pulled away the napkin tucked under his chin and pushed back his chair, addressing Daniel.

"I'm going to find that brother of yer'n."

"I wish you success," Daniel replied crisply, not moving.

Jem jerked a thumb over his shoulder. "Ye had better come with me. I may need yer assistance."

Daniel sighed heavily, but he was not as adverse to going as he made it appear, having recalled Harry's sharp distress with a seriousness he had not given it earlier. Together they set out to look for him. On the way, coming upon a goldsmith's that was still open, Daniel went in and bought a gold ring after being assured that it could be altered the next day if it did not fit the lady's finger. Harry was not in the first few taverns they looked into, all of which were crowded, but eventually they ran into a pugilistic acquaintance who had seen him and directed them to one of the less reputable inns. They found him slumped over a corner table. Not normally a drinker, he was almost insensible with the amount of liquor he had consumed, and they each took an arm, hauling him out into the courtyard where Jem held his head under a pump and Daniel wielded the handle. Popeyed, gasping and spluttering, he vomited twice before Jem and Daniel guided him on unsteady legs between them back to the hotel.

Kate had passed the time reading some monthly editions of *Annals of Sporting*, picking out anything written about Daniel. She sat up in her chair with dismay when Harry with lolling head was brought swaying into the room, his head wet with fronded strands of fairish hair sticking to a slim, firm-chinned face.

"We found him," Jem said grimly and unnecessarily, "and if ye'll pardon us, ma'am, we'll get him straight to bed."

Together they tugged him in the direction of one of the communicating doors that led out of the sitting room into adjoining bedrooms, but they had gone no more than a few steps when Harry lifted his head and blinked dazedly about him as if trying to discover where he was. Suddenly his gaze settled on Kate where she sat. He shook himself free of supporting hands, a kind of radiance dawning in his face as he took a few stumbling steps toward her, and then his senses went from him, his legs folded, and he cracked his chin on the edge of the table as he fell. Wordlessly Jem picked him up, heaved him over one shoulder, and bore him away.

Daniel glared after his brother until the door closed, jamming his thumbs down angrily in his waistcoat pockets. "A fine help he is going to be in the ring tomorrow with the head that he will have." His thumbnail touched a small leather folder and he remembered the ring he had bought. Taking it out he tossed it carelessly into her lap. "Try this on."

Her lowered lashes as she took up the folder from her lap shielded from his sight whatever her reaction to his bestowing of the ring might have been. She took the gold band out and slipped it onto the third finger of her left hand. Only then did she look up, her blue eyes cool and distant.

"It fits perfectly."

"So it does." He was well pleased with his cleverness in having guessed the size so accurately and came across to take her hand by the wrist and hold it toward the lamplight, she stretching her fingers automatically to display it for him. "You have beautiful hands, Kate," he commented reflectively, his gaze leaving her hand to travel up her arm and settle on the full, rounded curve of her breasts.

Quickly she withdrew her hand from his hold and clenched it against her, rising to her feet and avoiding his following glance. "I'll bid you good night. Jem said you always retired early on the eve of a mill and I must not keep you talking."

"Good night," he replied. He would willingly have escorted her chastely to her door, but her whole attitude discouraged it. As soon as she had gone he pulled his cravat undone and began to unbutton his waistcoat on his way into his bedroom.

Kate did not undress for some time. Feeling less than secure behind her locked door, she paced the floor warily and did not make ready for bed until she was sure she was to be left alone. Only then, with hands shaking with relief, did she begin to unhook the back of her dress. She had not dared to believe that Daniel would want nothing more from her than a masquerade for his dying uncle.

She awakened to an overcast day, a dampish breeze coming in from the dark green sea to billow the curtains at the window. Breakfast came to her room on a tray and was served to her in bed, lace-edged pillows propping her high, and she was awed by such luxury. Later when she emerged from her room dressed simply in the only other gown she possessed, a faded blue cotton, a riot of laughter and talk boomed up the stairs from the dining room where champagne breakfasts before attendance at the mill were the order of the day for all members of The Fancy staying there.

She tapped on the door of Daniel's suite, wanting to wish him good luck before he departed, and it was opened by Harry, white-faced and puffy-eyed, but freshly shaven and neatly dressed. His hair, now that it was dry, was much lighter in color than she had realized and flopped over his forehead, curling a little about his ears. He appeared to have been expecting her and opened the door wide for her to enter.

"Good morning, Mrs.—Mrs. Warwyck." His embarrassment over the surname was acute. "Daniel is still getting ready."

She gave him a warm smile as she came into the room and hoped to put him at his ease. "I implore you to call me by my Christian name. I have no claim on the surname of Warwyck, but it is to suit Daniel that I am to use it."

He pushed back the fall of his hair with spread fingers, trying to seem nonchalant, but only succeeded in looking rueful. "I remember nothing of what happened last night," he confessed, a frown of anxiety creasing his brow. "I trust I did nothing to cause you offense, either in speech or behavior."

"Nothing at all." She took the chair he offered her and saw his eyes go unhappily to the ring on her finger. Instinctively she folded her hands.

Abruptly he pulled up another chair and sat down facing her, leaning forward. "Jem told me that Daniel bought you a wedding band. I wish with all my heart that you did not have to wear it." He spoke stiffly, his lips thin and full of pain.

She began to understand the full extent of his feelings. Foolhardy, impulsive, and immature they might be, but that did not lessen the strength and anguish of them. Immediately she recalled how moved and touched she had been by the way he had looked at her in that brief flash of recognition before passing out completely, for it had been unmistakably a wave of love that had washed over his face. All her instincts told her she must tread carefully and nip his adolescent passion for her in its bud.

"The ring means nothing either to Daniel or to me," she said carefully, "but I'm obliged to him for his bidding for me in the market place and must do what I can in return. Never had I dared hope to find myself in such agreeable circumstances."

"It was I who bid for you first!" The words tore from him.

"I know you did. It was a kindly act and put an end to the insults being hurled at me."

"But it wasn't only for that I did it!" He was frantic to convince her. "I would have paid all I had in the world to buy you and set you free!"

She stared at him. "You mean you would have sacrificed everything you had to let me go my own way?"

He nodded vigorously. "Naturally I'd have hoped you would come with me. All my powers of persuasion—for what they are worth!—would have gone into trying to make you see that life with me would have much to offer you—not now, of course," he interjected hastily, "but in the future. But if you had shown that you wished to have none of me I'd have stood aside and let you walk away."

There was a long pause before she spoke. "You're an exceptional young man. I cannot say what my reactions would have been if things had gone as you described, but I believe that although I should have recognized your worth, as I do now, I would have chosen freedom and not rested until somehow I had paid back all it had cost you." She saw she had hurt him, but she had had to make the cut sharp and clean in order that it should heal the quicker.

"That's what I feared," he admitted hoarsely.

"Daniel gave me no such choice, and I intend to keep my half of the bargain."

He dipped his head and passed the fingers and thumb of one hand across his forehead to bring them closed onto the bridge of his nose, forcing himself to come to terms with what she had said. Deliberately she misunderstood his action, seeking to disperse the further embarrassment he was experiencing.

"Your head is aching? I can mix you a draught out of my box of herbs that I brought with me—"

"There's no need, but I thank you." He lifted his head again and his smile had a vulnerable sweetness, lulling her still further into thinking him a gentle, malleable youth. "I hope we can be good friends, Kate."

"There's nothing that could delight me more," she answered gladly, her voice throbbing.

"You already have a champion in Jem. He has formed a high opinion of you."

"That pleases me," she said simply and genuinely.

He hesitated. "Do you like the theater, Kate?"

"Indeed I do!" Her eyes shone. "Whenever a company of traveling players came to the district I would go."

"I have two tickets for the Theater Royal on Wednesday next, the eve of our leaving for Devonshire. It's a dramatic production that has been seen in London and the same actors and actresses from the Metropolis are in it." He saw her face close, wariness and uncertainty taking over, and he sought to reassure her. "You would be doing me a favor if you should come. Daniel saw the play at Drury Lane. I have no liking to sit beside an empty seat."

"Perhaps Jem—" she suggested.

"It has to be a burletta or some other kind of bawdy comedy to get Jem to watch a curtain rise. Don't let that ticket go unused."

She drew in her breath and nodded acceptance. "I have never been inside a theater of any size." Flinging back her head she gave one of her rare, deep laughs. "What a time I am having!"

He hid his triumph, well pleased, and she was content in thinking that the meeting had turned out extremely well, not knowing that she had yet much to learn about his character. She should have seen it in the Warwyck chin. His resolve to have her for himself had not lessened one iota.

At that moment the communicating door from the main bedroom was swung open from within by Jem, and Daniel came through, easing his fingers into gloves of finest French kid. Kate's eyes widened and she rose slowly to her feet. His appearance stunned her with its elegance. He was clothed in dove-gray with buttons of silver, his slimly cut pantaloons held taut by straps under the instep, and his waistcoat was a rich sky-blue, matching the silk neckerchief wound around the fashionably high collar and tied in a soft bow.

He did not even notice her, addressing Jem, and then turning his attention to Harry, demanding to know if the curricle was at the hotel steps. "Who's in charge of the horses? Is it an ostler who knows how to keep them calm in that waiting crowd outside? Did you place that wager for me?"

He was already halfway out of the room. She stepped forward quickly. "Daniel! Good luck!"

He gave her a blank stare as if momentarily he had completely forgotten who she was, but at once he snapped his thoughts away from all that absorbed him and had the grace to show some appreciation of her good wishes.

"Thank you. Most kind."

His coattails swung out of the door and down the stairs, Jem following. Harry picked up a waiting hamper containing all his brother would need and took his own hat from a peg.

"Don't expect to see Daniel looking quite the same when he gets back," he advised her dryly. "Slash Higgens is a formidable opponent and Daniel will have his work cut out to win the fight." The tone of his voice gave the impression that perhaps for the first time he was not going to be sorry over any punishment that his brother received. Outside the hotel a cheer resounded as Daniel made an appearance. Not daring to delay any longer Harry dashed off after him.

She stood alone in the room listening to the cheering as the curricle departed and did not go back to her own quarters until it had quite died away.

Chapter 3

It was a match that had been guaranteed to attract an attendance of twenty-five thousand spectators, for such was the popularity of the prize ring, but as the morning went on it began to be estimated locally that the number would rise even higher. From every direction the people were converging on Deane Dell, the wheeled traffic making a living river of the road there out of Brighton with equestrians weaving in and out, and hurrying pedestrians forming a continuous line, sometimes two or three abreast, along the grass verges. Merriment on the road to a mill had long since become a traditional part of the occasion, and the good humor radiated from the aristocratic class down through the genteel, the middling, the respectable, and the tidy to the lowest and humblest of the poor, most of whom were barefoot and in rags with pockets that could never reach to gate money, but who had their own methods of sneaking in for a free view of a bout.

It was a scene of color and activity, unaffected by the storm that broke suddenly in the midst of it all, leaving rain to lash down long after the thunder had rolled away over the Channel to France. Lively groups in coaches and laughing young men in chariots bowled along in quick succession. Gigs in every hue jogged along at a spanking pace. Handling the ribbons of their high-mettled horses as lightly as silk were the well-dressed Corinthians, those sporting men of rank and fashion, who drove with speed and skill, heedless and uncaring of the mud thrown up by the high wheels of their elegant equipages onto those on foot. Barouches and fours, chaises, phaetons, curricles, and every other sort of carriage mingled with carts drawn by donkeys normally engaged in giving rides on the beach, while other vehicles used to transporting fish and shingle and driftwood dropped showers of powdery sand shaken free from under the axles and jarred and jolted their uncomplaining passengers. The most crammed of all the vehicles were the huge, lumbering farm wagons drawn by teams of six or more great shire horses, their thick manes braided with colored strands, their polished harnesses and brasses twinkling, enormous hooves leaving heavy imprints in the squelching mud of the road.

The road dipped to meet the natural amphitheater formed by Deane Dell at its one low point, for it represented a saucer that had been molded down to form a narrow lip. It was at this section that the spectators paid their gate money to those posted to collect it before swarming down past the ring and up again to secure places on the encircling high slopes which would offer superb and unimpeded views of the bout, the grassy stretches around the site more than adequate for the hundreds of vehicles gathering there.

A cheer went up in waves of sound all round the dell when the rain began to ease, allowing a pale and watery sun to show itself soon afterward, but that appreciative noise was nothing compared to the echoing roar that greeted the arrival of the first of the two combatants. Slash Higgens, dressed in sober brown, his black-spotted yellow neckerchief the only splash of color in his attire, came into the dell after alighting from his backer's chaise and accompanied by that same gentleman, a baronet well known to The Fancy for his generous support. They were followed by Slash's second and his bottle holder.

A few minutes later Daniel arrived in his own curricle, a crimson equipage with upholstery to match drawn by two black horses. He stepped grandly from it and acknowledged the applause as he strode down toward the ring. His backer was absent, being abroad on diplomatic business, and only Jem and Harry followed behind him.

Daniel, who never felt any animosity toward an opponent, which helped to make him the clearheaded, decisive, calculating boxer that he was, extended his hand to Slash, who shook it in a sportsmanlike manner, each nodding courteously to the other. "How do you do?" Daniel inquired. "Well, I hope."

"Quite bobbish," Slash replied in deep tones, "and very well, I thank you."

Another tremendous burst of applause resounded as both pugilists threw their hats into the ring, Daniel first as the challenger, and each having taken note of the direction of the wind, for it was held to be indicative of ill luck and a lost fight if a combatant's hat blew back out of the ring. Then they stepped between the ropes and both began to strip off.

Their neckerchiefs, symbolic in pugilism of colors flaunted in tournaments of lance and sword in centuries gone by, were removed first, Jem taking Daniel's from him, Slash's second following suit with his, and the squares of silk were tied, the challenger's over the challenged, to one of the wooden stakes that marked off the roped-off ring. In the contest itself, although no hits were allowed below the waist or when a man was down, almost everything else, from the ferocious chopping blows to wrestling holds and throws, was permitted; indeed, each combatant sought to bring his opponent to the ground by every means possible. It was only a fall that could end a round, and a bout lasted until one or other of the two men was either knocked out or, when time was called, failed to come to the scratch, the line made prior to the match across the middle of the ring, not even when helped by his seconds, which was allowed.

When both men stood bare to the waist in their white, knee-length milling breeches, the crowd reassessed their potential and there was a last-minute frenzy of betting unlike any other that had taken place previously. Slash had earned his nickname through his ability to deal exceptionally fast punches with an uncommonly brutal power. The veteran of many a bloody battle, the evidence of which was in his scarred countenance and broken nose, he was athletic and big with muscles rippling under the white skin as though with a life of their own. His cauliflower ears were much damaged and most unsightly, but his head was well shaped on a bull-like neck, his light brown hair cut to a stubble that showed his scalp through and would give no hold to an opponent who tried to grab him by the locks.

Daniel thought too much of his appearance to shave his head in a similar fashion, resolved to take his chance, and his supporters did not hold it against him, being more than satisfied that in physique he was tight and hard and lean-hipped with the broad shoulders and muscular frame essential to his profession, a triangle of hair spreading across his chest and descending into a thin arrow line to vanish under his waistband. Although over six feet in height he topped his opponent by less than an inch, which was no advantage, but it was his panther-like litheness indicative of a latent strength and a disciplined fury that made the wagering swing in his favor.

It was time for the mill to commence. Both took up their places facing each other across the scratch, fists up and elbows level. Then they promptly set to, Daniel after a couple of feints landing the first telling blow.

It was at the end of the twenty-seventh grueling round that he first sighted the redheaded girl. Had she not risen to her feet in her carriage as he turned for his corner after ferociously punching his opponent on the ropes till Slash went down on both knees, he might never have seen her. She would have brushed against his life and out of it again without his being aware of it. The day would have meant no more to him than being the one on which he defeated Slash, for he was confident that victory was within his grasp. From the start it had been a savage battle, both of them setting to with unusual severity, and the crowd of spectators had roared and groaned exultantly at the violence of rib roasters and throat hits, the nobbers and the facers, the throws and the falls.

The wet grass underfoot had added to the hazards, but during the past few rounds it had not been the treacherous ground that was making Slash reel and stagger and fall with increasing frequency. He had been dragged up from the ropes by his seconds and was sitting slumped on the knee of one of them, his head lolling, his breathing labored and gasping as though his lungs could barely function. Daniel's own chest was heaving harshly and agonizingly, but he gave it no more mind than the lacerated and bleeding knuckles of his pain-racked hands. From a cut on his bruised cheek the blood gushed freely and was smudged gorily about his body, which was glistening with the sweat that had soaked his grass-stained breeches to a second skin, and bore evidence of his opponent's mighty blows in darkened patches on his ribs and stomach; otherwise he was little harmed, his defense having been as scientific and skillful as his ceaseless and merciless attack.

It was the soft butterfly flutter of her primrose-colored clothes caught out of the corner of his eye that had broken his concentration and snapped his glance toward the road on the rim of the dell where a private cavalcade of half a dozen highly polished carriages had drawn up in a line, arrogantly occupying the space that had been left clear, all the hoods down and open to the sun, which had strengthened to full heat throughout the course of the lengthy mill.

She must have sprung up to see better, and the two gentlemen riding with her had spilled out to join companions from the other equipages, who were also alighting in their eagerness to catch a late glimpse of the mill that they had come across on their way to some other destination. She alone stood high, her shining, bronze-red hair escaping in curls from the confines of her wide-brimmed bonnet, young and haughty with the self-assurance that comes to the cosseted and the spoiled. The rest of the lady passengers remained modestly in their seats, snapping open fans to shield their gaze from the vulgar spectacle in the dell, although one of them, who had hair of similar coloring, fluttered a hand from the neighboring carriage in an attempt to wave the girl down into her seat again, but the slender, bright-haired figure continued to stand in the open barouche. Across the distance between them Daniel saw that she was regarding him with a supercilious, half-pitying scorn, and his own glance hardened into a wrathful stare. She in turn promptly raised her thin eyebrows delicately to spike his effrontery in daring to look at her at all and in such a way. To the burning heat of his pounding blood was added the sudden, searing flash of temper avid to use her as he would, to drive from that sharply feline face its taunting expression and fire those glinting, light green eyes to a smoldering emerald in bemused acknowledgment of his prowess as a fighter and as a man.

"Dan!" It was the urgent voice of his brother that broke through to him. "Your half minute will be up if you don't move!"

The noise of the crowd burst again against his eardrums, and his nostrils were reassailed by the reek of stale sweat and crowded bodies, crushed grass and blood and resin. He turned toward his corner, ignoring the outstretched hand of Jem, who seemed to think he might be in need of some aid. Although shaking inwardly from exertion and a physical weariness that went right to the soles of his feet, he was too mindful of the girl's watchful gaze to take a much needed rest on his brother's bent knee, but remained standing instead with a boastful show of untiredness, welcoming the coolness of the damp sponge that Jem applied to his face and body while giving into his ear urgent, low-voiced advice for the kill.

"Ye've almost finished him! Move in quick before his addled brains get working. One more of yer levelers and it'll be all yer own." There was a throaty chuckle. "Ye'd be able to fell oxen for butchers with those mitts of yer'n if ever ye had a mind to it, lad!"

Harry had sprung up again and was putting the bottle to Daniel's mouth. For the first time since the fight began he received the kick of brandy and did not swill it out again. Normally Jem kept him clear of liquor during a contest, knowing how too much brandy-laced water could affect a pugilist's judgment during a long bout, but this was to be an undiluted booster for finishing the contest.

The half minute was up. Daniel's opponent was given a lifting thrust forward by his agitated seconds and came lumbering to the scratch. One eye had now closed through persistent contact with Daniel's well-directed fists during the earlier rounds and his countenance was a sorry sight, but Slash was tough and he was game and he swung up his fists, but all too late, for Daniel had already lunged inside his guard. The lightning speed with which the onslaught came was more than Slash could deal with at such a late stage in a punishing and exhaustive bout. Daniel's right-hand body blow hit him a little below the heart with such force that he was only prevented from falling forward onto his face by a savage repetition of the fierce punch smashed home with all Daniel's remaining strength behind it, flooring him instantly onto his back where he lay in a complete stupor. The fight was over.

A thunderous roar went up from the crowd. The judge's announcement that Daniel was the winner went unheard. Harry and Jem were clapping him on the back, and the whips were trying to keep the spectators out of the ring, but already on one side the ropes had been torn down and many had swarmed into it, exasperating Daniel with their thoughtless crowding and hampering with their high spirits those carrying Slash away. Daniel sensed without looking that the girl was still standing there in the barouche, his nerve ends tingling as though he and she were communicating by some invisible current passing between them.

"The colors," he ordered Harry, holding out a hand impatiently while Jem threw a soft, woolen cape about his shoulders and then turned to clear some semblance of space for him by keeping his admirers at bay. Obediently Harry had sprung to the stake and untied the neckerchiefs, the loser's color falling forfeit by custom to the winner.

"Here they are!" He looped them across Daniel's puffed and swollen palm, and without looking at them Daniel closed his fingers about their softness and stepped between the ropes, going not in the direction of his own carriage waiting in readiness to transport him away to rest and treatment, but making for the girl in the barouche. The burly whips, who kept order, were prepared to be rough in order to clear a passage for him, but the crowd drew aside good-naturedly in deference to the winner, and he was given an uninterrupted view of her as he approached slowly up to the road. Some of the other carriages in the cavalcade were already on the move, bowling away, and she, seeing how purposefully he had set his step toward her, quickly seated herself. With a little tilt of her chin, pretending to have forgotten his existence, she leaned back comfortably and rested one arm on the folded hinge of the hood while making a show of addressing her two fellow passengers, both of whom were about to mount the steps of the barouche and rejoin her for their departure from the scene. Her clear voice rose on an impishly chiding note, reaching him as was intended.

"I declare we shall be the last to arrive at the races if we don't leave on the instant! All the other carriages in our party have left us behind. Hurry along, do! It's been a most tiresome and unnecessary delay." She pursed her mouth at the first fellow as he entered. "As it was your idea that we should take time to watch the mill I've half a mind not to let you change places with Alexander and sit beside me the rest of the way."

The threat was not meant and the first fellow showed that he knew it, answering her on a low, amused note and giving a smiling shake of his head as he swung himself down in the seat beside her. He had left the door wide for the other gentleman referred to as Alexander to follow, and through the gap Daniel caught the flick of her gloved hand smoothing down into place a wayward frill of her skirt that was floating in the draft. Then she looked toward him again under her lashes, which were dark and swept to tips as copper-hued as her hair, giving a curious luster to the wide-apart eyes that were regarding him with a kind of calculated taunt and had the effect of aggravating still further his dangerous, edgy mood. She should have shown some change in attitude toward him, some respect for what he had achieved in that final, triumphant round, but he would have it from her yet. She was not beautiful, he thought savagely, although by her very air she gave an illusion of it, but there was a restrained voluptuousness about her, a sensual defiance that was both a challenge and an invitation, and he had never yet turned aside from the thrown-down gauntlet.

In the barouche Alexander put his hand behind him to close the door, but Daniel reached the equipage in time to wrench it wide again and set his foot on the step.

"Damme! What the devil—?" Alexander had turned, a thick-set fellow in his thirties, handsome in a black-browed, hawkish way, and he showed surprised annoyance at the sight of the pugilist, whom a few minutes ago he had been applauding, monopolizing his carriage step as though he owned it. Had Daniel kept his place, bowed and shown suitable humility toward his betters, Alexander Radcliffe might well have tossed him a guinea or two to add to his prize money, but this getting above himself was too much. "Remove your insolent foot! Clear off, I say!"

Daniel ignored him, watching the girl. She had not drawn back in her seat at his nearness, but her flawless skin with its exquisite pallor had tightened over the high brow and crystal-cut bones of her face, and her delicately fashioned, almost translucent nostrils were flaring at his audaciousness. The game was over. He had carried it too far and she no longer wanted to play. Yet he did not believe that she was regretting that deadly quirk of flirtatiousness that had brought him unerringly to her, for he sensed her high-pitched tension, her pulsating excitement, which was almost tangible. It was only that momentarily she found herself at a disadvantage, being totally unused to a situation slipping out of her control and intensely displeased by it.

With a superb sense of timing and much of the drama that he used when entering a ring he swept his upturned hand to her with a flourish, holding out the colors he had won, but still keeping his fingers closed to prevent the breeze from whisking off the fine silk squares before she could accept them. The first fellow to have entered the carriage leaned forward in his seat beside her and murmured appreciatively.

"The colors, eh! An impertinence in this case, but not intended to be, I'm sure. The victor seeks to honor you, Miss Clayton." He prodded Alexander with his cane. "Sit down, Radcliffe. You're taking up too much room."

His order was obeyed with hostile reluctance and a squeak of the opposite leather seat under a not inconsiderable weight. Still the girl made no move. By rights she should have touched Daniel's fingers lightly to unlace them, but she kept her own hands folded and pressed tight against her, and under lowered lids her shaded lashes kept her gaze hidden. Reversing his fist, he opened it, releasing the colors in a flow of silk across her lap.

She reacted instantly, coming alive on an indrawn catch of breath, her lips twisting affectedly in a spasm of distaste. She swept out the back of her hand to dash the colors from her lap, the yellow one swirling out to hook itself on the window strap of the door and his own to float down to the step on which he was standing. His face whitened and went rigid. He jerked his foot from the step and snatched up the blue emblem before it could be soiled by the dust.

Her gaze had turned unblinkingly onto Alexander, her whole attitude showing the incident to be lost to any importance. "Why are we delaying?" she demanded impatiently. "Is there to be no racing for us today?"

Promptly Alexander leaned forward to whip the door shut, at the same time giving a snapped order to the coachman. "Drive on!"

With a lurch of wheels the barouche swept away, the yellow color trapped between the door and the carriage body, fluttering wildly as the horses gained speed until it tore free and was lost from sight in the wayside grass. The primrose bonnet did not turn, but the gentleman beside her raised himself up slightly for a backward glance over the hood, his the only laughter, although as the barouche drew farther away Daniel heard with silent fury Alexander utter a guffaw.

Harry came running up, Jem stumping in his wake. "What do you think you're doing, Dan?" his brother demanded anxiously, catching hold of him. "Who were those people? Did you know them?"

He shook his head with great effort, the sheer physical exhaustion of all he had endured in the ring finally overtaking him, his legs sagging. Jem seized his wrist and pulled one arm about a burly neck, supporting him. His curricle had been brought forward, and between them they helped him up into the seat where he sprawled in a tangle of limbs. The curricle dipped as Jem stepped up into the place beside him and took the reins. Harry, after covering his brother with a plaid rug, sprang up into the rear seat, and with a large proportion of the spectators running and cheering after him Daniel was borne away, back to the resort and to The Old Ship Hotel.

Kate, waiting for their return, could scarcely believe he was the victor when she saw the state he was in as he was carried past her, and she pressed her fingertips to her tremulous mouth.

Lying in bed between deep white blankets after Jem and Harry had administered to him, his body smoothed with oil and camphor, his cuts dressed with lint, his knuckles covered with soothing ointment and wrapped in soft cotton, he suffered the usual agonies of a battering and his thoughts drifted to the Clayton girl. She had not seen the last of him, however much she might wish it. Somehow he would see her take back that insult she had inflicted upon him today. He would see her humbled yet. On this resolve he succumbed to the slumber he had been keeping at bay and was lost in an exhausted sleep of total oblivion.

Chapter 4

Two days later Daniel announced he would take Kate shopping. It was his first venture out into the open air since the bout and she was amazed how quickly he had recovered from all he had been through. His bruises remained, but Jem knew how to treat them and already they were fading. His knuckles, still raw and bound up, he concealed in a larger size of glove, and as he stood waiting to escort her she thought he looked no more unsightly than if he had had a tumble from a horse while hunting.

"Well? Are you ready?" he demanded tetchily, anxious to get the whole business over with and displeased with her dowdy appearance since he, still the hero of the hour, had to appear in public with her. He reminded himself that it was no fault of hers she looked as she did, and she had tied a ribbon prettily in her hair, but nevertheless it was not good enough.

She, able to guess from his hard expression what he was thinking, bit back the retort that she would much rather be accompanied by Jem or Harry, who would not care what she wore, and answered him with her head high. "Yes, I am."

He took her to a good class dressmaker's, and knowing that to suit his purpose in winning over his uncle she must appear as conservative and genteel as possible, she submitted to his eyeing and considering each garment before she tried it on. From a gilded chair which looked scarcely strong enough to bear his handsome weight, he nodded or shook his head imperiously when she paraded before him. Miraculously they reached agreement on everything, but he left her to choose undergarments, shoes, stockings, and a few other fripperies while he went off by himself.

He was soon at the Library where the resort's Master of Ceremonies maintained a book in which new arrivals set down their names in order that they could be contacted by acquaintances and in turn discover who there was known to them and of consequence in the town. He read that Miss Claudine Clayton was staying at Alton House in North Street with Mr. and Mrs. Alexander Radcliffe. Their mutual home address was Radcliffe Hall, Easthampton, Sussex. He decided he had been right in thinking that it was an older sister who had admonished Claudine from a neighboring carriage, which meant that Alexander Radcliffe was Claudine's brother-in-law. Although Daniel had never heard of Easthampton one of the librarians, in answer to his question, informed him that it lay no more than twenty miles distant to the west along the coast and was a simple fishing hamlet nestling against the Downs, such as Brighton had been before it had started to grow.

Well satisfied with the information he had gathered and determined to study Easthampton's location on the map he had bought at the market, he came out of the Library into the shade of its columned portico, wondering exactly how he could come face to face with that redheaded witch again before leaving for Devonshire. He had gone no more than a few paces when he was hailed from near at hand.

"Warwyck, by the Devil!"

Daniel swung around recognizing instantly the voice of his most influential backer. "Sir Geoffrey! Your servant, sir!"

Sir Geoffrey Edenfield shook him heartily by the hand. "And yours, my young Corinthian." Tall, lean, and middle-aged, with an impeccable taste in clothes, a classic restraint even to the folds of his cravat, he was a striking and distinguished man, gray wings of hair passing back from hollow, aristocratic temples. "This is a most unexpected encounter. I thought you would have returned to London before now." He frowned with immediate concern at Daniel. "I trust you suffered no injuries of any seriousness in your mill with Higgens? None was reported to me."

Daniel reassured him. "Nothing at all. I'm off to Devonshire the day after tomorrow and it seemed pointless to go back to London. It could be said that I'm taking the sea air like everybody else."

"Well deserved! It was a great disappointment to me that I was unable to return to England in time to attend the mill, but His Majesty's affairs must come first, even when such a fine display of fists is taking place. I landed at Dover yesterday and came at once to rejoin Lady Margaret at our summer residence." He clapped a hand on Daniel's shoulder. "Come! It's no more than two minutes' walk away, and I insist on a blow by blow account of the whole mill without any further delay. There is one thing I must know immediately—is it correct that Higgens gave you some unexpected trouble in the seventh round?"

Daniel gave a wry grin. "Indeed he did." Briefly and accurately he described how he had been floored, and as they walked along Sir Geoffrey listened with keen interest. He had been Daniel's first patron, persuaded into becoming his backer when Tom Cribb, whom he knew from the great pugilist's heyday in the ring, had put in a word for the young newcomer on the scene, and he had never had cause to regret it, either from a personal or financial angle. But the liking and respect were mutual. Daniel considered himself fortunate to have secured long since the patronage of one who had done much for the sport of pugilism and who was among those using all the pressure at their disposal to try to get new and more humane rules passed for the prize ring.

In his elegant drawing room overlooking the Steine, Sir Geoffrey listened and questioned and listened again until he had absorbed every detail of what had occurred at the mill. It took the rest of the morning and a discussion about it continued throughout luncheon, which they ate on their own, Lady Margaret being absent. Afterward when they took a turn in the shady garden Sir Geoffrey frowned, stroking his chin, when he heard that Daniel's sojourn in Devonshire depended on how long his uncle survived.

"I had hopes of seeing you in the ring with Bob Craven before the end of next month. In no way am I trying to keep you away from your uncle's deathbed, but I understand from all you have told me in the past that he is a tough old rooster and he may linger a devilish long time."

"Not from Jassy's letters. She says there is no chance of his rallying as he did after his illness a year ago when he seemed to recover completely for a short spell. I have to accept the olive branch he has offered in a wish to see me if I am to re-establish myself as his heir, but if there was a chance of my sister's name being written in place of mine on a last will that he is about to sign I would go nowhere near Warwyck Manor again. Unfortunately no woman can inherit the place. It goes back to some obscure deeds."

Sir Geoffrey pondered the matter. An inheritance of family lands and fortune was every gentleman's right. One did not put anything else before it, but whether Daniel could sustain his powers for a championship throughout all the diversities and responsibilities and duties of the estate that would inevitably fall upon his shoulders was another matter. A pugilist had to be single-minded about his training. There could be no lapses of any duration, no lengthy relaxation. However much Daniel was resolved to keep in fighting trim he would find himself beset with difficulties far away in Devonshire and out of daily London contact and involvement with The Fancy, and could lapse into the role of country squire before he was even aware of it. He said as much. Daniel brushed his misgivings aside.

"You are thinking that with Warwyck Manor being such a distance from London I shall lose contact with the ring, but that will not be the case. You see, I have no intention of ever living there. I shall find a trustworthy steward to leave in charge, and apart from restoring a wing in need of repair, setting aside a large dowry for Jassy, and securing funds to establish Harry in a suitable profes-

53

sion, the income from the estate will be plowed back into it for the benefit of generations of Warwycks to come. I want none of it."

Sir Geoffrey raised an eyebrow at him. "You do detest the place, don't you? But I agree with you that one has a moral duty to hold such property in trust. Is your sister betrothed?"

"No, she is only sixteen and has had a wretched existence until now. I would have taken her into my charge long ago had I been following any other road in life, but the fistic environment is no place for a young and innocent girl. I plan to leave her at Warwyck Manor in the charge of a most suitable young woman named Kate, who has—er—come to my notice." Daniel did not intend to give his backer any details there. "She will act as chaperone, and the house can be opened up for parties and other social occasions to let Jassy enjoy life at last." He was well satisfied with what he had worked out on his own for Kate's future. She would have no choice in the matter and should think herself fortunate to have a good home for as long as she wanted it, because even after Jassy married one day Warwyck Manor would need a housekeeper.

"I must say I envy your going to Devonshire for a spell," Sir Geoffrey said as Daniel was about to make his departure at the gates into the Steine. "Brighton has become too large and crowded for my liking, not at all what it used to be. Lady Margaret also finds it disappointing these days. Both of us would like to find a smaller resort with a convenience of situation and all amenities, but without Brighton's vulgarity. There are many among our acquaintances who feel as we do, but nowhere seems to fit the bill."

"What about Worthing or Bognor?"

"Worthing is too dull and Bognor has declined since the turn of the century when its founder died. There was a man for you— Sir Richard Hotham. He invested his entire fortune into turning a fishing hamlet into a resort, the first ever in England built specially for sea bathing, and he created a charming and elegant place, but unfortunately he left no one to carry on after him and ensure its continued success." He put out his hand and shook Daniel's once again. "Congratulations again on a splendid fight with Higgens. You must let me know if there is anything I can do for you during the period after your uncle's demise and before you can return to London."

"I thank you." Daniel, about to step away, checked his leaving on an inspirational thought. "Actually there is something that I would appreciate now."

"Yes?"

"I need an introduction to a lady spending the season in Brighton."

Sir Geoffrey's eyes twinkled. "Do you indeed? Very well. Who is she?"

"Miss Clayton, sister-in-law to Alexander Radcliffe of East-hampton."

"Radcliffe, Radcliffe," Sir Geoffrey reiterated thoughtfully, stroking his chin. "Is he a follower of the Turf by any chance?"

"That I could not say, except that they were on their way to the Brighton races the first time I came in contact with her. He's a tall, dark, aggressive-looking fellow."

Sir Geoffrey gave a deep nod. "I do know him, not well, but enough to oblige you in your request. I recall that Lady Margaret did receive Mrs. Radcliffe and the young lady in question here in Brighton last summer—or was it the summer before? I met them briefly, but I cannot guarantee to recognize Miss Clayton when I see her again, and you'll have to point her out to me. Where am I to present you to her?"

"That I cannot say. What her engagements are and when I may be sure of meeting her make up a problem to be solved. With my departure from Brighton drawing near I wish it could be solved with some promptness."

"I think I might be able to assist you there. Everybody of consequence in the resort will be attending a ball at the Marine Pavilion tomorrow evening. His Majesty will be absent—it does seem that even his interest in Brighton has waned in spite of the completion of more additions to his most extravagant of follies, the summer palace—but one of his lady cousins is spending a month there and she is the hostess." He gave Daniel a conspiratorial nod. "I will get you an invitation. Your name shall be added to my party. I would wager a pony that your Miss Clayton makes an appearance. But if she does not"—his smile broadened in a worldly fashion—"there will be plenty of other pretty faces to console you in your disappointment."

"I thank you, sir." Daniel was jubilant. He left then and went at once to a tailor of local repute, having decided to order an outfit of new evening clothes to be ready the next day for the ball at the Marine Pavilion.

Before returning to The Old Ship he took a walk along the parade where he met Jem and Kate taking the sea air together. He thought how the new, full-skirted dress of striped dimity suited her, the ribbons of the lacy straw leghorn that shaded her face running over her shoulder in the salty breeze. He turned to fall in step with them, now and again raising his hat when he was recognized by passers-by, who gave him a well-bred spatter of applause or raucous shouts of acclamation according to their station in life.

It was a perfect afternoon to see and be seen. The sea lapped turquoise-colored waves on the creamy sands, and on one stretch of the shore a cluster of high-wheeled bathing machines were drawn up at the water's edge and the squeals of the female bathers echoed shrilly as they bobbed and splashed. The machines had doors fore and aft, which enabled the ladies to enter through the rear door and disrobe in seclusion while the patient horses pulled them down the sands and into the water until the wheels were hub-deep. The horses were then unharnessed and plodded back up the sands again. The most piercing shrieks came from those who had changed into their bathing garments and had emerged through the doors facing the sea, for as soon as they appeared they were seized unceremoniously by professional women dippers and ducked two or three times under the water. The dippers had a reputation for being dragons, all tough and stout and clad in dark serge garments, straw hats giving some shade to their nut-brown faces, and eyes screwed up against the smoke of

their foul-smelling clay pipes. They waded about waist-deep for
hours on end, keeping a close watch on their charges, and although they usually ministered to their own sex some women
dippers were posted at the machines used by gentlemen in another part of the beach, and joined their equally tough male coun-
terparts in plunging their unfortunate victims without ceremony
into the chill briny. Daniel counted himself lucky that he was
able to avoid these ministrations by diving immediately from the
top step into the water and swimming away through the waves.

He was wondering if Claudine Clayton could be among the
bathers when Jem, who had been chatting to Kate, cleared his
throat and spoke in an entirely different tone of voice, both hesi-
tant and serious.

"Look here, Dan, there's something that has been troubling me
about this here turning up at Warwyck Manor with this good
lady as yer supposed wife."

"What is that?" Daniel was unconcerned. His glance followed a
saucy-looking young woman sauntering by.

"I think old Mr. Warwyck will suspect that all is not as it appears to be. Not that he won't approve of ye, ma'am," Jem
quickly nodded to Kate. "Have no fear on that issue. He'll see ye
as the salvation of his nephew, but he's a wily customer and
maybe it ain't going to be as easy as Daniel thinks to pull the
wool over his eyes."

"What do you mean?" Daniel questioned, his interest held at
last.

Jem answered him forthrightly. "I mean ye'll find yerself in a
right mess if he asks to see yer marriage lines. And even if he
don't, that lawyer of his, Mr. Houston, is more than likely to
want to check on them. After all, didn't ye tell me once there's a
lady's portion what is due to the wife of whoever inherits Warwyck?"

"That's correct. It's very little—a small endowment bequeathed
by a female ancestor of mine about a hundred years ago. It can be
waived—"

"That lawyer won't let it be waived! Not him! I remember him as a real pernickety devil, who'll prod and peer and pry into yer affairs, Dan. I'm warning ye!"

Daniel became extremely thoughtful and rubbed his chin meditatively. "There's nothing I can do about it, unless—" His eyes met Jem's and then both of them looked at Kate.

She blanched, coming to a standstill, guessing instantly what was in their minds. Her mouth dropped open slightly, her eyes frightened. "You want me to commit bigamy!" she accused in a whisper. "That could mean prison—or transportation!"

Jem spoke placatingly. "Not a marriage ceremony in a church. Nothing like that. But a proper service nevertheless, conducted by one of them traveling preachers what has been defrocked like as not, but still marries runaways and seamen twice or thrice over in one port or another and baptizes by-blows and suchlike. It would never stand up legally—ye're still the lawful wife of Farmer Farringdon and nothing can change that—but if ye'll agree to go through such a ceremony there'll be a marriage certificate to show at Warwyck, which'll look open and aboveboard, Daniel'll get his inheritance, and ye'll have done him a right good turn for saving ye from being encumbered by a rash youth who don't know his heart's turn from one day to the next."

They both watched her intently. Ever afterward she was to associate that moment with the cry of seagulls overhead, the shrieks of distant bathers, and the splash of the running tide on the shore. She took a deep, shuddering breath and expelled it slowly. "Where would you find one of these priests?" she asked, low-voiced.

Her watchers relaxed visibly, the moments of suspense over, and Jem's eye gleamed with satisfaction. "I could get a certain Reverend Appledore before the evening's out if ye're agreeable."

She did not look at Daniel. "I'm agreeable, Jem," she said with a resolute tilt of her chin. "I think I'll go back to the hotel and wait in my room until you let me know the clergyman has arrived."

They escorted her to the hotel entrance. When she had disappeared inside it Daniel punched Jem jubilantly in the chest.

"Well done! She would never have agreed for me, I feel sure. Now nothing can go wrong at Warwyck!"

Together they set off to find the Reverend Appledore with whom Jem had fallen into conversation a couple of times at one of the more disreputable taverns in the town.

The only trouble came from Harry, which Daniel had expected, and it took all of Jem's powers of persuasion to convince him that the ceremony was nothing but a sham, the ensuing certificate no more than a piece of paper not worth the ink on it, and that Kate remained as legally tied to Farmer Farringdon as ever she was. Eventually, smoldering with disgust for the whole sordid business, he agreed to stand as witness with Jem, and he was thankful that the ring, which Kate had already removed from her finger in preparation for the charade, had been given to Jem to hold and not to him.

The Reverend Appledore arrived at the appointed hour. Jem met him downstairs and showed him up to the sitting room where he greeted the Warwyck brothers affably, smiling a huge, benign smile, eyes crinkling.

"Good evening, Mr. Warwyck," he said to Daniel. "The Lord's blessing be upon you. And you, sir," he added to Harry.

He was every inch the rotund, benevolent priest, except to the keenly observant, who would notice that the eyes themselves did not smile, but were stone-hard within the fleshy folds, and his shabby black clothes were not the garments of an impoverished man of God with his mind on spiritual matters, but were more stylishly cut, wear-worn not at the knees through prayer, but at the cuffs and elbows, which was the result of countless hours at gaming tables and at taproom bars. He had spent over a month at Brighton, a longer sojourn than was customary for him, it never being advisable to stay too long in one spot, but the pickings had been exceptionally good and the local folk splendidly gullible. Nevertheless his nose for scenting the first whiff of unpleasantness, which had stood him in good stead over the years, had warned him that the hour of a timely departure was imminent. It was pleasant to close his time at the resort by making an honest guinea or two for a change.

"I'm obliged that you were able to come," Daniel replied. "Allow me to offer you some refreshment first."

"A capital notion! A little brandy if I may."

Daniel poured him a sizable measure and he made no attempt to stem verbally the flow into the glass, which he took with eager appreciativeness and downed with remarkable speed. He finished a second measure as Jem brought Kate into the room.

"Ah! The bride! God bless you, my dear." He took her hand into his clammy palm and patted it, his eyes running over her. "A most happy occasion, is it not?" He had made up his own mind about this hole-in-the-corner marriage, deciding that it was an elopement and the pugilist had brought her secretly to the hotel.

"Shall we begin?" Daniel suggested, seeing that Kate was having difficulty in withdrawing her hand.

"By all means!" The parson beckoned to Kate. "Now if you will take your place beside Mr. Warwyck, my dear? That's right. Have the ring ready, Mr. Pierce, seeing that you are to be best man." He beamed at them, cleared his throat, and opened the tattered black prayerbook he had taken from his pocket. "Dearly beloved, we are gathered here in the sight of God . . ."

Kate listened to the words as she had not done when she had married Jervis Farringdon. Then her abject despair had dulled her sight and hearing, making the church and the altar candles and the stained-glass windows a rainbow blue, the voices of the rector and her bridegroom seem far away, a drumming on a distant door. That ceremony in its own way had been no less a travesty than this one, but she had made her vows and kept them, never intending to destroy as she had done, and yet later finding it impossible not to exult without conscience that she had brought it about.

". . . nor taken in hand unadvisedly, lightly, or wantonly, to satisfy men's carnal lusts and appetites, like brute beasts that have no understanding, but reverently, discreetly, advisedly, soberly, and in the fear of God . . ."

Brute beast. Jervis Farringdon had fitted that description, but she must think on him no more. That chapter of her life had closed on that morning in the market place. The future was an unknown path, the shadow of Daniel Warwyck lying across it, but her courage was fierce and high.

". . . ordained for the procreation of children . . ."

She would like to have had a child of her own on whom to lavish all the pent-up love within her, one to laugh with and play with, to guard, to guide, to teach, and to set free. She had never known freedom, the possessive ties of an ailing mother having given way to the bonds of an unwanted marriage, only to be followed yet again by an obligatory commitment to the man standing at her side.

The parson's rich voice flowed over her, tender emphasis being given to the mutual help and comfort that each partner should have of the other, a vibrating resonance adding dreadful warning as he challenged first Jem and Harry and then charged her and Daniel to confess to any known impediment why they should not be joined together. The service moved on. Daniel's fingers were firm as he held hers when their vows were made. Then he was sliding the ring on her finger. It was over. The sham was played out. Nothing remained except for their names to be put to the piece of paper, worthless to all but Daniel.

The nib scratched as they each signed in turn. The Reverend Appledore bowed to Kate. "My sincere good wishes, Mrs. Warwyck." He turned to Daniel. "Congratulations, sir."

If he expected further refreshment he was to be disappointed. Daniel put the payment into his ready hand and saw him out of the hotel. When Daniel came back again Kate had gone to her own room, Harry had taken himself off to the taproom downstairs, and Jem was glancing over the certificate. He handed it to Daniel, who folded it and tucked it carefully away in an inner pocket. With a sudden chuckle he caught his trainer's eye.

"That was time and money well spent," he declared.

"It was that," Jem agreed with a grin.

Together they sat down in high good humor to finish every drop of the brandy left in the bottle.

Chapter 5

Daniel, dressed for the ball, stood back to scrutinize his reflection full-length in the cheval glass, adjusting the cuffs of his shirt for the right amount to show below the sleeves. His tail coat was green, fitting smoothly over his broad shoulders, his waistcoat of figured satin in a lighter shade, and his pantaloons narrow and blue-black. He was not a dandy, but he liked stylish clothes and these suited him well. A final touch with a brush to settle the forward sweep of his hair in the current fronded mode and he was ready.

A quarter of an hour later he presented himself again at the Edenfields' house, for it had been decided that he should arrive at the Marine Pavilion with his patron and Lady Margaret, who was small and plump and kindly, well used to her husband's hobnobbing with every kind of person on the Turf and in pugilism. Daniel was made welcome, renewed a previous although slight acquaintanceship with Sir Geoffrey's two sons and their wives, and then the seven of them set off in two carriages.

The Marine Pavilion glittered with lights, its onion-shaped domes soaring against a star-filled sky. The sound of music drifted across the lawns and blended with the plash of waves on the foreshore. The two carriages joined a long line of equipages drawing up in turn in front of the similarly domed porticoed entrance to allow guests to alight and follow the spread red carpet into the exotic Royal residence.

Daniel, walking in the wake of Sir Geoffrey and Lady Margaret, the other two couples behind each other after him, was more than a little taken aback when their little procession passed from the delicately hued vestibule into the vivid pink and gold brilliance of the Long Corridor where foliage of cerulean-blue covered the walls and from which airy-light staircases of cast iron and bamboo arose. From the ceiling was suspended a golden dragon supporting a waterlily-shaped chandelier, which added its glow to the gaudy magnificence of tasseled Chinese lanterns of opaque glass. The King's long-established passion for chinoiserie was made more than evident by the banners and pennants, the Ch'ien Lung vases, the model junks, the abundance of bamboo furniture, and the life-size Chinese figures in the gilded wall recesses.

They were received in the circular Saloon under a domed ceiling and reflected by crested, ormolu-framed looking glasses. The Royal cousin knew and remembered many of the faces bowing and bobbing before her, and those whom she did not recognize she blamed on her own poor memory, but how she could have forgotten the wild good looks of Mr. Warwyck she did not know, the scar on his cheek obviously from a duel wound in who knew what passionate strife, and when he bowed over her hand her powdered, middle-aged bosom swelled and sank on a suppressed sigh.

Daniel found himself being presented by the Edenfields to people on all sides in a gracious Drawing Room and was drawn into conversation, winning side glances from under feminine lashes at his height and fine bearing. By a gilded serpent-entwined pillar Sir Geoffrey finally drew him aside for a private word.

"Do you see your lady anywhere, Warwyck?"

Daniel, who had been scanning every face, shook his head. "Not here, nor was she in the Saloon."

"She may not have arrived yet. People are still coming in."

At Sir Geoffrey's side he went with his patron to rejoin Lady Margaret and one of her daughters-in-law, and the talk turned almost inevitably to the ever-increasing popularity of Brighton with the difficulty of getting suitable accommodation, in spite of all the new terraces and houses being built, unless one was fortunate enough to own one's own seaside house or booked months ahead.

"Nobody can have enough of the sea air," Lady Margaret declared. "Every resort is mushrooming and there seems no end to it. Oh, for a place a trifle different from the rest along this delightful stretch of coast where the individual would still be considered and persons of quality feel quite at home. I remember as a child that the resorts were primarily for invalids, and the famous Dr. Russell, who advocated the health-giving properties of the sea and its air in the middle of the last century, advised my grandmother when she was a girl to drink four pints of sea water mixed with milk daily, which was of many such remedies advised for the ailing. She told me it was quite dreadful."

Lady Margaret laughed merrily, the daughter-in-law tittered, and Daniel managed a polite smile, his eyes searching for a bright, red-gold head. Sir Geoffrey saw his increasing tenseness and skillfully propelled his wife into making a move for the South Drawing Room, which was as yet unexplored territory. There more greetings and introductions took place.

Then Daniel saw her. Lost in conversation with a gray-haired gentleman standing by her, her face tilted in an artfully graceful angle, Claudine was seated on a dolphin-ended sofa recessed within draperies of pleated dark green silk, the whole theme of the room linked with the sea and Nelson's victories, and it crossed his mind that her choice of seating position had not been accidental, for it set off superbly her gown of parchment-colored satin trimmed with rosy pearls and the burnished magnificence of her hair, which this evening she wore elaborately dressed in an urn-shaped topknot adorned with a wide bow and rosebuds, bunches of ringlets dancing over her ears.

"There she is!" he exclaimed in a low voice.

Sir Geoffrey followed the direction of his gaze and then touched his wife lightly on the arm. "My dear, I spy Miss Clayton on that sofa. I think we should renew our acquaintanceship."

Lady Margaret, who must have known the purpose of Daniel's
having been included in their party, gave a little nod. "I do agree.
And there's Mr. and Mrs. Radcliffe near at hand. How pleasant!
We shall present Mr. Warwyck."

With earrings bobbing she led the way across the luxuriously
carpeted Saloon, Daniel following with his patron. They came
first to the Radcliffes, who were in conversation with a Mrs. Stewart, wife of the gentleman talking to Claudine, and introductions took place. Alexander's arrogant face hardened as he recognized Daniel, his expression saying clearly that it had come to a
fine pass when even in a Royal palace a gentleman could not be
free from brushing shoulders with the common herd. Only the
presence of the Edenfields prevented him from turning his back.
Olivia Radcliffe, flustered and pleased that the Edenfields should
have sought them out, did not share her husband's knowledge of
Daniel's profession, not having seen him at close quarters on the
day of the fight, and spoke charmingly to him. She was not unlike
her younger sister in facial bone structure, and although she
lacked the force of Claudine's glittering personality she was in
truth the better-looking of the two; her eyes were round and
thickly lashed, more gray than green, without the wicked slant of
her sister's, and her hair, its coils entwined with plaited ribbons of
silver thread, was a soft, tawny hue full of golden lights. Daniel
judged her to be closer to her husband's age than that of
Claudine, which he thought to be nineteen and no more. As the
small circle widened to bring Mr. Stewart and Claudine into it,
Daniel was hidden momentarily from Claudine's view and she
had not yet seen him.

"Lady Margaret! Sir Geoffrey!" Claudine glowed as she rose
from the sofa to make the curtsy expected from youth in
deference to those older and socially superior. "How delightful to
meet again!"

Then Daniel stepped forward and Sir Geoffrey introduced him.
"Allow me to present a young friend of mine, ma'am. Mr. Daniel
Warwyck."

It was to both of them as if all else ceased to exist and they were alone in that Saloon, but it was with a burning clash of personalities and not with any gentler aspects or with romantic undertones. Claudine's ivory skin went chalk-white over her cheekbones and she glittered hostility at Daniel, recognizing that in some obscure way a trap had been set and sprung, catching her in it. There was no escape from acknowledging at last this powerful man with his alarming good looks, and from now on he would be able to address her by name at any place they met or their paths crossed, no matter whom she was with, no matter if it were the King himself. And he could even be in his pugilist's garb at the time. But warring with her aversion to his low station and all he represented there was the familiar excitement that the sight of him had brought her when he had held her eyes with his bold and savage stare from the ring. It made her insides quake and every nerve quiver. As on that first occasion her body seemed to communicate with his in a language of its own that she was powerless to control. Never would she forget the sensation that had swept over her at the intense and brutal maleness of him when he had set his foot on the carriage step, smelling as he had of sweat and blood and violence, which had stirred something basic and primitive in her that she had not known existed.

"It gladdens me to make your acquaintance, Mr. Warwyck," she lied, her throat stiff.

"The honor is mine, Miss Clayton," he answered evenly, well aware that this was his moment of triumph and determined to make her squirm a little more within the trap. "But surely we have met somewhere before?"

The odious wretch! she thought spitefully. No social graces at all! No gentleman would refer to a meeting at which he had been half-dressed, but then no gentleman would be seen in a prize ring in the first place!

"I think not," she replied, her carefully placed smile for the benefit of those watching, but meant as a baring of teeth to him. "I always remember those to whom I'm properly introduced, but otherwise all else is beneath my notice."

"Then I'm grateful to Sir Geoffrey for having performed our introduction," he returned glibly, "because now I can be sure of being remembered. The music tells me the dancing has begun. May I lead you onto the floor?"

She would have refused him on some pretext, no matter that he did enjoy the Edenfields' patronage, this low-class upstart whose well-spoken voice could only be born of a mimicry of his betters. But then Olivia—dull, silly Olivia who could never grasp under-currents swirling about her—spoke up before she could bring out a reply.

"You must have guessed how my sister loves dancing, Mr. War-wyck. I sometimes think she would dance all day and night if it were possible. By all means take her onto the floor without delay, and I know I speak for all of us."

None could have suspected the turmoil of Claudine's feelings as she moved with her usual feline grace at Daniel's side through to the Music Room where the Royal cousin had opened the dancing with one of the more distinguished guests in a setting of oriental lavishness that burst upon the eye in its scarlet and gold. It was the Turning Dance, which had become known as the Waltz. For a deliberate moment—a moment that seemed to hang in the air and suspend time—Daniel and Claudine turned to face each other and he looked deeply at her, increasing the insane excite-ment within her that had not abated. Then he took her fingers possessively into his, set one hand on the back of her shivering waist, and drew her into the music. Her feet began to glide with his. On silk, on clouds, on the music itself.

They completed a circuit of the shining floor without speaking, but their physical communication was so vibrant and demanding that she did not dare to meet his eyes, not knowing what she might see there. Briefly she knew a pang because he was what he was and there could never be anything between them. None of the suitors she had refused—and there was an unending queue—had been able to reach the innermost parts of her by a mere look, glance, or touch of the hand as this man could. At the same time she hated him. He represented something she could not have and throughout her nineteen years there had been nothing that she had set her heart on that she had not been able to have. Doting parents had indulged her and with their passing Olivia and Alexander had taken over their role at the same time as they had taken her into their home, although at times Alexander's attitude toward her was anything but fatherly.

"Tomorrow I'm leaving Brighton," he said, having watched her under his lids ever since he had swung her smoothly into the rotating dance. Was it his imagination or had he felt a tremor pass through her at his words? Relieved that he was going, was she? Or could it be the reverse?

"I declare I could not endure to leave Brighton before the season is out," she answered lightly. "My sister and brother-in-law, with whom I have made my home, have a mansion buried away from civilization."

"Is it deep in the countryside then? Whereabouts?"

She was not going to be caught out as easily as that in revealing where she lived, not realizing that he was already in possession of the facts, and she evaded a direct answer. "It's close to the seashore and a short ride from a market town, but dull, oh, so dull compared with Brighton."

"Yet you live by the sea."

She gave a contemptuous little laugh. "You would understand what I mean if you could see the hamlet that gives its name to our address. Nothing but a handful of fishermen's cottages, a church, an inn, and miles of white sand with rarely a person on them."

"It sounds as if the sea bathing is safe there."

"Nothing could be safer or, as I said before, duller."

"I don't believe I should find it dull," Daniel remarked thoughtfully. "No, I think I should find such a place extremely interesting." Jem would have recognized the expression in his eyes as being an indication that he was up to something, and even Claudine, without knowing why, felt that whatever it was that lay behind his words it boded no good for her.

"Well, if you favor Devonshire you would favor anywhere," she retaliated with a supercilious smile.

"I have some matters of importance to settle in that county and it may take two or three months."

She considered him to be boasting about matters of importance and did not imagine a word of it to be true. After all, he came from a profession that knew how to feint and bluff, and she would make a guess that he had been engaged to fight bouts at fairgrounds and other such disreputable places in that part of the country. Good riddance to him! That was where he belonged. His head had been swollen by Sir Geoffrey's patronage or else he would not have dared show his face in these regal surroundings. It was well known that many a pugilist taken into the home of a wealthy patron to be trained and fed like a fighting cock got ideas above his station. For a short while those men rode in grand carriages, were dressed like princes, and fêted by all, but the cherished delusions of grandeur came to a sorry end when the pugilist began to go downhill, invariably through debauch, and began to lose one mill and then another. Many of them ended in the gutter, and more than one once-famous hero of the ring had died in the workhouse. Would such a fate come to Daniel Warwyck? She hoped it would. With the strength of a curse she hoped it would. Through the fans of her curiously shaded lashes she looked up into his face.

"Should that interest me? To be informed of your plans?" She did not dare to make it of more biting taunt while comparatively helpless in his arms. There was no telling what such a fellow might do and she had an unholy dread of scandal. She had seen what scandal could do, and for that, far more than anything else, she watched and guarded her behavior, taking no risks that might destroy all chances of an advantageous marriage, for she had set her sights high and, although she had money herself, she wanted great wealth and perhaps a title. She knew her own value, had discovered early how easily she could attract the opposite sex, and was sure at the moment of her bargaining power. In it she was backed by Alexander, who was in no haste to see her wed and out of his house, willing enough to protect her and turn away those suitors in whom she had lost interest and others not fit by his own standards of class, wealth, and breeding to call upon her.

Daniel was answering her, not showing whether or not he had taken up the jibe lurking behind her words, although there was taunt enough in his own. "Now we are formally acquainted my absence will be noticeable to you. I consider it only courteous to give some warning of the length of time before I'm able to return to Sussex."

Warning indeed! He was telling her that he intended coming back into her life! "Have you another mill arranged in these parts then?" It was a skillful way of shamming indifference.

He shook his head, and his voice took on a faintly ominous crispness. "Tell me, Miss Clayton, how would you value the colors of the champion of all England?"

She raised her eyebrows delicately. "Is that where your ambition lies?"

His mouth curled without humor. "I have a single aim in life, ma'am. To gain what I want and what I mean to have. It happens—among other things—to encompass the championship."

Her shoulders, exposed by the fashionably low neckline, rose and fell prettily.

"That's a sight I'll never see. Nor should I want to." Since he had again referred indirectly to their first meeting she saw no reason, now that none else was in earshot, not to make some comment upon it. "It was sheer chance that day I should come with others to that part of the road overlooking the dell where you fought the bout."

"You've not answered my question about the greatest colors a pugilist can win." He was pressing her closer to him, arching her like a bow.

There was a threat in his voice, a deep, abiding anger with her that she recognized as being close to a passion of another kind. She knew he sought from her a retraction of her action that day. A submission. A sop to his pride. All tantamount to surrender. Never! But it would be amusing and deliciously dangerous to let him stew. The waltz was coming to an end and she twirled out on his hand to dip low in a closing curtsy to his bow.

"Win the colors first, Mr. Warwyck," she said, maliciousness behind the smile she turned up at him. "And then we'll see."

We'll see indeed, he thought. She was full of tricks, but he would break her yet. Never could he remember lusting after a woman more. It was like a sickness of the blood.

"My hand, sir," she said. She had risen from her curtsy, but he was still holding her fingers, exerting pressure, and only by tugging could she expect to release them, an indignity she was not prepared to indulge in.

"Which of the next dances is to be mine?" he asked. They were moving off the floor, but her fingers were totally captive.

"Another waltz." She was desperate to be free, thinking they must look like lovers hand in hand. "The last one of the evening —nobody else shall claim that from me, you have my word on it."

To be granted the last dance of the evening was an honor in it-self and could be given without risk of speculation by a lady of any age, but for a single couple to dance more than twice with each other was to invite gossip, and he knew he must be content that she had selected the only dance other than the supper dance that was special in itself. He eyed her warily, suspiciously, but her face was guileless, and he was compelled to let her fingers slide from his. She linked them with those of her other hand in front of her, swishing along beside him in her satin hems as he escorted her back to the group they had left in the Saloon. As he had ex-pected, there was a small cluster of other would-be partners wait-ing to commit her to the rest of the evening's dancing. He left her to them with a bow and turned to invite Lady Margaret to take the floor with him, which she did.

He enjoyed the evening. Pretty women abounded and the champagne flowed. He drank more than he would normally have done, not to become intoxicated, but to follow his mood through on the triumphant note of having secured the most honored dance from Claudine, which was like a notch marked up to him in the curious, tempestuous battle known only to themselves. The sparkling wine gave him a lightness of spirit that suited him and he flirted with his partners, who responded dazzlingly. Had he wished it the opportunity for more than one assignation could have been his, but he had another ultimate conquest on his mind and let it pass. Once, his glance happening to rest by chance on Olivia, who was only a few feet from him, he saw her gray eyes fix in a certain direction and the corners of the soft mouth tighten. Out of curiosity he followed her gaze and saw Claudine laughing provocatively up into Alexander's face, her white-gloved fingertips dancing against his cravat to emphasize a point, and he, smiling closely at her, would have folded his hand over hers had she not whipped it away teasingly, continuing to hold his besotted attention. So that was the way of it. Daniel looked again at Olivia, but her expression had regained its repose as someone addressed her, and he believed himself to be the only one who had observed that tiny crack in the woman's armor. Beneath it she suffered. Claudine's magnetism reached out far and wide, but even closer home it appeared to have qualities that her own sister feared.

At supper in the magnificent banqueting room the Edenfields joined the Radcliffes, but Daniel was duty-bound to look after the lady with whom he had danced the gavotte previous to it, which was no hardship, for she was both witty and beautiful, but it left him no chance to talk again to Claudine, who in any case had her own admirers about her. Yet across the champagne their eyes met, hers gleaming and secretive as though she were savoring some private pleasure of her own. Again afterward on the Music Room floor their glances touched and parted and met again. Puzzlement grew in him, and gradually there came the uncomfortable feeling of being left out of a joke that she was finding intensely entertaining.

What that joke was he discovered when he went into the drawing room to claim her for the promised waltz. Not seeing her at once, he stood looking about him. Sir Geoffrey touched him on the sleeve.

"Miss Clayton left a few minutes ago with Mr. and Mrs. Radcliffe. She requested most charmingly that I should bid you good night on her behalf."

Had he been entirely sober he would not have reacted as he did, but her trickery enraged him. His temper snapped. She had sworn that no one else should claim the waltz from her, but neither had she intended to dance it with him! Swiftly he dodged through couples and evaded chattering groups until he reached the comparatively deserted Long Corridor where he broke into a run. The pounding of his feet set up a vibration that made the nodding porcelain mandarins wag their heads as if demented. Out through the vestibule and the octagon hall until he reached the portico in time to see the Radcliffes' barouche, closed against the night air, bowling away down the street. He broke into a sprint after it without a second thought.

At the corner the barouche slowed its pace due to the crush of other wheeled traffic taking home theater-goers, who had just emerged from the performance. Among those walking homeward were Harry and Kate in the company of Jem, who had come to the theater to meet them. Kate was telling him what a superbly acted play it had been when Jem turned his head at the sound of running footsteps and drew in his breath sharply.

"Hallo! What's up? There's Dan after that carriage! Has he been robbed or what?"

Even as he and Harry sprang forward automatically, intent on giving whatever assistance was needed, Daniel reached the barouche and leaped for it, seizing the handle and getting a foothold to swing himself up and hook an elbow over the open window. He saw the pale oval of Claudine's suddenly frightened face in the gloom of the interior before Alexander rose from where he was sitting and loomed up as a dark shape between them. Before Daniel realized what was happening Alexander's outspread hand half-covered his face with the full force of a great thrust behind it. Unable to save himself, Daniel lost his hold and went flying backward. His head cracked on the cobbles and he lay still in the gutter as the wheels went rolling on and bore the barouche away.

Chapter 6

Daniel sat brooding and smoldering in the curricle beside Jem, who was driving him away from Brighton, which lay several miles behind them along the dusty road darkened by a dismal day. In their wake Harry held the reins of a second equipage, a chaise used for the conveyance of their baggage, Kate beside him. Daniel did not want to think about Kate, whom he had abused the night before with a harshness that he acknowledged to himself had been unfair. Recovering from being stunned by the impact of the cobbles, he had discovered her kneeling in the gutter beside him, and his head was in her lap, she heedless of the blood flowing from the cut he had suffered, that was being soaked into the skirt of one of her new gowns.

"Have you no sense, woman? Is this how you accept charity? Ruining an expensive garment before the occasion it was intended for!" He thrust himself up from her, half-mad with rage at the final humiliation heaped upon him from the Radcliffe carriage. None of the clothes bought for Kate had been purchased with any thought of charity and all had been reasonably priced, but he was making her bear the brunt of the whole disastrous evening. Jem and Harry caught and steadied him as he reeled about, still half-dazed, the blood flowing down his neck to stain his shirt and darken the fine cloth of his evening coat. Passers-by thought him drunk, but drunken bucks on the street were a commonplace sight at night, and although some tittered and made remarks, nobody stopped to stare.

Kate had not retaliated to his insults and somehow her silence as she had risen quickly to her feet and drawn back from him had had the effect of exacerbating his anger, but Jem gave him no chance to give further wrath against her, and with Harry's aid helped him along at a stumble to the hotel, which was only a short distance away. Kate had followed behind and he had not seen her again until this morning when she had been seated ready in the chaise when he had come out of the hotel. He might have offered some kind of apology then and even thanked her for having sponged clean and pressed his evening coat, but with that detached air of hers that had been so apparent at the auction, she sat looking ahead and virtually ignored him. Well, let her get on with it for the time being, he had thought to himself. But he was nevertheless riled by her attitude, no matter what he said or did to her, for she was practically his property as much as the gold fob-watch that dangled from his doeskin waistcoat.

His thoughts turned to Claudine. Her remembered, intensely personal perfume seemed to fill his nostrils, exquisite, slightly musky, the unmistakable bouquet of the highly sexed woman, and the palms of his hands knew again the firmness of her waist through the fine satin of her gown and the provocative play of her fingers within his. Restlessly he shifted in his seat.

"When you get to Lewes, turn off and take the sea road to Easthampton," he ordered Jem. "It goes by way of the market town of Merrelton."

"There's no sense in that," Jem answered bluntly and doggedly. "It'll take us miles off our route for no purpose." He was not as ignorant as to the possible reason for the proposed change of road as he appeared, having made it a point of interest after the mill to find out about the redheaded creature who had taken Daniel's eye, and he had read in the same visitors' book that her home address lay at Easthampton. Last night Daniel had let fall that the young Clayton woman had been in the barouche and it was her brother-in-law who had pushed him in the face. After getting him to bed Jem and Harry had sat in the taproom over a pint pot each and more or less put together the story of what had happened at the Marine Pavilion. Normally Jem would have insisted on Daniel's spending the morning or even the whole day in bed after receiving such a clout on the head, as he would have done had it occurred in a mill, but both he and Harry decided that in view of what had happened it was best to get Daniel safely away from Brighton at the light of dawn to avoid the risk of his getting into any further trouble. And now Daniel wanted to drive through Easthampton, doubtless to moon over the house where the wretched little minx lived. Jem found himself hard put to it not to put his irate thoughts into words.

"We don't have to retrace our tracks," Daniel was saying, not to be put off. "There's a lane out of Easthampton that carries on along the coast and will bring us back eventually to our own road."

"A lane!" Jem snorted. "More like a rutted bog that will glue down our wheels and hold us up for a day or more."

"Now do as I say, for I mean to see Easthampton before I leave this part of the coast," Daniel replied with heavy impatience, showing he had had enough of the argument.

It was unfortunate that when they had left Lewes and reached Merrelton, Harry having acknowledged the change of direction shouted to him by Jem with a lifting of his whip, a light rain began to fall. By the time they approached Easthampton it had turned into pelting drops, which drummed on the two carriage roofs as they bowled along, one behind the other, the wheels splashing freshly churned mud. Daniel was undisturbed by the rain, staring out avidly when they passed the gates of the several large houses grandly set within their own spacious grounds. When they came level with a pair of huge, lion-topped stone gateposts, one of which bore the inscription *Radcliffe Hall*, he bade Jem draw up. He jumped out before the wheels came to a full stand-still and darted through the increasingly heavy rain to reach the wide wrought-iron gates where he stood looking through at the curving drive and the gaunt, turreted mansion that loomed up at the end of it.

"What on earth is he doing?" Kate inquired, leaning forward to peer out at him. She and Harry were snug under a leather knee cover and were well protected by the projecting roof from the weather.

Harry had also been watching his brother. "That's the permanent residence of Miss Clayton, whom I told you about—the one who was the cause of the trouble last night. He's taking a good look at it. God knows why! Even if he fancied his chances with her before in his forthcoming status of Squire of Warwyck, that insulting behavior of Radcliffe's toward him has created an unbridgeable gap. Daniel's pride would never let him call upon her at Radcliffe Hall and in any case he would never be received. So there's an end to it, and we're wasting traveling time over it and he's risking lung fever in this rain, all to no purpose."

"He's getting back into the curricle now," Kate observed.

"That's a mercy. Let's hope we can get through Easthampton at a spanking pace and lose no more time." Flicking the whip across the horse's rump, he settled back in his seat to follow the curricle moving forward in the rain ahead. He had welcomed the downpour. It had created a cosy and intimate atmosphere in the carriage with Kate, which would not have been if the hood had been down in blazing sunshine. At first he had done all the talking, but gradually he had drawn her out, slowly at first, smiling his charming smiles and gaining her confidence with his open countenance that held no more than a friendly and compassionate interest. He asked her if she was born in Heathfield.

"No, I was born in London, but I remember nothing of that place, because my parents left there when I was only two years old. My father's aunt bequeathed him a house at Heathfield, and as he was ever short of money he thought to save rent and live more cheaply there than in London, but my mother was never happy in their new home."

"What trade did your father follow?"

"No trade, but the arts. He was an artist—a very fine artist. His lack of commercial success had nothing to do with any lack of talent." She spoke proudly and with some defiance. "He turned one room into a studio and I spent hours there. Sometimes I sat for him, and others I'd clean his brushes, mix his paints, or prepare his canvases. I regret to say that my mother was jealous of his affection for me as she was jealous of anything and anybody who took his mind from her. In the end her jealousy destroyed his ability to work even as it had destroyed their relationship, and finally he could endure no more." The bleakness of the rain outside the carriage window was reflected in her eyes. In a voice that was barely audible she said, "He took his own life."

"What a tragic misfortune," Harry said with deep sympathy, moved by her tale. He could only guess at the grief and misery and torment of a gifted man that lay behind it. "I should like to see some of your father's work—"

She cut him short. "My mother burned every one." Abruptly she turned her face from him, her bonnet brim a shield, and he refrained tactfully from further questioning, barely able to visualize the scene that her words had conjured up of a woman demented in a thwarted possessiveness creating a bonfire out of what had been dearest to her man's heart. Harry longed to put an arm about Kate, to draw her head against his shoulder and promise her such love that all unhappy memories of the past would be driven away and forgotten, but he had to stay his embrace, hold his tongue, and bide his time, or else he would lose her forever. Yet there was so much he wanted to know about those years after her father's death. Why had she married a man years older than herself, and what were the circumstances that had brought about her being put up for sale? Abruptly he changed the subject.

"Do you care for animals, Kate? There are always dogs and plenty of cats at Warwyck. I remember when Jassy and I reared a motherless lamb and Bella, as we called her, delved us into no end of trouble, because she would follow us about—in the house and out of it. Once she got into the rose garden and ate every bud she could reach. It looked as if they had been snapped off with shears." With satisfaction he heard her give a little throaty chuckle. "That's when Uncle William decided it was time for her to join the flock. It was one misdemeanor too many. She had lambs of her own the following year." That was a lie, but having coaxed Kate away from her memories he was not going to depress her again. Uncle William had had Bella slaughtered.

Kate, innocently unaware, caught up the topic of pets on his lighthearted note and proceeded with some tale of her own, and they were smiling together over it when they drove into East-hampton and drew up once more at a signal from Jem in a lane that ran by an overgrown green around which the humble dwellings of the hamlet were clustered.

Daniel, alighting from the curricle again, saw the smiles Kate and Harry were exchanging in the chaise and resolved to take steps to keep them apart. He would never have bought Kate in the first place if part of the reason had not been to keep Harry from his folly and it would be a sorry state of affairs if it still came about. Daniel had thrown around his shoulders over his coat a traveling cape which was kept under the curricle's seat for such quirks of weather, and he turned up the collar against the rain as he approached the chaise.

"I want to take a look at this place," he informed his brother, pulling down the brim of his tall hat to protect his eyes more from the rain.

"Are you out of your head?" Harry exclaimed, glancing about to see where they were. "There is nothing to look at in this dismal hole."

"That's why," Daniel replied enigmatically, and then added, "There's no need to wait in the carriage. Jem has spotted a tavern at the end of this lane by the seashore. It's a long time since we had breakfast and if you are hungry have something to eat there. I'll seek you out as soon as I have seen all I want to see."

He stepped back from the carriage and they drove on, sharing bafflement over his extraordinary behavior for which they could find no explanation this time. They came into the courtyard of the slate-roofed tavern with a loud clatter of hooves on the wet flagstones. A sign, creaking as it swung in the wind off the sea, showed them that it was called The Running Hare. When a young ostler ran forward to catch the horse's head Harry helped Kate to alight, setting his hands boldly on her waist, and then they both darted out of the rain through the low-linteled door to join Jem, who was already inside and had placed an order for the three of them.

Left alone Daniel took careful note of his surroundings. The hamlet was more or less as Claudine had described it, but in addition to the church, the tavern, and the cottages there were some small commercial establishments and a few better-class houses. None of that interested him as much as the hamlet's setting, which in spite of the weather was spectacular with a broad, blunt-summitted hillock rising above the green, lush woodland on all sides, and backed in turn by the undulating sweep of the Sussex Downs. Only to the south did the hamlet lay open and that was to face the sea.

He stared long and hard at the hillock, such an image of what could be there forming in his mind that when he happened to glance back at it a few minutes later it was almost with surprise that he saw it was as bare of all but grass and trees as it had been before.

Holding his cape about him he set off along the lane and reached the seashore, passing on the way a man leading a creel-laden donkey, and two girls hurrying homeward under a shared coat they held jointly over their heads. Pushing aside the feathery branches of a tamarisk hedge he stepped onto a natural bastion of rocks and shingle, and saw stretched before him the white expanse of tide-rippled sands meeting wind-whipped waves within the graceful curve of a wide bay. He caught his breath sharply. It was a magnificent vista, and in the distance, lying like a sea-logged whale, was the Isle of Wight.

He turned back through the hedge. What a location was Easthampton's! It had the combined unspoiled beauty of country-side and seashore, and he saw within his grasp the chance he had been waiting for ever since he had begun to make his own way in the world. He could embark on a venture that would enable him to build his own empire out of rocks and flints and sand. His mark would be made for all time. He would make the name of Warwyck his own at last.

With rain trickling unheeded down his face he grinned at the green hillock situated so centrally above the hamlet. Not for him a sheltered dell for the house he would build by the sea. He wanted no quiet woods and filtered breezes, but a site that faced the elements, its stout walls withstanding the wind's buffeting, its interior snugly protected with great fires leaping up the chimneys in winter, and its many windows open to let through the cool sea draft in summer. When the matter of the estate in Devonshire was settled he would come back to Easthampton, and somehow or other he would raise the money by his own efforts to buy that hillock facing the sea if he had to fight seven days a week in the prize ring to do it. On the summit of those slopes there would rise one day the most splendid house for miles around, and he knew already what he would call it. Easthampton House.

He could not be sure when the idea of seizing Easthampton for himself first came to him, but the kernel of the idea had been slowly forming over the past few days. Perhaps his enchantment with Brighton was mainly responsible, opening the pleasures of the seaside to him as it had done, but it could be that subconsciously a decision to strike roots at Easthampton had originated when he read in the Master of Ceremonies' book in the library that Claudine came from there, almost as if he knew even then that he would have to stalk her long and true to wreak the full vengeance that he had in mind. How the score between Claudine and himself had grown since then!

Turning his head into the wind and meeting the full force of the slashing downpour, he soon covered the short distance across to The Running Hare. In the hallway he unclasped his wet cloak, hung it on a peg, and went into the taproom. The landlord had lit a fire and Harry sat in the inglenook with Kate, who had her eyes on him as she listened attentively to what he was saying, his gestures animated, his voice low. There was nothing coquettish in the manner in which she was regarding him, but Harry's face showed that he was absorbed in her alone. Neither turned their heads to look at Daniel as he entered, but his glance lingered on them with some displeasure at their oblivion to all else around them. He went straight to the bar to join Jem, who was leaning an elbow on it, in full conversation with the landlord. They both turned as he reached them.

"Good day to you, sir." Obsequiously the landlord nodded and half-bowed behind the bar, reaching out to wipe with a cloth the worn surface in front of Daniel where some wet circles from the base of a tankard gleamed. "What may I serve you?"

Daniel returned his greeting, but before giving an order he leaned his arms on the bar and raised his eyebrows inquiringly at Jem. "Have you had anything to eat?"

Jem nodded. "I can recommend the hot steak pies. Mrs. Warwyck had one, but Harry and I have tucked two each away."

"Then I'll have the same and a pint of ale."

The landlord fetched two steaming steak pies on a plate from the kitchen and would have set knife and fork upon a table if Daniel had not stopped him, saying he would remain at the bar. When they were put before him Daniel picked up the first without ceremony and bit into it. Tender meat and rich gravy mixed with crisp, golden pastry in his mouth. It was as good as Jem had said it would be.

"Just the day for something 'ot and tasty," the landlord beamed when Daniel expressed his praise. "I've been 'earing from your man 'ere that you be on your way to Devonshire." It happened frequently that Jem was taken for Daniel's servant and Jem never resented it, for Daniel had the gentry's way of walking into any place as though he owned it and Jem knew he looked as though he had never owned anything of value in his life.

"And I've been learning a bit about Easthampton," Jem put in with a sideways glance at Daniel.

"I liked what I saw of it," Daniel replied, and sampled the ale. He set it down again with an appreciative nod. "The Running Hare's ale is as good as its pies. You must do a good trade here, landlord."

The man had a large, good-humored face, but it sagged hound-like as he shook his head regretfully. "It's mostly local people that come in 'ere, and they don't flash money about—it's too 'ard to come by. Once a month there's a small market 'eld and then we're busy 'ere for the day, but few travelers pass through East'ampton, 'cos it's away from all the through roads and turn-pikes."

"Do you get no custom from those who live in the outlying mansions around the hamlet?" Daniel inquired.

Again a heavy shake of the head. "I reckon you can see for yourself, sir, that this ain't no establishment to attract the quality trade, and them below stairs don't come into East'ampton. It's the town of Merrelton what's the 'ub of everything in this part of the county for many miles around."

"Is there no coach trade?" Daniel was well into the second pie.

"None at all. The stagecoaches pour into Merrelton and go from there to all parts of the country, and it's a real thriving place. Mr. Brown, who 'as the general stores in East'ampton, runs a weekly wagon for those who want to send in goods and ain't got the transport themselves. Mostly the fishermen walk in their donkeys and creels, not able to pay 'is fancy prices, but it's fifteen miles each way."

"I saw a few bathing machines pulled up on the shingle with the name of Thomas J. Brown painted on the sides. Who patronizes them when they are in use?"

"The quality folks from those big 'ouses you mentioned use 'em, making expeditions in on fine days with picnics and servants. Otherwise we don't see other than ordinary local folk."

"That's a great pity." Daniel had finished up the last crumbs and he took a swig from the tankard. "Visitors bring employment, and there appears to be a sad lack of it from what I have been able to judge."

"You've 'it the nail on the 'ead, sir. I sometimes think it would 'ave 'elped if old Sir 'Amilton Barton or some of 'is family would come back and stay 'ere like in the old days, but we never see sight nor 'ide of 'em."

"There's a Member of Parliament in one of the London boroughs of that name," Daniel said, sharply interested.

"That's the old gentleman's grandson. We read about the family in the newspapers sometimes."

"The Barton family gave its patronage to this hamlet in the old days, did it?" Daniel pursued.

"That's right, sir. But it was long before my time. Old Sir 'Amilton was a sickly child and they brought 'im to East'ampton for the sea air, never thinking he would ever thrive, but 'e's over ninety now and still going strong." The landlord laughed heartily and slapped a big flat hand on the bar. "'Ow's that for proof of the 'ealth-giving properties of the salubrious East'ampton air!"

Daniel smiled and then Jem, who chuckled, asked the question that had formed in Daniel's mind, although less grammatically. "How come they don't show no interest in the place?"

The landlord shrugged. "Ask me another. They own enough of East'ampton—or at least, Sir 'Amilton does—but 'e lives up north and so do most of the family, and I've 'eard tell that 'e 'as estates in Yorkshire and Lancashire as well as in Scotland ranging over many acres, so there isn't nothing 'ere to tempt 'em down. Barton agents collect the rents and there's always trouble with tenants that can't pay. Bailiffs turn 'em out, and then the Reverend Singleton and 'is good wife make up beds in the church for the 'owling women and the weeping children, and it's a real troublesome time for everybody." He emitted a sad sigh and shook his head. "I don't know if you noticed a strip of overgrown land near the green? There were cottages there, but the Barton agents 'ad such fights with the occupants that in the end old Sir 'Amilton 'ad the places pulled down." His rubicund countenance was grim. "It was a cruel day—in winter, too, and 'alf of 'em starving. It's no wonder that most of East'ampton is up for sale, but there ain't nobody interested in buying anything in a poverty-stricken 'amlet like this one, more's the pity." Then, seeing Daniel drain his tankard and set it down, he reached to take it. "Same again, sir?"

"No, thank you, landlord. I bid you good day. We must be on

our way and delay no longer, pleasant though it has been to sample your pies and your ale."

"Good day to you, sir. I 'ope you'll be back again one day. God speed your journey."

Jem drank up quickly, preparing to follow Daniel as he turned to leave. In the inglenook Harry and Kate, both realizing that a move was being made, rose from their seats, still in animated conversation. At the door Daniel paused to look back over his shoulder at them. His voice snapped out across the length of the taproom.

"Kate!"

She started violently, her head jerking round toward him, and her hands that were fastening her coat buttons became still. "Yes, Daniel?"

"You'll ride with me in the curricle now. Jem can take the hired carriage with Harry." The hardness of his stare defied her to make any form of protest and she submitted with a stiff-necked little nod. As he swung out of the tavern he heard her say placatingly to his brother that they would finish their discussion another time. The door swung shut on Harry's reply, but Daniel caught its displeased murmur.

He sat in the curricle with the reins in his grasp when she climbed up beside him, Harry giving her a helping hand before going off with disgruntled strides to join Jem. When she was settled with a traveling rug over her lap and the protective leather weather guard over their knees was fastened, he flicked the whip and they rolled away.

He did not speak until they were out of Easthampton, not wanting his attention diverted from whatever else there was to see of it, but in a little while it was left behind.

"I would deem it a favor," he said stonily, "if you would discourage my brother's attentions. If you do not, it could cause unnecessary complications."

"He was only friendly," she replied, a slight tremor in her voice as though somewhat upset by what he had requested.

"It's more than that. He's romantic and susceptible. He saw you in the market place as a damsel in distress, and I dare say the illusion still clings. You're older than he is and wiser. I cannot believe that such a comely young woman as yourself lacks experience in rejecting unwanted overtures."

He became aware that she was shaking. "He has done nothing to cause me embarrassment and neither has he said anything that you or anybody else could take exception to. Am I to be denied friendship?"

"I said nothing about friendship. By all means make a friend of him as of Jem and of me."

"You!" So fiercely was the word uttered that he looked at her in amazement. Her eyes were blazing, giving away depths of passion locked within her that her calm docility had never led him to suspect. "Do you mock me? I—a wearer of charity garments, a chattel, purchased by you for money like any common whore! Jem has befriended me, and so has Harry—but you treat me for what I am! A burden and a nuisance necessary to the securing of your inheritance! I wish you had let Harry buy me—or both of you had left me to the Frenchman! At least I would have been wanted as someone within my own right!"

He jerked the horse to a standstill and then turned about in the seat to grab her by the arms in a vise-like grip, half-pulling her to him. "Do you think I'm proud of what I said to you last night? I was angry—I was half out of my head. You are doing me a favor by wearing the clothes that we chose together—charity does not come into it, except that I am in your debt for the form of marriage that we went through and the part you're prepared to play! But don't talk to me of Harry or the Frenchman My brother would have wearied you with his calf love and the Frenchman would have used you cruelly—I at least have made no physical demands upon you, which would have been my right, and neither shall anyone else all the time you go by the name of Kate Warwyck, which makes you mine and mine alone!"

Her face was aflame, her chest heaving, but before she could make any reply Jem's visage loomed out of the rain at the side of the curricle. "What's up, Dan?" he inquired, peering in at them. "Why have ye stopped?"

With a kind of choked sob Kate sprang up, set one hand on Jem's shoulder and leaped down from the curricle. With flashing heels she ran back down the muddy lane to where Harry had drawn up the hired carriage in the rear and clambered into it. Jem looked after her.

"Best let her be for now," he said calmly, hauling himself up into the equipage and sitting down heavily beside Daniel. "Want me to take the reins?"

"No," said Daniel on a sigh, taking them up with the whip again. "Just sit there and tell me whatever you learned about Easthampton before I came into The Running Hare."

It proved to be talk about people who were prominent in the hamlet, and included the information that Thomas J. Brown was one of the few who owned his own property, having bought it from a small strip owned by the Radcliffe family. Jem had learned it was Alexander who had financed the bathing machines managed by Brown, mainly for the convenience of his own guests, an idea instigated by his young sister-in-law Claudine the summer she had come home from her convent boarding school in France and deplored the lack of local facilities.

"From France?" Daniel picked up.

"I probed a bit on that one," Jem said, "thinking ye'd be interested. It appears the mother was French and heiress to some vineyards, which the father, who was English, acquired upon the marriage. Yer redheaded Miss Clayton has a real bit of money, a right catch for any man what likes that color hair, and it seems her sister had an equal share of the fortune. Y'know, it's been my experience that there's nothing a landlord don't know about people what lives in his area or can't find out from somebody or other."

"Go on about the land," Daniel prompted, the information about Claudine and her relatives having apparently drained out.

There was little more to tell. Some of the small holdings were owned by those who worked the land themselves, and a few acres adjacent to the church, which were ecclesiastical property, were farmed out at a peppercorn rent to the poor of the parish.

"So that's Easthampton for ye," Jem rounded in conclusion. He sounded as if he hoped he had seen the last of it. Daniel knew it was only the beginning.

For the rest of the day Kate rode with Harry. When they stopped to change horses or take some refreshment at a wayside tavern she showed no aftereffects of the clash with Daniel and was her usual dignified and composed self, but she did not speak to him unless politeness compelled her to address him, and he answered with equal courtesy.

Fire and ice, Daniel thought, observing her when she bade the three of them good night at the coaching inn where they were staying overnight. In her neat, blue gown that suited her fine height, and with candlelight shining on her moon-colored hair she had the look of a Norse goddess about her, an impression strengthened by the long-legged grace with which she moved across the floor to the door that led out of the private room where they had dined long and late. Under dipped lids his gaze followed her straight back and he half-regretted not exercising those very rights he had renounced and which she could not have denied him. But then Harry sprang forward to open the door for her and Daniel saw how she smiled her thanks. There would have been no such smiles for him had he invaded the privacy of her bedchamber, and he had never yet taken a woman who had not welcomed him gladly. It was better that he had left matters as they were between them.

In the hallway beyond the door that Harry had left open there was a table set with candles for guests to light and take upstairs with them. From where they still sat at the table Daniel and Jem could hear what he was saying to her although they could not see them.

"Let me light one for you, Kate! This one has a strong wick. There! I'll take it and show you to your door. The staircase is old and has treacherous bends."

She answered him. "I can manage quite well by myself, Harry.

Good night to you." The treads creaked as she began to ascend the stairs.

Harry spoke again. "Kate?"

The creaking fell silent as she paused to look back over the shoulder at him. "You spoke, Harry?"

"Sleep well." Softly.

"You too, kind friend."

Her footsteps faded away up the winding staircase, getting fainter. With Harry not returning immediately to the private room it showed that he was watching her out of sight. Jem rose, pushing back his chair, and went over to knock out his long-stemmed pipe on the hearth. "Harry is badly smitten," he said solemnly, taking his tobacco pouch from his pocket and refilling it.

"A passing infatuation," Daniel replied, leaning back in his chair and crossing one long leg over the other.

Jem gave his big head a shake. "Don't be that sure on't. I were his age when I met and lost my heart to my dear wife, naught but a slip of a girl herself, and I never loved another then nor after I lost her, God rest her good soul."

"I'm not concerned that it is the same with Harry."

Jem stopped tamping down the tobacco in his pipe and with lowered head looked at Daniel from under bushy brows, pointing the long stem at him warningly. "I'm telling ye I know the signs. Take heed."

Daniel's answer was firm and definite. "I'll not let matters get out of hand, you can be sure of that."

"Oh, oh, oh!" Jem scoffed at such high conceit. "How can ye steer that brother of yer'n away from love when his mind's made up to it?"

"I'll find a way somehow." His voice became steely and implacable. "I tell you Harry shall never make a match with Kate."

Jem was not reassured. He feared serious trouble between the brothers, which was the last thing he wanted to see. Moreover, there was something in Daniel's whole manner that made him exceedingly uneasy, but nothing more could be said on the subject, because Harry had come back into the room.

Next morning when breakfast was almost finished and their equipages had been brought round to the door of the inn to await them, Jem made a request of Kate across the table.

"Would ye grant me the honor of yer company in the chaise today, Mrs. Warwyck?" He had not consulted Daniel, who he was sure had intended she should be parted from Harry to ride with him again in the curricle.

She had been quiet throughout the meal, eating well with a naturally healthy appetite, but taut and strained as though she might be dreading the day's traveling that lay ahead. Now her blue eyes melted at him in a deep relief. "I'll ride with you gladly, Jem."

Alone with her as the journey progressed that day, except for the customary halts, Jem was able to tell that she accepted him without question as someone she could trust, perhaps adopting without being consciously aware of it the brothers' own attitude toward him as the weathered old rock in their midst, a fatherly benevolence that they frequently mocked and abused, but without malevolence on either side. She had been looking out at the passing sun-dappled countryside for a considerable time in silence when she said quietly, "What an adventure this is to me, Jem. I always longed to see other parts of England and never thought I should. There is much talk of London and its pugilistic circles between you and Harry and Daniel from time to time. Do you think the opportunity to visit the Metropolis where I was born will come my way shortly?"

"Ye'd like to see the big city, would ye then, Mrs. Warwyck?"

"It's an ambition I have never dared to cherish until now."

Jem wanted to promise her there and then that he would see that her aim was fulfilled, but there was no telling what Daniel had planned for her at Warwyck. He answered her as best he could.

"I reckon we'd best wait and see what forthcomes at our destination before we speculate on London. But I'll bear in mind what ye've said, Mrs. Warwyck. That ye can be sure on." It was as far as he could go in letting her know he would be her advocate in all matters with Daniel to whatever extent lay within his power, and she pressed him no further upon the subject.

"Tell me about Warwyck," she requested. "I have heard so little about the place. Is it a large mansion? What scenery does it encompass?"

"I ain't much at building up pictures," he protested heartily. "Harry's the one at descriptions, and Daniel has 'em at his fingertips."

"I want to hear about it from you, Jem. Their opinions of Warwyck Manor are set in childhood, but yours were not. You came as a stranger to its gates even as I shall when tomorrow comes."

Jem, who liked to talk and could hold a crowded taproom any time the mood took him, needed no second bidding. He had the uneducated man's inability to cut corners, but Kate was a patient and interested listener and she did not mind that he came to answer what she had asked by way of the gouging blow that had put an untimely end to his pugilistic career. So great was his sense of loss, so racking his anguish at no longer being able to take his place in a ring that he had turned his back on London and reverted to his original trade as a journeyman-carpenter, getting as far from his old life as was possible. It was after two years in this role that he had come to Warwyck, where a vacancy for such a craftsman had occurred. With accommodation provided in two loft rooms to himself in the woodyard he had settled in. Before long he had made the acquaintance of Daniel, who had been nine years old at the time. The lad had been crossing perilously one of a number of planks lodged across two high beams in the carpenter's shop. It fell, the boy falling with it, and Jem had caught the full force of a glancing blow across his head. It knocked him out and could have killed him, but the child came to no harm.

The incident with forgiveness on Jem's side and indifference on Daniel's did nothing to bring them together. Yet Jem, a widower who had loved his wife and never looked to marry again, began to see in him the son he had never had. Naturally fond of children he took to all three of the young Warwycks, but it was Daniel to whom he had felt himself particularly drawn, although on the surface there was little enough to like about the child, for he was a wild one, forever in rebellion against authority, making the lives of both the indoor and outdoor staff a misery with his tricks and pranks and angry ways. At first Jem's tentative overtures at friendship, which had been welcomed by little Harry and the toddling Jassy, were rebuffed with distrust and hostility, even when he risked his own neck to rescue the boy from the Manor roof where he had ensconced himself on a gable forty feet from the ground in defiance of all the world, and yet again when a homemade raft had sunk in the river and he pulled him and his unfortunate younger brother in to the bank half-drowned. In the end the dawn of their long relationship was brought about by a stable boy, tired of the tricks played on him by the Squire's devil of a nephew, who had given Daniel a bloody nose and a black eye, leaving him sprawled in the horse dung and straw mucked out from the stalls. Jem had set his booted feet apart on the cobbles, linked his thumbs in his belt, and looked down at the sorry sight, hiding his admiration at a courageous refusal to give in to tears, although the boy's mouth was tremulous, the lip bitten through, and the pain he was suffering obvious enough.

"Well, now," Jem said with an air of weighty consideration, his big head on one side. "I reckon ye didn't put up yer mitts fast enough, *and* ye didn't keep yer mouth firmly closed, which is one of the first rules to remember. How were ye standing? Right foot nicely turned out with the weight resting on the ball of it and in line with the left heel?" The boy's glistening eyes were regarding him with total puzzlement. "Were yer knees slightly bent?" he continued. "Was yer right arm across the mark and yer left hand level with its elbow? Heh? What? Speak up!"

"I don't know." A gulp and a wiping of the bleeding nose on a sleeve. "I don't know any of it."

"Don't yer now? Stand up and let's have a look at that smashed countenance of yer'n." Obediently the child rose to his feet and tilted his face for inspection. With those huge hands, which could be tender and gentle, Jem smoothed back the silky hair and crouched down on his haunches to scrutinize the injuries. "Hmm." He blew through his squashed nostrils like an amiable cart horse. "A piece of rump steak on that peeper for a start, some cotton to that sneezer, and a piece of lint on yer chaffer, and ye'll soon be as good as new again."

The boy's swollen and distorted lips crept into a serious, cautious smile. "Is that prize-ring talk, Mr. Pierce? Would you teach me the—the—"

"—patter? The flash?"

"Yes! And the way to put up my mitts!"

"Mitts—or bunches of fives." Jem showed his gap teeth and fist-broken stumps in a grin from ear to ear. "I'll teach you, boy." He straightened up and ruffled the boy's head in a fond, fatherly caress. "Ye're a pigeon yet, but that's in yer favor. There won't be nobody able to get the better of ye again once I've learned ye the noble science of self-defense."

He taught the boy, and his dreams of a prize-ring championship reawakened, not for himself this time, but for Daniel, who over the years grew like a weed and broadened out into the physique of an athlete, with a promising scientific mastery of fists and movement which was of the kind that could come to put glory in the ring. Daniel's wildness became disciplined, but Jem was wise enough to see that it was no more than that of a fiery stallion, broken only to bridle and saddle while retaining a free heart and a will of his own.

Jem, reminiscing for Kate's benefit, found his thoughts drifting to a subject not for her ears. With Daniel's coming to young manhood he had found himself giving advice on other matters. Afterward, how often the lad went poaching for petticoats he did not know, but no trouble of any kind was ever forthcoming, and he was relieved that his good counsel had been heeded.

"Unknown to Squire Warwyck," he continued, "I launched Dan on his pugilistic career when he was just seventeen. That first apprentice bout was fought with a redcoat two years older and a stone heavier than Dan during some recreational mills organized at a military camp near Plymouth—we were still at war with Napoleon in them days and the soldiers were awaiting embarkation."

How well Jem recalled that expedition for Kate. Cover for it had been unwittingly provided by the lad's tutor, who had wanted Daniel to study some ancient buildings in the area from an architectural viewpoint. Jem had had no liking for that Mr. Ellis, with whom he had carried on a running battle to hold the boy's chief interest, determined that the ring should not lose him. The buildings were never seen. At Jem's instigation the tutor had succumbed to the bottle, leaving Jem and Daniel free to carry out their own plans. In the ring Daniel had shown his inexperience, being too eager and impetuous, but he had been hardy and daring and milled his opponent all round the ring, his head and body seemingly insensible to blows, and he had shown even then the beginnings of his skillful draw and rushing onslaught. He finished off the redcoat, a boxer of some experience, after a dozen rounds and won himself half a guinea. Six months later Daniel was matched against a local celebrity at the village fair. After seventeen rounds he leveled his opponent and the three guineas prize money was his, but even before the bout had ended news of what was taking place had reached Squire Warwyck's ears, and for the first time the old uncle realized that it was not merely training in the gentlemanly art of self-defense that his nephew had been receiving at Jem's hands, but a serious preparation for the prize ring, which in his eyes was the most foul and evil of sports, an invention of the Devil himself. The resulting quarrel between the Squire and Daniel had reached such proportions that it was only the old gentleman's age that had prevented the young man laying hands on him for the insults inflicted and shaking him like a rat. Under the Squire's threats and curses Daniel had turned his back on Warwyck and departed with Jem for the Metropolis. Sitting at Daniel's side in the stagecoach Jem had been scarcely able to keep his private jubilation to himself, the lad's public appearance in a prize ring at the village fair having had the effect he had hoped for and intended. The tutor's scholastic aims for Daniel had been defeated in the nick of time. Jem was convinced in his own mind that a future champion of all England was on his way to London.

In the city Jem had looked up old friends in the pugilistic world and found he was not forgotten. At The Union Arms in the Haymarket, where the proprietor was the retired champion, Tom Cribb, champagne had been opened in the snuggery behind the taproom, and there had been a merry reunion with other pugilists dropping in, which had first opened Daniel's eyes to the good fellowship among most of those who fought each other in the ring. At 13 Old Bond Street, where Gentleman Jackson's rooms were situated, the Master himself, after listening to what Jem had to say about Daniel's fighting ability, put on the gloves out of interest to spar a few rounds with the lad and take his measure. His verdict echoed Jem's: the boy was raw, too headstrong, and in need of all the experience he could get, but the shining spark was there. "Guide him well, Jem, and you'll have a true knight of the knuckle before you and I are much older," Mr. Jackson concluded with warm encouragement, clapping Jem on the back.

Soon afterward Daniel took part in a sparring exhibition at Fives Court, one of the big London meeting places for The Fancy, and as a result a modest purse was raised to match him against another young pugilist who was rising in the lists. Daniel won, and the occasion was much discussed in milling circles as well as being reported in the monthly edition of *Annals of Sporting*. Jem's protégé was on his way up. Before long the rough and unpolished were no longer matched against him, and although success did not crown all his efforts he had now emerged as a fighter to be reckoned with, a man on the brink of greatness in the ring with victories behind him over such renowned pugilists as Ned Painter, Bob Burn, and Tom Oliver, who not long since had for two years challenged all England as champion, and then at Brighton the previously invincible Slash Higgens had been defeated.

"That's why I ain't having no joy out of returning to Devonshire—save for your pretty company, Mrs. Warwyck," Jem added hastily, and went on to explain that if the old Squire lingered it could mean postponing a number of good bouts considered to be preliminary mills for the championship.

Kate showed that she grasped the situation and what it meant to Jem. "If I can help in any way to relieve Daniel of some of his duties on the estate I will do whatever he allows me. I had considerable experience in aiding Mr. Farringdon with administrative matters and did all his clerical work for him." It had not been easy for her to bring her husband's name into their conversation, for she had hoped never to speak it again, but it had had to be done.

"Did ye now?" Jem looked sharply interested. Young Jassy could scarcely tell a milk can from a plowshare, but an intelligent woman like Kate in charge of the Manor could ease Daniel's path back quickly to the ring. No wonder Kate lacked the weathered countenance and work-worn hands of the average farmer's wife. Old Farmer Farringdon must have been a cut above the others financially, but had set his wife to another kind of labor with a pen, and Jem thanked heaven for it. She was going to prove a treasure in disguise. He only hoped that Daniel would come to realize it, because Kate was a good woman in every way. He himself had never had any doubt on that score. Sometimes he was reminded in her of his late wife. Such a woman deserved to be happily wed with children about her skirts. Instead she had been through some devastating experience that he could tell had left its mark on her, and now she was tied to Daniel, who cared nothing for her and was going to make sure that nobody else did, least of all his own brother.

Jem mulled it over at the back of his mind as they jogged along. She could be the making of Harry. There was no more than four years' difference between Harry's age and Kate's, albeit the wrong way round with Harry the younger of the two, but that was not an insurmountable barrier if Kate were willing. But would she be? It was too early to tell and the way he saw it there would be heartache and sorrow for all concerned whichever turn Fate might take.

They stayed that night at a hotel in a small market town on the borders of Dorset and Hampshire, and when they had had dinner Harry invited Kate to play backgammon with him on a board that was available in the drawing room, which she did while Jem dozed in a chair. Daniel, after reading a newspaper, went for a walk to stretch his limbs after the long journey, and when he returned Kate, who was tired, was about to go up to bed.

"You shall ride with me tomorrow, Kate," he said to her without preamble. "It is fitting that my *wife*"—he gave laconic emphasis to the word—"should be at my side when we come to Warwyck."

"As you wish," she replied, displaying no reaction in the cool composure of her face, her withdrawn attitude toward him galling him increasingly. "Good night, gentlemen."

Jem and Harry both answered her, but Daniel, who had taken hold of her elbow to forestall his brother in walking her from the room to the foot of the staircase, did not reply until they reached it. "Good night, Kate."

He watched her ascend as Harry had done the night before, making sure that there would be no more tender and private good nights between them through any last-minute appearance of Harry. She did not look back as Daniel supposed she would have done had it not been him standing there, and turned with sweeping dignity at the bend of the stairs, candles in a wall sconce making silver moonlight of her hair. Her shadow showed briefly and was gone.

Daniel returned to the drawing room and caught his brother's face before it jerked away, all attention directed onto the backgammon board, which he promptly started to pack up. Daniel eyed him thoughtfully. Relief had engulfed torment in a sudden deep flush of color. It seemed that during those few intervening minutes in which he had been gone from the room, Harry had been torturing himself with the fear that on this night Kate was not going to be allowed to go alone to bed. The hands folding the backgammon board were trembling visibly.

Chapter 7

They came to Warwyck in the midafternoon of the next day, Kate at Daniel's side in the curricle, its hood down as was that of the chaise in their wake driven alternately by Jem and Harry. The lane approaching it was set deep between high hedges that prevented all view of the Manor until the gates loomed ahead. Upon reaching them and driving through, Kate was able to turn in her seat and see that beyond the walled boundary of the grounds the lush fields and meadows of the estate spread out over gently undulating countryside as far as the eye could see. The house itself was not as large as she had expected, Jem's description of it as being "a real good size" having led her to think it would be of immense proportions. It was a four-square granite mansion built around a small courtyard, no more than two stories high, with a proliferation of chimneys rising against the clear blue sky. Leaded lights held the brightness of the sun and one window suddenly shot out reflected beams as it swung open and a girl waved excitedly.

"It's Jassy!" Daniel exclaimed on a warm, deep note, raising his whip high in salute to her. In the hired carriage behind, with Jem holding the reins, Harry was standing and waving his whole arm exuberantly in answer to the same wave. Then the girl disappeared and even as both carriages drew level with the entrance the huge door swung open and Jassy threw herself out to meet them.

Daniel reached her first, having leaped down from the curricle to spring up the steps three at a time and meet her halfway. She was sobbing with joy as she fell into his arms and he hugged her hard, swinging her up and round, laughing and kissing her wet cheek with true affection. Then as he released her she flung herself at Harry, who held her head between both his hands, his own bent down to bring his face to hers as he grinned and greeted her and hugged her in his turn. After that it was Jem's turn for a rushing embrace and a kiss planted on his round, smiling face.

In the curricle Kate had not moved from her seat, not wanting to intrude on the reunion between the brothers and their sister, and she smiled at their mutual happiness. Harry had not seen Jassy since he had left home, but with Daniel it was longer, a full six years, his willingness to have come to Devonshire and met her at some point of venue away from the house balked always by Jassy herself, who was nervous and lived too much in dread of their uncle's displeasure to risk it. Daniel's voice reached Kate as he took Jassy by the fingertips, lifting them up in the air even as he let them go, and drew back along the step to tease her admiringly in a brotherly fashion.

"Where's the plain little cygnet I left behind? I declare you have grown quite tolerable to look upon, Jassy!"

Tolerable indeed, Kate agreed with him in her thoughts. Delicate and diminutive, the girl had rich chestnut hair that sprang back from a point on her bare brow and framed in bunches of ribbon-tied ringlets a chaste, sweet-mouthed face with velvety, violet-dark eyes from which the tears continued to flow. It puzzled Kate that after the first exhilaration of meeting was over Jassy should continue to weep with no watery rainbow smile showing through, her expression becoming increasingly forlorn. It was dawning on the three men standing there on the steps that all was not as it should be, and Kate began to alight unobtrusively from the curricle, drawing her own conclusions as to the cause of it and thinking she might be able to take over from the brothers with feminine condolence and comfort, but Harry was already on his way to bring her into the gathering

"Come and meet Jassy!" He took her hand and swept her forward.

From where he stood Jem spoke soberly to the girl. "This is Dan's wife, my dear. Make her welcome."

Outwardly it was an unnecessary request, for he knew Jassy to be exceptionally tenderhearted, and did not quite understand why he had made it, not realizing it was an involuntary expression of his own anxiety for the future. Under the streaming tears Jassy's face showed astonishment at the import of his words and she looked quickly and uncertainly at Daniel, who grinned at her.

"You're wondering why I did not let you know? I'll explain later. In the meantime, pray make the acquaintance of Kate Warwyck."

Jassy, standing one step higher than where Harry had brought Kate to a standstill, dipped a little curtsy, a fresh gushing of tears from her eyes. "I bid you welcome into our family with all my heart, Kate—but to the house in front of which we stand there can be none."

Kate saw Daniel's face go chalk-white, the bones standing out as though burnished under his skin, and she pressed her hand to her heart as though she felt the beat that his had missed. Dear God! She thought in an agony of compassion, he has come too late to save Warwyck. He has lost his inheritance!

It was Harry who exclaimed the conclusion that Kate had drawn. "Uncle William is dead! When did it happen?"

"Yesterday. Not twenty-four hours ago yet. He took un unexpected turn for the worst." Her throat was so full that her voice choked and with uncertain, tentative hands she took hold of Daniel's lapels. "It's more than that. Much more. Oh, my dear Daniel, I don't know how to tell you."

Daniel was held stiff by shock and he spoke through bared teeth. "To whom did he bequeath this place?"

"Not to you."

"You wrote that he wanted to see me, that he had only to see for himself that I was no longer the wild youth he remembered and all would be well."

"Yes, that is what he promised, but unbeknown to me he meant well for him and not for you. One of the last things he said to me when he was dying was that he had wanted only to gloat over your humbling yourself in vain, because he would never see Warwyck Manor sullied by contact with the Devil's prize ring. It was his revenge for all your independence and defiance."

Kate burst out her protest. "But Daniel wasn't coming back with cap in hand! Far from it! I was to be the instrument by which he would get his inheritance."

None of them seemed to hear her. Daniel had gripped Jassy by the shoulders. "To whom has Warwyck been bequeathed since Harry is as much connected with the fistic world as I am?" When she did not reply at once he shook her fiercely. "Tell me!"

"I fear to," she sobbed helplessly.

"Is it to be sold?" he roared, shaking her again.

"Worse!" she gulped hysterically, getting beside herself with fright of him.

Kate spoke up, outraged. "Enough, Daniel. Enough. You're terrifying her."

Jassy, perhaps taking courage from sympathetic support, opened her mouth and forced out the words as if she had difficulty in articulating. "It has been bequeathed to—to the newborn son of the hired nurse. It's Uncle William's own child!"

He released her abruptly in his stupefaction. Blindly she turned to Kate and was caught close in protective arms. Without another word he charged past them all and burst into the house.

It smelled stale and neglected, the floor of the magnificently proportioned hall dirty and unswept. Never before had he seen it in such a state. He stood in the middle of it, looking around at the fine old furniture with thick dust in its carving, and knew a kind of regret that he and such a beautiful house had never come to terms with each other, but in his day it had known the rule of an ill-tempered man and it was in this hall alone that Harry had been cruelly whipped, Jassy had been shut in a cupboard for some small misdemeanor, and he himself at the age of ten had had to stand all day with his hands above his head until he had collapsed and Jem had carried him away.

"You're trespassing!"

He jerked his gaze upward and saw that a woman in a dressing robe, suckling a shawl-wrapped infant at her ample breast, had come to the head of the staircase set there in Tudor times. She had a sharp, avaricious face with a vulgar breadth of nose, her hair beneath her cap with the draggling lilac ribbons a riot of yellow curls. He knew instantly who she was.

"I'm Daniel Warwyck," he snapped with all the arrogance of pride and power inherent from generations of Warwycks before him. "You dare to call me trespasser in this house!"

She began to descend the stairs, her feet in rose satin slippers. Everything she wore was of expensive quality, but the billowing robe was stained and the ruffles of the nightgown beneath, open down the top to accommodate the baby, were grubby and soiled.

"It all belongs to my son now," she stated with triumphant satisfaction, her coarse voice matching her appearance. "He is as much a Warwyck as any of you."

Daniel clipped his utterance. "Is he legitimate?"

She gave a shriek of temper, crimson gushing up her neck. "Don't you deal out no insults to me. I've marriage lines good and proper, and if you don't believe me go and see the rector and Mr. Hunston, the lawyer in Barnstaple. Your uncle wed me secretly when it became obvious that his bit of slap-and-tickle had had results."

"Why secretly? Was he ashamed of you?"

She bared her teeth and stuck her head forward, rolling it from side to side as she attempted to imitate his cultured tones. "No, he wasn't. But he wanted to plan a nasty little surprise for you when the day came, and why shouldn't I have played along with him? I had nothing to lose. He's lying now in the family vault in the village churchyard ready for the funeral the day after tomorrow, and I wager he has a grin on his face."

Behind Daniel the others had entered the hall and the woman, having reached the bottom of the flight, beckoned sharply to Jassy, her attitude that of mistress toward a despised servant. "Stop your sniveling there and tell your brother how your Uncle William told you the truth of it on his deathbed yesterday." When Jassy, trembling, continued to cling to Kate without obeying her, she stamped her foot with impatience "JASMINE! I'm speaking to you!"

Harry stepped forward and rebuked the woman heatedly. "Do not dare to address my sister in that manner, you slut!"

The woman gasped and stamped her foot again, jerking up the baby as she did so, which caused the source of nourishment to be lost to him, and his infant wail of protest rose as she made her furious answer. "I'm Mrs. Bessie Warwyck to you! And I talk to Jasmine how the hell I like! I'll remind you that I'm the widow of her late guardian, which makes her my charge to do as I tell her."

Jassy, conditioned to being obedient, accepting the truth of Bessie's words, broke from Kate and ran to Daniel. "It's all true. Everything I told you was true. Had you not been due to arrive today I would have written to tell you all about it, but there was no time. Believe me, if Uncle William had still been alive when you got here after what he had said to me, I would never have let you suffer the humiliation at his bedside that he had planned for you. I would have stopped you even as I watched for you today."

Daniel heard her out but made no acknowledgment, simply jerking his head at Harry. "Take the best horse you can find in the stables and ride for Mr. Hunston at his chambers in Barnstaple. It should take you no more than three quarters of an hour to get there and back. I want him here and without delay." He jabbed a finger downward at the spot where he stood. As Harry went he took a few paces toward Bessie. "Now, you conniving wretch, I will see your marriage certificate."

Her eyes went sly. "Oh, no. Not until the lawyer gets here. Since you won't take my word for anything we'll let him lay it all on the board for you, nice and legal."

Jassy, floundering uncertainly after being ignored by Daniel, half-turned to Kate. "I'll make you some tea. You surely need some refreshment after your journey. The servants never stay nowadays. Not since—" she broke off with a nervous glance toward Bessie, only to see that the woman had already advanced upon her. She shrieked out as Bessie seized a handful of her hair and pulled it viciously.

"You'll make none of my tea for these intruders! I've had to tell you before about making free with what is mine, mine, mine!" She gave vindictive emphasis to her words with further jerks and tugs until suddenly she grunted herself as Daniel seized her wrist and broke her hold, twisting her around, the back of his hand lifted threateningly.

"You lay a finger on Jassy once more and I'll strike you right across this hall! Now take that bastard of yours and get him out of my sight."

He scared her, but she had intrigued too much and plotted too long to get her hands on old William's property and fortune, as well as suffering his nauseating penetrations on two awful nights, to back down before the fury of his nephew. "I'll do no such thing. You'll be pinching God knows what out of these rooms if I turn my back. I know your kind. It don't matter how hideous an object is, if those old ancestors of yours brought it back from Rome or some other place on those Grand Tours that William used to tell me about, it's got good money value and I'm the one who's going to sort things out and sell whatever I don't want around any more."

Daniel gave her one murderous look and strode across to some double doors, flinging them wide into a library of immense size. She hastened after him, shoving the wailing infant back onto her breast, her slippers flapping.

"Don't you touch none of those old books. I made inquiries some time ago and I can get hundreds of guineas for some of them." Her voice echoed back into the hall after her as she continued to follow Daniel. Jem, who had been lingering indecisively, uneasy in the house which he had only ever entered by the kitchen door, let his hands rise and fall wordlessly in a general despair at the whole situation and set off slowly in the wake of Daniel and Bessie, his tread heavy.

Kate, having produced a clean handkerchief for Jassy to dry her tears, gave her a cheering smile. "Never mind about the tea. I really don't want any, and Daniel would choke before he swallowed anything that was begrudged him. How long has that woman been treating you like that?"

"Ever since Uncle William took to his bed again a few weeks ago. She was awful before, ordering me about and bullying the servants and acting as if she were the mistress in the house, but she told me a nurse always ruled a household for the good of her patient and I believed her."

"Who appointed her in the first place?"

"I did. The doctor sent her. She took meticulous care of Uncle William and her nursing of him could not be faulted, even though she wasn't as personally fastidious as she should have been."

"Why didn't you write and tell Daniel how unhappy you were?"

"What was the point? It would only have worried him, because he couldn't take me round with him in the fighting world. I wanted nothing to stand in the way of his becoming champion of England one day."

Kate smiled with her eyes. "You Warwycks have a strong sense of duty and responsibility. Let us hope the infant in this house has inherited the same trait. What's his name?"

"William after his father. Bessie calls him Willie." Jassy's face was serious. "That was a good wish to give him. He is a dear little baby and can't help looking a bit like my uncle."

A clock chimed and Kate glanced toward it. "We had better make the most of our time before Harry returns with the lawyer. I've a feeling that as soon as Daniel has legal proof that Willie is the rightful owner of the estate that he'll have us all away from this place at a gallop. I suggest you collect your possessions together and I help you pack."

Jassy's eyes widened incredulously. "Do you mean Daniel will take me away from here?"

"He certainly won't leave you with that terrible woman, I know that. In any case, everything is changed now that I'm with Daniel and Harry and Jem. I'll be able to look after you and we'll be company for each other when the men leave us to go off to a mill."

For a few moments Jassy found it impossible to speak, shaking her head as if unable to comprehend the miracle that had happened to her. Then she grabbed Kate's hand and kissed it, holding it to her cheek. "Oh, Kate. You're the most wonderful thing that has ever happened to us three Warwycks. I know it. And I'm sure Jem feels the same."

It took an hour for Harry to appear with Mr. Hunston, who had had to gather up all the necessary papers. Bessie had dumped the infant in a cot somewhere and had changed her robe for another of brocade, which was obviously brand-new. She thrust herself in front of Daniel to meet the lawyer in the hall. After greeting her and shaking hands with Daniel, whom he knew from the past, Mr. Hunston expressed amazement that she was up and about.

"Should you be on your feet, Mrs. Warwyck?" he inquired with consideration, knowing his own wife never rose from childbed until the usual two weeks were out.

Bessie, who came from rough stock that could birth like a sow, feigned a smile of weakness bravely endured. "Unfortunately this unpleasant business of my late husband's nephew questioning the will has forced me to drag myself downstairs." She led the way into a drawing room and draped herself against cushions on a sofa.

Normally Mr. Hunston would have exchanged pleasantries with Daniel, having followed his career with interest, but the atmosphere being what it was he could tell that he must not let his grasping client imagine for a second that he was not entirely on her side. He displayed the marriage certificate for Daniel's scrutiny and a copy of the will.

"Why did my uncle wait until the last minute to sign it?" Daniel questioned sharply.

"He did not intend that it should be the last minute for him. He was waiting to know the sex of the child. Had it been a girl a previous will made after his marriage would have protected my client and her offspring, Warwyck Manor being put up for sale and the amount fetched left entirely to his widow. But with a boy it was a different matter, of course. Mr. Warwyck wanted the will to be entirely devoted to him. He inherits everything as it stands under his mother's jurisdiction until he is eighteen years old."

"There! What did I tell you?" Bessie sneered triumphantly.

Daniel ignored her. "Everything, Mr. Hunston, except that which belongs to me."

Bessie, forgetting her lady-like repose, sprang up as if she would defend with her life anything he was set on taking away. "You take nothing from under this roof, do you hear?" She turned for confirmation to the lawyer. "That's right, isn't it? He has no claim to any of it?"

"He has every right to remove his own personal possessions, Mrs. Warwyck. So have his brother and sister," Mr. Hunston answered her.

Daniel had already left the room. He went upstairs and along the corridor to the portrait gallery where he let his eyes run along the faces of his ancestors for the last time until he came to a portrait of his father. It had been painted for his mother and she had brought it to the house with her. Taking it by its gilded frame he looked into the narrow, dark gray eyes that were much like his own and spoke quietly aloud to the likeness without self-consciousness and from the heart.

"You never belonged here and neither did I. You were considered to be the black sheep of the family and in that shadow I walk myself. But not for long. I intend to start my own dynasty of Warwycks in a house as grand in its own way as this one is. Your portrait shall hang there in pride of place, I promise you."

He took nothing else. When he came downstairs again with the portrait under his arm Bessie screamed and swore at him in the foulest language, not because she wanted the painting but because she was livid at being thwarted in her determination that he should have nothing. Daniel could have been deaf for all the notice he took of her. He shook the lawyer's hand again, thanked him for coming promptly to settle the matter, and went out of the house, Kate and his sister following him, with Jem and Harry coming after with Jassy's baggage.

"Home to my London lodgings," Daniel said when they all reached the two waiting carriages. Jassy promptly climbed into the chaise, Jem having started to put her belongings aboard it, and she made room on the seat ready for Kate to get in with her. Daniel went to his own curricle, wrapped the portrait carefully in his cape to protect it from damage on the journey and stowed it away. The equipage swayed as he got up into the driver's seat where he took reins and whip into his hands and waited for a signal from Harry that they were ready to start. He had expected Jem to ride with him, but when there came a scrunch of gravel by the curricle he saw Kate there, looking up at him.

"I came to Warwyck Manor with you and I shall leave the same way."

He held her eyes and saw a calm acceptance of what had occurred that was not indifference but conveyed a complete understanding of what it meant to finish with the past and embrace the future. Without speaking he reached out a hand and assisted her up into the seat beside him. He flicked the whip and the horses bounded forward, bearing them away from the house he would never see again. Behind them Harry followed suit. Within minutes all that remained to show they had been there was a cloud of dust settling on the horizon.

Kate did not intrude on Daniel's thoughts as they bowled along, sitting quietly with her hands in her lap, watching the passing scenery. The sun began to set, flooding the sky with orange, pink, and gold.

"You must have had quite a talk with Jassy," he prompted after a while.

"I did. She had no idea there was anything between her uncle and his nurse. She is astonishingly innocent and thought that Bessie was merely putting on weight beneath her large nursing apron. It was a complete surprise to her when the upheaval of the birth took place in the early hours of yesterday morning."

He glanced laconically at her. "Did she imagine it had materialized out of thin air?"

"She knew then, of course. It is a mercy as far as Jassy is concerned that your uncle departed this life when he did, because her sense of duty would have kept her there forever."

The setting sun had made black silhouettes of all the trees and hedges, and she sat like a cutout within a frame against its rose-red light.

"You speak with some knowledge of such duties, Kate. Was it such a duty that compelled you to marry Farmer Farringdon?"

"I did what I had to do." No bitterness, no resentment. A simple statement of fact.

"For what reason were you so obligated?"

She drew in her breath. "After my father died my mother and I lived in great poverty. She had genteel notions that we could no longer afford, but I earned what I could to supplement them. Although she shut her eyes and would not hear me talk of it I went hay-making and bird-scaring and potato-picking until such time as I was old enough to put the education she had given me herself to some use. The village school at that time had one teacher and there was no employment for me there, so I found what pupils I could in homes where people could afford to pay a little for daily instruction. Then my mother fell ill. It came about through a simple accident when she fell in the garden, but the injury would not heal and gradually she began to need intensive nursing. I had to give up going to houses that were too far afield, because she could not be left for any length of time. Again I resorted to farm and agricultural work to earn whatever I could between the few lesson times still available to me, but even so I could not afford the medical attention that she most sorely needed." She paused deeply. "Then Mr. Farringdon, who knew our impoverished circumstances, offered me marriage, promising that my mother should have the best physicians in the land. I saw it as a door through which to gain relief for my mother from her terrible suffering and the only way to save her life. So I accepted him."

"Did you love another, Kate?"

She shook her head. "I had been too much at a sickbed and too occupied with the daily need to find food for the table and fuel for the fire to give time to the gentler aspects of living. I cared for none of those who would have engaged my attentions, whether they were those with whom I worked in the fields or those gentlemen of all ages who imagined their children's daily instructress was fair game for their immoral advances." Her lips pursed a little wryly. "You were correct in the assumption you voiced on our first day's journey that I was surely not a stranger to spurning unwelcome overtures. But Mr. Farringdon came to me honorably and he kept his word. My mother received the most solicitous care and was seen by several physicians from London. She never recovered from her affliction, but for a while she was in less pain and able at times to walk a little with aid and to take carriage rides. She despised Jervis Farringdon, whom she regarded as a common man who had made money and was socially ambitious, but she accepted all he paid for, back in her element among the luxuries of life that had been hers before her own marriage. She lived just a year to the day of my marrying Mr. Farringdon, but her time was eased and extended through his generosity, and for that I was deeply grateful."

After a moment's reflection Daniel said, "I do not see that he was generous. He blackmailed you into marriage. What was done for your mother could have been donated without its bonds. That would have been true generosity."

"He was determined to have me." It was said with a simple clarity that held undertones of abject despair.

Sharply he pulled his mind away from the thought of her youth in that gross man's arms. "You mentioned his social ambitions. What line did they take?"

"He wanted to be accepted by the people of quality who lived in his district. It was galling to him that he was never invited to ride with the local hunt, to shoot or to game at cards, and was never received into any of the big houses. He had amassed money and absorbed other farms into his own to make a great estate, and was unable to understand why the gentry passed him by."

"Why did they? Other farmers ride to hounds."

"He was not trusted. His sharp methods had caused one gentleman to commit suicide in most tragic circumstances. Quality folk have long memories. None of them accepted his invitations to our marriage, and the long tables under the trees set with silver and fine linen were lined with empty chairs, nobody of importance in his eyes putting in an appearance. It savaged his pride."

"I suppose he thought that marriage to a comely and educated bride would help pave the way to the place he wanted, quite apart from his own desires."

"That was behind all his promises. I know I disappointed him from that wedding day, because he made no secret of blaming me for those absentees whose presence would have been all-important to him."

"I have met many men like Farringdon," Daniel commented sagely. "They cannot endure their own inadequacy and must ape and seek ever to ingratiate themselves with those whom they consider to be better born and whom they envy in their foolishness. Give me a man like Jem, who is what he is and carries his own honest dignity without pretense or obsequiousness. There are many among the elite in The Fancy who look down their noses at him, but he could meet royalty at any time without embarrassment on either side. Farringdon could have learned a lesson from Jem and should have had one delivered to him for such deep injustice toward you."

"Unjust or not, he was unable to be rational over slights or snubs, imaginary or real. You may find it hard to believe, but he was enormously impressed by my mother's excessive gentility and sought to make me more like her, forbidding me to do a hand's turn towards anything he did not consider fitting in my new role as his lady-wife. Like the character in the rhyme for children I had to pass my days sitting on a cushion and sewing a fine seam. My days dragged with boredom, and nobody called. After a while I managed to persuade him to let me deal with his correspondence and write up his accounts and allot the wages. Since no social stigma is attached to the sight of a lady using a pen he allowed me the authority, but his disappointment in me did not abate and out of it hatred grew until he could scarcely bear to set eyes on me. Finally one evening he broke the news that he could tolerate me no longer under his roof and that the next day he was taking me to market at Brighton and putting me up for sale."

Her tale had come to an end. The last glow was fading from the sky and ahead the lights of an inn twinkled. She was glad of the deepening dusk that was hiding the hollowing of her cheeks and the glisten of unshed tears in her eyes through having forced herself through bleak and desolate memories. Much had not been told. Moments of intimacy that still made her cold with horror. Hard hands and hard, wet mouth and brutality rising out of hatred and frustration. Although her present circumstances were not to be envied by others, in her own eyes she had become greatly blessed: Harry was kind and sweet to her, and goodhearted Jem was her stalwart friend; in addition, she had unintentionally but gladly won the trust of Jassy, a girl of gentle ways and softly natured, whom she liked in return. Of Daniel she would not think beyond the fact that he had made her Kate Warwyck, albeit a sham, and whatever lurked in the innermost depths of her heart she would neither think about nor admit.

That evening Daniel would have drawn Jassy aside to talk to her alone, but she reached out to catch Kate's hand and would not let it go. There being no secrets between Kate and him over what he had to say he made no objection.

"I apologize for shouting at you as I did today," he said gently. "I ask you to forgive me."

Her violet eyes were very wide as if he had so unnerved her at that earlier hour that she feared even now he might become transformed into that terrifying figure that had made her almost faint away. Her voice caught in her throat. "Yes, I do." Her reply did not sound very convincing.

Later, returning from a walk alone in the open air during which he mulled over his future plans again, formulating details, he heard Jassy laughing and found her alone with Jem, playing a game of cards with him that involved much shouting out when matching ones were laid.

"Where's Kate—and Harry?" he inquired abruptly, trying not to notice how instantly Jassy had been made still and silent by his presence as though he were an entering prison-warder rattling chains.

Jem shrugged a trifle uncomfortably. "I ain't sure."

"Jem!" Daniel's attitude brooked no evasion.

"They said something about taking a stroll in the garden." Then Jem turned his big body sharply in his chair as Daniel swung back out of the doorway. "Dan! Let them be, boy! Let them be!"

In the garden Daniel saw them before they saw him. They had risen from a bench seat against the old inn wall where they had been sitting in the mild night air and were illumined by the lamplight shining through a window, standing close in low-voiced conversation. Her back was toward him as she looked up into Harry's face, her head at an angle, the nape of her neck revealed through a wispy veil of shining tendrils that had escaped from her neatly pinned-up tresses, and her waist curved with her weight on one foot and the other slightly extended. There was a conspiratorial intimacy about them that made them look like a pair of lovers, and convinced of amorous intrigue—at least on his brother's part—he saw her nod as Harry cupped her arm with his hand and turned her with him to make their way back together into the inn.

He observed their reactions with narrowed eyes when they sighted him not far from them along the path. Kate gave a start and flashed a glance at Harry as though questioning him about the possibility of their having been overheard, but Harry only regarded his brother mildly and slid his hand down her arm to link her fingers in his.

"A perfect evening, Daniel," he remarked easily. "It should be another fine day tomorrow. One of the ostlers looked to that faulty harnessing on the chaise and has replaced a link. There should be no bother with it from now on."

Kate relinquished her hand from Harry's and stepped ahead of the two brothers into the side entrance of the inn. She and Harry had been discussing how best they might help Daniel adjust to his loss of Warwyck Manor, and she hoped he had not overheard their good intentions. They had decided never to mention it again, and she intended to pass on their decision to both Jem and Jassy.

In the morning she had hoped to persuade Jassy to ride with Daniel and start to cement the breach between them, but he was waiting for her by the curricle and had instructed the inn porter to place her overnight valise in it with the rest of her baggage and his. As she set a hand into his and gathered up her hems an inch or two the better to negotiate the equipage's step she saw a closed, indefinable look in his eyes that filled her inexplicably with overwhelming apprehension. Almost in panic she would have turned and bolted toward the chaise, insisting that she change places with one of them or demanding to ride with them, but Daniel's hand was already guiding her up and she had no choice but to take her place.

"Comfortable?" he inquired courteously, getting in after her from the opposite side and unlooping the reins. "We are fortunate in the weather."

She gave a nod, trying to draw comfort from his ordinary tones and half smile, but the constriction in her chest was not banished and the dread of a happening unknown stayed with her. As the morning progressed she tried to convince herself that it had all been in her imagining. He did not talk very much, but she was used to that, because conversation when it did come was always between lengthy intervals during which he appeared deep in his own thoughts.

It was shortly before noon that he slowed to a halt at a crossroads and waited for Harry, who was driving the other equipage, to draw level with him. "This is where Kate and I bid you adieu for the time being," he said amiably.

Harry had whitened, jerking forward in the driver's seat. "What do you mean? Where are you going?"

"That's our affair," Daniel replied in the same smooth tones. "There's the London road ahead of you." He indicated the direction pointed by the signpost with his whip. "With luck you should reach my lodgings by midnight, but if you have any delays don't hesitate to draw into an inn earlier. It will be a long day for Jassy."

"You can't leave us like this!" Harry made as if he would bound from the carriage and snatch Kate, who had gone deathly pale, from the curricle, but Jem clamped a heavy hand on his arm to hold him back.

"Harry!" he growled warningly. "Dan don't have to take orders from ye."

"That's right, Jem." Daniel's face had become grim and he took a more secure grip on the reins ready for departure. "I think it's high time that Kate and I were on our own for a little while. Good day, Jassy. We'll meet again soon at the lodgings. Safe journey to you all."

His whip cracked. The two fine horses leaped forward and with all the speed that made the curricle such a popular vehicle with those who liked to cover ground quickly, he and Kate were whirled along the road that branched to the right and away from the three who stared after them.

Harry seemed to come to his senses. "God! What am I doing being shoved off like this? I'm going after them!" He brought up his hand with the whip, but Jem's arm shot out and he snatched it from him.

"We'll do as Dan instructed!"

"No!" Harry's whole face was distorted with personal torment and he tried to grab the whip back again, but Jem held him off with an elbow blow in the chest and jerked the reins from his hold.

"Now I'll drive. Ye're in no fit state to be in charge of horses!"

In the seat behind them Jassy whimpered at the scene, but neither heard her. Harry blindly took a handful of Jem's coat and jerked it. "Don't you know why he has taken her off like that, you blunderhead?"

"I know," Jem answered phlegmatically, flicking the horses forward over the crossroads. "To all intents and purposes she's his bride, even if it ain't legal."

"She doesn't even *like* him!" Harry's voice was hoarse as if strangled in his throat. "I know! I can tell!"

"I didn't see her struggling to get out of the curricle, did ye?" Jem stated bluntly, having made up his mind he had to be cruel to be kind. Now that Daniel had acted decisively to put an end to Harry's surreptitious courtship the crisis had been reached and passed. It had been high time that things were settled one way or the other. There could be no going back now on the path that events had taken. "Be a man, Harry. Accept the situation. Mrs. Warwyck has made her choice."

Jassy sat with bowed head in the back seat weeping silently. With Kate she had felt safe, able to face anything the future held, knowing she had someone who would stand by her. Now Daniel had taken her away. Harry would be no support. How could he be? He was sitting with his head in his hands and sobbing shamelessly.

While the chaise continued on the road to London, Daniel was driving across country. Kate barely noticed the villages they passed through or the farms that went by. Where previously she had observed everything from a bird in flight to the tiniest of blooms on wayside hedges her gaze had become unfocused, and she seemed only to see the horses bounding along in front of them, the jingling of harness now discordant to her ears. Daniel hardly spoke, making no attempt to prepare the way for whatever lay ahead, and she seemed frozen inside, knowing she could not warm to arms that took her into them without love and without the tenderness of love. Past experience in the marriage bed had taught her that.

They took one short break when bowls of thick meat soup were set before them with crusty white bread and yellow farm butter, but Kate took no more than a few spoonfuls. Daniel having cleared up his, saw that she had left hers and finished it for her. Then with fresh horses in the shafts on they went again.

"Where are we going?" she asked once.

"I hope that we shall reach Winchester by late afternoon," he replied.

So it was to be there. In the ancient cathedral city. When signposts began to mark it and each one they passed lessened the mileage he did begin to talk more, telling her that Winchester was a hub of commerce as well as being of religious importance, and that stagecoaches left to all parts of England from it. She made a few comments, but her restraint, which came upon her acutely at times of despair or outrage, was causing the atmosphere between them to become noticeably strained.

The curricle went clattering over the cobblestones of the Winchester streets, the benign cathedral towering above the city. He drove through an archway into the courtyard of a busy coaching inn where embarking and disembarking passengers thronged about, and others, waiting for some later transport, leaned on the railings of the gallery that surrounded it or went in and out of several large taprooms. There was noise and bustle, the shouting of ostlers and the stamp of impatient and restless hooves, the mingled aromas of fried onions, ale, roasting meat, and fish soup drifting overall in steam from the inn's kitchen windows.

She went with him into the oak-paneled hall and sat down on a chair while he awaited his turn at the reception desk, for here as well people were coming and going. It took only a few seconds for him to be given attention, for he had that air about him that compelled others to his service, and after he had signed the register she saw a key change hands. Then he remained engaged in conversation with the clerk about some matter that caused further delay. Obviously intending to return to the desk, he broke away and handed the key to a porter waiting with her baggage.

"I have some more business to attend to, but there is no need for you to wait in this crowded hall. The porter will show you to the room, and I'll be up in a few minutes."

She followed the porter up the dark staircase and along a corridor into a large, comfortably carpeted room with carved furniture and a wide bed hung with crimson curtains looped up with cords. It was most surely the best room in the whole establishment, and the windows did not face inward to the courtyard, but looked outward onto a garden and orchard at the rear of the inn. Left alone she stood looking about her, untying the strings of her bonnet and removing it from her head. Neatly she hung her coat away and no sooner had she closed the clothes closet door on it than Daniel entered the room. He put aside his hat on a chair and stood looking across the length of the room at her, his face serious but not unkind. In his hand he held a newly purchased stagecoach ticket. Without warning a terrible quaking fear possessed her that swept away all else. Suddenly she seemed to know what he was about to say even as he opened his mouth to speak.

"We have come to the parting of our ways, Kate. You have your freedom at last. Your marriage with Farringdon is a thing of the past and ours a hollow ceremony of what never was. The stagecoach ticket I have bought for you will enable you to travel in comfort tomorrow to whichever place in England you decide to make your destination." He dived into a pocket and brought out a folded paper and a leather purse that jingled as he moved forward to put them down on the bed. "There's fifty sovereigns in the purse, and a draft on my bank for another hundred. That will give you security and you need be in no haste to take the first post as governess or companion or whatever other kind of employment you decide upon."

"You're sending me away," she said faintly. It was all she could absorb.

He saw that her eyes held a frantic look and there was not a vestige of color in her face. The shock of being parted from Harry was telling on her. It was as well that he had taken action when he did. Had Warwyck become his, there would have been more time for his brother to have become irrevocably ensnared by her intriguing beauty, and extricating him could have proved more difficult, so some good had come out of it all.

"You must have realized that sooner or later I should desire my own freedom," he pointed out. "As I said before, no legal ties bind us. Even if I had inherited Warwyck your time with me would have been short, although I would have given you employment there. I never said my purpose for taking you there was for any other reason than that it might help to secure my inheritance for me. I believe you understood that there could be no lasting personal attachment."

Perhaps she had in the beginning. She did not know now, nor could she think in her stunned dismay. Slowly she took a few steps forward and lifted her hands helplessly. "But why turn me loose into the world here? Why could I not have made my farewells to you and the others in London? I did not say goodbye to any one of them."

"That's precisely why. I did not want Harry to continue to pursue you, and he would never have let you depart without securing an address or contact of some kind through which to reach you. As it is, he will never see you again, which is as it should be. He is nothing but a lad, headstrong and romantic, but he will mature and he has his whole life before him. To fall in love seriously at his age and live openly with a married woman abandoned but not divorced by her legal spouse could ruin his chances at any profession he might choose to follow."

She stared dumbly at him. Harry in love with her? Doubt struck her. Had she been misguided in accepting his friendliness at its surface level? Unhappily she recalled one occasion—no, two! —when she had caught a look in his male eye that was as old as time, but so quickly had it vanished, so abruptly had he laughed or made some teasing remark that she had thought herself mistaken. Or, to be absolutely accurate and truthful, wanted to think herself mistaken?

Daniel took her silence as admittance of the knowledge of

Harry's love and perhaps even of her own for his brother. "Do I have to ask you not to try to see him or to write to him?"

She gave her head a shake and he jerked his chin twice, indicating that all was satisfactory. She wanted to send good wishes to Jassy and kind old Jem and even to Harry, but her throat was immobile, tight and dry. Her hands fell like little dying birds to her sides.

He made a bow and half turn to leave. "This is goodbye then, Kate." Her failure to make any reply made him hesitate and he looked at her sideways. She could have been carved out of ice, so motionless was she, but her mouth was soft and moist, trembling and vulnerable, and every nerve and fiber in him was filled with a searing consciousness of her as a seductive woman. He put down his hat which he had picked up, and returned to her in two swift paces. Pulling her into his arms he took her mouth in a kiss of deep and abandoned passion that was at once both wonderful and dreadful to her, and she closed her eyes on the fire and fury of it, the length of her body crushed to his.

When he released her she pressed both hands over her wildly beating heart and saw how penetratingly he looked at her. It was as if in the very moment of their parting he had come to know more about her than at any time before.

"Goodbye, Kate," he said again. He went from the room and clapped his tall hat on his head as he closed the door behind him.

Out in the courtyard a couple of stagecoaches were departing and he had to stand back and wait until they had clattered and swayed past before he could seek out the ostler who had taken charge of his curricle. He tipped the fellow, took the reins, and drove smartly out through the archway into the street beyond. He had gone no more than a few yards when he almost glanced back in the vague notion that he might catch a last glimpse of her, but he checked himself and kept his gaze ahead. He was done with Kate Warwyck. Strange how he should continue to think of her linked to his own surname, but he supposed that if she ever crossed his mind in the future it would be the same.

At the window she caught a final glimpse of him when the curricle passed in a flash of crimson between a break in the trees on the road out of town. With a tight little moan she swung herself away and with upraised arms, her hands balled, she pressed her face and her body against the paneled wall until her knuckles and the side of her face felt numb. All her courage had deserted her. She wished she might die, and wondered that she did not of the anguish within her. With all her heart she loved the man who had turned away from her forever.

She stayed as she was until dusk fell and all light went from the day. Only then did she move and with stiff fingers lit the candle lamps in the room. The purse and bank draft lay with the stagecoach ticket on the bed where he had left them. With careful fingers she put the bank draft to a lamp flame and watched it burn. She did not know the address of his London lodgings or any place where she might return the fifty sovereigns to him, but surely some day and somewhere she would hear of him fighting in a bout and have them returned to him, any amount that she was compelled to use in the meantime replaced in full. Only the stagecoach ticket was in any way acceptable, for it would carry her far from those whom she had come to think of as her own little family, and that had to be.

When morning came a stagecoach bore her out of Winchester, her eyes weary from lack of sleep. Progressing in another direction, after a good night's rest, Daniel could already inhale the salt air. He was on his way back to Easthampton. When he caught the first sparkle of the sea a memory of Kate on the sands of Brighton stirred briefly in his mind, and then was lost again and forgotten.

Chapter 8

Daniel stayed two weeks at Easthampton. During that time he felt he discovered all there was to know about the place from its history to the properties of its soil, which was a rich loam, chiefly upon a reddish earth suitable for making bricks, a piece of valuable information he picked up from a local builder who made what he wanted for his own limited needs, but lacked the finance necessary to start producing them on a larger scale. When the tide was out the same builder, whose name was Arthur Tanner, showed him the argillaceous substances revealed when the sea had washed away the upper stratum of sand and marly earth in which the clay nodules used for making cement were found. Even the rocks themselves provided materials for the erection of houses and walls.

"No need to go far afield for anything," Daniel remarked casually.

"No, sir," Tanner replied. "The materials are there for the taking, but labor is needed to fetch it out, and that takes money." His round, honest face was scored with lines brought about by the struggle to remain financially solvent. He was a master craftsman and a good builder, but the well-to-do did not place their orders with him, going instead to builders in Merrelton, and most of his work consisted of repair jobs and alterations and reroofing, mostly for customers who took a long time to scratch up the money to pay their bills. The only building of any importance he had built in recent years was the new Easthampton vicarage, due to a word put in on his behalf by the ecclesiastical occupant, and it was gratifying that this stranger had remarked upon it with praise.

"How right you are," Daniel agreed in acknowledgment of the statement that had been made, standing with hands in his pockets as he grinned into the sea breeze and let his eyes travel over the shore. "Money! Money! Money! It's the key to everything."

It was in the vicar of Easthampton, a conscientious, scholarly man with deep concern and compassion for his often wayward flock, that Daniel made another friend. In the study at the vicarage the Reverend Eliot Singleton opened his bookcase and took down large volumes of Sussex history to locate those paragraphs about Easthampton. It was known there had been a settlement on the hamlet's site since Saxon times when the local rock reef, which spread out in a semicircular curve and could be seen at low tide, would have formed a safe anchorage then as it did now. Fishing and farming had been carried on from those ancient times throughout the centuries, and apart from a local man fighting at the Battle of Crécy during the Hundred Years' War with France, quarrels over land and other property, and erosion by the sea from time to time, the history of Easthampton was relatively unexciting.

"Nothing much to thrill the blood," Eliot Singleton said, closing the last of the books. He was not yet forty and was much disabled by rheumatics of the joints, but outwardly he refused to acknowledge the pain that racked him, and made himself mobile with the aid of two sticks indoors and went about his parish outdoors in a low-slung gig with a special step constructed on it by the local blacksmith for easy access to the driver's seat. He took Daniel for a drive in it one afternoon, pointing out everything of interest from a copse of particularly splendid trees to the well-preserved grandeur of a medieval barn. It was not far from this barn that he drew up in front of a fine old house with russet slates, its windows shuttered and closed from within, which stood in several acres of neglected garden that rose like a jungle about it. Briars and brambles and long-lost flowers tumbled in profusion over the surrounding walls and almost covered the gate, which bore the name Honeybridge House.

"Take a good look at that house," Eliot advised. "You'll not see finer Sussex diamonds anywhere than those that have gone into the building of that place. It's the old name for knapped flint-work, and each of those rectangular flints has been faced to shine like polished marble."

Daniel alighted from the gig and went to lean on the gate. In all his explorations he had missed the tiny cul-de-sac of the lane in which it stood alone, facing the sea, but sheltered and protected on three sides by trees. The knapped flintwork that could be seen between spreading, half-dead ivy was magnificent, seeming to hold old sunshine in its depths, warm and glowing and promising to stand forever. He knew it to be the home he would have until such time as he could start to build Easthampton House on the hill above the green.

"How long has it been empty?" he asked.

"Many years. It saddens my wife to see it unlived in and forgotten, except when a Barton agent comes once a year to check that it is weatherproof and watertight."

"It belongs to Sir Hamilton Barton, does it?"

"Yes, it was his summer home as a child. Originally it was no more than a cottage, but his father had it enlarged to the size it is now. I doubt if Sir Hamilton remembers that it still stands. An order for its maintenance was probably given fifty years ago and is still being carried out."

"It's an unpretentious house for a grand family."

"Old Sir Hamilton is an unpretentious man as was his father, who made his fortune in shipping and was a John Blunt in his ways and in his speech until the end of his days. The family is grand enough these days and chooses to forget its power originated in common trade, but the old gentleman likes to remind them of it to bring them down a peg or two now and again."

Keeping one hand on the gate Daniel said, "You talk as if you know him well."

"I do. Through him I gained this living at Easthampton. I was at a church on one of his estates for a long time, and he thought the sea air would help cure my aches and pains."

"He shows less consideration towards his tenants."

"No man is perfect, Mr. Warwyck, but there is some good in every sinner. These days he is very old and knows little of what takes place on his behalf. His agents handle everything."

Daniel stepped forward eagerly, the dust of the lane billowing up about his high boots. "I will take the names of those agents. I mean to have this house if its interior lives up to the promise of the exterior."

"There is a key at the vicarage. Since the time the Bartons used to stay at Honeybridge House a spare key has been left there to be at hand in any emergency. The Merrelton builders in charge of maintenance always use that key."

"I'll be glad to borrow it. But there is more of Easthampton I want to own than Honeybridge House and its grounds."

Eliot drew in his breath and sank back against the supporting rail of the seat. He had sensed the determination and ambition of Daniel Warwyck ever since the young pugilist had approached him after a morning service with a request for information about Easthampton. It had been like a spark, a burning spark, and his wife had been aware of it as well. They had shown him hospitality as a stranger in their midst, and on their own they had talked about him, wondered about him, and inexplicably found their hopes raised by him in his enthusiasm for the hamlet, but not quite knowing why.

"If it is for the good of Easthampton and its people you shall have any assistance that lies in my power to give. Get back into the gig and tell me what you have in mind."

By the time they arrived back at the vicarage the grandiose plan had been outlined. Over tea and currant buns baked by Sarah Singleton and served still warm from the oven to them on their own in the study Eliot pointed out the difficulties and problems that Daniel must expect, not in any attempt to discourage the plan, but only to put him in possession of all the facts.

"I must warn you that important local families who live in the surrounding district will oppose your every move. If they should have wind of it already—"

"There is no chance of that. I lived many years in the country and I know how village tongues wag about any stranger in their midst. The landlord of The Running Hare knows now I am a pugilist of some fame, and believes me to be resting on doctor's orders after my last bout. He is flattered that I should return to Easthampton after a previous brief visit to it, supposing it to be due to what he had said about the health-giving properties of Easthampton's salubrious air. Naturally he has spread the word wide, and"—here he chuckled—"he has assumed from a word planted here and there that my hobby is collecting artifacts and fossils, which has explained away my uncommon interest in the seashore and the local soil."

"I see you came prepared for opposition, but I am not sure that you understand fully how virulent it might prove to be. Gentlemen of quality in this area will not want development and advancement on their own doorsteps. In winter and other times of great hardship the ladies provide soup and clothing and deal out their charity to the poor of Easthampton, but their gentlemenfolk do nothing to supply employment beyond the needs of their own mansions and estates. Their stewards are able to pick and choose from the cheap labor that is available, for so many apply for every vacancy that occurs."

"I intend to change all that." Daniel leaned forward in his chair, his tea and currant bun forgotten on the table at which the two men sat. "There shall be work for all, summer and winter, and they shall live in decent habitations. All the hovels will be cleared away, together with everything else that is unsightly and an eyesore on the landscape. I'll engage the best architect I can find, but he'll be drawing up my ideas and my plans. I tell you, Easthampton shall come alive."

"You have my blessing on all you have proposed," Eliot said earnestly, "but will these backers whom you mentioned earlier be persuaded to put up the finances required for such a venture? To back you in the prize ring is a very different matter."

Daniel's face was set in confidence, nothing able to assail him in his present elated mood. "They have great wealth, but I have my fists." He raised them, laughing. "My promise to use these on any opponent they care to set up against me will do much to persuade them to my point of view."

Eliot's kindly mouth, always thin with pain, showed a little smile. "There are men of the cloth who would question my condoning the prize ring as a means to an end, no matter what good might lie at that end, but in all conscience I see no harm in a fair stand-up bout between honorable combatants who respect each other as fellow human beings. 'Better the fists than the sword.'"

"I thank you for that," Daniel said sincerely, extending a hand.

They shook hands warmly, each aware that it was a seal upon friendship born out of mutual respect and liking. An hour later Daniel went to view Honeybridge House, and as his footsteps echoed on the oaken floors in the large, paneled rooms he knew he had found a well-built and solid temporary home. Everything was dry and sweet-smelling with no ominous patches of damp or sagging floors. In the kitchen he tried the pump by the sink and after the first discolored gush which splashed out, showering him with spray, the water came clear and pure. When he had locked the house again behind him he inspected the garden and located a bridge over a stream that led to some long-discarded and broken-down beehives, which explained the house's picturesque name. He was smiling to himself as he strolled back to the vicarage to return the key. Early next morning he was making for the Brighton road.

Sir Geoffrey listened long and keenly to all Daniel had to say, and his attitude was entirely different from his resigned frame of mind when he had received the news of Daniel's departure to claim his Warwyck inheritance. Then there was nothing to be done but to hope for the best and as far as he was concerned that had come about. Back into the boxing world without the delay Sir Geoffrey had feared had come the potentially greatest scientific fighter that the prize ring had ever seen, at the same time stripped of his birthright and on a different footing. In exchange for the financial backing that Daniel required to exploit and make a fortune of his own out of this unknown hamlet with its boundless opportunities, Sir Geoffrey saw his own chance to secure a bond on Daniel's fists that would give him exclusive rights to all mills that were arranged with the financial advantages appertaining to them.

"The land is cheap enough," Sir Geoffrey commented, glancing through the papers again that he held, all containing information that Eliot Singleton had gathered and supplied, "and we should get it cheaper."

Daniel knew how that could be done. "Individual purchases under different names, I assume? Not letting a right hand know what a left hand is doing?"

"Precisely. I see that not all the property and land you are after is Barton-owned. I have agents of my own who can move in on your behalf."

"And the Barton property? I suggest a round figure. The family wish to rid themselves of a white elephant and there will be no questions asked."

"Capital!" Sir Geoffrey lowered the papers and leaned back in his chair. He was enjoying himself. Nothing appealed to him more than a venture of initiative and daring, and he had taken plenty of chances of his own in his time. To think that he was to be part of Daniel's tremendous gamble, albeit from the sidelines, gave a renewed zest and excitement to life, even if he had had more than the average man's share of such stimuli in his diplomatic missions in the service of the King. "I foresee no difficulties. After I have pulled a few strings it should not prove hard to raise the money you need at a moderate interest in addition to what I am prepared to advance you. In return I expect to be your only promoter and backer in all future bouts."

"You are generous."

Sir Geoffrey shook his head, his eyes astute behind the lively sparkle. "I am being practical and losing nothing by it. To weigh you down with financial worries would hamper your concentration in training and in the ring with dire results. That must be avoided at all costs." He put the papers aside and folded his hands across his waistcoat. "No banker would give you his time towards this venture at Easthampton with your having nothing to offer except your fists as collateral security. Should I refuse this aid you would merely turn to others in The Fancy for financial backing in this enterprise, and therein could lie your ruin as a fighter, because there would be many greedy to exploit your talent in the ring. In the end you could be weakened instead of strengthened for the championship, which must be taken at the precise moment you are ready for it and not before." He made a fist and shook it triumphantly. "Then you shall hold it against all comers! None will be able to withstand you!"

Daniel smiled with calm acceptance of the praise. Then he said, "I notice you have not said one word of criticism or shown any opposition to my plan."

Sir Geoffrey chuckled and rose up from his chair to refill Daniel's glass from the decanter of Madeira before adding to his own. "I have watched you in the ring too many times to believe any man can turn you from a course you have in mind. In any case, the plan is a good one. It will give you the prosperous retirement you deserve when your pugilistic days are over, because the business openings you are creating for yourself in this previously ignored hamlet can bring in financial rewards beyond measure." Replacing the stopper in the decanter, which made a little clink of crystal against crystal, he picked up his glass with fingertips around the rim, looking down with slyly amused eyes at Daniel where he was seated in a winged chair. "You are as set on making Easthampton your own as you are determined to win Miss Claudine Clayton. That evening I presented you to her at the Marine Pavilion I saw you had marked her down for yourself.

Easthampton is to share her fate. I ask only that you make the Championship of England your third conquest."

Daniel stood up and lifted his glass with a quick, wide grin. "All three shall be mine, Sir Geoffrey. I swear it."

Both drank to the promise. Neither doubted its ultimate fulfillment.

Together they left for London the same day, Sir Geoffrey to contact his banker and his lawyers and his agents, setting into motion the wheels within wheels that were to launch Daniel into his venture. Daniel had other business to deal with, seeking out the architect whose work he favored and entering into consultations with him, impressing upon him an immediate need for secrecy, which sent that architect in the guise of a late summer visitor down to Easthampton to view prospective sites. All the time Daniel stayed as a guest in Sir Geoffrey's Grosvenor Square residence until the contracts began to be signed and the deeds of Honeybridge House were in his pocket. Perhaps most satisfying of all to him was the document that sealed the purchase of the hill above the green. Only then did he leave Mayfair and go to his London lodgings, which consisted of five rooms on the second floor of a house near Blackfriars Bridge.

He had entered and was halfway up the stairs when Jassy, who had sighted him from a little distance away in the street, came running into the house after him.

"Daniel! You're home!" She came pounding up the stairs, her face flushed with excitement, past unhappiness between them momentarily forgotten. "How are you? Have you been abroad? We had no word from either of you. Where is Kate? Has she gone ahead upstairs?"

She would have passed him, for he had drawn aside to let her come level with him, but he caught her arm. "Kate is not with me."

"Not with you?" She smiled uncomprehendingly and glanced down at the hall as if half-expecting Kate's shadow to appear at any minute in the rectangular patch of sunlight that spread itself in the entrance. "Did you leave her in the street? Has she shopping to do? Tell me where she is and I'll go to her—"

"Kate and I have parted company."

Jassy drew back against the baluster rail, staring at him in abject dismay. "I don't believe you."

"It is true enough. There were no legal ties to bind us in any way. I gave her back her freedom."

"But her freedom was in being with us. I know it. I felt it. She would not want to be alone."

"I think Kate is well able to take care of herself and lead her own life." Daniel shifted his valise to the other hand and would have put a reassuring arm about Jassy's shoulders, but she shrank away from him.

"I may write to her, mayn't I? You know where she is?"

His sister's accusative attitude was beginning to try him, but he kept his patience. "I do not know where she is, and she has most surely forgotten us in the weeks that have elapsed since she and I went our separate ways at Winchester on the same day that we left you at the crossroads."

For seconds Jassy stared at him. Then she said, "You are the cruelest man in all the world, Daniel Warwyck." With a flurry of petticoats she swirled away from him and went running back down the stairs and out of the house, turning in the direction of the sparring rooms, which lay farther down the street.

He supposed she was bent on spreading the news to Jem and Harry, but he hoped she had not fallen into the habit of frequenting the sparring rooms, because it was no place for a young girl. In fact, the whole district was not one in which he cared to have his sister living and the sooner she was out of it and settled in Honeybridge House the better.

He was reading through a stack of letters that had been awaiting his return when Jassy came back, entering the room first and followed by Jem with Harry behind him. Jem's welcome was genuine, but restrained.

"Good to see ye, Dan. It's high time ye were back. Mr. Jackson has kindly offered ye a benefit at the Fives Court next month, and there's none that gets that without his special consideration. It could bring ye in a tidy sum."

It was excellent news. The money raised at benefits was to give hard-fighting and deserving pugilists extra funds in recognition of their services to the prize ring, and never did Daniel need every penny as he did at this particular time.

There was no welcome from Harry. He had lost weight as well as most of the tan that the Brighton sun had given his complexion. Daniel half-expected him to burst into some tirade about Kate's banishment, but her name was not forthcoming. Instead with a look of resolve and a new seriousness that seemed to have become stamped into his features since Daniel had last seen him he spoke out strongly on another matter.

"I know you wanted funds from a certain source to launch me into a profession," he said, his agreement with Kate never to mention Warwyck Manor by name again remaining unbroken, "but in truth I always dreaded the prospect. I have a head for figures and an aptitude for most things, but not for devoting several years of my life to the study of law or medicine or anything else that takes a deal of time. I was aware of what you planned for me by one means or another but I balked at it constantly, and now I feel free to make a decision about my future. I want to become your manager. Jem and I have talked it over, and he has given his approval. He believes I can do it. What do you say? It must be yes or no, because I can't wait any longer to know which way it is to be."

Daniel looked at his brother steadily. When Harry put himself out he had been a great help to Jem many times, and now there was a change in him, an inner strengthening that had been lacking before. He should be given his chance. With Jem to steer him along for the first few months it would soon become apparent whether or not he was as suited to the position as he apparently believed himself to be, and he certainly knew all the background to it already.

A grin spread slowly across Daniel's face and he gave a nod. "Very well. I'll give you a chance. It's up to you to prove yourself to be the best manager in pugilistic circles today."

There was no answering display of exuberance, only a solemn bow of the head from Harry, and a hand reached out to shake Daniel's formally. Jem fetched out a bottle to pour drinks on the agreement, and although Jassy gave Harry a kiss on the cheek to show she was pleased he had been given the opportunity he had sought, there was no air of celebration in the strained atmosphere. Daniel knew that all three of them were ranged against him in his failure to bring Kate home to them, but he told himself they would soon get over it.

He took them out to a chophouse for dinner and when the wine and good food had had some effect he decided that his moment had come. "I think it's time I told you everything that has been happening since I saw you last."

They listened to him, at first incredulously and then each reacting independently. Harry, in spite of himself, was fired by his brother's enthusiasm, able to see his own talents having full scope long after Daniel's days in the ring were over, and with a chance to make his own fortune. Inevitably his thoughts linked Kate with that future, because he was resolved to find her again and when he did he would never let her go. His life had become molded to that aim and the necessary successful livelihood to keep her in comfort. Jem saw the project in Easthampton as the fulfillment of a need in Daniel's character that could only result in his becoming an even better fighter, but he also saw the presence of Claudine Clayton in the same district as a disturbing threat that could not be ignored. Jassy, although she found London overpowering and distressingly noisy after the peace of Devonshire, dreaded another move, and with all her heart longed for the companionship of Kate, who had shown every sign of becoming the only true and steadfast friend she had ever known.

The first bill of sale of land and property in Easthampton was signed and sealed on the day of Daniel's benefit at Fives Court. The crush of carriages outside its doors in St. Martin's Street began early and soon stretched across Leicester Fields. Over a thousand male spectators gathered in the open court to watch the sparring set-tos on the stage, many of the gentlemen present being of superior rank in society, Sir Geoffrey among them. Daniel took part in the final exhibition bout of the day, and when it was all over he found himself several hundred pounds the richer.

Disappointingly it took until after Christmas before the final bill of sale could be added to all the rest that had been gathered together over the intervening months, and the following day Daniel surrendered his lodgings, which was one economy he could make, knowing that whenever he or the others needed accommodation in London a room could always be had at The Union Arms in Panton Street, which was at one of the hubs of the milling circles. The landlord there was the great boxer, Tom Cribb, who had won the Championship of England some years previously and was rarely seen in the ring these days due to corpulence and a touch of gout. Jem, driving a wagon in which the furniture, carpets, and other household effects were stowed, followed Daniel's curricle and Harry in the chaise with Jassy as the four of them set off for the coast where Honeybridge House awaited them.

They arrived in the early January dusk to find lamplight glowing from the windows, smoke rising from the chimneys, and at the gate was Eliot Singleton, who waved to them as they approached. From the doorway his wife, Sarah, came hurrying out to them, her round face smiling, both hands extended and upraised.

"It was unthinkable that you should arrive to a cold house and have nothing to eat awaiting you," she declared. "I beg you not to think I have abused any privileges."

Daniel, jumping down from the curricle, caught one of her hands in his and put it to his lips with gallantry. "You are kindness itself, ma'am."

Amid greetings and introductions they flowed into the house. A neat-aproned woman, one of those hired in the hamlet to clean the house, was waiting in the hall, and she took Jassy's cloak. Jassy smiled vaguely, but barely noticed her, taking in her new surroundings with wide eyes. It was a tiny habitation compared to Warwyck but spacious in comparison with the London lodgings, and she warmed to its paneled walls and low black beams and the open hearths where fires of apple wood had been lit and danced their crackling flames up the chimneys. The absence of all furniture enabled her to get a full picture of its fine proportions, until she came to the dining room where Sarah had had three of her own card tables set end to end and flanked by borrowed benches. On the spread cloth a cold collation waited together with a tureen of steaming soup served up as they had been sighted turning into the lane.

Eliot did not have an opportunity to speak alone with Daniel until the other two had entered the dining room to join Jassy and Sarah. Then, leaning on his sticks, he regarded him sternly and with some disappointment.

"When I agreed to help you in any way I could," he said heavily, "I had no idea that dealings coming close to sharp practice would be used to oust several small business men from their properties. You cannot tell me you know nothing of the supposed expert who came talking about subsidence of soil and the possible danger to life through cracking walls or roofs."

Daniel's face was bland and his gaze did not flicker. "It was a means to an end. There was a limit to the amount I could borrow. Not one of those men shall suffer through being persuaded to surrender their leases or their livelihoods. Only Thomas J. Brown was not approached or asked to sell, simply because he might have turned to Alexander Radcliffe for advice, and that had to be avoided. I understand that when word reached him of his fellow business men selling up he added his persuasions, thinking to acquire cheap property to rent as housing, no matter if it was being condemned as unsafe."

"One man's proposed knavery does not excuse another's crooked actions!" Eliot reprimanded heatedly. "In the present matter you and he are two of a kind, and in addition I include your London friends who are backing you in this coming venture."

"Friend, not friends," Daniel corrected pedantically, wanting to find some way to soothe Eliot down. It had been essential to his plans that certain properties be acquired near the green, and only through vacant possession could they be demolished. He sought to change the subject. "That mention of the Radcliffes reminds me that I must ask you if they are in residence at the Hall?"

"Yes, as far as I know. Mrs. Radcliffe distributed food and clothing to the poor at Christmastime. But I cannot say they are there for certain, because they attend St. Cuthbert's Church in Merrelton and I do not number them among my congregation." Eliot tapped a stick sharply. "Do not prevaricate. I want your word as a man of honor that neither you nor anyone acting on your behalf will stoop to further questionable dealings to gain your own ends."

Sarah appeared at the dining room door, most opportunely in Daniel's opinion, for he was saved having to give Eliot a reply. "Come along, both of you," she chided. "The soup will get cold and all my efforts will have been wasted."

"That cannot be allowed," Daniel answered, smiling, and he went in to take his place at table beside Jem.

When the meal was over Daniel and Jem took off their coats and began to unload the heaviest furniture. Harry assisted, and soon carpets and rugs were laid, beds assembled, and tables and chairs set in place. Jassy and Sarah with the help of the hired woman unrolled mattresses and made up beds from the hampers of linen, and by midnight Honeybridge House had become a home with only a few pictures still to be hung and a crate of china yet to be unpacked. The Singletons by this time had gone home again, Eliot still uneasy in his mind, but saying nothing to his wife about it.

Daniel was the last to go to bed. In the morning the architect with whom he had had long consultations would move into the hamlet, and the foreman appointed to organize the work force needed for the first clearance of land. Moving in after them would be the stonemasons, the plumbers, the joiners and carpenters, who in turn would gather many local men following the same trades into their own work units. Daniel wanted nothing to do with sub-contractors, determined to keep his own tight hands on the reins, and he could count on solid and reliable support from the local builder, Arthur Tanner, whom he had set in charge after work of his in the Easthampton area had been inspected and approved by the architect. Arthur Tanner had found himself summoned to London, his fare paid, and there he had received and accepted the proposition put to him, which was to be held in strictest confidence until the appointed day. Daniel's original judgment of Tanner as an honest and sensible man able to keep his own counsel had not gone amiss, for Tanner revealed at the interview that he had guessed it had been more than an interest in fossils that had prompted so many questions about the soil and sands, but he had kept it to himself and waited to see what might happen.

The apple wood on the hearth was still flickering and with the toe of his boot Daniel nudged it apart, leaving the red-gold ashes to darken and die out. It was warm and comfortable in the house, but outside there was a sharp frost. He thought again that the winter was an excellent time of the year for obtaining all the labor needed, even if it had not been normally plentiful, for the local agricultural workers had no employment and the lowest of wages would be gratefully taken. He frowned, aware that he was going to obtain that labor for a pittance, but he had no choice. Costs had to be cut on all sides. In time to come when returns started to pour in he would adjust wages to a higher scale, but in the meantime that was out of the question.

Going across to the window he held back one of the curtains that Jassy had made to measurements sent by Sarah Singleton, and he looked out toward the moon-drenched sea. This was the beginning. Everything should turn out exactly as he wished it. And on Sunday he would drive to Merrelton and go to church. He wanted to see Claudine's face when she saw him in the next pew. He began to laugh, low-throated and full. The laugh of a man who believed he could already taste victory.

Upstairs Harry heard the sound as he lay in bed, and he rolled over, punching his pillow. Hating his brother. Hating him for snatching away Kate and losing her in the unknown. But at least a home had been made in Sussex. It meant that with every spare minute he had he could comb the countryside for Kate, for he firmly believed she would have returned to the only county familiar to her. He would go first to her home village of Heathfield and make inquiries there among all whom he could discover who knew her. One of them would most surely know her whereabouts or would have had some word from her. If that lead failed he would follow other trails, and if need be call on Farmer Farringdon himself. No stone should be left unturned, no slight clue left unfollowed. But he must be sure that Daniel did not have the slightest suspicion as to what he was up to. There must be no risk again of losing what he had longed to gain.

In her room Jassy sat brushing her hair before a looking glass, her thoughts also dwelling on Kate. How different everything would have been if Kate had been with them. As it was, from tomorrow she must start running the house on her own without servants, for Daniel had made clear they must be living to a strict budget from this time forward, with no spare cash to spend on anything. The thought dismayed her. She had never gone marketing for food at Warwyck, never had to wash or cook or clean, and she always had difficulty in checking the household accounts presented to her, although sometimes in the past she knew her inability to balance them lay more with the pilfering that went on belowstairs than her own inadequacy; in fact, the Manor had been run by whichever housekeeper happened to be employed at the time, and not until Bessie, a slattern herself, had moved in to take over, was any interference made in the running of the place, and that was with even less satisfactory results.

Jassy emitted a heavy sigh. In London, Harry and Jem had spoilt and pampered her, neither of them letting her go out alone beyond the immediate vicinity of the lodgings in a district full of dark alleys and sinister corners. She had gone with them to the local markets, but there had been too many new sights to see, too many diversions for her to pay any attention to prices or to notice the quality they looked for in what they were buying. Mostly they had eaten out in chophouses, such as the place Daniel had taken them upon his return, for London abounded in places to eat where the food was good, and any cooking in the lodgings had been done by Jem. A laundry woman had collected the washing, hers and theirs, and everything had come back smoothly ironed and starched. Her Warwyck pride would not let her seek advice from Sarah Singleton who, being so capable and efficient and practical, would most surely despise her for her foolishness and ignorance, but Kate would not have despised her. Kate would have taught her all the domestic sciences with patience and understanding. Kate.

She let the brush slide from her hair down into her lap. "Come back to us from wherever you are," she whispered aloud, her eyes shut. "Come home to us, Kate."

In the following dawn of a crisp, cold morning the humbler inhabitants of Easthampton began to emerge from cottage, shack, and hovel, the women and children remaining huddled around the doorways while they watched the menfolk converge on a disused stableyard by the green, a small crowd of them gradually growing. There was nobody in the stableyard yet, but the previous evening a stranger with the unmistakable stamp of a foreman on him had arrived at The Running Hare, and sharp eyes had spotted a portable trestle table and stool there. The hamlet grapevine carried the news. As it was customary for anyone needing labor to sit in the stableyard, nobody was going to lose the chance of any work by getting there late, whatever it might happen to be. Thus when Bertram Hardy, foreman, came out of the tavern on the stroke of half past seven by the church clock he found over a hundred men and boys waiting patiently to be hired as casual labor or, more hopefully, to put their cross on a paper that would guarantee them work for the rest of the winter. He eyed them with a steely, impersonal glance, able through long experience to separate the sheep from the goats, the wheat from the chaff, the strong from the weak or the lazy.

"Aw'right," he bawled. "Get in line. I'll speak to each one of yer, but I'll have no pushing or shoving. Any bloke what causes that sort of trouble can sling his hook right now."

They obeyed him, quietly and with only some little confusion of shuffling into a queue that averaged two abreast. Two boys ran forward at his bidding to take the portable table he was carrying and set it up for him together with the folding stool. There he sat himself down, knees spread wide, paper and a stub of pencil in front of him.

"Right. First man come forward and step lively."

The line of men had much to watch as they awaited their turn. Horses and carts began to jog into the hamlet, bearing equipment in the shape of shovels and sledgehammers, wheelbarrows and ropes, and saws and pickaxes. In charge of each cart was one of Hardy's own men, and when those signed on as suitable applicants came out of the brickyard they found themselves directed into work at once. There was land to be cleared, buildings to be knocked down, rubble to be carted away. Before it was full daylight the air rang to the sound of axe and hammer and the roar of collapsing walls.

Daniel and Harry, with Jem in tow, watched it all, going from site to site, stared at by any who dared lift their eyes from their tasks and by the rest of the inhabitants, who gazed in disbelief at the frenzied activity of workmen from behind their lace curtains, or came out to the gates or into the street to demand to know what was afoot. The word spread and absurd rumors grew rife with talk of iron ore being mined in the middle of the green and the place becoming a spa for foreigners with unmentionable diseases. Out of it all some facts emerged. The Warwyck workshops were to be set in the old brewery that had fallen into disuse and the buildings there utilized as workshops for smiths, joiners, and carpenters and other trades, with the sawpits at hand, and the land beyond becoming brickfields to supply the manufacture of bricks on a grand scale. Then once more rumor took over and swamped all common sense. Those with genteel aspirations bewailed the misfortune of it. Nothing was ever to be the same again. Into their midst had come the viper most dreaded by the upper and middle classes: the speculator with his shrewd brain and ruthless tactics, and in this case a common pugilist to boot.

There was no doubt in the minds of any of those not needing the employment provided that Easthampton was destined to end up as vulgar and gaudy as a fairground under the jurisdiction of such a man.

Those with a more practical turn of mind, including two maiden ladies who set out at once in their gig, took their complaints and their fears to the most powerful personage in the district, Alexander Radcliffe, whose land met the boundaries of Easthampton. He heard the first of his callers with incredulity and the belief that some small clearance work had fired off ludicrous rumors that were completely without foundation, but by midday he had heard enough complaints to ride over and investigate for himself.

Once in Easthampton, after asking a few questions here and there from men in charge of minor working parties, as well as calling in at the general stores for a word with Thomas Brown, he realized that there were sound grounds for concern. Swinging himself back into the saddle he sighted Daniel at a distance across the green, but turned his arrogant face away, and digging in his heels he galloped out of the hamlet and back to Radcliffe Hall. There he penned a letter to his lawyers demanding that they conduct a full inquiry into what was taking place, and to use every means in their power to get an injunction through from a magistrate to put a halt to what had begun at Easthampton.

Daniel, after a totally satisfactory day, was less than pleased when he and Harry took the architect home to dine at Honeybridge House only to find that Jassy had prepared a most disappointing meal. There was no soup or fish, and the joint of roast beef, which was curiously burned on one side and running almost raw on the other, completely defeated his sharpened carving knife in the serving of fine slices. She had forgotten to put salt in the vegetables, and the pudding when it came was a caramelized glue that stuck to the spoons and would have pulled out any loose tooth better than a string tied to a door. Only Jem ate with a show of relish, seeing that Jassy was dangerously on the point of

tears at her failures and taut with nerve-racked strain at Daniel's
obvious disapproval. After the cloth was removed and she left
them to their port Jem made an excuse to follow her out to the
kitchen. She was white-faced amid a wreckage of burned pots and
spilled sauce and scattered cooking spoons.

"Oh, Jem," she cried, sinking down into a chair on which rested
an opened bag of flour. "I did my best, but it was awful. The
range"—she made a helpless gesture toward its blackness set enormously into the wall under its copper hood—"seems to have a
mind of its own. It has gone out again, and there is no hot water
for washing up or for tea when Daniel takes his guest into the
drawing room."

Jem rescued the flour bag just before it tipped its contents to
the floor. "Don't ye fret. They're settled where they are at the
table for a bit. I'll get the range going." He stooped his big frame
down and began to rattle the grid and reach for firewood. "My
knowledge of cooking is limited to frying a slice of ham and boiling a spud, but I reckon ye could ask Mrs. Singleton to give ye a
few hints—"

"No!" Jassy was not without the Warwyck stubbornness as well
as pride. "I will learn, and without her help."

The flames had begun to roar behind the grating. Jem
straightened up. "Of course you will," he agreed with a forced
heartiness, being of the opinion that good cooks were born and
not made, and since Jassy seemed to be singularly lacking in any
culinary ability he privately saw little hope for her or their stomachs all the time she was in charge of the kitchen. But it was not
only the kitchen where she showed herself to be inexperienced in
housewifely duties, for already the house had an untidy look. How
to define it he was not sure, but without being aware of it he had
gained an impression of general disorder, together with crumbs
from breakfast on the carpet. "Maybe ye should have house help.
After all, ye've been used to it."

"No," she said again. "Daniel has put his foot down and I'll
not beg from *him*." Her eyes flashed in her animosity toward her

brother before her expression softened again at Jem. "Thank you for getting the fire to go. There will soon be hot water now, and I can make excellent tea if nothing else."

Jem returned to the dining room and she took the teapot and cups and saucers from the cupboard where she had put them after unpacking the china crate earlier that day. She warmed the pot, added the tea, and poured on boiling water. Milk in the jug and sugar in the basin. Picking up the tray she advanced to the kitchen door. Then her heel slid on some congealed spilled fat on the floor. In the dining room they heard the crash and clatter as she fell, and they sprang up and rushed to the scene of the disaster. She was screaming hysterically, but not because she was scalded as they had feared.

"Let me pass!" she shrieked when they clustered about her in concern, and she thrust them off, catching up her half-soaked skirt and running from the kitchen across the hall and up the stairs, spattering a trail of tea drops as she went. Her bedroom door slammed, and the sound of her sobbing went on long after the architect had made his departure and Jem and Harry had cleaned up the kitchen.

Daniel tapped on her door. "Jassy?"

"Go away."

He ignored the instruction and entered. She was lying across the bed in her petticoats, her dress in a damp heap on the floor. "I'm going to hire a servant to help you. It's obvious you cannot manage on your own. That woman Mrs. Singleton found who was here yesterday evening would do very well."

"I don't want her." Jassy sat up, supporting her weight straight-armed on the bed. Perversely she was relieved and annoyed that Daniel had changed his mind. "I don't want anyone whom Sarah Singleton has picked out. I find Sarah pious and condescending and she thinks she knows everything."

"You're being childish."

"And you're being blind. It was more than Christian charity that prompted all she did for us in this house for our coming. She cannot take her eyes from you when she believes herself to be unobserved."

Whether it was true or not he did not know or care, except that he would not want Eliot Singleton's kind and sensitive nature hurt one iota through any foolish and frustrated middle-aged yearnings on the part of Sarah. "I advise you to curb your tongue. If it will make you any happier you may interview and choose your own servant. There are enough womenfolk in need of employment in this hamlet."

She drew herself up with dignity. "I thank you, although I am the lady of this house and that privilege should be mine. I'm aware that it will be a small drain on your purse which you had hoped to avoid, but I'll choose wisely and well. A servant's help will give me the time I need to become better at marketing and cooking."

"That's settled then." He turned to leave again.

The words burst from her. "If Kate hadn't been sent away—"

He rounded on her. "Kate went of her own free will!" he thundered. "Let there be an end to it! I don't want to hear her name from you again!"

He slammed the door after him. He thought, fuming, that Jassy's earlier timidity had changed through antagonism into a strange willfulness. And somehow Kate was to blame for it.

When Sunday morning came Daniel left Honeybridge House driving his curricle. He was bound for St. Cuthbert's Church in Merrelton, and he was in the belief that Harry was still abed, not knowing that his brother had been up far earlier and had been riding along on the road to Heathfield, hard set on the commencement of the search for the woman he loved. Jem, always an early riser, had been up, surreptitiously making an attempt to tidy up the house for Jassy, who had not yet appeared. No servant girl had been taken on yet, although several had been interviewed, but Daniel was determined to say no more to his sister on the subject, forcing himself to be patient, for he wanted to heal the breach between them.

When he reached the church he looped the reins of the two horses in the shafts to a hitching post and waited under the bare branches of the churchyard trees, until he saw the Radcliffe landau arrive. A groom sprang down to open the door and Alexander alighted first, turning to hand out Olivia and then Claudine, who wore a fur-trimmed coat of tangerine velvet that was matched by the dancing, feathery plumes of her wide-brimmed, brown bonnet. She was bright as a flame, and the pang that Daniel felt was forceful and physical and made him draw deeply at his breath.

But he was not alone in waiting to see her. Out of the shadows of the church porch came a tall man of aristocratic bearing with meditative gray eyes lashed under arching brows that appeared darker than his curly fair hair, his nose straight and narrow, his clipped beard outlining the well-set jaw. Altogether he was a fine-looking and arresting man, his clothes fashionably styled, but falling short of being dandified through a personal good taste, his cravat folded about his high pointed collar like a slice of new-driven snow. Yet, for all that, there was no force in him, no sharpness of character in the smooth features burnished by some foreign sun, and to Daniel's observant eye he in no way deserved the look of pleasure lighting up Claudine's face when she sighted him.

"Good morning, Lionel," she greeted him, her pace quickening a fraction to close in shorter time the distance between them. "We danced the night away, and yet you are still here before me. Have you slept at all?"

His smile held charm enough to turn the head of any woman, creating a little crease on either side of the handsome mouth. "My dear Claudine, how could any man think of sleep with thoughts of you filling his head?"

Claudine gave him a flirtatious side glance and tapped his lapel with an admonishing gloved finger. "Well, do not fall asleep in the sermon, that is all."

He offered his arm and she took it, walking at his side, and following in the wake of Olivia and Alexander with whom he exchanged some conversation. Daniel gained the impression that the comfortable familiarity between the two men was based on long friendship, for they were about the same age, and it would be a highly likely state of affairs if Lionel lived somewhere in the region of Radcliffe Hall. He intended to make it his business to find out.

When the four of them had gone into the church he followed at a distance, marked where Claudine's bonnet was bowed in a fine show of private devotion, and took a seat a little to the left in the pew directly behind her. He then fixed his gaze on her and did not shift it.

She rose from her knees and sat back in her seat, exchanged a smiling whisper with Lionel who was seated on one side of her, her sister on the other, and then she began to find the hymns and psalms in her book from glances at the numbers on the board, setting in little tasseled lace bookmarks. Her hand faltered. Daniel saw how gradually she was becoming aware of somebody's attention transfixed upon her. She looked in the opposite direction first, half over her shoulder in a quick darting glance which caught up a smile or two and a nod from those acquaintances who happened to catch the passing flicker of her gaze. Unsatisfied, she turned her head round over her other shoulder in a covert glance and met the full impact of his eyes.

Had he been Nemesis sitting there she could not have reacted any differently. The color gushed into her cheeks and in the depths of her eyes there showed a kind of drowning helplessness before her spirit rallied and with a toss of plumes and a tilt of her chin she swept her face forward again. But she was trembling. He could see it.

The service began, but she stood and knelt and sat like an automaton, so fierce was the sense of his presence just behind her. He was stalking her, and she truly believed that behind his invasion of Easthampton, which was being discussed and deplored on all sides in the circles in which she moved, there lay some link to his obsession for her. Because he was obsessed by her. No matter what he said or did there was an unspoken declaration in his whole being that told her he meant to have her, even against her will. On this erotic thought the color soared again into her cheeks and then left her paler than before.

When she had tricked him over the last dance at the Marine Pavilion she had thought to put him in his place once and for all, a snub to rid herself of him completely, but when he had pursued her, throwing himself onto the barouche as if he would snatch her from it, she had known a sweet, exultant terror that had thrilled her through. Then Alexander had thrown him off and she had seen him go crashing back onto the cobbles. Believing that every bone in his body must be broken, she became wild with panic and remorse, begging Alexander to stop the carriage that they might go back to him. Never had she seen Alexander so angry. In the end he had quelled her with his anger, upbraiding her for having consorted with the common fellow, and she had sat ashen-faced and shivering, Olivia's hand stealing out under the cover of the shadows in the carriage to clasp itself over hers in an attempt at comfort and reassurance. Unknown to Alexander, it had been Olivia who had sent a servant to The Old Ship Hotel to make discreet inquiries after Daniel Warwyck, bringing back word that the pugilist had most certainly returned to the hotel with some support from his companions, but walking unbroken and unbowed.

It had been a relief that he had gone from Brighton the next day as he had planned. Freedom returned to her and she no longer went about in that high-pitched state of resentful excitement, knowing that any moment they might meet, but with his going the dangerous spice had gone too and everything had become a little flat. Fortunately Lionel Attwood returned from abroad, his health fully restored after spending some long time at his villa in the Italian sun, and he had come to spend the rest of the season in Brighton. They had not met before, she having come home to England from France shortly after he had departed for Italy, and Attwood Grange, which lay only a few miles west of Radcliffe Hall, had remained closed throughout his absence. He and Alexander had known each other all their lives, and the rest of the time at Brighton had been spent in a pleasant foursome with all thoughts of Daniel banished. Lionel was a beautiful man, both in looks and nature, and she found they had much in common in a love of music and poetry. Gradually they had been building up a relationship, for since her return to Radcliffe Hall and his to Attwood Grange all the social activities of the winter had caught them up in a whirl together, every great house in the district holding some grand function to welcome Lionel home again. Now Daniel had burst into her life once more, presenting such a threat that she could foresee only doom and destruction, and yet with it had come a sweeping and undeniably pleasurable return of the old excitement, the tingling warning of amorous danger, impossible to ignore or turn aside.

The service came to an end at last. As everyone made to leave she slipped her hand into the crook of Lionel's arm before he had time to offer it, and he looked at her with a quick smile, which she returned. They had a word with the vicar at the door and then passed with the rest of the congregation out into the pale January noon, falling into conversation with groups of acquaintances here and there, all lingering for the enjoyable social interchange that followed morning service.

Daniel stood alone, a dark-clothed figure against the gaunt trees, and Claudine, fighting to concentrate on all else but him, failed and let her gaze seek him out. For a few moments they regarded each other across the stretch of grass between them. Then deliberately she detached herself from the group that she was with and crossed over to him. He doffed his hat and held it. She came to a halt facing him, trying to ignore the nervous pounding of her heart.

"I trust you suffered no serious harm from the fall you took in Brighton," she said in a clear, steady voice.

"None at all, but no thanks to you, ma'am, or your brother-in-law."

She felt compelled to defend Alexander stoutly. "Your action was foolhardy. It was natural that my sister's husband should imagine you to be some footpad or other rascally villain bent on who knew what mischief."

His eyes narrowed cynically. "Pretense does not become you, Miss Clayton. Attempt no more tricks on me. Radcliffe knew me, and his attack was cowardly and unmanly."

Although riled by his words the fact that she inwardly agreed with him about Alexander's behavior made it difficult to maintain her defensive attitude, but she managed it. "You would be foolish to judge Alexander's character by that yardstick. He is afraid of nothing. If you have any sense, sir, you will abandon whatever diabolical scheme you have for Easthampton and depart from the coast with all haste. Already you have every person of quality for miles around ranged against you, and at the forefront of them all is Alexander."

He grinned without mirth. "Opposition is my livelihood. I will remind you that in my profession it is all I meet in the prize ring, and I thrive on it. Let Radcliffe do his worst. I'll not be dislodged."

"Why did you come to Easthampton of all places?" The question burst from her as if her tongue spoke by its own volition. "Tell me why."

"Let me invite you to see the plans for it one day at your convenience. You will soon understand the reason why."

There was enough underlying emphasis to his words to leave her in no doubt that it was an assignation he was after more than any aim to explain his actions to her, and she knew she must talk no more with him.

"That is out of the question," she answered firmly, uncomfortably aware of two bright spots of color burning in her cheeks. "Good day to you."

She turned with a rustle of her skirt hems and faltered in her tracks at the sight that met her. It was as if everyone gathered there before the church had changed into a collection of statues, for all stood in their little groups with every face turned toward Daniel and her, each conversation stilled. She knew that what had passed between the two of them could not have been overheard, but Daniel had been recognized as the speculator from Easthampton and the word passed around, all there having heard tell of him. Interest, curiosity, amiability, hostility, and indifference showed in the variety of expressions. Alexander's face was black as thunder, but Olivia had restrained him from coming forward with a warning hand on his arm, fearful of any scene taking place in the vicinity of the church and before many whom they knew, and reluctantly he had allowed himself to be advised by her. Lionel, puzzled that Claudine appeared to know the arrogant pugilist who had dared to disturb the centuries-old peace of Easthampton, stood waiting for her at some distance from the others, but far enough away not to intrude. She swept toward him with a sense of overwhelming relief, seeing him suddenly as her haven, her refuge, and his being there at that precise moment did more to cement their relationship in her eyes and in her innermost feelings than anything that had gone before. She treated him to an eye-dazzling smile.

"Foolish me," she declared, taking his arm. "Briefly I saw myself as Joan of Arc seeking to save Easthampton from the enemy, but my appeal was to no avail."

"You know the fellow?" he inquired incredulously.

"He was presented to me by his patron, Sir Geoffrey Edenfield, at the Marine Pavilion one evening." She gave a mock shiver, glancing in her brother-in-law's direction. "I can see Alexander is far from pleased at my acknowledging that brief acquaintanceship, but it was in a good cause." Her eyes were full of winning appeal. "Be my defender Lionel."

"At all times, my dear Claudine."

Daniel watched them depart, well satisfied with the morning's achievement. Had she not wanted the chase to continue, he the hunter, she the prey, she would not have been drawn to speak to him, and without being aware of it she had given him an advantage. Wondering just how long it would take her to follow up his invitation he made his way back to his own equipage and drove away.

During the days that followed he began to watch out for her, turning his head sharply many times when the flick of bonnet plumes caught his eye or the gleam of a carriage passing by made him pause in whatever he was doing, but it was never Claudine's face that he saw. Sometimes he was too busy to think of her from early morning until he fell into bed at night. To keep himself fit and in peak condition he not only ran daily along the sands, Jem jogging along with him, but would wield a pickaxe or shovel earth or give a hand with any other heavy task in progress that would help keep his muscles supple. This working alongside his laborers added further to his detriment in the opinion of those ranged against him.

The architect had departed, as it was quite customary for plans to be left in the hands of a capable builder, and in the opinion of both the architect and Daniel, Arthur Tanner met those requirements. Hardy, used to being foreman to more bombastic personalities than the quiet, steady man with his eye for detail and conscientious outlook, treated him with some contempt, which did nothing to aid relationships and added to the many problems and difficulties that inevitably arose.

Harry went to London for several days on his own, entrusted by Daniel and Jem with the responsibility of settling a number of future bouts. Sir Geoffrey as backer was at the discussions, and afterward wrote to Daniel that his brother had handled everything competently, even to insisting that each mill be held within a thirty-mile radius of Easthampton which would eliminate long journeys away from the venture on the coast.

The letter came three days before Harry arrived home. When his brother did appear Daniel was far from pleased at his prolonged absence. "What the devil have you been doing in London all this time? You should have left the same day as all business was finished. A rented room at Cribb's is not for your idle pleasuring."

"I did not stay there," Harry answered aggressively, slapping his hat on a hall peg and pulling off his cloak. "Not after the last bout was finally arranged, anyway. I had business of my own to see to."

He had been searching for Kate again. Unbeknown to Daniel he had traveled back by way of Winchester, where at the coaching inn he questioned those employed there as to whether they could remember a Kate Warwyck taking a stagecoach and in which direction. Nobody could help him. The traffic was too constant, the comings and goings too frequent. He discovered her name registered for her in Daniel's handwriting in the book at the reception desk and this did jog one of the clerks' memory into recalling that an open stagecoach ticket which allowed travel up to three hundred miles had been purchased for her, but where she had set off to and in which direction the next day he did not know. That was the end of all information to be gathered there. Yet Harry did not give up hope, and journeyed out to the first stopping places within a radius of Winchester, hoping that at one of them somebody would remember the tall, fair, young woman for whom he searched and he would gain some clue to the road she had taken, but it was all in vain. In bitter disappointment he had come home, and he was in no mood for any sharp words from Daniel.

"Hmm." Daniel was not wholly satisfied with his reply, but decided to let the matter drop. "Come in by the fire and let Jem and me hear all the details of the bout fixtures from you. Sir Geoffrey only referred briefly to them."

Daniel went back into the living room and Harry, about to follow, saw a maidservant on her way upstairs with a copper warming pan. Seeing that he had sighted her she stopped and looked down over the baluster rail at him.

"I'll tell Miss Jassy you're here, sir. Shall I?"

There had been no need to follow her first words with the question, which had been put with a provocative air. The girl was young and saucy-looking with sly eyes and a ripe mouth. Harry felt surprised at Jassy's choice and held out little private hope for any improvement in the running of the house with such a flippant-looking creature in charge under Jassy's hopeless command.

"Yes, let my sister know I'm home. What's your name?"

"Annie, sir. I've been here exactly a week."

A baggage if ever there was one, Harry thought to himself, strolling into the living room after Daniel. Once by the fire with Jem asking him questions and Daniel pushing a chair forward for him to sit down and tell them everything about the articles drawn up for future matches, Harry forgot all about the new maidservant.

Upstairs Jassy, who had been about to go to bed, hesitated as to whether she should go downstairs again or not to see Harry while Annie ran the warming pan between the sheets to take the chill off them.

"I think I'll wait until morning," she decided. "It will be all prize-ring talk downstairs now and I'll be quite bored by it."

"Do you like to see your brother fight, miss?" Annie asked, her head tilted bird-like to one side.

"I've never seen him use his fists and I would not want to." Jassy shuddered, her hands behind her as she unhooked the back of her dress.

"Here. Let me help you." Annie came to take over the unfastening. "You don't know what you've been missing. I tell you a mill is real exciting with all the crowds and the shouting and the hitting and the blood."

Jassy looked over her shoulder at the girl, her eyes wide. "It's no place for females. Only men go to prize fights."

Annie giggled and gave her a nudge. "I've borrowed my brother's clothes more than once for a lark and been at the ringside along with him. Next time there's a bout we'll rig you up as well, and we'll go together."

Jassy shook her head, laughing at the absurdity of the idea. "Never. I should give everything away by weeping if Daniel was hurt or being sick or something else as foolish and conspicuous."

She stepped out of her dress and Annie picked it up to hang it away. "If you don't want to see a bout we'll have to think of something else," the maid suggested roguishly. "It's time you had some fun. From what you've told me your life in Devon must have been dull as ditchwater, and it's not going to be any better now."

Fun. Jassy closed her eyes longingly on the thought and let her shoulders rise and fall in a sigh. Fun to her would mean a first beau and parties and dances and balls. Uncle William with his fierce Puritan ideas, which had contrasted oddly with his immoral activities, had associated dancing with sin in the same way that he had considered pugilism to be a sport of the Devil, and she had never been allowed to accept the few invitations that had come her way at Warwyck. At Easthampton with Daniel a social outcast among those with whom she would otherwise have expected to mix, she must face permanently the same state of affairs, for she was tainted by his shadow as Harry was too, and neither of them could expect to be received. One of the reasons she had chosen Annie to be maid at the house out of all those who had applied for the post, many far better qualified, was that there was an impish liveliness about the girl that had promised company and chatter and a lifting of the montony that had settled once more upon her life after that brief respite in London where everything had been new and exciting and she had contentedly anticipated the return of Kate. Annie had been quick to get above herself and take advantage, and her faults were many, for much that she said was outrageous, much of it vulgar and offensive to one of more delicate manners, but balanced against all that was the ready laugh, the friendly, vixenish grin, and a willingness to shoulder any chore without complaint, acquitting herself well enough at cooking to silence Daniel's disapproval of the way the food had previously been served. Maybe the grease was never cleaned off the saucepans and the kitchen floor, perhaps dust was swept under the carpets, and the furniture waited in vain for a polish, but none of it mattered when added up against the cheerfulness that Annie had brought into the life of a lonely girl. What was more, to be left to her books, her sewing, her embroidery, and her flute, which she played with some talent, was bliss to Jassy, who had felt physically defeated and mentally overwhelmed by the simple domestic chores that Daniel had expected her to undertake as though born to them.

"What sort of fun, Annie?" she questioned, half-eagerly, half-warily. One never knew what Annie would think of next.

"You leave that to me, miss." Annie's eyes twinkled mischievously. "I'll arrange a real spree for you before long."

For a moment a twinge of misgiving touched Jassy, but she dismissed it. When Annie had gone downstairs again, she blew out the candle in a happy frame of mind and tumbled into bed.

Chapter 9

It seemed sensible to leave Harry in charge at Easthampton when the time came for Daniel to depart with Jem for the series of exhibition bouts arranged long since, and as a gentleman's word was his bond, it never crossed Daniel's mind to suggest canceling it. They were to be away three weeks, going first to Bristol and then to Bath, concluding the tour at Leatherhead. Harry, although he had proved himself capable of working in close co-operation with Sir Geoffrey, was turning a tremendous interest toward the development of Easthampton, and he was constantly at one work site and then another, sorting out problems and settling arguments and disputes that arose with a remarkable tact that would have been beyond his brother's patience; thus he eased the burden on Daniel, who with Harry was always up before dawn and both of them were the last to finish the day's work at night. Again it was Harry who stepped in and faced out the Radcliffe lawyers and inspectors on the morning they arrived, when Daniel had gone to Merrelton to deal with some matter of delayed supplies. By the time he returned Harry was able to inform him that the enemy party had departed in defeat, there being no loophole through which they could put a halt to the work in progress.

"I do not care to be away for this coming length of time,"

Daniel said, shrugging on his shoulder-caped greatcoat. "In future it shall be as we agreed, one exhibition at a time and no tours. You know the address of each place where Jem and I shall be staying, and by all means send the fastest messenger available should any emergency arise."

"There is no need to worry about anything," Harry replied with a jaunty self-confidence. "Just you show those town dwellers how a future champion spars with the gloves, and bring home plenty of jingling gold. We need it."

Daniel's smile was grim. "We do indeed. I trust I'll whet the spectators' appetites enough to make them travel long distances to support me in my next fight." He half-turned to give his old trainer a glance. "Ready?"

"Yes, lad," Jem answered with his usual cheerful grin. He made a show of being first out of the door to the waiting equipage, but in truth he would have preferred to settle in a comfortable chair at Honeybridge instead of venturing out in the cold weather, which gave him gyp with the rheumatism in his knees. He liked Easthampton more than he had imagined possible, and wondered if it had anything to do with striking roots again after the wandering life he had led since losing his wife all those years ago. His enthusiasm for Daniel's career was as keen as ever, and once started on the journey he would be contented enough, but only to himself did he admit true and blessed relief that young Harry had proved to have the gift of management, for his mind had never been as quick to deal with the prematch argufying as he had been with his fists in the ring. He swung his muffler one more turn around his neck, thrust his hands into his pockets, and took a deep breath of the frosty, sea-spiced air. Well, three weeks was not so long, and it would be good to see Daniel using those lightning-flash mitts of his in a scientific display.

Harry did not watch them depart, having things to do, but from an upper casement window Annie's cat-like eyes crinkled as she grinned slyly, the tip of her pink tongue showing. For three weeks she would make the most of the power she had gained over that whey-faced baby, Jassy, and consolidate it for all time, or at least for as long as it suited her to stay at Honeybridge House. She discounted Harry as being the possible cause of any trouble, having observed that he had secrets of his own in comings and goings which that black-browed brother of his knew nothing about. In another part of the room behind her, Jassy swiveled round on the chair where she sat writing at the bureau.

"Have they gone?" she inquired eagerly.

"Yes, miss. They've gone."

"Good riddance to Daniel for a while," Jassy breathed thankfully, unaware that she was echoing Annie's thoughts.

That evening, with Harry absent from the house, Annie persuaded Jassy to go with her to a friend's home where there would be some merrymaking. Jassy, palpitating with nervousness and excitement, lent Annie her second-best blue silk gown to wear, and the two of them went off on foot to a fisherman's cottage on the brink of the shore. When Annie pushed open the door and they entered, Jassy had difficulty in not wrinkling her nose at the odorous smell of the place with its blending of fish and sweat, stale food, smoky pipes, and ale, but blinking after the darkness outside she forgot everything in the welcoming sight of a company of young men and girls seated around a long, oaken table in candlelight, pitchers of ale and mugs before them, and a comfortable-looking old grandmother knitting a sock by the glowing fire.

"Evening, folks," Annie announced. "I've brought along the young lady what I works for. Miss Jassy Warwyck."

They greeted her, none of the young men rising to their feet, but those on one side shoved along on the bench to make room for her while Annie made her own place on a stool at the far end of the table. The whole company was rough-spoken, somewhat coarse in their talk, but they treated Jassy with a friendly respect, and were quick to pour her some ale into another tankard taken down from the dresser.

"That's right!" Annie shouted from her end of the table. "Fill Miss Jassy's tankard to the brim."

Jassy protested, not seeing the wink that Annie exchanged with the lad pouring the ale from the pitcher for her. Ale was not to

Jassy's taste, but she had no wish to appear ungracious toward their hospitality, and after a few gulps taken to their uproarious encouragement, the odd, spicy-bitter taste burning her throat like the foulest physic, she felt amazingly less shy and singularly light-hearted and began to laugh with them at their jokes and fun, enjoying herself more than she could ever remember. She was quite taken with the youth sitting next to her, who wore the clothes and boots of a fisherman, his black eyes bold and his grin endearing. She discovered that his name was Charlie Brent and he came from a fishing village a few miles away. When his thigh came hard against hers she thought it was due to the crush on the bench at the table. Later when he slipped an arm almost by accident about her waist she let it remain there wanting to be fully part of the bonhomie that prevailed among the gathering.

When Annie announced it was time to leave, Jassy's disappointment at the evening's end was alleviated by Charlie's prompt offer to escort the two of them home.

"I'll see you through the dark," he said, reaching for his woolly cap from a peg.

It seemed to Jassy there was a burst of laughter from the room when the door closed after the three of them, but she felt dizzy in the head from the night air and missed her footing on the path. She might have fallen if Charlie had not put his arms about her, but Annie muttered some fierce reprimand and herself took charge of her, allowing him only to walk with them to the gate of Honeybridge House. In her bedroom Jassy shed her clothes and fell into bed, her head still spinning, but not unpleasantly. She hoped she would see Charlie again, no matter that he was only a humble fisherman and probably could not read or write his own name.

It was the first of many evenings during Daniel's absence that Jassy was to spend with her new-found friends. To overcome her shyness she always drank deep at the ale as soon as she arrived and no longer found it distasteful, although it soon dawned on her that it was a measure of smuggled brandy that gave the ale its special potency.

Although she kept only to it for her drinking there came grander bottles on the table, which Daniel would have recognized with furious indignation, but Jassy did not care. It had been on the third evening that Annie, clad again in the blue silk which she now appeared to regard as her own property, had given the broadest of hints that practically amounted to a demand. "Ain't it time you coughed up something for the table?"

Jassy was bewildered, not comprehending at first. "What do you mean?"

"It ain't mannerly to drink up other folks' liquor without taking your share along like everyone else, you know."

Jassy clapped dismayed fingers to her cheeks. "Of course! How thoughtless of me. Tomorrow I'll give you money to buy some ale—"

"What about taking a bottle from the cellar? The master would never miss one measly bottle, would he?"

Jassy was firm. "I would prefer to buy my own—"

Annie flounced about on her heel, snatching up Jassy's cloak from a chair. "I'll borrow this cloak then. You won't be needing it tonight. I ain't got the face—and that's the truth!—to take a miserly companion with me once again."

"Wait! Oh, Annie! Don't leave me behind!" Jassy was in despair at the thought of missing a few sweet hours in Charlie's company. "I beg you!"

Annie paused, looking over her shoulder. "Well, I told you—"

"I'll get a bottle from the cellar! I'll take two! Only don't go without me!"

Annie's face was full of wicked satisfaction. "Make it three. Nobody will ever know."

After that Jassy took bottles every night, trying to select what Charlie liked best, and not caring that he did not savor Daniel's finest port or claret as a gentleman would, but slung it down his throat and wiped his mouth on the back of his hand afterward, making some uncouth comment, for she knew whatever he said was well meant.

"Good drop of the right stuff that was, Jassy," he would say quite often. "Any more where that came from?"

There always was, and she brought it along to him without conscience. She did not think Daniel would miss the bottles, but if he did she would meet that disaster when it came. She was no longer afraid of him as she had been in the past. He had sent Kate away and for that she would never forgive him.

She lived for her evenings at the cottage. The talk was always bawdy, the laughter loud and raucous, and the behavior uninhibited, but her innocence protected her from an understanding of much that was said and done, and Annie was as watchful as a chaperone over her, which was as well, for the old grandmother in the chimney corner, whose presence Jassy had found reassuring, was not there any more. Sometimes there was card-playing or throwing dice for money, at others the table was pushed back and everybody danced to a concertina played by one of Charlie's friends. It was then that Jassy put from her all the ballroom steps she had been taught and gaily skipped and pranced and whirled with Charlie along with all the others. She always knew a keen disappointment when he was out fishing by night and was not present. Once he came in very late and his eyes went straight to her as if he had been as starved for the sight of her as she had been for him. When he walked home with her and Annie afterward he asked her if she had missed him.

"Yes," she admitted shyly, huddled in her hooded cloak, the night being cold, and she felt a little embarrassed that he should have asked her such a question in Annie's hearing. She failed to see the glance they exchanged with satisfaction.

"Charlie wouldn't miss so much of the fun if he had a convenient place to store one good catch instead of having to fetch in small ones all the time," Annie said carefully, watching Jassy out of the corner of her eye. "Would you, Charlie?"

"That's right," he replied overcasually. "I'd like to find an outhouse or some such place for storage that I've never used before. Somewhere like the stable loft at Honeybridge House, for example."

Jassy kept her lashes down, filled with trepidation. She knew it was not fish they were talking about, but smuggled liquor such as the brandy that nightly laced the ale. Annie seemed to guess her thoughts.

"It would only mean storing the catch for a couple of nights or three at the most. Nobody would see it come or go, you can be sure of that. It would be gone long before the master comes home again and Mr. Harry will know nothing about it."

"You can be sure of that," Charlie endorsed wholeheartedly. He took Jassy's hand into his own and held it tight, peering round the edge of the hood into her face. "What do you say? It means you and I can really be together all the time."

How could she resist that thought? She gave a nod, releasing her breath. "Very well. Just as long as Daniel never finds out."

Annie clapped her hands triumphantly, and Charlie gave a joyful shout, seizing Jassy by the waist and whirling her up and round before setting her on her feet again with a big hug. She had never been so happy in her whole life.

They kept their promise of secrecy. When the stable loft was used she never knew and did not question. It was enough for her when Annie patted her on the shoulder one day and told her it was all done with and she need not give what had taken place another thought.

Jassy had noticed from her first evenings at the cottage that a surprising number of visitors called, not those who came to join in the merrymaking, but men who either knocked on the door and remained in the darkness outside for one of the girls to go out to them or else went quickly through a side hallway to be accompanied upstairs. Jassy thought there must be a sitting room up there that she had not seen.

"The girls have many callers," she remarked naïvely to Charlie one evening, "and they don't even live here. Nobody comes to see any of the male company, do they?"

Charlie's eyes crinkled up incredulously with mirth and he gave a huge bellow of laughter, throwing his head back and slapping his knee. He was so helpless with it that everybody wanted to know what the joke was and when he could speak, wiping his eyes and still half-choked with laughter, he repeated what she had said. She thought they would never stop hooting and guffawing, the walls ringing with the sound, and she was bewildered by it, feeling herself close to tears. Annie leaned across the table, rolling her head with merriment, and gave her a belated answer.

"It has been known, Jassy. Oh, dear, yes, it has been known."

The whole roomful went off into fresh paroxysms of mirth and unable to bear it any longer Jassy sprang up to rush outside, but Charlie caught her by the waist and brought her back onto his knee, cuddling her to him and kissing her cheek and then her lips. It was the first time he had kissed her. She forgot everything in the wonder of it, not minding that there was still laughter in his throat, and swiftly her arm went about his neck as if she could not endure to let his mouth leave hers.

He blinked at her when their kiss ended, surprised by her involuntary response and a slow smile spread across his face. "You're a real sweet thing, you really are."

"Am I?" she asked breathlessly, wanting him to pay her more compliments. Around them nobody was paying them any notice any more, the joke forgotten in some fresh hilarity, and it was to her as if they were entirely alone.

"I'll say." His mouth found hers again, and this time his hand went to her breast and would have found its way into her bodice if Annie had not suddenly come up behind him and cuffed his head, putting an end to the interlude.

"Don't jump the gun," she rebuked him in a mutter, and then smiled brightly at Jassy. "Come along. It's time we were getting home."

After that night Jassy found he was no longer content to sit with his arm looped about her waist, but would let his fingers fondle and explore. Once under the cover of the table he unexpectedly dived his hand down into her lap and cupped the shape of her through her skirt and petticoats, outraging her modesty, and frantically she tore at his grasp to free herself, gasping at his audacity.

"I'm a bad lad," he chuckled, smiling into her eyes as he let her claw his hand away, "but you're far too pretty for your own good."

Her anger faded before such an excuse. Anything remotely loving that he said to her was more intoxicating and could turn her head quicker than any liquor that she drank.

The days of Daniel's absence were passing as quickly for Harry as they were for Jassy. He was at Honeybridge House only to breakfast and to sleep, absorbed in his duties in Easthampton during the day and then, whenever the opportunity presented itself, riding far in the evening hours to make inquiries at one main coach station or another in the vain hope of finding some clue to Kate's whereabouts.

On the eve of Daniel's return Harry finished work early. After a word with Tanner to make sure the builder would keep a watchful eye on everything, he went back to Honeybridge House to saddle up his horse and make ready for a longer journey. He heard chatter in the kitchen and, opening the door, saw to his amazement Jassy sitting drinking tea with Annie as if they were equals, and with them were three of the younger and prettier village whores, one of whom had accosted him when he had left The Running Hare the previous evening.

"What the devil!" he expostulated, rendered almost speechless.

Jassy set down her cup and saucer with a little clatter and sprang to her feet. "These young women are going to mend some linen for me. As it's such a bitter cold day with snow in the air I could not let them go again without something to warm them." The lie came easily, but she was uncomfortably aware of looking foolish both in her brother's eyes and those of her company.

Hastily the girls had started to make ready to depart, tying their bonnets and slipping their arms into sleeves.

"We're most grateful, sir," said one of them. "Now we'll be off."

Harry beckoned Jassy and she followed him out of the kitchen into the hall. He saw she looked flushed and defiant, and put his own reason on it.

"It's not for me to say anything to you about how to run this place, but you must remember that since we have no older gentlewoman to chaperone you when we men are absent a maid must suffice, and you know well enough that no mistress of a house drinks tea with servants and—and menials." He could not mention the side occupation of those hamlet seamstresses. "It is simply that creatures such as Annie would soon take advantage, despising you for bridging the gap, and in no time at all there would be no discipline."

Jassy did not need Harry to tell her that. Although she welcomed the daily visits of those young women of similar age to herself, there was no denying that Annie was treating Honeybridge House as though their positions were reversed, Annie the mistress and she the servant, and sometimes she was reminded uneasily of Bessie. It was lucky that they had all been in the kitchen today and not the drawing room. Annie often sat there herself, but so far had not taken her visitors into it.

"They've gone now anyway," she said stiffly, seeing them go past the window to follow the path, heads down and huddled against the bitter wind. "What are you doing at home at this hour?"

"I have to go quite far afield on some business, and I shall put up somewhere for the night and get back as early as I can in the morning. So there is no need to worry about my not coming home tonight."

She was suddenly concerned for him. "Must you ride in this freezing weather? There was a flurry of snow a little while ago. Do wrap up warmly."

"My riding coat is thick. I'll be all right." He glanced toward the kitchen door and lowered his voice, not at all sure that Annie's ear would not be pressed against the keyhole. "Keep that maidservant in her place, and let there be no more convivial tea drinking in her company."

Jassy made him no answer, thinking that she drank a stronger brew than tea often enough in Annie's company, but Harry did not notice her lack of response, and went up to his room to put on his riding coat and boots.

It was snowing when he left Easthampton behind, not enough to make a carpet on the ground, but the more bitter for it, being close to sleet with all the closing savagery of winter behind it. His destination was Uckfield and Farringdon Farm. It was a last resort. The very beat of his horse's hooves seemed to echo Kate's name in his heart.

He had been in Uckfield over three hours when he turned into an inn and ordered a hot brandy toddy to warm himself. Then he went and sat with it in the inglenook, staring unseeingly into the fire. Never would he forget his visit to Uckfield. There from the local priest, who had tried to help him, he had branched out to everyone with whom Kate had been remotely connected, from her dressmaker to her physician, but drawing a blank each time. None had had sight or sound of Kate since the day Farmer Farringdon had driven her away to the sale. Finally he had ridden out to Farringdon Farm, his heart sinking, for he expected no joy there. Neither did he get it. When he left again he reined in to look back at the farmhouse where Kate had known deep, dark depths of unhappiness that would be hard to plumb. He had come to Uckfield as a final hope, but he should have known that of all spots in England and even on earth it would be the last one where she would have attempted to keep any connection. He could think of nowhere else where he might search for some trace of her. Disappointment weighed him down like a physical burden that he did not know how to bear, and he was suffering an anguish that was torture to him.

He saw he had drained the toddy from his glass and he looked bleakly toward the bar, "Landlord! Another brandy toddy. Make it a double one this time."

At Honeybridge House, Jassy was reluctantly helping Annie to make the dining room ready with extra chairs. Harry's absence for the night had given Annie the chance of having everybody there instead of going to the cottage, something she had long had in mind.

"You can't bring them to Daniel's house," Jassy had protested when Annie had said what was to be done. "I won't allow it." She was horrified at the thought of the general carelessness with pouring liquor, the red heels that would gouge the table if one of the girls, who fancied herself as a dancer, chose to perform as she did at the cottage, flicking up her petticoats riotously, and the attacks of drunken vomiting. "In fact, I absolutely forbid it."

Annie's face lost its good humor and her eyes and lips narrowed simultaneously. "They're coming tonight and we're going to lay on the best of everything that the cellar and pantry can provide. If not," she warned, her voice dropping a note in its awful threat, "the master is going to find out that his little sister let the stable loft be used for smuggled storage, and you wouldn't want that to happen, would you?"

Jassy almost fainted at the thought. She knew Daniel. Quite apart from his personal wrath that she would have to face there would be his determination to find out somehow who had been involved, even if she drowned herself to keep silent. He would not give up until he had uncovered the truth and that would mean a rope's end for Charlie. She gulped, ashen-faced. "No, I wouldn't."

"That's settled then." Annie was amiable and cheerful again. "Think of this evening as a real chance for you to show return for the good times you've had at the cottage."

Jassy refrained from saying that she had more than returned their hospitality with the many bottles she had taken, to say nothing of the basketfuls that Annie had carried on her arm sometimes. The maidservant always brought the emptied bottles home again, filled them with water and pushed in a cork before setting them back on the lower racks, but Jassy knew that sooner or later Daniel was going to discover the theft. That did not worry her. She had been confident all along that she and Annie could escape the blame there, being certain that it would be assumed that the crime had taken place at the London lodgings before the bottles were moved, Jem having once surprised the washerwoman helping herself to Daniel's port and with two full bottles hidden in the pockets of her coat. But at all costs she must make sure no damage was done to the house during the party and she would call on Charlie to help her there. Charlie. Even to say his name to herself was bliss, and this evening they might snatch some time on their own together. She was convinced he was waiting to tell her he loved her as soon as the right opportunity presented itself. Tingling at the thought, she sang happily to herself as she went up and down the cellar steps fetching bottles.

At first the party was quiet enough. The company, numbering twenty, was somewhat overawed by the surroundings. It was not that Honeybridge House was grand, but it had soft carpets instead of straw, polished floors instead of flagstones or beaten earth, and elegant furniture instead of a few primitive tables and chairs. Among the tankards Annie had set out were some of Daniel's milling trophies, the silver engraved with his name and the occasion of the presentation, but although Jassy made some protest Annie insisted that no harm could come to them. Then gradually, as the wine and brandy began to flow, together with the contents of a keg of ale that had been brought and set up, the scene changed. The alcohol fed their bravado, and they became noisy and boisterous, the guffaws and giggling shrieks accompanied by the spilling of liquor on table and carpet, the occasional smash of a glass. Had Jassy been less under Charlie's spell she might have paid more attention to what was going on, but the two of them were sitting by a side table in the window, she refilling his glass and sipping her own while listening to his sea talk, having to strain her ears to catch what he said when the raucous singing started, Daniel's silver tankards among those being banged on the smooth surface of the long mahogany table. When there came a crash and a splintering of wood, one of those sitting in a chair having tilted it too far backward and falling to the floor together with the wench on his knees, Jassy became startled and alarmed, jumping to her feet to intervene. But Charlie had sprung up to whip an arm about her waist and draw her to him.

"There ain't no harm done," he said reassuringly, smiling into her eyes. "Let you and I find somewhere quieter away from the rest of 'em."

It was what she had hoped for, and all else was forgotten in the magic of it. When they went out into the hall, Charlie closing the dining room door after him, she would have led him toward the drawing room, but he halted her.

"Not there," he whispered thickly. "Upstairs."

She remembered telling him once that Daniel had his own study furnished like a drawing room on the upper floor, but she was reluctant to take him there, it being a room she avoided and was rarely in. She might have explained how she felt had there not come at that moment the pounding of running feet upstairs, a laughing shriek, a man's triumphant, male bellow, and the slamming of a door somewhere. She thought it sounded as if the couple had gone into Harry's bedroom. In dismay she ran toward the stairs and up them, Charlie following, and she called out as she went.

"Come down, whoever is up there!"

Charlie caught her up on the landing, and again he swung her to him. "Let 'em be, my pretty. You and I have better things to do." He jerked her closer still and took her mouth in a kiss that was totally unlike anything she had received from him before, and she was deeply shocked by the force of his hot, wet mouth with the hard, thrusting tongue, and his hand was hurting her breasts, kneading and squeezing through the fine silk.

She thrust herself from him with both hands against his chest. "Don't!" she exclaimed hoarsely.

He laughed and fell upon her again, crushing her against the wall and imprisoning her mouth with his while his hands took greater liberties, wrenching up her petticoats to find the smoothness of her thighs, his body hard in its unmistakable eagerness for hers as if he were prepared to take her then and there.

"No!" With a strength born of panic she wrenched herself free, causing him to stagger back slightly and catch the newel post to save himself from slipping down the top stair. With whipping skirts she fled for the safety of her own room, the walls of the corridor flashing past her, the door at the end of it seeming as far away as in a nightmare. He gave a laughing shout and came running after her as though it were a titillating game she played, and with a sob she reached her door, opened it and slammed it shut after her, turning the key even as he reached it. The doorknob shook and rattled.

"Go away!" Facing the door she drew back a few paces from it. "Go away, I say!"

He was less good-humored, but still not taking her too seriously, and his tone became wheedling. "Come on, my sweeting. Don't you keep Charlie out here in the cold no longer."

"I told you to go away! And take everybody else with you!"

There was a moment's silence, the vibrating tone of her voice having left no doubt in his mind this time that she meant what she said, but she had underestimated the strength of his lust, for he was totally inflamed for her. The doorknob rattled again as he tested its ability to hold. Then there came the mighty thud of his shoulder against the door with his full weight behind it. In terror she looked about wildly for something to push against the door to make a barrier, but by the time she had managed to get any of the heavy pieces there he would be in the room. Already a crack had appeared in the wood by the lock. Thud! Again his shoulder had come against the door and this time there was a cracking and splintering as the lock barely held. One more attempt and it would burst. For a few seconds she hovered and fluttered like a trapped bird in her panic, and then she rushed to the window and flung it wide. The icy wind with flakes of snow whirled in upon her, blew out the candle flames in the wall sconces, and beat against her bare shoulders and partly exposed breasts revealed by Charlie's ripping of the tiny button loops down the front of her bodice, but she did not hesitate, and hoisting up her skirts she swung her legs over the sill. Below was the jutting bow of the drawing room window, and clinging desperately she lowered her feet to it. The slates on it were sloping but uneven in their age, and she managed to gain some foothold even as the door crashed open under the final blow.

"Don't you hide from me!" Charlie roared in the darkness of the bedroom above her. "I'll find you!"

She let go of the sill, slithered on the slates, saved herself from plunging down, and then, cutting her hands on the gutter in the process, she half-fell, half-dropped to the ground. In the same instant Charlie, realizing what she had done, appeared in the window. Dear God! He was coming after her!

Scrambling to her feet and snatching up her skirts she hurled herself down the path and out of the gate into the lane. Behind her she heard the slates of the bow window's roof clatter under his weight, but she did not look back. Ahead lay the length of the lane and he would catch her up long before she could reach any other habitation, hampered as she was by her heeled satin slippers. If only she could reach a clump of trees where the lane began its turning and twisting before he drew level, she might hide herself somewhere among the rocks on the beach.

She heard him shout to her as he came out of the gate, calling her some vile and abusive names she had never heard before with dreadful meanings she could only guess at. Straining herself to an effort that seemed beyond her own strength, she drew abreast with the trees before his racing feet could reach her, shot through the tamarisk hedge, and threw herself down behind a rock. She heard him go pounding past along the lane.

Dry sobs of relief at her temporary escape shook her through, but she knew it would only be a matter of minutes before he would realize she had given him the slip and return. Although the night was black and wild the shimmer of the wet sand left by the ebbing tide, which lapped only a few yards from her, would show a trail of footprints for him to follow. She must cover her tracks in the sea.

Dodging between the rocks, splashing in and out of dark rock pools, she reached the water's edge. Not daring to turn toward Easthampton, the only source of help, in case he should sight her from the lane, she doubled back in the direction of the house, gasping as the ice-cold water swallowed her feet and swirled about her ankles, sopping her dangling hems as she hastened along. Now and again when she met a rock she took shelter behind it, leaning against it in exhaustion, her teeth chattering violently, and so shivering with cold and fear that every jerking muscle seemed generated by a power of its own.

It was when she was moving on from one of these rocks that the toe of her shoe caught on a submerged piece of granite and she fell headlong into the waves, and floundered in the shallow water before staggering to her feet again. On she went, having

long since drawn level with Honeybridge House and left behind
her its warm lights showing through the waving trees, and a kind
of numbness settled upon her. She had become cold beyond cold,
and when she fell to her knees in the water again she stayed there
for several minutes, letting the wavelets swirl about her, her head
bowed with the sea-wet tresses hanging stickily, and no longer was
able to think or reason beyond the fact that somehow she must
find the strength to keep going. Lurching up, she staggered on
again and did not see that she had swerved from the edge of the
water onto the wet sand. There her feet wove a winding pattern
until at last she fell full length and could no longer stir.

It was Daniel and Jem who arrived home first when morning
was well advanced and snow was gently falling. All Harry's good
intentions of making an early start back to Easthampton had been
swamped in brandy and nursing a head that throbbed like a kettle-
drum he jogged back up the lane in the saddle as Jem, brought
running from unharnessing the curricle horses by a roar from
Daniel surveyed with horrified disbelief the ravage that had been
wrought at Honeybridge House.

"God in Heaven! What has been done here!" Jem exclaimed
hoarsely. Then he broke forward to follow the white-faced,
flashing-eyed Daniel on a tour of inspection into one room and
then another. There were empty bottles everywhere. Chairs lay
overturned, and in the dining room the table's surface was deeply
scored. In a choking, silent rage Daniel stooped and picked up a
battered silver tankard which had been hurled against the wall,
denting the paneling. With broken glass scrunching underfoot he
left the dining room and, after glancing in at the littered kitchen,
made for the stairs. It was then that Harry entered the house.
Daniel rounded on him.

"What in the Devil's name has been going on under my roof?"

Harry's horrified astonishment at the state of the hall and what
he could see of the dining room through the open door beyond
was enough to show both Daniel and Jem that he knew no more
about it than they did.

"Who's done all this?" he demanded, forgetting he had been

asked the same question. "I've been away from Easthampton since yesterday noon. Where's Jassy?"

"That's what I want to know," Daniel answered grimly. "She did not answer when I called her." He went on up the stairs, Jem after him, and Harry in the rear. The discovery of the forced lock and broken door to Jassy's room and the window open to the snow blowing in made all three of them turn grave-faced with a new and terrible anxiety. Downstairs the doorbell rang.

Daniel reached it first and opened it to a weathered old fisherman. One look at the man's face told Daniel that he brought bad news. "My sister?" he demanded shakily.

"Not dead, sir," came the reply, "but not far from it. She's sick with a terrible fever, and the missus is tending 'er at my cottage now. I've bin ten times to this 'ouse today since my wife realized who she was, and I've not found nobody at 'ome."

"What happened?"

"I don't rightly know, sir. I went down to set out my lobster pots in the early hours and spotted 'er in my lantern light. First I thought she were drowned and washed up from some wrecked vessel, but when I found she still breathed I wrapped 'er in my coat and took 'er up to my wife."

"Thank you for what you have done, but she must be brought home at once." He turned to Harry. "Fetch Sarah Singleton. Then get a doctor—Sarah will know which one is the nearest. Jem —you light a fire in Jassy's room and get a warming pan into the bed. I'm going to bring her back to Honeybridge House."

For four days Jassy threshed in a burning fever. She cried out and was often incoherent, but now and again Sarah, who sat by her bedside and nursed her, caught one name over and over again. Kate. Sarah, who was experienced in looking after the sick and dying, thought that Jassy cried out the name as though for a lifeline.

Annie was not to be found, but it was not difficult for Daniel to start putting facts together, and he decided that Jassy's flight from the house must have broken up the debauch that had been taking place. Harry's mention of the whores drinking tea with Jassy resulted in the three young women being questioned. All denied having been at the house on that night, declaring they had witnesses to prove they were elsewhere, and lying in their teeth they protested ignorance of who might have been present. Daniel knew they were lying, and although he could have taken the matter further he decided to let it die a natural death for Jassy's sake. No good could come of scandal to sully Jassy's name if she lived, and if she died—he shuddered at the thought—he would not have any gossip following her to the grave.

He was writing in his office above the joiners' workshop at the converted brewery, which was already known locally as Warwyck's building yard, when a visitor was announced. Slowly he set his quill pen back in its tray and rose to his feet. Claudine entered, carrying a small basket covered with a lace-edged cloth, and stood facing him. The old fire and animosity were still there, but tempered to another kind of passion.

"This is an unexpected pleasure, Miss Clayton." He came round the desk and pushed a red leather chair forward. "Pray be seated."

She settled herself while he returned to his own chair. "You invited me to see the plans of Easthampton," she said with a little toss of her head. "I decided to come. Then I heard that Miss Warwyck was ill with a fever of the lungs. I should like you to give her this little gift from me."

He took the basket she handed to him, glimpsing the grapes and other hothouse fruits beneath the lace. "That's most kind. A little largesse from the Hall?"

She flushed at the sardonic tone of his voice. "No, not from the Hall. It is my own personal offering to the invalid. How is she?"

"Dangerously ill. We cannot be sure yet which way things will go."

"I'm extremely sorry. Perhaps my visit is ill-timed, and I should come another day—" She made to rise again, but he stayed her with a shake of his head.

"Not at all." His eyes did not leave her, missing nothing.

Against her tempestuous will she was ripening slowly like a plum for his picking, but this was a fruit he would bruise in the taking. In his eventual harvesting of her all payment to his pride should be made. She sensed her fate and yet still she came. "In truth, I have been hard put to keep my mind on work with Jassy lying at death's door," he continued, "and your company is most welcome." Swiveling round on his rotating chair he tapped the fingertips of one hand against a large plan on the wall behind him. "This is how Easthampton will be in the future when all the work is done, but first I will show you an artist's impression of how various sections of it will look."

For the next hour he spread drawings for her inspection, sometimes leaning with her over them, at others crouching at her side to hold them at lap level, and never missing an opportunity to brush her fingers or hold her glance or rest the back of his hand lightly against her. Finally he invited her behind the desk to study the plan on the wall while he explained in detail where everything she had seen would be built or was in the process of being erected.

"There," he said at last. "Now give me your opinion."

She gave a little sigh. "It is an inspiring enterprise. Such a pity it is doomed to failure."

He was not going to let her see that her jibe had riled him. "I assure you that you are quite mistaken."

"Am I?" She swung away, caught her reflection in the glass of a framed picture of a Sussex country scene, and adjusted her bonnet ties, ready to depart. "I prefer to take Alexander's judgment before yours. He and everyone else says that you are heading for bankruptcy. The Easthampton project will collapse disastrously about your ears." The familiar mockery glinted in her eyes. "My only regret is that I shall not be here to see it. We are off to London tomorrow for the rest of the season there, and in May we go direct from the Metropolis to Brighton for the summer. Alexander will, of necessity, have to visit Radcliffe Hall from time to time, but when I return you will be gone from Easthampton."

She made a few quick paces toward the door, but he reached it before her, not to open it, but to set his hand on the brass knob of it to bar her way. "You know I will not be gone and neither do you want me to be."

Her eyes flashed and she spoke contemptuously. "Your conceit is insufferable, Mr. Warwyck. It matches your manners."

He pulled open the door for her and she swept out and down the outside stairs to the yard below. He saw that she had not come in a Radcliffe carriage, but in a pony and trap that she drove herself. With her head held haughtily she went bowling away through the archway, her bonnet feather flowing. He welcomed her temporary absence from Easthampton. She was too distracting and he had too much ahead of him for the time being to deal fully with her.

That evening Jassy was lucid for a short time, but when Daniel came to see her she turned her face away from him on the pillow, whispering that it was Harry she wanted to see on his own.

When Harry came Sarah left them alone. Jassy's voice was so weak that he had to bend his head close to catch what she said.

"Fetch Kate to me," she gasped faintly. "I want her to be my nurse."

Her plea tore at him. "I do not know where she is. Nobody does. To tell you the truth, I have searched everywhere I can think of."

She was restless and agitated, trying to lift her head from the pillow. "I know where you can find her."

"What!"

"I have written to her several times." She gulped for breath. "She has never answered, but none of the letters has been returned, so I am sure she has received them."

"But how did you know where to write to?" he questioned eagerly.

"That day at Warwyck when Kate was helping me to pack my belongings she told me she had no living relative except an elderly cousin of her father's, and mentioned that lady's name, which was Miss Rose Carroll of Rose Cottage." She seemed to be finding it difficult to breathe. "She made me smile with some little joke about wondering if the cottage was named after the cousin or for the roses that grew in the garden."

"Where is this cottage?"

"At Ashford in Kent." Jassy's color had become high and beads of sweat were standing out on her forehead and upper lip. "You must find her." She began to flail about and no longer seemed to see him, her eyes becoming curiously glazed.

He was about to rush for Sarah when she entered. She gave one look at Jassy and ordered him to fetch the doctor. "She has had a relapse," she exclaimed anxiously.

Harry informed Daniel and Jem that Jassy had taken a turn for the worse before he went for the doctor. That duty done, he rode on in the direction of Kent, where he reached Ashford and located Rose Cottage without any difficulty. With haste he went up the path and loudly thumped the door knocker, which was fashioned like a rose and had probably been made specially by a local craftsman, for he had never seen the like of it before. Within, footsteps came in answer along a flagged floor. The latch lifted—and there was Kate.

Every vestige of color drained from her face and she choked on his name. "Harry!"

He stepped inside, caught up her hand, and pressed it to his lips. "Thank God I've found you. I regret to say I'm the bearer of bad news."

If anything she went even whiter. "Not Daniel!"

"No, it is Jassy. She is lying at death's door and calling for you."

She put a hand to her forehead, shock and distress registered as though permanently upon her face. "I'll come at once. Tell me what ails her. I have my own herbal remedies for almost everything."

She listened to his brief account in silence. Then she said, "I gave Daniel my word that I would not try to get in touch with you again and I have kept it. I'll go with you now on the understanding that we are as brother and sister, friend and companion, and after the length of time I am with Jassy, whose life I pray to save, you will let me go again without pursuit or protest."

"I swear it," he said solemnly, crossing his fingers behind his back in the age-old evasion of truth.

She nodded acceptance of his promise. "I have been housekeeper to my cousin here, but she is kind and understanding and will make no bother over my leaving with you. So I will tell her, and then get my things together. How are we to travel?"

"On horseback. Where is the best place to purchase a mount for you?"

She directed him, and when he returned to the cottage shortly afterward with a chestnut mare named Bonnie she was taking an affectionate farewell of her cousin, a well-preserved lady of advanced years. A few minutes later they were riding out of Ashford, he not knowing whether he would come too late with Kate to save his sister's life.

Weary in the saddle after the long journey and with tired mounts they came at last into Easthampton. At Honeybridge House after a quick embrace of reunion with Jem in the hall Kate went with Harry straight to the sickroom where Jassy lay thin and ashen, her eyes closed. Sarah at her bedside frowned at his intrusion with a stranger and half-rose as though to keep them from the patient, but he ignored her and went straight to touch his sister's arm, which lay weakly on the coverlet.

"Jassy. I have brought Kate to you. Kate has come home."

The girl's eyelids quivered and slowly her eyes opened. Kate leaned over and kissed her cheek. "I'm here," she said softly and reassuringly, taking Jassy's hand into both her own.

The faintest indentation of the corners of the pale lips showed a smile, but Jassy's gaze remained unfocused and her whisper was almost inaudible. "Don't let me die, Kate."

"I'll not let you die." Kate blinked back tears and clasped Jassy's hand a little tighter as if to infuse some of her own sturdy good health into the wasted form. "You are going to get well again. I'll help you all the way."

Daniel, entering the house later, stopped short at the sight of a leather moneybag on the hall table. Picking it up, he opened it out and saw the glint of sovereigns. He did not have to count them. Somehow he knew there would be the full fifty coins there.

A step sounded at the top of the stairs and he looked up. Kate stood with one hand resting on the newel post, her ivory-complexioned, classic-featured face strained and serious. He spoke first and accusingly.

"You gave me your word that you would make no contact."

"Neither did I, but Jassy guessed where I was through something I had said to her, and Harry found me." Her voice was full of quiet appeal. "Don't send me away, Daniel. Jassy has called for me throughout her illness."

"So I was told by the lady nursing her," he answered brusquely in an uncompromising manner.

"Let me stay until I have done everything in my power to save Jassy's life."

He considered her for a few moments before he made his reply. "If you save my sister's life you may stay at Honeybridge House for as long as it suits your convenience." With that he went into the drawing room and was inwardly surprised at how the sight of her again had pleasured him.

Turning back to the sickroom Kate was torn between joy and despair. She wished again with all her heart that she had never learned what had been revealed to her during her sojourn at Ashford. It was a heavy burden to carry.

Chapter 10

It was not long before all Easthampton knew that there was a newcomer at Honeybridge House. By the time news began to spread that the patient had taken a turn for the better, rumor had established Kate as a poor relation summoned to nurse the invalid, which often happened in cases of lengthy sickness and convalescence. Word of the Warwyck household reached Claudine in London, but such mundane arrangements were of no interest to her in her merry social whirl, and if she pictured Kate at all it was as a dreary, nondescript creature being retained as housekeeper.

With Kate in charge it was not only in the sickroom that things had improved. For the first time everything in the house began to look as if it belonged there, the furniture taking on the soft gleam that comes from polishing and care, looking glasses shone, spiders were banished and cobwebs swept away, paint was washed and carpets brushed. It was Kate who scrubbed the ale and wine stains from the carpets made on the night of the debauch, which Jassy had told her about in detail, and it was she who worked on the scored surface of the table, using some tip given to her by Jem out of his past experience with wood, until the marks became lost in the dark glow of the mahogany. She rehung a couple of framed pictures to hide the damage done to the paneling by the intruders, and when she came across the ruined silver tankards she took them herself to a silversmith in Merrelton to have the dents removed in order to make them as good as new again.

No longer was there a musty smell to the house with the lingering odors of greasy pans and stale food; instead the three men of the household would enter to the fragrance of newly baked, crusty bread, beeswax polish, and sweet-scented potpourri made up of lavender and dried herbs that Kate had brought with her. It was again a pleasure for them to sit at table, for Kate's cooking was simple but superb, her roast joints done to a turn, her pie pastry melted in the mouth, and she had a way with vegetables that kept their color and their flavor as was rarely found. In the face of such cooking Daniel found it impossible to restrict himself to the diet that Jem favored for periods of training, and after the two of them had had arguments and even strong words over it, Kate mediated by cooking special dishes of equal tastiness for Daniel, which had only a little of whatever it was Jem wished to ban, and thus was harmony restored. No harm came to Daniel's physique and peak of fitness through the leeway, and he remained as lithe and tapered and flat-bellied as before, taking his daily run along the sands, sparring with Jem, and pounding his fists into the leather punch bag suspended from a stout beam in the harness room of the Honeybridge stable.

Out of all the changes that had taken place in the house Daniel naturally took greatest satisfaction in his sister's recovery, which had been marked from the moment she had set eyes on Kate again. Jassy's attitude toward him had also taken a turn for the better, and in spite of there still being a barrier between them, she would chat amiably when he went to sit by the chaise-longue where she lay with a rug over her knees. It was not hard to guess that she did not quite trust him, fearful that at any time he might banish Kate again, but that was not his intention. He had given his word that she could stay as long as it suited her, but he expected her to leave of her own free will when Jassy was fully recovered. He was as violently opposed to any liaison between

Kate and Harry as he had been before, but although Kate was obviously bearing in mind what he had once said to her and gave his brother no encouragement, it was easy to see that Harry was infatuated beyond all reason, barely able to take his eyes from her, forever springing up to fetch or carry and adjust her chair for her. Whenever he returned from business trips he was never empty-handed, bringing her a length of lace or ribbon, a book perhaps, or a new ladies' magazine with the latest modes, all of such small monetary value that there was nothing against Kate accepting them and nothing to be done to stop them.

Jem tried to speak out on Harry's behalf. "Look here, Dan," he began one day when the two of them were alone in Daniel's office at the yard. "That brother of yer'n is eating his heart out over Kate. Ain't it time ye relented and let him court her the way he wants to?"

"No," Daniel answered bluntly, not raising his eyes from the plans he was studying on the desk at which he sat and making a note on them with his quill pen.

"But why? In the beginning ye were right to stop him rushing into the purchase of her, no matter that it did appear at the time to be suiting yer own ends, 'cos he were a right young fool and aimless as a jelly, but he is different now, as well ye know to yer benefit. Goodness knows how many times he has protected yer interests and in some cases prevented a real sly one being put over on ye. He is making a good career for himself and will end up at the top of a tree somewhere eventually."

"Yes, and he would drop Kate on the way. He cannot marry her. She would have no claim on him, and—knowing Kate—neither would she make any. I will not have her left in a whorehouse when my brother decides he has had enough of her and seeks to make a marriage to his advantage."

Not once had Daniel looked up from the plans. Jem thrust his reddening face forward pugnaciously, and rose from his chair to slam a fist down on them, making Daniel draw back in surprise. "Don't give me none of that high concern for the lady. I know ye. Ye have come to think of her as belonging to ye as Honeybridge

House belongs to ye and this yard and the resort ye're building and the money ye jingle in yer pocket—and ye ain't going to let nothing with yer seal on it go to another. If ye weren't like a son to me, Dan, I swear I'd go from here this instant and never clap eyes on ye again!"

He stamped out of the office. Daniel shook his head once and carried on with the work in hand. He had plenty of other matters on his mind beside Kate and everything to do with her. The whole of his project was taking shape at last. The sound of hammering and sawing and banging had become like a persistent hearbeat, and the smell of wet cement, bricks, paint, and timber wafted over the hamlet roofs. Everywhere men were busy with spades and ladders and with hods on their shoulders, and wagons came and went delivering what was needed and carting up sand and shingle and other necessary materials from the shore.

March winds gave way to the soft rains of April and with the coming of warmer days Sir Geoffrey made a special visit to Easthampton to see the progress being made. He and Daniel made a tour on foot to see it all, and he was particularly interested to notice that the long green, which stretched from the base of the hillock to the shore, was to be left open as a focal point of the resort.

"It will have laid-out lawns and flower beds," Daniel told him, "and will be overlooked on either side by the buildings that will rise from those foundations being dug. There will be fine terraces and the pride of place will go to the Assembly Rooms."

"Capital!" Sir Geoffrey's own personal backing was behind that much needed amenity for social affairs, and he was filled with enthusiasm for all he saw, remarking on the sites earmarked for shops and coffeehouses. They strolled along the area following the shore that had been cleared for a promenade where Daniel pointed out the spot facing the sea where Easthampton's first hotel would stand, adding that he intended to call it The Warwyck Hotel.

"The land to the rear of it will be left for future expansion with large stables and coach houses." He indicated The Running Hare.

"That prime site I'm leaving for the highest bidder to develop. I want the right financial sources to find they have to vie with each other when the time comes, which will send up the prices of other property."

Sir Geoffrey chuckled approvingly.

When the inspection of everything was over Daniel took his patron home to Honeybridge House where Kate presented the best of hospitality.

All through the summer the work went on relentlessly. It became a popular pastime on leisure days for men from the surrounding villages to bring their wives and families to see what was going on. The Running Hare did a brisk trade and the baker sold more cakes and buns in a day than he previously did in a week, and people picnicked on the green and on the sands. Folk from Merrelton put in an appearance, several business men taking a cautious, speculative look at certain sites, and although the local nobility retained their united hostility there were a few, mostly younger sons and daughters, who broke ranks now and again to ride on horseback through the growing resort or bring a carriage and pair to a halt in order to watch some work in progress. But the general opinion was that it was too ambitious a scheme to survive, and the setbacks that Daniel suffered were numerous. Harry did all he could to alleviate them, particularly when Daniel was involved in intensive training for another important bout, but part of the labor force was always unruly, materials were wasted or stolen, and frequently wanton damage by unknown persons sent up the cost and set back a completion date.

Summer faded and September came to tint the trees. Daniel, alone among the half-built walls of the Assembly Rooms, was examining part of the structure that had been discovered to be faulty, needing to be pulled down and recommenced. It was almost certainly sabotage, and for once he felt intensely depressed, although he had won a recent bout easily and was another rung higher toward the championship. As he ran his hands over part of the brickwork a young woman's voice rang out within the walls.

"You are still here then, Mr. Warwyck."

He did not even have to see her to feel the physical effect of her nearness, but he turned casually, almost with indifference. Claudine was standing in the open space that was to be the entrance, her face framed within a bow-trimmed bonnet, her dress and pelisse trimmed with the same soft apple-green color, the sunlight an aura about her. As he strolled toward her she stepped daintily onto a bridge of planks and held out an arched hand imperiously for him to assist her across to firmer ground. He did so, but did not release his grasp, keeping her fingers captive as he had done once before at the Marine Pavilion.

"You should know by now that I never give up."

They were back at their old game of thrust and parry, and her nostrils flared delicately on the sexual excitement of it. She tilted her head at him, her eyes dancing wickedly.

"I must say that I am pleasantly surprised by all I have seen this morning. It was difficult to picture it from the plans you showed me. You will have no more opposition toward your resort from me, but I warn you that Alexander and the others have hardly begun to do battle."

"What have I to fear from him?" he questioned boastfully.

"He has already done you some damage." The familiar mockery glinted in her eyes, showing she was still prepared to triumph over him whenever she could. "You have had labor troubles, have you not?"

He did not reply that he knew well enough that most of the wages that he paid were below subsistence level and he had expected trouble from time to time over it. Instead he said, "There are always a few rabble-rousers not content with honest work. These fellows and those they influence seem to forget that if it were not for me there would be no work at all for them most of the time, but they become humble enough when they are sacked on the spot and sent away." His eyes narrowed at the smugness of her smile. "Are you telling me that your brother-in-law is behind it?"

"I happen to know he sent in half a dozen agitators to stir up the rest."

Daniel breathed deeply. "What else do you know?" His score against Alexander Radcliffe was growing.

She twirled away from him provocatively. "La! Are you asking me to act the spy for you, Mr. Warwyck?"

Slowly he grinned. So that was her game. A show of favor toward his plan for Easthampton to create a cover of face-saving pretense for visits to him. "Would you, Miss Clayton?"

"I might."

"I think you will." He came behind her and turned her toward him, holding her by the arms. Her shapely feline face was uptilted to his and he could tell she had missed him wildly, her whole frame ashiver under his touch, her lips moist and slightly parted. Her voice came huskily.

"I would spy only out of the highest motives, simply because I believe in what you are doing for Easthampton and everyone in it."

"I understand that," he answered blandly, the corners of his mouth tight in a hidden smile. "What other possible reason could there be?"

He drew her against him, saw her eyes close as though she swooned as his arms went about her, but her pliant body remained taut and vibrant in his embrace, her hands coming up to bury themselves in his hair, pressing his head downward as her lips came up with a passionate violence to meet his. They kissed as though each could never have enough of the other, but without the least tenderness on either side.

She was breathless when he released her, her breasts rising and falling swiftly, and she stepped away from him. "I shall see you again when I have anything to report from the enemy camp," she said, half-flippantly.

"I thank you." He was serious. Or appeared to be.

She almost looked at him, but not quite. This time she did not wait for assistance across the planks, but ran lightly over them and away into the soft autumnal sun. There came the sound of the pony and trap spinning off along the lane. He stood grinning to himself where she had left him. It would not be long now.

Across on the other side of the green Kate was walking with Jem, who was carrying her shopping basket for her. She never lost a chance to look at the latest building development in progress, for in her opinion Daniel was creating a resort of great beauty out of Easthampton. There was an airy elegance already to the uncompleted terraces and other buildings, some in advanced stages adorned with balconies and railings in delicate acanthus designs with hooded verandas and curving flights of steps. She thought The Warwyck Hotel was destined to be as fine as any palace and nothing could be more in keeping with the theme of everything than the slim classical pillars supporting the portico of the Assembly Rooms. Even as she turned her head to look across at them Jem emitted a disapproving grunt, and she observed as he did the redheaded girl driving away from there.

"Who is that?" she asked with some disquiet, but she was only seeking confirmation. Harry had described those unmistakable, vivid curls.

"It's Miss Clayton of Radcliffe Hall," Jem answered gruffly. "So she's back again. Why don't she keep away from him?"

There was no need for Kate to inquire as to whom he was referring even if she had not known. Daniel's horse was hitched to a post by the steps of the Assembly Rooms. She tried not to think what exchanges might have passed between Claudine and him. His attitude toward herself was the same as ever, polite and courteous at times, sharp and brusque at others, particularly when he came upon her laughing with Harry or found them alone in talk together, his attitude almost that of a jealous man, and yet in all the months since her return to Honeybridge House he had only once looked at her as a full-blooded man could look at a woman. It happened on a hot day, oppressive with the threat of a storm, and believing herself to be alone in the house she had come barefoot downstairs in her petticoats to collect a tortoise-shell comb that Jem had mended and left in the hall for her. Her hair, newly washed, was pinned up high on her head, exposing the full length of her neck. She was padding across the floor to where the comb lay on the hall table when a door opened and Daniel came unexpectedly from the kitchen. She showed no foolish modesty, being adequately covered, although her shoulders were almost bare and the scoop of the lace-edged neckline showed far more bosom than she would normally reveal, but he raked her with his eyes, making her feel more than naked, and the color flowed over her cheeks. Quickly taking up the comb she hurried back upstairs to her room again. Not a word passed between them, but she felt him staring after her. All she could think of was the way he had kissed her at Winchester, and she was filled with an ache and an almost unbearable yearning.

"Have you any more shopping to do, Mrs. Warwyck?" Jem questioned, breaking into her reverie.

She came back to the present and smiled at him, brushing back a tendril of her hair that the sea breeze had teased loose. "No, I have everything now, thank you. We can go home."

As always her step became lighter as she turned toward Honeybridge House. However bad things were it always seemed better there. It was her haven.

It was a cold November morning when she saw Claudine Clayton's pony and trap again. Having a message to deliver to Daniel, Kate came through the archway into the building yard to see it waiting by the steps leading up to his office. She changed her mind about taking the communication to him personally and left it with the clerk. Her heart was heavy with an inexplicable dread as she went again.

In his office Daniel, seated at his desk, did not as much as glance at the message that the clerk brought up to him, but took it and put it aside, waiting only until the door closed again before resuming his conversation with Claudine, who sat opposite him. It was the second time she had been to the office to see him, the first on a pretext of concern that Alexander might attempt to close the public highway into Easthampton, an action the law would never allow, and again today with an equally useless scrap of information based on some foolish rumor. The only difference in the two visits was that on the first she had been amicable and amused by her own daring in coming and on this occasion she was taut and brittle with nerves, close to being snappish.

"What if your brother-in-law should learn of your coming here?" Daniel asked, watching her. He thought he understood the reason for her tenseness. It emanated from her like a perfume that only he could scent. Already he had in mind an isolated cottage he owned, emptied recently of its tenants, which would make an ideal place of assignation.

"It is taking a risk," she admitted sharply. "On both occasions Alexander has believed me to be visiting friends at Attwood Grange, and indeed I did go there afterwards as I shall today."

"A friend or friends?" he inquired pedantically. He had learned long since the identity of the poetic-looking fellow with whom he had seen her at church in Merrelton, and had made it his business to find out all he could about him.

Maliciousness glittered in her glance. "A dear friend, who holds day and evening festivities in my honor. He and I are extremely close. I think I shall marry him."

Daniel displayed no change of expression. There was little he had not found out about Lionel Attwood and his escorting of Claudine. An heir was needed for the Grange and to carry on the Attwood name, which had prompted Lionel's return from Italy where he had found none among the daughters of the aristocratic families there to suit him. There were probably other reasons why he had chosen to return to England to find a bride, but although not in possession of the facts, Daniel could guess at what they might be.

"Would Radcliffe approve of the match?"

His coolly delivered question surprised and displeased her. She showed she thought it an affront that he should ask that instead of giving way to the violent show of jealousy that she had hoped for. Her brows drew together and her mouth tightened in temper.

"The Radcliffes and the Attwoods have been neighbors for generations, and Lionel and Alexander are old friends from days gone by, so there is nothing my brother-in-law would like better than that I should accept Lionel's proposal. Indeed he encourages me towards a betrothment, but I have told him that I will not be rushed and need time to think it over."

"You have doubts, then, and rightly so."

"No! None at all!" she flashed at him, maddened by his calmness, and sprang up from the chair to leave. "I cannot think of anyone dearer or kinder or more considerate to my every wish than Lionel. No one could make me a better husband!"

"No one?" He was on his feet and had come round the desk to face her.

"Not you, Daniel Warwyck!"

"What makes you think I should ever want to make you my wife?"

"Because you'll never have me any other way!" The door slammed after her. He perched himself on the edge of the desk, his head went back, and he burst into laughter. It was a threat he did not take seriously.

There was no laughter in him some weeks later when he read the announcement of her betrothment to Lionel Attwood in the Merrelton *Chronicle*. He curled up the newspaper and slammed it into a corner of his study, the draft making the flames in the fireplace flatten and swirl out a puff of wood smoke. Then on second thoughts he rescued the newspaper and smoothed out the crumpled page on his desk to read the announcement again. It was a last bid to escape him, and not only was he enraged, but he was aghast at her folly.

It was unfortunate for Kate that she should choose that moment to come to the study in order to tackle him over a matter about which she could no longer keep silent, in spite of warnings from Jassy. She was fresh-cheeked from the cold weather outdoors, for she had done no more than discard her outdoor clothing before coming straight to him.

"Your workmen and their wives and families are starving on the wages you pay!" she declared heatedly with more outraged indignation than tact.

From where he sat he glowered at her under lowered, black

brows, his eyes the color of steel. She had broached at the worst possible time that touchy subject about which he had heard more than enough from different sources. "I advise you to hold your tongue on something about which you know nothing," he warned through his teeth.

"I know everything about it," she retaliated, unafraid of him in the right of the cause for which she was petitioning. "It is not only I who take baskets of food to the families, but the ladies from the big houses—"

His voice thundered at her. "You have dared to subsidize my workers' larders from my table!"

"Don't you care that the poor people are cold and hungry?" she lashed back at him.

"Ah!" He feigned approving surprise, his tone cutting. "You have your facts right at last. This winter they are cold and hungry, which I do not deny, but in other years without the work with which I alone have provided them they starved, and many of them died. None will die this year except through their own stupidity and mismanagement, and if I could afford to pay them more—which I cannot until I reap in some returns—it would be the same."

"By the time you have returns for your investment the enterprise will be completed and the workers no longer needed. You are lining your pockets at their expense. I have a little money of my own, which my good cousin paid me for being housekeeper to her while I was at Ashford, and every penny shall go to those in need."

"Keep your money. I tell you it would go to the landlord of The Running Hare, whose pockets would be lined with it, or the rogue who runs a small alehouse on the lane that comes into Easthampton from the west."

She looked coolly incredulous. "How could that be?"

He jerked forward angrily in his chair. "Since you do not believe me, ma'am, be ready at a quarter to six tomorrow morning and I will show you what I mean."

"I'll be more than ready to accompany you." She turned to leave, but his next words halted her.

"Let this be the last time you interfere in my affairs!" His furious finger pointed at her. "I've had enough. Enough, I say!"

She whirled about, goaded into retaliation. "Enough of me at the same time! You make no secret of the fact that I am a burden to you!"

He was on his feet. "Your accusation is unjust! I believe I have treated you with every courtesy. Did I not bid you stay under this roof for as long as it pleases you to remain with us?"

"Would you have me be gone, then?"

He crashed a fist down on the desk making pens jump and creating a draft that made the page of the newspaper with the announcement that had so incensed him flutter and slide to the floor. "No! Don't twist my words. Jassy is a different girl since you came back. She needs you still. Without you to be friend and adviser to her, Heaven alone knows what wayward paths she would follow. She could up and run away with the first Tom, Dick, or Harry who crossed her path."

"So! Is that to be solace to me? That I fill to perfection the role that could be played by any woman three times my age? I, the constant thorn in your side!"

"Damnation! Was there ever any female as provoking as you?" He was round the desk and they faced each other, taut and tense with the turbulence of their quarrel. "Not only do you turn the meaning of what I say, but you put words into my mouth!"

"A thorn!" she reiterated fiercely.

"How can I silence you!" He seized her face between his hands and clamped his mouth down on hers in violation, kissing her in anger, temper, and out of a violent personal frustration. It was totally unlike the kiss he had given her at the time of parting in Winchester, which had held almost a tender passion in its depths, and on a sense of deepest outrage she thrust her hands against his chest and wrenched her mouth away. For a few moments their eyes held, she breathing as deeply as he, and then she flung herself out of the room and her heels tapped away on a run.

He almost went after her, some vague idea of apologizing forming itself, but instead he flung himself back in his chair, took a
cigar from a box, which broke Jem's strict rule about smoking,
and lit it. Tilting back the chair, he narrowed his eyes in an unfocused gaze through the curling strands of fragrant smoke. Kate
was a disturbing influence, creating peace on the one hand with
the others, but forever in conflict with himself. Yet she was unjust
to accuse him of treating her as a thorn in his side. It simply
showed that she was as conscious as he of the friction between
them. Harry's attitude toward her did nothing to ease his irritation,
for it was obvious enough that his brother's love for her had not
faded one iota. It was easy to see that Harry imagined none
suspected it and, to give Kate her due, no sign of encouragement
was ever forthcoming. But what did she really feel toward Harry?
How could anyone tell? She was without doubt an enigma, full
of secret thoughts, the pearl in the oyster that could not be prized
open, and as much a mystery to him as she had ever been. The
facts he had learned about her amounted to nothing compared
with what there was to discover in the inner Kate who hid herself
away out of reach, ever exasperating him and, in spite of setting
himself against it, remaining as elusive and intriguing to him as a
siren's call. In all fairness he could not blame Harry for being
infatuated, for Kate was no ordinary young woman, either in looks
or temperament, but that did not mean he would ever condone the
infatuation. Far from it! He was as determined on that matter as
he had ever been.

He leaned forward to tap the ash from his cigar into the recep-
tacle on his desk, and it was then that his glance fell again on the
offending page of the newspaper. It drove Kate from his mind and
rekindled his hot animosity over the hopeless situation.

Next morning Kate was sitting in the hall well ahead of the
time that Daniel had given her and was warmly wrapped in a
hooded cloak, for outside it was wet and cold. Harry, buttoning
his greatcoat as he came downstairs, blinked at her in surprise, his
swift, leaping smile coming to his lips. Normally he and Daniel
made an early round of the sites and then returned to breakfast at

half past eight, when on the sideboard the hot, covered dishes awaited them and they saw her and Jem for the first time in the day, Jassy still taking breakfast in bed.

"What are you doing down here at this hour?" he asked in an early morning voice, sleep not quite gone from it.

"I'm coming with you and Daniel on your early morning round of inspection," she said, answering his smile.

A blast of icy sea air swept into the hall and sent her cloak billowing as Daniel opened the front door from outside and leaned in. "The horses are saddled," he said without greeting. "Let's have no dallying."

Outside with the two horses was Bonnie, the mare Harry had bought for her at Ashford, which she rode frequently. When she was settled in the saddle the three of them set off, Daniel riding ahead and Harry at her side. The darkness of Easthampton was alive with moving lantern lights as men went to their work, and at first it was all a routine matter of seeing Daniel or Harry check with various overseers whether everything was in order and that supplies and other necessities were being delivered or were to hand, the number of workers present always being noted. She began to have an idea what might be in the wind when they came at last to the foreman, who himself was about to ride out of the brickyard in a wagon.

"How many do you make it, Hardy?" Daniel questioned brusquely.

"Around a hundred, sir. I'm taking The Running Hare first."

"My brother and I will go there. You make for the alehouse and see to matters there."

Daniel wheeled his horse about and Harry and Kate followed at a canter. Harry took her by the arm after they dismounted at the inn and Daniel flung wide the door, his shadow and theirs falling in their wake in the rectangular patch of lamplight that split the predawn darkness. Kate was amazed at the scene that met her eyes. The smoky taproom was crowded with workmen, and some were in a state of semi-intoxication. Most of the noisy chatter died away when Daniel was sighted. It was not often that their employer or his brother came to rout them out, leaving it to the rough methods of Foreman Hardy and his henchmen, who were regular enough in breaking up these few warm minutes of comfort before the long, bleak day with its heavy toil began.

"Get out of here!" Daniel bellowed at them. He made no threatening gesture and did not brandish the crop he held, but such was the force of his authoritative presence that those nearest to him shuffled back and others with full glasses of spirits or tankards of ale began to gulp the contents down, knowing that they must move sharply. "I do not pay you good blunt to sluice your bolts at a boozing ken in working hours. Every one of you should have been on the sites half an hour ago. Now get!"

Kate watched them push toward the door to leave like a herd of cattle under the whip, except for a few stragglers who took their time, some unable to hasten their somewhat unsteady limbs, others strutting defiantly with the mulish look on their faces of the smoldering rebel. She thought they made a pathetic sight in their rags and poor garments tied with string to keep out the cold, and ahead of them lay a thirteen-hour day with nothing but their noon piece wrapped in a cloth to sustain them until they put down their tools and returned to hovels where their gaunt-faced wives and thin-limbed, wailing children awaited them in the faint glow of a stinking rush light. She had been in many of those homes with her basket-loads of food, sometimes in the company of Eliot Singleton, who watched constantly over the straying lambs of his parish, and although many of the women were slatternly and shiftless, seeking solace in a pennyworth of gin, Kate felt only compassion for them in their doleful existence.

"I must go with the men," Harry said to her. "Sometimes the drunken ones need to be hauled out of ditches or the troughs of dug foundations."

Then she and Daniel were alone in the taproom except for the landlord who was clearing up with a clatter the drinking vessels that had been used. Daniel went across to the fire in the hearth in the inglenook and kicked at a glowing log with the toe of his boot, causing flames to burst upward with a roar in a shower of sparks.

He pulled off his gloves and dropped them with his crop on the seat to warm his hands at the blaze, and he spoke over his shoulder at her.

"Well? Do you still feel charitably minded towards the work-shy? There is not a morning that this procedure does not take place, and it is a common enough occurrence everywhere. I would sack the lot of them if there was any guarantee there would not be the same percentage in the next batch. Drink is the curse of the lower classes, and if I had my way not a tavern would be allowed to open until a day's work was done."

The landlord paused in his labors to chuckle, secure in the belief that such a law could never be. "That would be 'ard on the likes of such as myself, Mr. Warwyck, sir. And I reckon when you've been traveling to or from a mill that there's happened many an occasion when you've been glad to see an inn along the road where you could take a nip to warm the cockles whatever the time of day might be, and that wouldn't be possible if it weren't open house for rich and poor alike."

Daniel did not deign to reply, ignoring the interruption which had been an intrusion into his remarks directed at Kate, whose answer he was awaiting. She was considering what she should say and drew nearer to come within the fire's dancing glow, which leaped up her cloak and made a play of light and shade across her face. With a single graceful gesture she swept her cloak back in folds over her shoulders, leaving her free to follow his example in holding her hands to the fire. Unexpectedly he was gripped by a renewed awareness of the unconscious sensuality in her every movement, and he was stirred by her as he had been in a hotel room at Winchester and again when he had surprised her in her petticoats one day. Innocent of the effect she had had on him, her serene and thoughtful face was in profile to his gaze as she looked downward at the flames.

"Some of those men have trudged considerable distances to get into Easthampton for the day's work. I cannot believe that it is not the rest and refreshment they need as much as anything."

At any other time he might have answered her derisively, but it was as though momentarily she had laid a spell upon him and he spoke more gently than he would otherwise have done. "It is as well that women have no hand in business, or else those like you would cosset their employees as though they were wayward children."

"Kindness never goes amiss," she replied in the same thoughtful tones.

His brows clamped into a frown. He did not consider himself to be completely a stranger to kindness, but there were limits that had to be drawn. Catching up his gloves and crop he swung away from the fire. "I have work to do before the breakfast hour."

They parted company outside the inn, he to go about his business, she to ride back to Honeybridge House. Later in the morning she returned to the building yard, which Harry had shown her one day on a tour of all the workshops soon after her arrival, and she went straight to a warehouse that she remembered as having plenty of space, being a place for stored timber and scaffolding. She inspected the premises carefully, deciding that it would be suitable for what she had in mind. She hoped to have a discussion with Daniel about it and went up the outside steps to his office, but a clerk informed her that Mr. Warwyck was taking a run in training with Jem Pierce along the sands. As she made to descend the flight again she paused to look over the yard below and the fields beyond, her gaze traveling on to the lane where two lady riders were making their way toward the shore. She supposed they were going to enjoy a ride by the sea. Then her grip tightened on the handrail. She had caught the bright flash of red-gold hair beneath a plumed riding hat. Once again there was to be a meeting between Daniel and Claudine Clayton.

Daniel and Jem had almost finished the morning exercise and were covering the last stretch back again along the sands when two riders approached at a gallop. He recognized instantly the vivid flare of Claudine's hair long before she drew near, and as the distance lessened he saw it was Olivia who rode with her. Claudine did not slow her horse's pace, the hooves of both her mount and her sister's throwing up clods of sand, but he halted to stare up at her and she let her eyes be trapped by his, her expression rigid as she galloped past. He followed her with his gaze and spoke to Jem without turning his head.

"Go on back to the house."

Jem gave his sleeve a tug. "The less ye have to do with the likes of her the better. Come on and finish the run."

"Do as I say!"

Jem breathed strongly through his disfigured nostrils, but refrained from saying any more, ambling off and looking back once or twice as if he hoped that Daniel might still be swayed by reason. Left alone Daniel did not have long to wait before Claudine brought her horse back at a gallop. What excuse she had made to her sister he neither knew nor cared. When she reined in he gave her no choice as to whether or not she would dismount, but seized her by the waist and pulled her down to him, swinging her into the shelter of some huge rocks where they could not be seen. There his mouth took hers and they kissed in a kind of frenzy, her arms locked about his neck, her mouth as avid as his. Then he seized her by the shoulders and jerked her from him hard against the towering rock behind her.

"Why?" he demanded furiously. "Why?"

Her lips were wet and her eyes were dilated and bright with frightened, unshed tears. "You are a curse on me! I must be free of you! Lionel loves me!"

He gave a shout of mirthless laughter. "You don't know what you're talking about!"

"He does! He does! There is the tenderest relationship between us. Not as it is between you and me!"

"Would you have how it is between us otherwise?"

Her exultant and yet cowering shudder gave him his answer. He had almost broken her. His arms crushed her to him.

"There is an empty cottage at the end of the track at Denwin's Corner," he said urgently. "We can meet there—"

"No!" Her voice rang with the steeliness of her will which matched his own, and she pushed herself from him. "I want an end to it all, not a beginning!" Then her face changed as she looked beyond him and spoke in a flat tone. "Here comes Olivia. She has a deep, sisterly affection for me and will pretend not to know I came back to speak with you. In that manner she can ease her conscience and save herself from reporting the incident to Alexander."

Although Daniel went with Claudine to assist her back onto her horse Olivia spoke to her younger sister as if he was not present. "Did you find your dropped glove, Claudine? Ah, yes. I see you are wearing it. I suggest we ride in the other direction now."

She urged her horse forward again, but before Claudine could follow her Daniel caught the bridle. "The day after tomorrow I leave for London, and from there to a mill at Harley Heath. I'll await you at the cottage after dark."

Her face twisted malevolently. "Never!" she hissed. "Never!" She brought her crop down with a mighty whack across her horse's rump and galloped after her sister.

Kate's hopes of having a discussion with Daniel that evening about the idea she had had were thwarted when he went out immediately after dinner and had not returned when she retired to bed at midnight. When he came in she was still awake, reading by candlelight, and she listened to Daniel's footsteps go past her door. It seemed to her that they did not hold the light tread of a man who had had a satisfactory evening.

It was after the daily sparring session in the roped-off ring on a grassy patch beyond the Honeybridge orchard that Jem, sinking down tiredly on a slatted bench in an outdoor bathhouse, pulled off the sparring gloves with their stuffing of soft wool and spoke his mind as he splayed his hands upon his knees.

"I don't have to remind ye that I'm yer trainer and what I says goes. Ye'll pull in yer horns from now on and keep within yer own doorstep."

Daniel, who had already doused himself over the head with one of the buckets of water set ready, spoke through strands of dripping hair and reached for a towel to dry himself. "Enlighten me," he answered on an ebb of good humor, a suspicion of what was about to be forthcoming bringing a frown to his brow. "You talk in riddles."

"Don't come no nonsense with me," Jem answered sternly. "Ye know fair and square to what I'm referring. I heard the hour ye came in last night. It don't fit in with yer training schedule or with nothing else neither. Ye were out petticoat-poaching and I've a right good idea whose it might be. Let there be no more of it, either now or when we get home again from the mill at Harley Heath."

Angrily Daniel retaliated, throwing down the damp towel and taking another one from a folded pile to pummel himself dry. "For a man with only one peeper you see a deal too much for my liking. I'm telling you to keep it closed and your chaffer shut. What I'm about is my affair and nobody else's—not even yours in this case."

"Affair, eh?" Jem chucked his head contemptuously. "Ye chose the right word there and no mistake."

Daniel snorted and flung on his clothes. The door of the bathhouse banged behind him, but Jem sprang up to wrench it open again with a shout. "That redheaded wench will be yer destruction. Why don't ye look closer home? The trouble with ye is that ye can't see the wood for the trees!"

Daniel neither looked back nor answered him.

That evening when they all sat down to dinner, Daniel at the head of the table, Kate made a request of him. "I should deem it a favor if you could spare me an hour to talk with you after we have dined," she said.

He was unfolding his napkin with a crackle of starched linen and he gave her a vague nod, his thoughts elsewhere. Jem answered heavily on his behalf.

"He'll talk with ye, Mrs. Warwyck. He ain't going nowhere this evening. Early nights are always the rule afore a fight, and we have the journey ahead of us tomorrow."

Jassy spoke from where she sat at the opposite side of the table. "Why do you have to go to London first?"

Harry answered her. "Sir Geoffrey wants Daniel to sit at his right hand at this grand dinner of the Pugilistic Club that we are going to, because that will be tantamount to an announcement that Daniel is his nominee for the championship. There is great rivalry among the members, who all want the fighter to whom they show their particular patronage to excel above all the other boxers in the prize ring. Many of those patrons will be at Harley Heath next Monday to see how Daniel fares against a new man being matched with him."

Jassy looked solemnly at her elder brother. "All my good wishes will go with you."

Daniel smiled and raised his glass to her. "I thank you." The other three saw that the breach between brother and sister was closing at last.

When Kate with Jassy's help had finished washing the dishes she returned to the dining room where Daniel was to await her, the others having withdrawn to the drawing room. But he was not there. Slowly she sat down in his vacated chair and rested her elbows on the table before her. He had used her request as a means of escaping Jem's watchful eye and had gone out again. To see whom? She tried not to guess. Spreading her fingers wide she clasped her bowed head, suffering her own particular anguish.

In the isolated cottage beyond the outskirts of Easthampton and less than half a mile from the boundaries of Radcliffe Hall Daniel waited, impatiently pacing the floor. He could not believe that Claudine would not come. Yesterday evening he had been disappointed, but not unduly surprised by her failure to appear, but he had been certain that she would not stay away the second time. The place where he waited was small and low-beamed, bare and unfurnished except for a built-in wall bed that was soft with clean, sweet hay. The shuttered windows kept the secret within of the candle's glow and the flicker of the fire on the hearth, which he had lighted as soon as he arrived. Once more he took his watch from his pocket and snapped it open to look at the time. It was almost midnight. She was not coming.

He knelt down by the hearth to rake out the fire when abruptly he tensed, listening. It was the click of the gate, but there had been no sound of hooves along the rutted track. As a precaution she must have dismounted and led the horse along the grassy verge. He straightened up as the latch lifted on the door, which opened swiftly into a narrow gap to let a woman enter and close it behind her. The hood fell back from the arrival's head and he saw to his astonishment that it was Olivia.

"Mrs. Radcliffe!" he exclaimed.

"I do not ask pardon for this intrusion," she said with a nervous intensity, "because it was for no good purpose that you sought to lure my younger sister to you."

He raised an eyebrow. "I think that matter lies between Claudine and me, but she took you into her confidence, I assume."

"She is distraught, but I thank heaven that she has kept her head and has too much good sense to risk her reputation and everything else that would be at stake by coming to this low place on her own."

It occurred to him that Olivia herself had risked a great deal by slipping out to see him secretly, not only her husband's wrath should Alexander discover where she had been, but the chance of being spotted by servants who would put their own interpretation on her midnight activity and set tongues of gossip wagging.

"You have not yet told me the purpose of your visit, ma'am," he prompted crisply.

She lifted her hands to put them together and then clasp them tightly in urgent appeal, her expression enforcing her request. "Do not try to come between Claudine and Lionel, I beg you. Withdraw from her life and cross her path no more."

In a flash he understood, recalling the look he had once seen on Olivia's face when she had watched her husband and sister laughing together with a certain intimacy. Olivia was desperately afraid that his pursuit of Claudine might inadvertently cause a rift in the betrothment, perhaps even a cancellation of the marriage, and more than anything else she wanted her sister out of Radcliffe Hall and safely away from Alexander as another man's wife. It was not only her conscience or sisterly devotion that had made her ignore his presence on the sands the previous day.

"Lionel is the perfect choice for her," she continued fervently, almost without drawing breath, "and they are ideally suited in every way. You are an entrepreneur, an outcast to genteel society, and a traitor to your class, but it is the very fact that you are a gentleman born that I implore you in the name of honor to give no more thought to my sister."

His hand, resting against the rough oaken mantel, balled into a fist and crashed down upon the shelf, sending the dust flying. "She must not marry Attwood!" Any revenge must be of his own making and he would not have others, however unwittingly, do it for him. "I suspect your husband's motives. It is not the wedded bliss of your sister that he has at heart." There was a limit to what he could say to her and no doubt a similar limit to her understanding. As it was, she misunderstood his attitude.

"You have no right to attack out of jealousy those who think only of her well-being since you wish nothing more for Claudine than your own seduction of her!" Olivia drew herself up to her full height. "It seems as if my efforts to appeal to the better side of your nature have been to no avail, and I'll stay no longer. I tell you that I shall do everything in my power to hasten the marriage date and ensure that my sister need no longer fear your wickedness!"

She departed as swiftly and silently as she had come. Daniel put out the fire and locked up the cottage. As he rode away he let the horse have its head, busy with his own thoughts. He had misjudged Claudine's strength of will. It looked as if she was not to be swayed from what she had said that day in the office: surrender only in the marriage bed. Why not? Yes, why not? It was an entirely new aspect to be considered. He would think it over while he was in London and before the big mill at Harley Heath.

At Radcliffe Hall, Claudine sat up expectantly in a chair by the Red Drawing Room fire when a step came outside the double doors and the handles were pressed down. But it was Alexander who had come home from gaming at a neighbor's house and not

Olivia, whose return she was awaiting with a mixture of triumph and trepidation. It gave her a vicarious thrill to picture Daniel's disappointment when he discovered her sister had come in her place, but if he sent back his promise not to see her again she knew she would suffer a disappointment far greater than his. How was it possible to be so drawn to someone whom she hated so much?

Alexander's smile showed he was pleased to discover her alone. Although Radcliffe Hall was very large and had more rooms than she was sure of, it was rarely that the two of them were ever on their own together. Olivia, like a prim-faced wraith, wafted in and out and appeared on silent feet in all parts of the house at any time as if there were a hundred Olivias instead of one first lady of the Hall. He came striding across to set his feet apart with his back to the fire and continued to smile down at her, the firelight running amber trails over the brown velvet of his flare-tailed coat.

"Did the ladies' card party end early, then?" he inquired, his gaze dwelling softly on her. The sight of her was ever fascinating to him, ever enchanting. She had cast her sexual spell over him when he had first clapped eyes on her hurrying down the gangplank at Dover, where she had arrived off the packet from France. It was amazing to remember how reluctant he had been to go, for it had meant missing the first meet of the season, and hunting was dear to his heart, but Olivia had been indisposed after a miscarriage, and in order not to upset her he had decided against relegating the chore, going himself to make some kind of welcome for the young sister-in-law whom he had never met. And there she was, stepping into his life, bonnet ribbons flying, the freshness of her youth vying with the awareness in her gleaming, mesmerizing eyes, and the wantonness that lurked in the inviting, rosy mouth. Olivia, for whom his desires had ebbed, had been reduced to a pale, dull shadow beside the vivaciousness of the bewitching creature who had come to make his home her own.

At first he had tried not to think about her too much, but whether they met mundanely at the breakfast table or on the stairs, or even if he came late to some gathering and saw her there, she burst gloriously upon his eye with the same magic, and before long he knew himself to be enslaved by her. But he was not alone in his enslavement. He endured as best he could a ferociousness of jealousy that he had not known since adolescence when other men eyed her, pursued her, called on *him* for permission to pay court to her with the most serious and honorable intentions, and even quarreled over her. And, the minx, she knew her power and flaunted it. When at last he could no longer keep his hands from her, never losing an opportunity to hold her fingers longer than necessary when handing her into a carriage or out of it, putting an arm about her slender waist with a brother-in-law's privilege, or touching her more intimately whenever they were unobserved, she did not rebuff him completely, but tempted and withdrew, flirted and faked shock at his boldness, played out the line and then jerked it hard in the age-old game that to his sophisticated wisdom and wide amoral experience presented nothing new, but this time had caught him securely on its hook as if he were some callow youth in the helpless throes of first love.

It was useless to torment himself with the thoughts of her marrying someone else, because it had to be. As is common in such cases, his resentment had grown against his marriage partner as if she were to blame for being the barrier between him and his new love, and at times he wished Olivia dead, although that would not have resolved the situation, for the Church allowed no man to wed his sister-in-law. To his relief Claudine showed no signs of being in a hurry to marry, and they shared special little jokes about the suitors she wanted him to show the door. Those she seemed to contemplate as being likely candidates he hated with murder in his heart, even as he hated those whom he was certain she allowed to kiss or embrace her in leafy conservatories or moonlit gardens, for the kisses he had won from her had been few enough, putting him on the rack for what she had made clear he could never have. Such was the strain on him that over the three years she had been living under his roof he had come latterly to show at times his virulent hatred of those who paid her undue attention, no longer able to keep his self-control. Only toward his old friend, Lionel Attwood, did he feel no animosity, not imagining that anything serious could develop between the two of them. The foursome without jealousy and inner suffering had been enjoyable at Brighton and afterward when Attwood Grange had been opened up again the happy association had long continued. It was impossible not to like Lionel, who for all his unmanly interest in poetry and other odd pursuits had a knowledge of horseflesh that could not be matched, and his stable of hunters, which he had replenished after his absence abroad, was the best to be found anywhere as it had been before; in addition he was good-tempered at the gaming tables, a cheerful loser and a modest winner, and in his cups he was never abusive or quarrelsome, but kept the quiet dignity that was natural to him. Nevertheless, it was inevitable that Alexander had known mixed feelings when Lionel asked for Claudine's hand. It was one evening over port after dinner at which he had been the only guest, and Olivia and Claudine had withdrawn, leaving them alone together.

"I shall do everything that lies within my power to make her happy," Lionel continued, taking Alexander's stunned silence to mean no opposition would be forthcoming. "My sojourn in Italy has to all intents and purposes cured the weakness of my lungs, and my physicians assure me that with reasonable care and attention to my health there is no reason why there should ever be a recurrence of the illness. Claudine's personal fortune shall remain her own, for I have no need of it, and with the many mutual interests that she and I enjoy together I feel confident that I can offer her a life of contentment at Attwood Grange."

It had not been easy to answer him. Alexander set an elbow on the table and rubbed his fingers across his forehead, playing for time. Claudine would never be happy with Lionel. He was not the one for her. Far, far from it! She needed a man who would use her violently, one able to inflame and satisfy the passions and desires of that erotic, beautiful body. A man such as himself. Then, like a snake slowly beginning to uncurl in the darkness of undergrowth, there moved into his mind exactly what it could mean to him if Claudine was restless and unhappy and frustrated at Attwood Grange. He swallowed hard and made himself look at Lionel with every appearance of friendly concern.

"Have you reason to believe she would accept you?"

"Lately she has shown unmistakably that I stand high in her opinion," he replied composedly, "and I have every confidence that her answer will be favorable towards me."

Had it been anyone else but Lionel stating his certainty that he was Claudine's choice of a husband, Alexander would have been overcome by jealousy and outrage, but as it was he extended his Judas hand to his old friend, managing an encouraging smile.

"Then I wish you good fortune when you speak to her. I assure you there shall be every encouragement towards the match on my part. There is none other I would have chosen for her had the option been mine."

They shook hands on it, and then adjourned to join the ladies, much to Alexander's relief, for he could not have made any affable remarks about married bliss and heirs, usual at such times, for the words would have made his gorge heave.

Now, at the fireside, he realized Claudine had replied to his question about the card party while he had been reminiscing. "A headache kept you at home, did it?" he acknowledged. "Then what caused you to sit up until this late hour?"

"I am feeling better. A little sleep on the sofa dispelled the pain and I did not wish to retire yet and lie awake."

Headaches were a favorite excuse used by women to get out of anything not agreeable to them and he hid his disbelief in what she had told him. Olivia could get a headache whenever it suited her, but had long since learned they were to no avail, for she had yet to give him an heir, and even though her attraction for him had waned she was his wife and he had constant need of her.

"Has Olivia gone to bed and left you without company?" he remarked mildly. "That was thoughtless of her." It was not only thoughtless, but extremely unusual, particularly since his wife would have known that sooner or later he would come home to find Claudine on her own. Not that Olivia had ever said anything to him about his close relationship with her sister or even as much as hinted that all was not as she would have wished it, but he was certain the matter was forever in her mind. Her relief when she heard that Lionel and her sister were to be betrothed had been transparently clear.

Claudine moved one hand lightly over the other in her lap, her diamond and sapphire betrothal ring sending slivers of reflected firelight across her creamy throat and chin. "She went to play cards and is not home yet. We could not both disappoint the hostess."

As with the headache tale, he felt she was not speaking the whole truth. There was no reason at all why he should doubt her, for she was relaxed and at ease, smiling at him from where she rested her head against the wing of the cushioned chair. But there remained in his mind the arrow-poised tenseness of her at his entrance, when she had twisted straight-backed on the seat to look toward the door, an unmistakable flicker of consternation passing over her face at the sight of him before the smile had taken charge. He had assumed it was because she was not altogether pleased that he had found her alone, for if not in the mood or at the irritable time of her month she could be tetchy and often cruel when he sought to caress her or touch her soft skin with his lips. But there was no mulish pout to her mouth, no glint of impatience or—worse!—vixenish malevolence. Instead there was the amiability he associated with their sweeter moments together, and he decided to put matters to the test.

"Had I known you had been deserted I should not have stirred out of the house this evening." He moved to sit down on the arm of her chair, running a caressing hand down her arm as he spoke, but instantly she was on her feet, taking his vacated place in front of the fire, her fingertips resting on the edge of the mantel. No, not resting—gripping. Yet still she smiled.

"Olivia will be back at any minute," she teased provocatively. It was a trick of hers to use the possibility of his wife's imminent intrusion either to give danger to their snatched encounters or to ward him off from her. This evening it was difficult to decide which was uppermost in her thoughts.

"We shall hear Olivia's carriage when it comes alongside the portico below," he said and took her into his arms. She was trembling! Not involuntarily from the amorousness that he was able to arouse in her, but from something else. Fear? She had never shown fear of him before and he was excited by it. Greedily he kissed her, aware of having full control of her as he had never had before, and he regretted not having turned the key in the lock of the double doors when he had come into the room. For some obscure purpose of her own she did not wish to antagonize him and he was going to take full advantage of the golden opportunity. Then the doors opened and Olivia swept in, her cloak billowing.

She stood stock still, staring at them. They had broken apart instantly, but only Claudine had the grace to show some shame, putting her fingertips against the hollows under her cheekbones. Her husband, on the other hand, was glaring at her as if she were the wrongdoer, his face congested to an ugly shade of crimson.

"Where have you been?" he demanded, taking menacing steps toward her. "No carriage came into the forecourt."

Olivia tilted her chin haughtily. Later the pain would set in, later the tears would come, but for the present moment she was sustained by shock in spite of having pictured times without number in her distressed mind's eye the scene that had met her horrified gaze. "Have you always listened for such warnings of my approach?"

His hand whipped out and he slapped her hard across the face out of his own temper, his own colossal disappointment at the chance he believed she had snatched from him, and because momentarily the sight of her was an abomination to him. The sharp sound in the quiet room jerked Claudine back to her customary self-possession. She had been afraid of Alexander discovering the business that she and Olivia had been about that evening, which had been secretly vindictive against Daniel on her side, but innocent and well-meaning on the part of her sister, for whom it had taken every scrap of courage not only to deceive Alexander as to her whereabouts, but also to ride out alone in the darkness, something she had never done in her whole life before. It had been to make Alexander pay little attention as to whether it was one horse or two that came clattering into the forecourt that Claudine had responded more to him than she might otherwise have done, and it had never occurred to her that Olivia would have the wit to return with some secrecy, but then ruin everything by guilelessly bursting in still wearing her cloak and without checking to make sure that Alexander had not returned from his evening out. However, now that the cat was out of the bag in more ways than one it was pointless to indulge in any more subterfuge. It would also be to her advantage to get round Olivia in any way she could in case she needed her as an ally again sometime in the future.

"Leave my dear sister alone!" she said fiercely to Alexander, pulling him by the sleeve. Then to Olivia herself she held out her hands in graceful appeal. "Forgive me. I was so distraught waiting for you that I was scarcely in my right mind. Without knowing the reason why, Alexander sensed my need for comfort."

Olivia was rendered speechless as much by Claudine's brazen bluff as by the stinging in her cheek, to which she had put a violently trembling hand. Alexander, breathing like a bull in frustration at not knowing what the two women in his life had been involved in without his knowledge, roared for enlightenment once more, turning to Claudine for an answer since his wife seemed to have lost the power of her tongue.

"I demand an explanation for Olivia's sneaking into the house on foot at this hour of the night." For one absurd, incredulous second or two he had wondered if his wife had a lover, but dismissed the idea instantly, secure in the knowledge of her cloying love for him, which he often found suffocating, settled as it was more on an emotional than a physical plane, but at least it meant he would never be cuckolded in his own house or out of it.

Claudine faced him blandly. "For my sake Olivia went to see Daniel Warwyck."

"What?" Alexander looked as if he might explode, so dark was the color in his face.

"He has never stopped his pursuit of me. If you had not thrown him from the barouche in Brighton it is likely he would have surrendered the whole matter long ago." She did not believe what she was saying, but she wanted Alexander to feel he was in some way to blame. "As a result his persistence has not waned. The day before yesterday he accosted me when I was out with Olivia and insisted on arranging a place of assignation."

"He dared!" Jealousy was threatening to choke him. He could not believe that Claudine had not given the fellow some encouragement, for it was as natural for her to flirt as it was to breathe, and even if she had not intended it there was invitation and allure in every supple move and wriggle and flick of eyelash. He had never forgotten the curiously possessive look that Warwyck had given her at their first meeting as if she were already his for the taking. And again at the Royal Pavilion when Warwyck's attitude toward her had been wholly proprietary, and it was that more than anything else that had been so galling. "Where was this place of assignation?"

She told him. "Olivia was brave to go there. Her sole aim was to convince him once and for all that I would have none of him."

Alexander snapped his attention back to his wife. "What did he say?"

Olivia continued to stare at her husband. His concern had nothing to do with her. It was not important to him that she had risked a fall from her horse if it had missed its footing in the darkness, not of any consequence that she might have been attacked by some of those rough men employed in the building of Easthampton and even now be lying raped or dead. She was not vengeful by nature, and normally she would have done whatever she could toward forgiving and forgetting and making whole again, but within the short span of an hour she had been betrayed and struck by her husband, played false by her sister, and defied by stubborn-jawed Daniel Warwyck. By her choice of words she could let them wreak their own punishment on each other and score her own particular victory.

"You had better both beware of Daniel Warwyck," she said with firm emphasis. "He mistrusts you, Alexander, and he wants Claudine. Unless she shows her good faith by marrying Lionel without delay there will be no getting rid of him, and I for one draw my own conclusions from his belief in his own power to achieve his aim."

Quietly she turned on her heel and went from the room, her head high. Left alone Alexander rounded on Claudine.

"You have encouraged him!" he accused gratingly. "You little—"

"Don't you dare!" She hurled herself back from his vicinity as though no longer able to bear his presence near her. "I do what I like and I encourage or discourage whom I will. It is no affair of yours. Although you and Olivia have legal responsibility for me until I wed, it is only with regard to my property and well-being, and you cannot control me in any other way. As it happens, I will marry Lionel soon, but simply because it suits me to do so, and not to prove anything to you or anybody else!"

She darted out through the open doors and away to her room. Alexander strode almost automatically to the doorway and stared after her. He would settle Daniel Warwyck. There was a way that he had long been churning over in his mind, one that would gain the support of several neighbors, although they would leave the sordid details to him and pay their share without asking questions. As for Claudine's declared intention to marry Lionel soon, he welcomed it. The sooner she was wed, the sooner she would look to him for what would be lacking in the marriage.

Chapter 11

Kate, having been given no opportunity to talk over her idea with Daniel, decided to go ahead with it anyway. She was defying the order he had given her never to interfere with anything again, but she could not believe that he would disapprove in this case. If he did, she would face up to him as she had many times before. The scheme did not take much preparation.

She cleaned out a large urn she had discovered in the cellar, purchased another with her own money, and a supply of tea; then, the afternoon before she put her plan into action she went back to the warehouse. There, with the aid of a half-witted lad who was employed to sweep the yard clean, she set up a table with planks and blocks that were available, and unpacked the assortment of mugs and cups which she had either raked out from the back of cupboards or bought herself in the local stores. A brazier to heat the urn was found for her by the lad, whose name was Ned, and then everything was ready for the morning of the next day.

"Thank you for your help, Ned," she said, putting on her gloves again. "You shall have the first cup of tea that is poured tomorrow."

His grin spread loosely over his face, showing his pleasure, for he lacked the ability to speak intelligibly, and the garbled noise that came from his throat made him the butt of many a cruel joke. He had the feeling, which was like having sunshine inside him, that everything was going to be much better for the presence of this lady, who had rewarded him for his trouble with a home-baked loaf and a wedge of fruit cake that she had brought specially for him.

"Now I am going into every one of the workshops," she told him. "Would you like to come with me?"

He shook his head, hanging back, for he had a dread of the tricks played on him, and the fear showed sharply in his eyes. Kate, who had not chosen him to help her without reason, guessed the cause, having seen all too often how those afflicted like Ned were bullied and kicked about. She put out a hand to him.

"Come along. Don't be afraid. Nobody is going to harm you. You are my helper now, and everyone shall know it."

It took him several minutes with much coaxing from her to summon up the courage to put his dirt-soiled hand into her spotless, cream leather clasp. Then side by side, she keeping her pace to his shambling gait, they went into the first workshop.

It was the smith's shop, heavy with smoke-laden air, and the faces that looked toward her were blackened and grimed. Over the noise she made herself heard.

"Good afternoon, gentlemen. From tomorrow morning at five-thirty onward hot coffee and tea will be served in the scaffolding warehouse at one farthing a cup. Ned has been promoted to my assistant, and I am glad to have his help. I look forward to seeing you tomorrow morning."

Next was the mason's shop, which was damp and steamy, and she felt sorry for those working there, for the old building offered no proper ventilation. She made the same announcement and went on to the workshops of the carpenters, the painters, and the plasterers where moldings were being made, and afterward into the journey works and the sawpits. With Ned in tow she went to each group at work on the making of bricks, passing the clay-washing mill worked by horsepower, and another mixing concrete. The men reacted to what she had to say in different ways, some smothering guffaws, others showing interest or merely gaping. When she had seen all there she left Ned and mounted her chestnut mare to ride to every site where men were working, spoke to them all, and then she went home.

Jassy greeted her. "Did all go well? I wish you would let me come and help tomorrow morning."

"It is no place for you. Daniel would never allow it."

"How do you know he is going to allow you to pour tea and coffee for his workmen when he gets back?" Jassy chided affectionately.

Kate unclipped her cloak. "He will if the scheme works well—and it must."

Next morning at five-thirty Kate arrived at the warehouse to find Ned was there before her. Later she was to discover that he was orphaned and homeless, spending the nights in whatever corner of the brickyard he could find out of the cold and the wind and the night watchman's eye, but that morning she was not aware of it and was grateful that he had the brazier burning and had brought water in pails she had provided from one of the pumps. Time ticked by. Nobody came into the warehouse. She and Ned waited in the light thrown down by two lanterns suspended from a beam. The urns bubbled and hissed. Then, when she was beginning to think the whole plan was a fiasco, one of the big doors creaked open and out of the grayish dawn a few men shuffled in. She turned the tap of the nearest urn and began to fill the mugs with steaming brew. Within minutes the place was crowded, the men jostling to be served and then drawing back out of the crush to sip the scalding drinks, their hands cupped about the reviving warmth seeping through the pottery. Ned, whose balance was too unsteady to hand the mugs over, took the farthings and was sharp enough to know when a dud was passed to him or someone attempted to palm off a polished pebble or an old button. His resulting show of anger, his gestures and gabble, succeeded in getting the attention of Kate or some of the men around, which caused the culprit to make a shame-faced joke of the deception and pay up. At six o'clock a bell clanged up and down the yard and the men left.

Kate smiled jubilantly at Ned. "I think that all went well, don't you?"

She was less jubilant when the foreman came to see her just as she and Ned had finished washing up. "I'm sorry to disappoint you, ma'am, but there were just as many men in the taverns this morning. I fear you only 'ad the custom of those who normally turn up for work on time."

Momentarily she looked downcast. "No reduction at all, Mr. Hardy?"

He shrugged. "Well, 'alf a dozen to a dozen maybe."

Her expression lifted. "Then that is a measure of success, to say nothing of the good that the hot drinks did to all those who were here this morning. Their thanks were heartfelt." She gave a little sigh, rolling down her sleeves and removing her apron. "But if it is stronger drink that some of them want I must provide it."

"Mrs. Warwyck!" Hardy was severely taken aback. "When the men start on the booze that early they are often on a bottle of cheap spirit all day. That's why accidents occur when a man 'asn't his full wits about him and staggers like young Ned 'ere."

"It is still the custom with many people to drink ale with their breakfast and when these men have no home-brew to start them on the day, they will fulfill that need of it," she said. "And if they can get a pint of ale at the lowest possible price from me I think you will find that fewer of them will go to the taverns on their way to work, and there will be no cheap spirits to buy here. In the end I think I shall have weeded out the habitual work-dodgers and lay-abouts, and you can decide what should be done to them. Between us we can cut down the accidents, which often involve other workers through no fault of their own."

He was not a man given to smiling, either in approval or otherwise, but he gave her a lift of the brim of his hat. "Whatever you say, Mrs. Warwyck."

As he made to leave she called after him. "If you see Mr.

Tanner, would you ask him if he can spare a moment. I want him to see if anything can be done about ventilating the buildings where the smiths and the masons work in those dreadful conditions. It must ruin their lungs in the end, don't you agree?"

Hardy considered there to be a marked difference between feminine good sense and female meddling. "Yes, ma'am," he said with less amiability. He deliberately failed to deliver the message, but the next day he found some of Tanner's men at work knocking out ventilator apertures with precious bricks piled ready for shaft-making in both the workshops. What Mr. Warwyck himself was going to say about men being taken off vital work for such unnecessary and time-consuming alterations he did not know. The thought made him take out his red-spotted handkerchief and mop his brow.

By the end of the week the numbers in the warehouse had increased considerably, and Kate drew in the help of two younger boys, aged between nine and ten, who were also employed at the building yard. After the day's rest on Sunday even more men turned up on Monday morning to be served with their choice of refreshment, and the fact that those who wanted ale were allowed only one pint each brought forth no resentment, for she had earned their respect, and those who did not watch their language in her hearing were muttered at by their companions. Human nature being what it was, the casks of ale had to be kept under lock and key at other times, and she brought in the carpenters to erect a division in the corner of the warehouse, where folding doors could be opened back in the morning, and within was enough space, not only for the casks, but for the proper trestle table they set up for her. They added a working bench for the washing up and cupboards for the mugs. She was well pleased with all that was done, and remarked on it when Hardy came to give her the morning report of the malingerers at the taverns.

"Yes, ma'am," he acknowledged, squinting under his bushy brows at it all, thinking it was a good thing that his employer would be home again the day after tomorrow. There was no telling what she would think of next, and that fool Tanner never questioned the orders she gave. "I came to tell you that there weren't no more than twenty men at The Running Hare this morning, and fewer still at the other alehouse. It's whittled down to more or less the same crowd, and there's a troublemaker or two among them. I 'ave them sorted out, and the lot of 'em'll get the boot on payday."

The next morning after the bell had rung and the men had dispersed, a lighter step sounded on the warehouse floor. Kate, supervising the heating of the washing-up water, turned and saw a red-haired girl in riding clothes just inside the door. It was Claudine Clayton.

"Mrs. Kate Warwyck?" Claudine questioned uncertainly. She had expected the Warwyck housekeeper to be older.

"Yes?" Kate went toward her.

"Can we be overheard here?"

"The boys have sharp ears. Let us step outside."

"I must not be seen!"

"It's still quite dark and everyone has gone from this section, but we can step into the stables at the side if you prefer."

By the empty stalls in the deserted stables, men and horses all at work, Claudine made the purpose of her visit known, keeping her voice low.

"I have come to give warning to Daniel. I did not dare go to Honeybridge House for fear of being sighted, but this way I came through the woods and I trust that I was not seen." There was bracken and dried leaves clinging to the cloth of her habit, bearing evidence of how she had pushed through the hedge which grew only a few yards from the warehouse.

"Daniel is away," Kate said, becoming chill and distant in the shutting down of an emotion that was more than hostility. Whatever warning Claudine might have brought, she herself symbolized another kind of danger in Kate's eyes. "Today he fights a bout at Harley Heath, and tomorrow, after he has rested overnight, he will make the journey home."

"He must come home tonight!" Anxiously Claudine peered out of the stable again before continuing with what she had to tell, low-voiced and trembling. "I knew about the fight and that he was not here. I—I happen to have heard that certain persons are to wreck everything he is building in Easthampton this night. It is planned that Daniel should come home to devastation and a smoking ruin."

"Who would dare!" Kate exclaimed in horror.

"He has enemies. Powerful enemies who can employ others to do their dirty work for them." She was frantic in her effort to impress upon Kate the need for urgency. "You must get word to him. I would go myself if it were possible, but my movements have to be accounted for. Only my being able to persuade my betrothed to ride early with me this morning enabled me to get here before meeting him." She took a swift step to the door, looking back. "I dare not delay another second. Get word to Daniel at all costs."

"It shall be done."

Claudine hastened away, and Kate sped on running feet to find Tanner. "I have to go home at once," she said to him. "Please see to the locking up for me."

She had walked to the warehouse that morning as she often did, having recently discovered a short cut across the fields, and never had the path seemed long, but it did then when she half-ran, half-walked the distance back again. Jassy, memories of the vandalism wreaked on Honeybridge House all too recent in her mind, went pale at what Kate had to tell her, but she ran to saddle Bonnie while Kate changed for the journey. She stood at the gate to watch her ride off swiftly along the lane.

It was midmorning when Kate reached Harley Heath, and the mill was to begin at eleven. A woman in the little town, which went by the same name, directed her to the place where the ring had been set up, and she rode on to it. She had no intention of giving the message to Daniel before the bout, which could distract him and hamper his concentration, but she would be near at hand to speak to him as soon as the fight was over.

When she drew near the location she realized the folly in expecting to get anywhere near the ring, which she could see in the distance on a slight rise in the land that formed a natural stage for it, and there was an outer roped ring at ten yards' distance from it, the space within patrolled by the whips to make sure the spectators did not come too close and stayed seated on the far side of it. Neither Daniel nor his opponent had yet stripped off, for they were waiting for the toss of the coin to decide on sides, it being a disadvantage to mill against the sun or slashing rain, although on this day the weather was overcast, dry and with no wind. Lying between Kate and the ring was the noisy, restless crowd, several thousands strong, all in their places, seated in the front and standing at the back. Encircling the whole site was a double row of farm wagons, about sixty in each, the inner circle with the wheels set in trenches dug in the earth to prevent any impeding of the view of those occupying the outer one.

Although Kate had barely brought Bonnie to a halt she was already the center of attention from those in the immediate vicinity, male glances caught by her reining in to look with apparent brazenness toward the ring, and she was about to wheel Bonnie round again, thinking to wait some convenient distance away until the fight was over, when there came a diversion. With a rattle of wheels and the blowing and snorting of steaming, sweat-darkened horses, a carriage drew up, and out of it there alighted with all speed a severe, determined-looking gentleman with a beaver hat rammed solidly on his head and in his hand a document with an official seal attached to it. Two burly individuals jumped down at the same time from the outside seat at the rear of the carriage and promptly made no business about clearing a way for the gentleman through the crowd, from whom a loud groan of mingled disappointment and fury went up on every side. The pugilistic name for a magistrate was on every lip.

"It's a beak! A damned beak!"

Kate dismounted quickly at the roadside, looped Bonnie's reins to a nearby fence post, and with everybody's attention directed toward the magistrate she seized the opportunity to cross the road and follow in his wake amid all the getting-up and stirring and making-way that his two bodyguards were creating. In the ring

Daniel and the others had come to the ropes, seeing that something was seriously amiss. Kate's guess was the same as everybody else's, which was that someone had lodged a complaint against the prize fight, compelling the law to take action to stop it from taking place. Edging her way through while all were straining their necks and taking no notice of her, she thought that the magisterial interruption was providential, for with the mill canceled, Daniel could return home earlier and be more than ready for whatever move he might make to prevent the raid on his property.

The magistrate reached the side of the ring, and the crowd closed as everyone pushed forward to hear better, trapping Kate in the thick of it. By standing on tiptoe she did get a glimpse of what was taking place. Nothing of what was being said between the magistrate, the officials, and those in the ring reached her ears, but she and everyone else could tell what was ensuing by the arguing and gestures of appeal on one side, and on the other the stern head-shaking in refusal by the magistrate. It seemed he was not to be budged from his lawful stand, and she saw that already Daniel was climbing out of the ring with Jem and Harry to fall in and depart with Sir Geoffrey Edenfield. Now an official had climbed through the ropes into the ring to cup his hands about his mouth and bellow an announcement.

"By order of the magistrate no mill is allowed to take place today on this heath, and all are ordered to disperse quietly and peacefully." Such a tumult went up that it took several minutes to get the noise to subside enough for the rest of what he had to say. "But I have good news, too. Farmer Natton of Barsden Farm half a mile east of Lewes in Sussex has offered us one of his fields, and we shall reassemble there."

Kate then understood why Daniel and his opponent had rushed to move swiftly from the ring. All around her people leaped into activity and began to run and push and scramble to get onto the road and away in the direction of Lewes. She was almost knocked flying, but clutching at the arm of a perfect stranger she managed to save herself, and when he wrenched himself free, nothing on his mind but getting to Lewes with everyone else, she tried to make sure she did not trip on the rough grass, fearful of going down and being trampled underfoot. As it was, she was jostled and thrust at, elbowed out of the way, and kicked by racing boots pounding past. She cried out to Daniel, but there was no chance of her being heard, and helplessly she saw him borne away with Sir Geoffrey in a swift equipage matched by that owned by the patron of the other combatant, whose second and bottle-holder followed in a phaeton while Harry and Jem in the curricle drove off after them. Within minutes all four vehicles were lost from sight, lengths ahead of anyone else.

There was such confusion on the road. Equipages of every kind were struggling for right of way, and many were held up by those spectators climbing back into drags and barouches, carts, gigs, and other vehicles of every description. She had difficulty in getting a chance to cross the road to where she had left Bonnie, kept for several minutes to the grassy verge by the rolling wheels dashing past her and the prancing of other horses under their riders' impatient hands. When a gap came, caused by the enforced halting of all traffic by the collision of two vehicles ahead, she darted through to the other side. Then she saw that Bonnie was gone! Stolen by some rogue who had seized the chance to take four-legged transport left unwatched and unguarded.

There was no time to shed futile tears about her dear mare, tired by the ride from Easthampton, being used roughly by a strange rider. She began to run into town, others running too, and she soon realized they were making for the same places as she had in mind, the inns and stables and the smithy, anywhere where a horse might be bought or hired, any center where a conveyance might have seats available. As soon as she came to any likely place the mob clamoring around it was so dense that she could not get near. It was not merely those who had been deposited at Harley Heath by stagecoach or in some other kind of commercial vehicle who wanted to ride or drive the distance to Lewes, but also people whose horses were wearied by long journeys and not in a fit state to be driven on again without sufficient rest. Those spectators who had filled the wagons were also at a loss for the same reason, and most angry and impatient of all were owners of equipages who had been in earlier, minor accidents in the crush approaching the site of the mill and could not use them again until wheels were replaced or shafts repaired.

When one landlord came to an upper window to shout down that every horse and vehicle on his premises had gone she darted on to the next place, but so did all the others until the mob grew and in some cases became out of hand when tempers flared and scuffling broke out. Realizing there was no chance at all for her, she left the quarreling scenes behind her and set off along the road to Lewes. She was not alone. Tramping along were hundreds of men from all stations in life as far as the eye could see. Gold in their pockets was no use to the well-dressed gentlemen, who had to plod along beside the plowboy and the merchant, and many of those of higher rank were portly, looking as if they had not walked farther than from a door into a carriage for years. But such was the passion for the prize fight that it was as if every man was consumed with a madness that would make him get to the new site unless he dropped from exhaustion on the way.

Whenever a farm came into sight men would break away from the general stream and swarm toward it to outbid each other before the bewildered farmer, but Kate made no attempt to compete, knowing it would be useless, and reserved her energy for walking on. Those who were successful were jeered and booed by the rest, and more than once fighting broke out. The strangest vehicles, some so ancient that the wheels wobbled and straw dangled out and fell in a trail behind them, came rattling down the farm tracks onto the road to join the passing traffic that cut its way through the pedestrians, rolling on to Lewes.

Many of those passing in vehicles or on horseback gave her an eye, finding it strange or amusing or provocative to see a respectable-looking woman among so many men. Doxies and draggle-tails were ever on the outskirts of such gatherings, but a graceful, ladylike creature with her shining, fair tresses and a cool, intriguing air was a different matter. The vulgar and the crude shouted and called and whistled to her, offering their knees for a ride, there never being other space available, and making more intimate suggestions, all of which she ignored as though deaf. There were similar unacceptable offers of conditional transport from the swells and the coves, who waved their hats to her from their speeding equipages and leaned over the back to grin and wink until she was lost from their sight.

Mile after mile was covered, and when she had paced a long way she sank down on the wayside grass, aching with tiredness. Had she been fresh at the start of the walk she would not have felt so exhausted, having been strengthened by hard work in the fields and tramping long distances in her youth, but she had been up at five o'clock that morning and the ride from Easthampton had been long. In addition her riding boots had not been intended for walking, and one heel was rubbed raw. She could tell by the sticky feeling under her sole that it must be bleeding quite profusely. But she allowed herself only a few minutes before she stood up and went on again. She had to get to Daniel whatever happened.

There was still plenty of company on the road, for her pace had matched that of many others, but it had thinned out. The bulk of the traffic to Lewes had also gone by long since, but there still passed by other vehicles that had come by chance from side roads into the stream of the crowd and been commissioned on the spot with the waving of money that the drivers had been unable to resist. It was one of this hotchpotch of vehicles which happened to emerge from a track in the woods as Kate drew level with the gap in the hedge that had kept it hidden from view. It was a dog-cart with a fresh-looking young horse in the shafts and driven by a boy about fourteen years old, his schoolbooks on the empty seat beside him. She flew to the dogcart's side and since the boy had slowed for entry into the road it needed only the slightest of pulls by him on the reins to bring the horse to a standstill when she made her appeal.

"Please let me hire your dogcart! I have to get to the mill that has been forced to reassemble outside Lewes. It is a matter of great urgency that has nothing to do with the fight itself." Hastily she pulled wide the strings of her reticule and took out the three sovereigns she had brought with her in case of emergency. "This is all I have, but my husband will give you more if only you will get me there."

She was pushed aside in a rush of men. Others had sighted the boy and the vehicle and he was surrounded on all sides, his horse nervously rolling its eyes and tossing its head at the sudden crush. Sums far in excess of her three sovereigns were shouted at the boy and purses were jingled in front of him.

"Wait a moment! Gentlemen! Please!" The boy spoke in quiet, cultured tones, which made her guess that he was the son of a local squire or some other gentleman of similar rank, and he looked toward her. "You mentioned a matter of some urgency, ma'am."

Hope soared in her. "My husband is one of the combatants, but I have to deliver a message to him about a threat to his property."

"Who are you then, ma'am?"

She answered with a quick little rush of pride. "Mrs. Daniel Warwyck."

The boy's serious expression was lightened by a smile. "I have followed his career with interest. I should be honored if you would allow me to drive you to the mill, Mrs. Warwyck."

Several willing hands helped her up into the seat and hats were doffed to her as the boy shook the reins to drive her on her way, her name having caused a minor sensation among those who had overheard what she had said.

"I am most grateful," she said tremulously, her relief overwhelming her. "Whatever payment—"

He interrupted her. "Let there be no talk of payment. It will not be far out of my way, and I hope your husband wins his bout today."

They talked a little more about it, the boy mentioning that Daniel's opponent, Carey Reid, was notorious for fighting foul, and then they conversed on other topics until they came at last to the site of the reassembled mill. She alighted and thanked the boy, who lifted his hat to her and drove away. She limped across the rough grass, her heel having swollen within her boot, and every step was excruciating agony. On the fringe of the gathering she came to a standstill, able to see the ring with ease, for it had been roped out at the end of a long field which sloped downward to it, enabling those at the back to see over the heads of those in front, much as if all were seated in the rows of a theater. The bout had reached its tenth round and the mood of the crowd was ominous, voices rumbling and roaring, dangerously lacking in good humor. Kate soon saw why. The information she had been given by the boy was correct, for Carey Reid was using every trick he could get away with to level Daniel and win a round. She decided she must get nearer the ring in case Daniel was able to land a knockout blow to end the fight, for in the resulting excitement she might again be cut off from him.

Forming a background to the ring was a tall hedge of considerable thickness that shut off any viewing from the next field, and no spectators had bothered to strain their necks from that direction when a fine view was offered everywhere else, which made her decide to take up her place of waiting there. Down the slope she went, tears of pain smarting behind her eyes, and with everybody's attention riveted on the ring nobody as much as glanced toward her. When she reached the hedge she saw that a swirling stream swept along behind it, but the slope of the bank was wide enough for her to make her way along and come out directly by the ring. Peering through the foliage she noted that only the two umpires and the referee in their chairs, some gentlemen, including Sir Geoffrey, and a few officials were between her and the ring, but none blocked her view. In the ring itself Jem and Harry were in one corner, Carey Reid's second and bottle-holder in the one opposite, all watching intently as Daniel and Carey milled away at each other, seemingly deaf to the crowd's din.

It was the first time she had ever witnessed a mill, and being at such close quarters she could see the state of the combatants' knuckles, the bruises and cuts and the running blood. Worst of all was the sickening thud of blows, which made her wince at the force and power behind them. Daniel fought with lips tightly closed, not uttering a word, but now and again his opponent taunted him with sneers and derision, and she was amazed how coolly he ignored the jibes, knowing how quickly he could lose his temper out of the ring, but in it he seemed a different man.

Suddenly Carey, taking advantage of a heavy punch that had found its mark, got Daniel against the ropes and held him as if he had been screwed into a vise. "You—Champion of England! Ha!" Carey's huge fist rammed him in the ribs. "There's one mark against it. And another!" Again and again his fist took its toll.

Great shouts of protest were going up from the huge assemblage. "Foul! Foul!" Kate clutched at a branch as if for support, terrified that Daniel's ribs would break under the onslaught. The struggle taking place was awful to see, but suddenly Daniel managed to free himself. Even as he did so, however, Carey's knee came up and on a vicious toss of pain Daniel went flying backward to crash down upon the turf. The round was over.

"Cowardly! Foul! Have the umpires no eyes! Foul! Foul! Foul!"

While Carey strutted to his corner, ignoring the boos and abuse of the infuriated crowd, Jem and Harry rushed to help Daniel to his feet, but he thrust aside their assistance and rose unaided. In his corner he sat on Harry's knee, head lowered and white-faced, while Jem sponged him down and gave him low-voiced, urgent advice to which he nodded before taking a swig from the bottle that Harry gave him, and swilling the water out again.

The half minute was up and both men went to the mark again. Daniel's ferocity was controlled and deadly, for he was set on teaching his antagonist a lesson for his temerity, and so swiftly did his fists lash out at Carey's face and head that for a few minutes it was like that of a puppet being jerked back persistently on a string. The blood spurted and one of Carey's eyebrows split in twain. Carey reeled, rallied, and bull-like rushed back in with a kind of flying leap that defeated a parrying move and bore Daniel back against a stake. With a different trick Daniel's neck was caught on the ropes and the full weight of Carey's body was on him so that he was in danger of choking.

With a roar of disapprobation, which must have been heard for miles, the spectators sprang to their feet, their expectation of fair play outraged, for there were few who cared to see a good fight ruined by such knavery in the ring. Something of their snapped patience got through to Carey, who let Daniel slip from the ropes, but managing again to put in another foul blow before he fell to the grass.

It was the final straw. The ropes of the outer ring, which kept a sizable area of space around the inner ropes of the fighting area, were broken down as spectators swarmed forward. The whips leaped to their duties, lashing out to keep back the invasion, but fighting broke out at once, their attempts to restore order acting like a spark to tinder. Kate, who had been in terror that she was about to see Daniel strangled by the ropes before anyone made a move to help him, had burst out from the hedge to go to his aid with her own hands, and now found the melee bearing down on her as it closed in upon the ring itself. Her retreat cut off she pressed close to the chairs of the umpires, who were arguing between themselves over the previous round, and in the raised tempers of everyone and the general excitement none paid her any attention. When the combatants took up their positions again both umpires sprang to their feet, demanding that the crush about the ring be cleared, which was an order more easily given than carried out, and Kate moved with them, fearful of being swept away by the nearby tide of scuffling men. She narrowly escaped being knocked by the umpires' chairs, which were sent crashing over as one of the whips fell back against them after a thrust in the chest from a maddened spectator.

The twelfth round of the dreadful bout began. Carey could no longer see out of one eye, so profuse was the flow of blood from his cut brow, and Daniel was obviously set for a speedy knockout, hitting with right and left punches that landed with deadly accuracy, but both he and Carey were hampered in attack and defense by the small space of no more than three feet in circumference left to them in which to fight. On all sides they were closed in by the yelling mob, those nearest to them pushing and shoving and dealing out their own blows to keep out of the way of the combatants, many afraid of receiving a chance hit intended by either Daniel or Carey for each other. Both combatants were wet with the sweat pouring down them, suffering visibly under the strain put upon them by the tight wall of humanity around them and the deprivation of air. Carey no longer dared make use of foul play and fought strongly, but he was on the defensive all the time and it was obvious that Daniel was waiting for the moment to plant the final and telling blow.

Then behind Kate there came a great wave of movement by those who had forgotten all else in their fighting against the whips, and she and the umpires and others standing by them were swept forward like flotsam on water. Kate found herself propelled abruptly and unexpectedly to the forefront of those immediately encircling the combatants. In the same instant by the sheerest chance Daniel caught sight of her face out of the corner of his eye. His concentration snapped for no more than a second or two, but it was enough. Carey took full advantage, bringing his fist round to land a mighty punch on the point of Daniel's jaw. Down Daniel went as though poleaxed to lie completely senseless. Carey had won.

So unpopular was the win that many among the wilder element in the crowd took out their resentment against anything that they came across as they made their way back along the lanes. Fences were torn up, windows smashed, and stones and bricks were thrown at anything that moved.

But Kate knew nothing of that as she sat waiting in the farmhouse parlor of the man who had loaned the field. Upstairs boards creaked as Jem attended to Daniel, the rumble of their voices sounding as they talked. She guessed Daniel was being given an account of all that had occurred.

With her swollen foot in clean linen bandages stretched out before her, she sat with her elbow on the arm of the chair, her fingers propping her forehead. Never would she forget Daniel's startled look of disbelief when he had spotted her. When he had gone down Jem had been first to him, dropping down to one knee on the flattened grass, but when she came at once to follow suit he had held her back with an outstretched arm, rejecting her willingness to help in the angry misery of disappointment.

"Ye have lost him this fight. Ye have set him back from the championship as surely as if ye'd pushed him downhill."

But Harry had darted to her without making any attempt to assist Jem, and to him she poured out why she was there and what was plotted against Daniel. He frowned deeply and then gave a nod that showed he was now in charge. Then he took action, handing the hamper and valise with Daniel's clothes to a ring assistant, telling him to take his place with Jem for the time being. Jem was then helping to lift Daniel onto a hurdle that two bearers had brought forward. Harry again had a word with Kate.

"Go with Jem when he takes Daniel to the farmhouse. I'll get there as soon as I can." With that he promptly disappeared into the crowd, which was beginning to thin out, except where skirmishes and fisticuffs were still going on.

Barely able to walk, she limped after Jem and the ring assistant, who went on either side of the swaying hurdle with its burden, and she bit deep into her lip to bear the pain. As Jem turned to steady the hurdle and make sure Daniel did not roll from it as the bearers stepped across a narrow brook to the grass verge of the lane beyond, he happened to see her. For a moment he made to go on, but then he changed his mind and broke away to come back toward her.

"What have ye done to yer ankle, Mrs. Warwyck? Sprained it?"

"No, Jem." Briefly she explained what it was and in answer to a further question told him all that she had previously related to Harry. Jem looked uncomfortable and touched his forelock in salute to her.

"My apologies, ma'am. I spoke roughly to ye in what was left of the ring and I should have known it were no idle folly that brought ye here. Did Harry say what he was about? No? Well, I reckon we must leave him to worry about it all for the time being. Pray allow me." He stooped to sweep her up in his arms, and after a spate of swift striding to catch up with Daniel again he carried her level with the hurdle until Daniel's signs of coming round caused him to set her on her feet again.

"Put the hurdle down gentle-like," he instructed the bearers, and he was ready when Daniel sat bolt upright, fists raised, and began to struggle to his feet, tossing aside the blanket that covered him. Holding him by the shoulders Jem sought to keep him where he was. "The mill's over, boy. It ended with the twelfth round."

Daniel, still dazed, shook his head as if to clear it. "Did he get me when I leveled him?"

"No, Dan. It weren't like that."

Now Daniel's gaze became sharply focused on his trainer. "Did Carey floor me out of my senses?"

"I fear that's the case, lad."

Daniel leaped to his feet, reeled, and would have fallen if Jem had not thrown his arms about him. Then he saw Kate, and the memory of her face appearing out of that struggling mass of humanity caused his eyes to fire to a dark brilliance of fury.

"You!" he accused almost in disbelief.

She did not quail, facing him out with that cool calmness of hers that never failed to spur him with the desire to break through and master it, and he was not to know that inwardly she cried out silently in sorrow at this further breakdown of any kind of goodwill link between them.

"Take it easy, Dan," Jem urged. "Mrs. Warwyck had good reason to be here, and if ye'll just get back on that hurdle and let us get ye to the farmhouse we'll tell ye all about it."

He tried to shake off Jem's support. "There can be no acceptable reason whatever why Kate should have shown herself at the ringside. And I'll thank you to let me walk!"

"Ye're in no fit state to walk and neither is she. Get back on that hurdle and let's have no more time wasted here."

The bearers had lifted the hurdle and Daniel's first swaying step was defeated when Jem thrust him back onto it and whipped the blanket about him again. Then once more Kate was taken up in Jem's arms, and keeping abreast with Daniel, who had fallen into a brooding silence, she was carried to the farmhouse. There Jem left her to the kindly administrations of the farmer's wife while Daniel was helped upstairs to a bedroom. The woman had to cut her boot from her foot before bathing it to reduce the swelling and binding it up for her.

The clop of hooves sounded in the lane outside. Raising her head Kate saw Bonnie being led along by Harry, and joyfully she hopped into the hall. When the farmer's wife opened the door to him Kate impulsively flung herself at Harry and hugged him. "You found Bonnie!"

Instantly his arms closed hard about her and he lowered his head to press his cheek against hers. "I'm glad to do anything that makes you happy," he said huskily. Then, even as she would have withdrawn from his embrace, she was split apart from him with a start by Daniel's voice raking Harry from the top of the stairs.

"You would have done better to have come here for a discussion about this Radcliffe plot against me than to chase after a stolen mare that others could have traced for you."

Harry's face flamed and he stepped forward to address Daniel, who was fully dressed and, as he descended the flight, looked little the worse for what he had been through except for a lack of all color in his visage, the untied cravat leaving free the painful weals from the ropes on his neck, and the bandages covering his hands.

"As it happens, brother, I spotted the mare while about the very business you mention. I have enlisted some help which I know you will approve. Are you fit to travel?"

"No, he's—" Jem began, but Daniel spoke over him.

"I'm leaving immediately. Is the curricle outside?"

"Yes, it is."

Tight-faced and without a glance at Kate, Daniel strode past her and went out down the farmhouse path. Harry paid the farmer's wife for the use of the room and for the tea and other small things she had provided, while Jem collected up the hamper and emptied valise and brought them downstairs. Kate would have hopped out to the waiting curricle, but Jem thrust what he had gathered up into Harry's hands and once more carried her.

Bonnie she did not see, for Harry explained as they got into the curricle that the mare had been hard-ridden and was being rubbed down and fed and watered by one of the farmer's hands, who would stable her overnight and ride her to Easthampton on the morrow.

"That's enough talk about that mare," Daniel growled impatiently in the front seat beside Harry, who had taken the reins. "Now drive like the wind and let me hear about this assistance you say you have sought out."

Although the farmhouse that fell away behind them was situated about the same distance as Merrelton from Easthampton, Harry managed to save two miles by following a narrow cart track that the farmer had told him about, and it had the additional advantage of getting them clear of all the pedestrians and wheeled traffic that would be congesting the main routes in the immediate vicinity. Nevertheless they had not been on the road long before dusk overtook them and it was dark when they reached Honeybridge House, which was ablaze with lights. Many of those whose help Harry had enlisted had arrived before them, but even as Jassy came out to meet them other riders and more carriages loomed out of the darkness. It seemed to Kate as she entered the house that all the pugilists who had ever fought a battle had gathered there to help Daniel defend his property.

It was going to be a long night for all of them, but most of all for Kate and Jassy, who could do nothing but wait at home alone after everyone else had left. By the time a quarter of an hour had passed they knew that Daniel, Harry, and Jem, as well as the pugilists, their seconds, and anyone else connected with the milling circles who knew how to use his fists or wield a cudgel, would be concealed in every finished and half-constructed building as well as in the yard premises, waiting to deal with the intruders.

The two of them drank tea and talked, Jassy wanting every detail of what had happened to Kate during the day.

"Was it not clever of Harry to round up everybody at the mill site he could find to come and help?" she said to Kate when they were on their second pot of tea.

"I agree," Kate answered, straightening herself in her chair at the kitchen table. She had been in danger of nodding off, and indeed it was for that reason she had suggested they sit in the least comfortable chairs in the house.

Jassy smiled at her sympathetically. "Why not go and get some rest? It is pointless to sit there struggling to keep sleep at bay after all you have been through. I'll call you if anyone comes with any news of what is happening out there."

Kate allowed herself to be persuaded, but decided against going to lie on the bed, certain that to close her eyes on a pillow would make it impossible to wake again in her present state of exhaustion. Instead she went without a candle into the drawing room and lay down upon the sofa. But hardly had she pushed a cushion into shape under her head and was surrendering blissfully to the embrace of sleep when she heard a slight sound outside the window. She was instantly wide awake and alert, her heart beating a tattoo of alarm. Somebody had brushed against the bush that grew there and some of the branches had snapped back again. Had Claudine been mistaken in thinking that the damage was to be wrought on Daniel's other property, but instead was Honeybridge House to be the target?

The inside shutters were closed over every window and the doors both front and back were bolted fast at Daniel's instructions, but she and Jassy were in a vulnerable position in that isolated house and quite out of earshot of any of those who would have come to their aid. Silently she rose from the sofa and went across to take down from the wall a cutlass that Daniel's maternal great-grandfather had used in the battle of Blenheim, and she slid it from its sheath. The edge was fierce and gleaming, and it flashed in the darkness as she settled her grip on the hilt and crept toward the kitchen. Jassy was washing the cups at the sink and she turned to look over her shoulder with a smile.

"I thought I told you to get some sleep—" Her voice trailed off as she saw Kate put a finger to her lips and limp, cutlass in hand, to turn out the lamp and then listen at the kitchen door. In fear she fumbled in the blackness to Kate's side and asked her questions in a whisper. "What is it? Is someone there?"

"I believe I heard somebody at the front of the house. The kitchen shutters will have hidden the lamplight from outside, but we cannot take any risks. I want them to think we are in bed and asleep."

At that second the latch lifted and there came the thump of a weight testing the bolts of the door. Kate clapped a hand over Jassy's mouth to stop her from screaming out, and drew her farther back into the kitchen. "Not a sound," Kate whispered, taking her hand away. "Get the poker. You can do some damage with that if the need arises."

"Listen!" Jassy breathed in terror. In the direction of the dining room there came the tinkling sound of glass being broken. "They're coming in!"

"Not if I can help it," Kate answered. Resolutely she went into the dining room, and as she entered, a heavy blow smashed open the shutters, sending them flying inward and silhouetting two men, dark against the lesser darkness of the starlit night outside, who were preparing to clamber into the house. Like an echo there came similar smashings from the kitchen, and she did not need Jassy's scream of warning to let her know an onslaught from both sides had begun.

"Get back!" She swung the cutlass, making the air hiss.

The men's surprise at the unexpected sight of her made them hesitate only briefly, and then boots came on the windowsill and hands grabbed the frame. The cutlass flashed and came down across the toe of a boot. The man's scream as he fell back created confusion among those with him, and when she lunged at the second intruder he leaped back down again out of range. She slammed the shutters closed again and as Jassy came to her side she snatched the poker from the girl's hands and used it to wedge them closed.

"They're breaking down the kitchen door!" Jassy was hysterical with panic.

Kate, her bandaged foot sliding on the polished floor, charged past her back to the kitchen in time to see half a dozen intruders bursting into it. She slashed the air with the cutlass like a woman demented.

"Out of this house! Out! Out! Out!"

One part of her mind registered the faces before her, stupid and thick-witted as much as brutal, and they drew back sharply before the deadly threat of her weapon. Then too late came Jassy's cry of warning. Powerful arms grabbed her from behind and a blow across her wrist made the cutlass drop from her nerveless fingers and go spinning across the floor.

She had no chance to see the face of her assailant, for she was hustled forward out through the door into the garden, her mouth clamped shut by a hard hand, and behind her came Jassy, held captive in a similar manner. A torch was lighted with a flare of brightness, which touched with a flickering, orange glow those who ran to light from it the brands that they held, and it was easy to guess the fate that was intended for Honeybridge House. Desperately she struggled, but it was to no avail. The first flare was thrown into the house, streaming through the darkness like a comet, and was followed by another. It was then that everything changed.

With a complete lack of speech normal to fighting in the ring, a wave of pugilists appeared on all sides to descend silently and inexorably upon the intruding force. Kate's captor was wrenched from her, and there came the awful crack of a breaking jaw as a fist smashed home. All around punches were being rammed into ribs and stomachs and whirled into faces to close eyes, knock out teeth, and flatten noses in a splashing of blood.

Kate, who had fallen to one knee on the grass, scrambled up and shouted to Jassy, who had also been released and stood weeping helplessly. "Come on! We must put out the fire!"

In the kitchen a flare had set light to a cupboard. Kate snatched up a bucket of water kept by the sink and threw it onto the flames, dousing them in a gust of smoke. Jassy had followed her into the house and Kate put the bucket into her hands.

"Pump!"

Leaving Jassy at the sink, pumping frantically at the handle, Kate seized a birch broom and ran into the dining room. The broken shutters swung on their hinges, the poker on the floor, and the curtains were ablaze as was the carpet. With the broom handle she managed to unhook the curtain rod, which came crashing down in a searing flutter of flames, and she snatched up a rug in front of the untouched fireplace and smothered it. Then she attacked the whole spread of fire across the carpet with her broom, pushing the dining room table out of the way and knocking the chairs aside. Coughing and choking from the smoke she grabbed the bucket from Jassy when she appeared with it, tossed the water on the flames, and hurled it back at her again.

"More! More!"

When Daniel ran into the house a little later he found her kneeling in the blackened, smoking room, her head bent to her knees in complete exhaustion, her half-burned broom beside her, and the fire out.

"Kate!"

She raised her streaked face and looked at him with smoke-reddened eyes. "I'm sorry I made you lose the fight," she said in a throat-sore voice. Then, the last atom of strength ebbing from her, she keeled over and lay stretched out face downward at his feet.

Chapter 12

Kate slept the clock round, opened her eyes briefly, and then fell asleep again for many more hours. When she finally awoke fully, Jassy appeared with a tray of hot chocolate, propped her up with pillows, and sat on her bed to recount all that had happened.

"In every place where those felons crept in they found the pugilists and their allies waiting for them. Jem says he and the others leaped out from the shadows at them and it was like all Hades let loose, just as it was here in the garden. Daniel has had a Merrelton magistrate brought in and those who were knocked out or failed to get away are being charged with breaking and entering with intent to willful damage. All of them come from the stews and dens of London, and a go-between arranged matters. We can all guess that it was Alexander Radcliffe who was behind it, but he cannot be accused without proof."

"How can anyone be sure that these men are not withholding the proof needed?"

Jassy gave a little laugh. "Jem says he has never seen so many scared fellows in his life, and each would have betrayed his own brother to get out of the punishment they received."

"What sort of monster is Alexander Radcliffe that he would let these men set fire to a house where he knew only you and I would be?"

"It was a condition of payment that no bloodshed should take place, and if everything had gone according to plan you and I would have been taken captive from our beds and left blindfolded in the garden while torches burned Honeybridge House to the ground."

"How is the man whose foot I slashed?" Kate asked faintly, the horror of the moment sweeping back to her.

"He lost his toes, but you must not plague your conscience over him. He has a bad record of robbery with violence, and those in charge of justice are relieved to have him under lock and key at last."

"And the house?"

"Only a little damage to the kitchen, because the flares fell on the flagstones and you doused the flames quickly, but the dining room is a different story. The whole room will have to be redecorated and partly repaneled, as well as having some floorboards replaced, but after it was all cleaned up Daniel locked the door on it. He says he cannot spare carpenters from other vital work for the time being. Only glaziers are replacing the broken windows."

Kate went cold inside, remembering how she had called in workmen without Daniel's authority to make changes to the workshops and build her cupboards and a partition. It had not occurred to her that she was doing anything of which he would disapprove, and none had challenged her orders, obviously thinking they came through her from Daniel himself.

"Was there no tea or ale served to the workmen while I lay here sleeping?"

"Young Ned carried on with the two other boys in your absence, and some of the men themselves gave a helping hand."

"What—what did Daniel have to say?"

Jassy looked uncomfortable. "I fear he was far from pleased."

Kate guessed it was a tremendous understatement and she knew that once again she would have to face up to his anger and disapproval. In the meantime she would drink another cup of chocolate and fortify herself for the ordeal ahead, for it would be best to go to his office at the yard and get it over without delay.

Later she was to find him in his office, but at that moment he was on horseback, waiting by a bridle path in the depths of the woods near Radcliffe Hall, which he knew Claudine followed on certain mornings when she set out to take a solitary ride across the Downs.

He saw her before she sighted him, her honey-colored riding habit a pale flicker between the trunks of the trees, and he rode forward to meet her. Her mouth twisted in a mocking smile.

"Behold the conquering hero! You and your low prize-ring acquaintances made short shift of those who tried to attack your property."

"Your warning came in the nick of time."

"Warning? What warning?" Her look of feigned innocence was a taunt in itself.

"Nobody can overhear us here. You need not be afraid to admit your good deed to me." He had wheeled his horse about and he brought it alongside hers.

She showed her small, white teeth as they rode along together. "I do nothing that is not for my own purpose. It suits me to watch Easthampton grow. Unlike Alexander and the rest of his cronies I welcome its development. Merrelton is an ugly, old town and has never appealed to me, but I look forward to the new shops of Easthampton, the theater, and the concert hall. Had you a decent habitation I might even be tempted to pay you a call when all the place is built."

"I intend to have the most beautiful house in the entire south of England." It was the first time he had mentioned to her what he had planned for himself alone. Although others knew of it, he rarely spoke about it, realizing that it would be a long time yet before work could be started on it, but in his own mind he had every room planned and never a day went past that he did not look toward the green hill with its handsome trees and picture his future home there.

"And where is this house to stand? By Mr. Brown's bathing machines?"

There were times when he longed to strike her for her provocative insolence. His face tightened, the cheekbones standing out. "No, ma'am. The setting of the hill above Easthampton shall complement the house."

She was impressed by the choice of site and showed it, raising her eyebrows. "You have good taste, sir," she said with marked condescension. "I only hope that it all works out for you."

He grinned at her with as little mirth as her smile had had for him. "I mean to get everything I want."

"That's easier said than done." Her riding crop flashed and her horse was away, galloping off through the clearing trees to the gentle slopes of the Downs beyond. He was after her instantly, and the two of them rode like the wind, his horse the stronger, and he could easily have drawn ahead, but he kept at her side and she laughed with exhilaration as they leaped streams and brooks, cleared a low stone wall, and thundered on. Once they scattered a whole flock of sheep, which fled before their fierce approach like dandelion seeds blown by the wind. When they finally reined in to rest their mounts it was by a disused windmill, which commanded a magnificent view in all directions, and there she dismounted quickly, tossed aside her riding hat and flung herself down on the grass.

He was beside her at once, scooping her around the waist and locking her to him with mouth and arms. Their kissing was frantic, wild and abandoned, but when he had torn open the buttons of her jacket and sought to discover more of her she struck him aside with all her strength and scrambled to her feet. Against the old stones of the mill she leaned panting, her fingers refastening the buttons with trembling haste.

"No," she gasped. "I told you before. No!"

He advanced slowly toward her with arms outstretched to bar any direction in which she might run, his dark hair blowing about his head in the wind, and his eyes were wicked with amusement. "No one would hear you scream for miles around."

"You wouldn't dare!"

"That sounds remarkably like a challenge."

His inexorable pace toward her did not lessen, and she breathed deeply and with real fear. It had taken all her will to break from his touch upon her, the molding hand, the seeking, tender fingertips, and if he put his mouth on hers again she would be lost beyond recall. Her body would answer his, and the dark, dangerous fire in the pit of her stomach, which burned whenever she was within sight and sound of him, would flare up and consume her in its blaze. Then how would she be able to wed gentle, quietly spoken Lionel, who looked at her without passion and read love poems to her written by other men when he should have expressed his devotion for her in his own words. Sometimes she thought it was because he was so unlike Daniel, the reverse in every way, that she had sought him out as her refuge.

Daniel was almost upon her. "No!" She bolted from him, evading his grasp, and had he not been between her and the horses she would have darted toward her mount. Instead she was forced to run in the other direction, the downward slope of the hill giving speed to her feet. Then her toe caught in a rabbit hole and down she crashed to roll over and over until she came at last to the bottom of the hill, face downward on the grass. He had followed, and she heard him come to a halt beside her. With nervous defiance she looked up over her shoulder and saw him standing tall and dark against the cloud-tumbled sky, his elbows jutting, his fists resting on his hips as he regarded her with that same overwhelming confidence in his power over her.

When he crouched down she gave a half cry and would have rolled away from him, but he gripped her by the arms. "It is yourself you are afraid of. You and I have been hungry for each other from the moment I set my foot on that carriage step and offered you the colors. Our coming together is as inevitable as night following day, but it will not be through rape, no matter how much it amused me to see you quail with a remarkable resignation. You shall come to me of your own free will. Marry me, Claudine."

Her emotional struggle was reflected in her face. She wanted to spit at him, yell derision, humble him, but driving against her love-hatred of him was a tidal wave of passion, inexplicable and compelling, impossible to resist. She knew herself to be drowning, going under, and out of her weakness she made one last totally feminine protest, entirely at variance with her normal strength of character.

"I am betrothed to Lionel. I cannot marry you. Alexander would never allow it."

"We shall elope. When the knot is tied none can part us."

"Where? When?" She threw herself against him in her eagerness, all pride gone in the manner that he had long awaited, and he lifted her up on her feet, holding her to him.

"I'll ride into Merrelton today, obtain a license, and arrange everything. It shall be tomorrow at St. Cuthbert's Church at any hour when you can get away without arousing suspicion or causing pursuit. Can you manage that?"

She gave a nod. "Olivia and Alexander both have their own plans for the day that do not include me. I can get away easily shortly after noon."

"I'll meet you with a carriage in the lane at the end of the bridle path where we rode today. We'll be married at two o'clock."

Again they kissed wildly, her arms about his neck, their mouths holding as though by a magnetic force, and had she not consented to the morrow he doubted whether he would have been able to hold back his taking of her, so savage was his need, so inflamed his senses.

They parted company on the hill slopes. She insisted that he was not to ride back with her along the bridle path as a precaution to being observed, for although she did not put it into words, she wanted nothing to prevent their union now that the die was cast. She rode away from him, exultant and charged with excitement, and it was only then that she realized that they had not talked of anything else except the preliminaries to their mating as if neither could look beyond that point, the future being left to revolve about their marriage bed as best it might. She gave her clear, trilling laugh, knowing she was facing a stormy passage rent with strife and temper and the clash of his personality with hers, but with it all she felt liberated. Everything that had seemed important to her, rank, position in society, an avoidance of scandal and the meticulousness of etiquette in all matters, had lost all significance. With her money she could free him in his turn from all the debts he had inevitably incurred through the building of Easthampton, and leave him only the profit to be gained. Best of all, there need be no wait for the beautiful house he wanted on the green sea hill. She would give it to him as a wedding gift.

She was still smiling to herself when she rode through the gates of Radcliffe Hall. Daniel had not mentioned love and neither had she, but she guessed he was a man who had never yet declared his heart's love for a woman and he would choose his time. A delicious shiver of aroused anticipation went down her spine. There would be no soft words, no moon-dipped meanderings, no petaled whisperings, but a volcanic statement of a true man's love for his woman, ancient as the tongue of Adam, ecstatic and dynamic, and with an echo that would pass into all eternity.

It was with something of a shock that she saw Lionel going up the steps into the ornate entrance where Olivia had made an appearance. She had completely forgotten he had been invited to luncheon, and not a single thought of hers had touched him since the moment she had sighted Daniel riding to meet her along the bridle path. Although normally her conscience did not trouble her, she did feel some slight remorse at the upset her elopement would cause him, for he was a sensitive man, easily pained, one of the few people to whom she had always shown consideration and who had never seen her claws unsheathed. Some tenderness stirred her, and when he looked round, having heard the clip-clop of her horse's hooves, she was struck as always by the remarkable handsomeness of his aesthetic features, which with his tanned skin and curly, fair hair, gave him a golden look, almost god-like, reminding her once more of a statue she once saw in Paris of Apollo.

He smiled, innocent of the treachery she planned, and hastened back down the steps with a swirl of his crimson greatcoat and a flash of polished black boots to come forward and help her dismount.

"My dear Claudine. Such news! A new book of Lord Byron's poems came by post today. I have them in my pocket and shall read them to you this afternoon."

She knew she would miss his readings in time to come. In spite of having cast some scorn upon them in a moment of pique, she did enjoy listening with her eyes shut to his fine voice, which could make every word come alive with meaning, and she had often thought that had he been born to a humbler station in life he would have made a splendid actor. Men courted women in different ways, as she knew well enough, and it was no fault of Lionel's that the restrained society in which they moved and his gentlemanly upbringing, which caused him to put her on a pedestal, forced him to hide his own more basic feelings for her behind the poetry of Byron and other poets of the day.

"I shall look forward to hearing them," she said, responding to his pleasure, and she tucked her arm into his as they went up the steps together into the house.

Alexander had come into the hall to join his wife in greeting their guest, and he looked askance at Claudine. "You are late in from your ride today. How far did you go?"

Suddenly she knew how thankful she was going to be to get away from Alexander's jealous and possessive questionings. The amusement of pulling him this way and that with her moods and pouts and playful glances had long since waned, and the scene that had occurred on the night of Olivia's visit to Daniel in the cottage had stayed between them, raw and unhealed, and it had suited her to keep it that way.

"I rode up to Bambury windmill," she answered. "It is a view to be seen at all seasons of the year, but now, with spring not two weeks distant, there is a touch of green in all the earth hues. I could have spent all day there if it had been possible."

"Would that I could have been there with you," he said, low-voiced. He was safe in speaking thus to her, Lionel and Olivia having gone into the library and out of earshot.

Her smile was cruel. "La, brother-in-law. Only my betrothed would have had any right to be with me in such a lonely spot."

He watched her prance on light steps up the great staircase, bound for her room to change out of her riding habit into a day dress for luncheon. Her movements were calculated to provoke and punish him.

Chapter 13

Kate faced Daniel across the desk in his office. He had invited her to sit down, and she seated herself with her own peculiar grace. He had the courtesy to ask if she felt rested after all she had been through, and if her heel was better.

"Much better, thank you," she replied. "I was able to wear a shoe again this morning."

"I'm pleased to hear it."

He was being excessively polite to her, not what she had expected at all, and she feared it boded ill for her, but she said what she had to say. "I came to discuss the serving of tea and ale to the workmen. I hope you will let it continue."

"I am assured by Hardy and Tanner that the scheme has had good effect. I am agreeable to its being continued, but since the running of it went smoothly enough in your absence I see no reason why you should appear there each day."

In her relief that he was not going to put a stop to the arrangements she leaned forward in her chair and spoke eagerly. "But I like to be there. It is necessary to have someone in charge, and I—"

He interrupted her. "There is open house for you at my home for as long as it suits you to stay, but that license does not extend to my business premises."

She drew her lower lip under her teeth. "Is that because of the alterations I had done?"

"The partition and cupboards and so forth in the warehouse were not essential, but I see that they go towards the efficiency of the project, and I will say nothing about what was done there in view of the good results reported to me, but"—here his voice and his eyes grew hard—"after all I said to you on a previous occasion that you should have dared to take matters into your own hands over the conditions of the workshops is another matter. You are never to set foot on these premises again."

The rose tint in her cheeks deepened painfully. It would have been easier to bear a slap in the face than his crisp dismissal. She got up from the chair. "Do you care nothing for the health of your workmen?"

He eased himself up to his feet and went to open the door for her. "I care about seeing Easthampton being made ready for the first influx of summer visitors," he replied. "Nothing else matters."

In the doorway she paused to look him full in the face. "You're a heartless man, Daniel Warwyck. No good will come of sacrificing everything to your ambition."

"Allow me to concern myself over that."

It was a second rebuff. She went abruptly from the office and hurried down the outside steps. The office door closed before she was a tenth of the way down the flight.

He was late home to dinner that evening, but they waited for him and were informed that he had been to Merrelton. With the dining room being closed Kate had had the table, sideboard, and chairs moved into another of the downstairs rooms, which previously had been sparsely furnished and little used, and he remarked approvingly on the improvisation when they went in to take their places. She thought as she ladled out the soup into plates that Daniel looked well satisfied with his expedition, a secret pleasure in the corners of his mouth, and his mood was affable and relaxed, his laughter quick and ready.

When she served coffee in the drawing room afterward, which Daniel and Harry preferred to the more fashionable cup of tea at that hour, he was impatient for all to be served, and when it was poured he handed it out himself to Jassy and his brother and Jem. Then, when Kate had settled back on the sofa with her coffee, he put his own aside untasted and made his announcement.

"What I have to tell you all is for your ears alone and must not go beyond these four walls. Tomorrow at noon I am going to marry Claudine Clayton secretly at St. Cuthbert's Church."

The cup and saucer dropped from Kate's nerveless fingers in a splash of scalding coffee and smashed china. Jassy rushed for a cloth and Kate stood to look down helplessly as her skirt was rubbed dry while Harry picked up the pieces of broken china and mopped the carpet himself with a second cloth that Jassy had thrown him.

"That was careless of me," Kate said shakily. She had suffered no harm, the layers of petticoats having protected her, but warm wetness had seeped through to cling against her limbs, and she gave her skirt a little shake to free it.

"I nearly dropped my cup meself," Jem said with a grunt. "Ye're out of yer head, Dan."

Unexpectedly Harry spoke up in his brother's defense, his own reaction to the news being exuberant and laudatory. "I think Daniel is a lucky devil. She's a fascinating beauty and none can say otherwise. Congratulations, Daniel." He shook his brother heartily by the hand. "She bewitched you long ago at Brighton, and if ever a man has pursued the woman of his choice you have. I wish you great joy in your love for each other and a long and happy life together."

Daniel was warmly appreciative and slapped him on the shoulder. "I thank you, brother. It is true what you say. Destiny plays strange tricks. From my first sight of Claudine I meant to have her and no other. She has felt the same, but circumstances have been against us and are still against us. That is why we must be married without Radcliffe's knowledge, because even if he and his wife were not her legal guardians they would do everything in their power to prevent her marrying me." He grinned widely. "Will you stand with me and be my best man?"

"Gladly!" Again Harry pumped his hand and they laughed together in shared jocularity.

The other three watched them in silence, and although Daniel looked expectantly toward Jem, no congratulatory salutations were forthcoming. "Come now, old friend," he prompted good-humoredly. "Let me have your blessing."

"I said it before and I say it again," Jem said stolidly. "Ye're out of yer head. I know ye better than if ye were my own son and through all the years ye couldn't have meant more to me, and so I can't make no pretense. The lady in question is, I have heard, betrothed to Mr. Attwood up at the Grange, and a promise broken to one will be broken to another. Let her marry him. She ain't meant for ye."

Daniel was in too jubilant a mood to be annoyed by Jem's attitude. He merely exchanged an amused glance with Harry before making his reply. "You can bully me as much as you like in the ring, Jem, but you must leave me to make my own decision in this matter. It is true that Claudine thought she would marry Attwood, but it was for reasons that only she and I understand and which I do not care to divulge."

Jassy, who had been twisting the coffee-stained cloth in her hands, spoke up. "Does she know about Kate?"

Daniel raised his eyebrows. "What is there to know about Kate? If you mean have I told Claudine yet about the little masquerade intended for our late uncle's benefit the answer is no, but she will hear all about it in good time, just as she will learn everything else that has happened to us as a family."

"Are you bringing her back to live at Honeybridge House then?" Jassy persisted, stony-faced.

"Naturally. Not for a few days, though. I thought from the church we would go on to London where it should be easy enough to evade Radcliffe and anybody else he cares to send in pursuit of us. I'll bring my bride home at the end of next week."

"Why don't you wait until you have built your big house for her?"

"You know that cannot be started for a long time yet."

"Well, I don't want her here." Jassy ignored Kate's warning touch on her arm. "Miss Clayton is rich, isn't she? She could buy you a grand mansion somewhere near and you could live there with her."

Daniel's good humor and patience went together. "What wealth Claudine has is of no interest to me. I'll have nothing bought on my behalf. What is more, Easthampton House shall be built in my own good time and out of the profits of my own efforts. In the meantime you and Kate and Harry and Jem can go on living under this roof, but Claudine and I will keep to one part of it and the rest of you to the other. It is large enough for all of us to live independently and harmoniously without forever getting in each other's way."

Jassy's face had not changed its expression. "Jem is right. You're out of your head. Don't expect me to speak to her, that's all. Because I won't! Never!"

She cast aside the cloth and flounced from the room. An uncomfortable silence followed, during which Kate bent to retrieve the dropped cloth. Harry forced a laugh.

"Jassy will come round. Don't take any notice of her, Daniel. Let you and I go out to The Running Hare and crack a bottle or two. You ought to have some kind of celebration on your last night of bachelorhood."

"Just as long as nobody suspects the reason why," Daniel joked.

Harry put a finger against the side of his nose and they laughed again, easily this time, Daniel's spirits restored. Before leaving they invited Jem to join them, but when he was on the point of refusing, the thought of drinking to what he considered to be Daniel's downfall abhorrent to him, he changed his mind and accepted. It was his duty as Daniel's trainer to watch what he drank and to keep him sober, and in this case duty must come before all else.

In her bedroom Jassy went to the window at the sound of the

gate clicking behind them, and when she saw Jem with her brothers she clenched her hands at what she believed to be his treacherous betrayal of all he had said earlier. Did nobody care that if was Kate who would have made Daniel the best wife in the world? Was it only she who had guessed that Kate loved him? With a heavy sigh she went out of her room, intending to go downstairs again where she expected to find her, when she saw a chink of light under a door. Kate had come upstairs. Crossing to it, she tapped with her knuckles on the panel.

"Kate? Are you there? May I come in?"

No reply came, but Jassy turned the knob and entered. Then she gave a gasp of dismay. Kate was lying face downward on her bed, shaking with sobs. Kate, who never cried, never gave in, never faced anything without courage, had broken down completely under the knowledge that on the morrow she was to lose Daniel forever.

"Kate, Kate. Don't weep. Oh, please don't weep so dreadfully." Jassy rushed to the bedside and knelt there, but Kate's terrible sorrowing went on unrelieved, her face within the crook of her arms, and the sobs wrenched from the depths of her soul and did not cease.

So long did she weep that Jassy became nervous, fearing that Kate might die before her eyes, for she had heard of people dying of broken hearts. Again and again she tried to make Kate lift her head or ease her grief. When all persuasion failed Jassy sat quiet for a little while. Then she said:

"When did you first know you loved Daniel?"

Hearing his name spoken had some effect. Kate stirred, moved, and slowly rolled over onto her back where she lay, one arm upflung above her head on the pillow, the tears still pouring unceasingly from the corners of her eyes down her cheeks.

"From the moment he bid for me in the market of Brighton," she answered in choked tones. "Not that I recognized it as being love that I felt then. I only knew that I thought him the most splendid man I had ever seen and that he wished to purchase me seemed like a miracle out of my wildest dreams. Then when he spoke to me afterwards I knew such a warmth in my heart towards him that gradually I began to realize it must be so much more than gratitude. When he asked me to go through that form of marriage with him I was glad to be able to do something for him in return for what he had already given me."

"Had you never been in love before? Not with anyone?"

"No. I was a stranger to its sweetness—and its agony."

"Did you hope that Daniel would love you?"

"Ah, I hoped. Yet I should have known from his attitude towards me from the first, the impersonal courtesy and consideration, that he felt nothing for me and would never come to love me as I already loved him."

Jassy took Kate's hand that was resting on the bed into her own. "You will get over it. There will be someone else for you one day. I loved Charlie and thought for a while that I would have died for him, but I soon recovered from that and so will you."

Kate rolled her head round to look at her with a trembling of the lips that could have been a faint attempt at a smile. Jassy was not to know that she was thinking how different was the first love of an innocent adolescent to that of a mature young woman with the experience of one disastrous marriage behind her and who had learned much of the ways of the world.

"It's kind of you to try to cheer me, Jassy," she said huskily.

"I'm going to fetch you a medicinal glass of brandy." The girl rose to her feet. "It is good for shock and upsets of every kind."

By the time she had poured the brandy and brought it to the foot of the stairs Kate was on her way down. "I cannot let you wait upon me as if I were ill," Kate protested bravely, drying the last tears from her cheeks with a pocket handkerchief. "And I can see that the measure you have poured is far too much."

"You are to drink every drop," Jassy insisted. "Then we can talk about how we shall manage to live under the same roof as the odious Claudine."

By the embers of the drawing room fire in the diffused light of a single, rose-shaded lamp Kate sipped the brandy while Jassy watched her solicitously. When the glass was empty Jassy took it from her with satisfaction.

"There! I'm sure you feel stronger and better already. Now

about Claudine. We could live in the eastern end of Honeybridge House, and she can install her own furniture in the western half. No matter what Daniel says about her money, he is not going to be able to stop her having her own maids to wait upon her, and in that part of the house there are basement quarters for servantry. The old butler's pantry in our part of the house will make an adequate kitchen, and you and I and Harry and Jem can use the rear staircase from there and never cross the path of Claudine or her underlings at any time of the day or night."

Before Kate could make any reply the voices of the three men returning from The Running Hare could be heard outside. She sprang up. "Daniel is home! He must not see me like this." In desperation she smoothed her fingertips under her reddened eyes, her lids swollen and heavy. "I won't have him know that I have been weeping." She gripped Jassy by the shoulders. "Promise me you'll never tell what you know. Swear on our friendship that you'll never reveal to Daniel by word or hint or sign that I love him as I do."

For Kate, who had done so much for her, Jassy gave her promise, but it was with reluctance and an uneasy conviction that she had done the wrong thing in committing herself to the secret which could now never be told, no matter what circumstances might arise. In the hall the men were entering.

"Don't worry," Jassy said quickly to Kate, who had started again and drawn back, at a loss to know which way to turn, for her retreat upstairs was quite cut off. "I will not let them come in here."

Jassy closed the drawing room door behind her as she went into the hall. Jem was as sober as when he had left the house, but Daniel and Harry showed signs of having enjoyed the outing. "Hush," she whispered, putting her finger to her lips. "Kate went upstairs soon after you left. She still needs all the rest she can get after all she went through on the night of the fire."

They nodded, said their good nights quietly, and went up to their own rooms. Jassy popped her head back into the drawing room. "It will soon be safe. Give them a little while to settle down."

Kate nodded gratefully and sat down again to wait until she could be sure of not meeting Daniel on the landing or anywhere else. The clock ticked ten minutes away and she was about to make a move when once more the door opened. She expected to see Jassy again, thinking the girl had returned to tell her that the coast was clear, but instead it was Harry, whose quick smile of pleasure showed that he had been looking for her.

"There you are. I had to talk to you on your own this night of nights, and when there was no answer from your room I confess to opening the door and looking in. I have no shame in saying that had you been asleep I should have awakened you."

She was completely bewildered. "What is so important that it could not wait until morning? I do not understand."

He came and stood close to her, his face alight with the fullness of the love he believed he had managed to conceal since he had found her again. "Surely you realize what Daniel's marriage to Claudine means to us, my beloved Kate. You are free of him. Free at last." He dropped to both knees by her and clasped her about the waist with outstretched arms. "There is no longer any reason for you to keep a barrier between us or for me to hold back my love for you." Joyously he dropped a kiss on her hands lying in her lap. "How I've longed for this hour to come."

She shrank back, snatching her hands out of range. "What are you saying? Nothing regarding the two of us has changed. Nothing at all."

His embrace was unloosened and he continued to gaze up at her with the singular sweetness of expression which so many times she had found endearing and disarming, but his words continued to puzzle her.

"Do you think I do not know why you have been at such pains to keep me at a distance? It was not only because of what Daniel might say that you thought to make me vow all sorts of foolish promises that day at Ashford."

For a passing moment she thought Jassy was not alone in guessing that she loved Daniel, but then that did not add up with Harry's confidence in his amorousness toward her. "You seem to imagine that Claudine's breaking of her vow of betrothment to

Mr. Attwood in order to marry Daniel has automatically released each one of us from promises made," she said, "but that is not the case."

He tightened his clasp on her and pulled her forward in the chair, holding her more securely, and to her bafflement he smilingly blinked his eyes once in what could only be a tender and loving reassurance that he understood more than she was prepared to say. But what could that be? What was it he imagined she had to hide? Unless—oh, no. He could not know that. Nobody knew the special knowledge that she had lived with by night and day since her cousin had passed on the information to her upon her arrival at Ashford. Yet his next words practically confirmed it.

"You have no need to be afraid. Daniel shall never learn the truth from me. It is sealed away forever."

"Tell me what it is you know," she whispered. She made no protest when he drew her from the chair down onto the floor beside him, his arms momentarily as protective as wings about her.

"I discovered the strange trick fate had played when I had been searching far and wide for you for a long time. It was the day I went to Uckfield as a last resort and sought out Farringdon Farm."

She gave a despairing moan and dropped her face into her palms. "If only you had kept away."

He smoothed her bent head with gentle fingers. "I learned when I inquired for news of you that none had seen or heard of you since the day that Jervis Farringdon had driven you off to the sale, but that he had returned feeling unwell. Two days later he was seized by pains in the chest and expired before help could be forthcoming. It did not take me long to discover the hour at which he died. The local physician confirmed it. Farringdon's death occurred the evening before you and Daniel were married at The Old Ship Hotel."

She raised her distraught face. "But the clergyman who married us had no true authority."

"On the contrary, he had never been defrocked and was an ordained minister with full rights to marry you. It was a ceremony that was legal and binding, but only I and now you know the truth of it."

"Are you sure about the Reverend Appledore? I have pinned my hopes upon the certainty that he was a cheat and a fraud."

"Then they were in vain." He was proud of how painstaking he had been. "I made inquiries through ecclesiastical records at Canterbury."

"And you'll never tell Daniel?" she implored. "He loves Claudine, and that he should have the happiness he seeks is more important to me than anything else."

"That is the first of two vows that I shall keep to my life's end," he said fervently, catching up her hand and kissing it.

Her face calmed in relief, for there had been no reluctance about making the promise, and his face shone with the vehemence of his words. "What is the second vow?"

"To love and to cherish you always as my dearest wife."

She jerked back from him, her pupils dilating. "What are you saying?"

He gave his answer eagerly. "Nobody is ever going to find out that your marriage to Daniel was lawful. Remember that the only other witness was Jem, and he has no cause to suspect the true situation in any way. As for the Reverend Appledore, he'll never cross our paths again. A few months ago he was transported to Australia for embezzlement."

She scrambled to her feet, stumbled on her skirts, and took a pace back from where he still knelt, his whole expression radiating his devotion for her. Wildly she shook her head. "It is my decision alone to give Daniel his chance to marry the girl of his choice, but for myself there is no such future. I have no right to it and there is an end to the matter."

He thought he understood her principles. "There is no need for us to go through the hypocrisy of marrying in a church. We'll go away for a few days together and tell everyone we decided on an elopement too. And we'll not stay in this house. I'll arrange to purchase one of the fine new villas going up with a view of the sea. I love you. There is nothing I would not do for you."

She stood quite still, pressing her fingertips to her eyes as she willed herself not to weep again, not for her own loss, but that she must inflict the same misery as she was suffering upon Harry. Then slowly she lowered her hands to her sides and looked at him.

"I do not love you. With all my heart I wish that it were so, but my feelings for you are bound up only in friendship and affection. It never has been and never can be anything more."

So quietly and resolutely did she speak that he was left in no doubt that she meant exactly what she said, but hope persisted and he was undeterred. "I have enough love for both of us," he declared ardently. "Did you think I had not realized that you do not feel towards me yet as I would wish? But it will come, Kate, my dearest." He moved forward on one knee and caught her about her skirts, holding her captive. "I have enough love for both of us. You were created for joy and fulfillment and you shall find it in my arms."

"No, no. I've told you. What you ask is impossible." She tried to move from him and loosen his hold, but she was powerless within his limpet-like clamp. "You are still young and do not know your own mind. Your life is before you—"

"—to share with you. You're mistaken if you take me for less than the man that I am. Never again will anything touch the importance of your telling me now that you will be mine. Trust me to show you the path to loving me as I love you."

The emotional stress was tearing her to shreds, and she thrust at him in a vain attempt to ease his grip. "Delude yourself no longer. Believe me when I say that even friendship must end between us if you will not accept my irrevocable refusal to enter into any kind of liaison with you."

His cry rang from the heart. "I can't live without you, Kate!" Passionately he buried his face in her skirts against the very fount of her.

Had he not buckled her knees with the force of his embrace she would still have tumbled to the floor by the way in which she reeled away from him. When he would have gathered her to him again she pushed him off, stiff-armed, and swiftly darted off and away up the stairs to seek the refuge of her bedroom.

"Kate, Kate. Forgive me. Did I frighten you?" His voice, soft and urgent and full of a distress that matched her own, reached her through the door. In his contrition he did not attempt to turn the doorknob, or perhaps he guessed she would have turned the key.

Compassionately she went to answer him through the panels, a sad little smile with some wryness in it touching her lips. Frighten her? Not he. Not that kindly youth out of his depth in love.

"All is forgiven and forgotten, Harry," she whispered to him. "It will not be referred to again and the book is closed on all that was said once and for all."

There was a pause. "Not to me. Only a chapter has ended. I'll not give up. You cannot make me. The day will come when we shall both be glad that I refused to abide by your present wishes. Good night, my dear and only love."

Quietness descended on the sleeping house. Only Kate was awake for a long time, thinking over what she must do. She had known with Daniel's announcement of his elopement on the morrow that she could no longer stay at Honeybridge House. His unspoken wish that she should be gone had had its roots in his blunt dismissal of her from the business premises, whether he had realized it or not. In any case she could never have borne to have remained under the same roof as Daniel and his bride. All along she had tried to persuade herself that such an eventuality might never take place, but she had been deluding herself as much as Harry had done over the chance of her loving him. Yet from the time she had learned the day of her late husband's death from the newspaper cutting her cousin had kept, she had known what she must do if such a disaster fell. She must go far away to one of the colonies where she could lose herself in a new life and never be traced. Only in that way could she ensure that the suspicion that Daniel's forthcoming marriage to Claudine was bigamous would never fall upon him. Before she left she must find the marriage certificate that the Reverend Appledore had written out. There had been no copy and Daniel had taken the certificate in readiness to show it to the lawyers of the estate that he finally failed to inherit. It must be in his big mahogany desk downstairs. The key to it was kept on a ring with many others and invariably jingled in one of his pockets when he shrugged on his greatcoat. At all costs she must get it tonight, because tomorrow he would take them with him when he departed, for Harry had duplicates to all the office and other business premises. When Daniel returned to Honeybridge House with Claudine she intended to be on an emigrant ship bound for Canada.

On silent feet she crept out of her room and down the stairs. Daniel had left his greatcoat carelessly across a chair instead of on its usual peg in a clothes closet, and she found the key ring without difficulty. It took longer to find the right one to open the desk, but slightly less to discover the marriage certificate, which had been slipped through a ribbon holding together a number of letters that she supposed had dealt with matters concerning Warwyck Manor and which had probably been kept in case of future reference, or even forgotten. At least she could be sure that the marriage certificate would not be missed since Daniel considered it no more than a hoax inscribed on a worthless piece of paper. She relocked the desk, returned the key ring to his pocket, and went back upstairs. Before returning to her room she went up to the attic and fetched down in turn her brass-cornered trunk and the large valise, both of which Daniel had bought her long ago in Brighton at the start of it all. She did some packing before tiredness overcame her completely and she climbed into bed.

When morning came she was up at the usual time. Harry gave her a special smile when their eyes met, and she smiled back at him, thinking that after she had gone he would soon forget her in a new love, and she longed for all to go well with him. Then she busied herself in the serving of breakfast. Jem was obviously deeply depressed by what was to take place that day, and after the meal was over he slunk off on his own to go down on the beach and amble aimlessly, occasionally stopping to hurl pebbles with an outbreak of exasperated energy into the sea. Both brothers made ready to go to the yard where they were to discuss some business matters that were to be left for Harry to deal with, and they would not be returning to Honeybridge House before the elopement. Jassy absented herself when they were ready to leave the house, too upset to present Daniel with any good wishes, but Kate, loving him as she did, could not let him go without a final word. He was picking up the traveling satchel he had packed to take with him when she came into the hall.

"May good fortune go with you, Daniel."

"I thank you, Kate." He seemed pleased that she had not followed Jassy's and Jem's example in cold-shouldering him. In the moment of crossing the threshold to go out into the crisp, bright morning he looked back to give her one last glance, which to her registered as a final sweet memory of him to be kept through all the years ahead. Then he and Harry were gone.

She ran to the nearest window to watch them ride their horses from the stable and out of sight. She shed no tears. All her tears had been wept out the previous night, but there remained with her an awful numbness greater than sorrow and more agonizing than death, and in its wake would come a heart's ache that she would know to her life's end.

When she had finished the packing commenced the night before she went in her coat and bonnet to find Jassy and break the news to her. Jassy had grown up and matured greatly since the breakup of the romance with the villainous Charlie and the lung fever that had followed, and Kate was confident that this time the girl would accept her departure stoically. She was not mistaken.

"I had the feeling you would go today," Jassy said bleakly. "I heard the boards creak in the attic overhead last night and guessed what you were about. I think I knew yesterday evening that nothing I could say about dividing Honeybridge House with Daniel and his bride would make you stay. Where are you going?"

"Far away."

"Will you write to me?"

"No, I must not. But I shall think of you often and remember you and everyone else here at Honeybridge House with love for all time."

They were hugging each other wordlessly when Jem came into the house. One look at his dejected expression told Kate that he had also guessed what she was about. "I knew ye'd never stay on in this house with Dan wed to another. Yer sense of fairness wouldn't let ye."

"No bride should be expected to share a home with a woman with whom her husband had been through the ceremony of marriage," Kate replied, "no matter that it was done merely to hoax an inheritance."

"Ye're in yer outdoor togs. Is it to be now then?"

She nodded. "I'm going to hire transport at The Running Hare to take me as far as a coaching station."

"I'll carry yer baggage."

With the trunk balanced on Jem's huge shoulder and her valise in his hand he escorted her to the tavern, Jassy with them. There it was a matter of minutes before the carter who obliged travelers with his dilapidated dogcart came rattling into the forecourt. Again Kate and Jassy embraced, and Jem, who would have kissed her hand, was given a warm hug and kiss on the cheek. Then she was taking her seat in the dogcart. Blinded by tears which she could no longer control she twisted in the seat to wave to the giant of a man and the wisp of a girl until the end villa in one of Daniel's completed terraces hid them from her view. Still she looked back, gazing for the last time on the new splendor of Easthampton, gracious and elegant even where the rawness of brick and unstuccoed walls showed red and ocher and russet. Canopies with graceful curves enhanced bow windows, and the filigree ironwork cast lace patterns of shadow across inset doors and stone steps. Freshly planted trees sprouted in company with older trees kept to give shelter as well as charm to the laid-out public lawns and gardens that had banished the rough meadow grass from the long green. Before the dogcart took a bend in the road and Easthampton was lost from view, she looked finally at the hill where one day Daniel's grand house would stand. Then even that was hidden by surrounding woods, and the last link severed.

Shortly before two o'clock Daniel and Claudine arrived with Harry at St. Cuthbert's Church. It had been hard for her not to dress as strikingly as she would have wished for the occasion, but common sense warned her not to attract too much unnecessary attention, and she had left Radcliffe Hall attired as she would be for any afternoon party, her wide-brimmed bonnet lined with oyster silk and trimmed with velvet ribbons and braid in the same nectarine shade as her neat-waisted coat and striped gown. In the church porch the vicar welcomed them, and then Daniel offered her his arm. She tucked her gloved fingers into the crook of his elbow, returning his twinkling, triumphant stare with a dancing glint of her own victory. Then, together they entered the church, the mellow scent of candle wax and flowers and old wood enveloping them in a gentle wave. Harry, who had stepped inside ahead of them, was in his place in the front pew, but apart from the verger, who was to act as the second witness, there was no one else in the church.

The eloping couple reached the chancel steps. The vicar opened his book and the service began. No other sound disturbed the stillness of the church until the vicar spoke the words that were never omitted from the ceremony.

"Therefore if any man can show any just cause why they may not lawfully be joined together, let him now speak or forever hold his peace."

Before he could say any more, out of the side chapel where she had been hidden by the empty choir stalls, a girl stepped. It was Jassy. Her voice rang out clearly. "Daniel Warwyck already has a wife. His legal spouse is Kate Warwyck, whom he married at Brighton nearly eighteen months ago."

Daniel spun about, aghast. Claudine gave a sharp cry and clapped fingers to her lips, all color gone from her face. The priest closed the book with a snap, and only Harry showed no surprise at the revelation, but bowed his head in utter despair and reached out a hand to support himself on the arm of the pew by which he was standing. As Jassy advanced toward them to take her place in the aisle Daniel found his voice.

"What terrible joke is this?" he demanded hoarsely of his sister.

"It is the truth. Jervis Farringdon dropped dead twenty-four hours before you and Kate were married by the Reverend Appledore." She was repeating what she had overheard when listening without shame at the drawing room door the evening before. "The ceremony was legal and binding. Ask Harry." Her pointing finger shot out in her brother's direction. "He will verify that what I am telling you is true."

Harry, aware that all eyes had turned upon him raised his head. His face was haggard and the bones showed white through his skin. "Jassy is right in all she has said. Kate is your wife, Daniel."

Claudine became transformed by temper, her cheeks glazed by a fiery pink, and she faced Daniel with all the barbed hatred of humiliated pride and thwarted purpose. "You fiend! You devil! You knew it all along! When you could not get me by any other means you planned this despicable outrage! I hate you! Hate you!"

She rushed past Jassy and ran back down the aisle with skirts whipping and bonnet plumes streaming. The church door slammed hollowly behind her. Daniel did not attempt to go after her. It would only have exacerbated matters, and all he could think of was that once again Kate had interfered in his life. He moved to meet Jassy in the aisle.

"Where is Kate?" he inquired in a dangerously soft voice.

"She has gone," Jassy answered brokenly. Now that it was all over her legs felt as if they would not support her, and she was not far from tears herself. "This time it is forever. None of us will ever see her again."

His jaw tightened and his eyes blazed at her. "So she has gone and still you came running to ruin everything out of spite and revenge. You disgust me!"

He thrust her out of his path, sending her reeling backward with a shriek that resounded in the stillness of the church, and she fell against the side of a pew, hitting her head, her legs

sprawling in a tumble of white petticoats. Without ceremony
Harry, as much out of patience with her as his brother, wrenched
her up and shoved her onto a seat. As the vicar snatched up a
glass of water kept ready for emergencies, Harry rushed after
Daniel, who was making for the door. He caught him by the arm
and jerked him to a standstill a few feet from it.

"You always did think you could ride roughshod over everyone!" Harry shouted furiously at his brother, whose face was so
congested with rage that he barely recognized him. "You were
never content with anything but the cream of all there was to be
had. Father favored you before me, Mother spoiled you, and then
when Jem came to Warwyck it was you whom he chose to train.
You even took Kate away from me and it is due to you she has
gone again. My loss is beyond measure!"

Daniel grabbed him by the throat. "You dare to speak to me of
loss!" he roared. "You dare!" His hand squeezed and then he
thrust his choking brother from him. He went as violently out of
the church as Claudine had before him.

Kate traveled many miles on the coach that day. When evening
fell the coach drew up in the inner courtyard of a large coaching
inn, allowing the passengers to alight and seek accommodation for
the night. Kate had taken a cheaper seat on the top of the vehicle
instead of riding inside, and she had thought that no ship at sea
could sway so much as a stagecoach bounding along. Although
not queasy, she was tired in every limb, and after a modest meal
she treated herself to the luxury of having hot water brought up
to her room for a bath. When she stepped from the hip bath in
which she had soaked until the water cooled, she felt much
refreshed and spent a long time drying her washed hair, brushing
it afterward until it spun about her shoulders like silvery silk,
every hair wafting as if with a life of its own.

The tub and the water had been cleared away and she was
ready for bed when another maidservant came with a warming
pan. "'Ave I kept you waitin', madame?" the girl inquired anxiously, hurrying across to the four-poster bed where she lifted the

covers enough to thrust in the pan and run it between the sheets to take the chill off them with a rattle of hot coals.

"No, you have come just at the right time." Kate took off her robe and placed it on a chair.

"Thank you, madame." The maidservant held back the sheets for a moment to allow Kate to slip quickly into the warmth. "I expect your 'usband will be coming upstairs soon."

Kate stared at her incredulously. "What did you say?"

The maidservant was carrying the warming pan to the door. "When I came past the archway into the 'all I 'eard a gentleman asking if 'is wife, Mrs. Kate Warwyck, was staying 'ere. That is you, ain't it, madame?"

Kate had turned ashen. "Perhaps there is another guest at this tavern with the same name."

The maid shrugged, not interested, and went out of the room. Kate swallowed hard, twisting a fold of the top sheet in her hands. It could only be a coincidence. There was surely no other explanation. Then without warning the door swung open again and Daniel entered, his face dark and glowering, his eyes hard and curiously brilliant. Deliberately he shot the bolt home in the door as he closed it.

"So, Kate," he said gratingly, "we are truly wed after all."

She gave a gasp of fear and slipped from the bed in a flurry of pale feet and ankles and a swirl of nightgown. She would have darted for her robe on the chair, but he had stepped forward with a creak of floorboards and the way was blocked.

"How did you find out?" she whispered, gripping a post at the foot of the canopied bed.

He threw aside the hat and riding crop he was carrying and began to unbutton his coat. "That is a tale that can wait. It is enough that the truth is out and the wedding band you are still wearing on your finger has every right to be there. Just as I have rights that have long been denied me."

She looked as if she might faint, clutching at the bedpost as though she had lost all strength. "I was going away. You had no need ever to see me again. It can still be like that if only you will go from this room and this inn and forget that we ever met again."

"It is too late for that." He had untied his cravat and unfastened his shirt, which he was pulling from his body. Had it not been too late he still could not have left her that night. In spite of his anger, his disappointment, his blind fury at the turn events had taken, her unconsciously seductive magnetism had worked on him as it had on previous occasions when he had chosen to hide his reaction from her. He had caught his breath inwardly when he had opened the door and seen the softly disheveled look of her, so different from her daytime neatness when never a ribbon was loose or a hair out of place. Now, standing by the post with the candlelight faintly silhouetting her form through the white fullness of the fine linen nightgown, her hair tumbled and flowing about her shoulders, she had become completely irresistible to him and strangely not even Claudine herself could have turned him from the fever of his desire at that particular moment.

"Is there nothing I can say to make you leave?" she implored.

"Nothing, Kate," he said irrevocably, still undressing.

A shudder went through her. Turning, almost stumbling, she picked up the candle snuffer on the side table and put out the flames. But no darkness descended, for the moon was full and it flooded the room with its silvery light through the coarsely woven curtains. With a terrible resignation she raised her hands and began tremblingly to unfasten the buttons down the front of her nightgown bodice in a feminine action of surrender that was as old as time. Fear was high in her. Jervis Farringdon had not loved her either and he had used her cruelly, punishing her for his unmanning caused by her shrinking involuntarily from his nearness and freezing in his gross embrace. In the end he had come to hate her for it, no matter that she had never wished to destroy him. She shuddered again as the garment fell billowing at her feet and she stepped out of it.

"Kate." Daniel breathed her name. Never had he seen a woman more beautifully shaped, but she could have been a statue of marble in the chill, withdrawn way that she looked slowly toward him, her mouth tremulous, her throat working as if her voice had been strangled to everlasting silence.

Naked himself, he crossed to her and gently enfolded her in his arms. She jerked convulsively and went rigid, every limb stiff, her back like a ramrod, but he knew what he was about and began to kiss her with tiny touches of his lips, which passed light and fleeting over her eyes, her temples, her throat, and on the lobes of her ears. Gradually and almost imperceptibly she began to thaw, the statue becoming woman under his caresses, the marble turning into warm, vibrating flesh. Only then did he draw her into the bed with him. Only then did he discover the true Kate in a night that was to him the most passionate he had ever spent.

Chapter 14

He brought Kate back to Easthampton after two days. If the Kate of the night hours had given something of herself to the Kate he faced across the breakfast table he would have stayed away much longer, but with the coming of daylight she was once again the distant, self-contained creature that ever eluded him. They had talked while taking walks in the soft spring air, she pausing to pick primroses and then holding the little bunch before her as they strolled on again, not realizing that the fragile blooms matched the color of her wonderful hair, which time and again in more intimate moments had run like silk through his fingers on the rumpled pillows. He told her of the disastrous elopement, of Jassy's and Harry's shattering evidence, and how it had been easy enough to trace the route she had taken, first through the carter and then at the coaching stage where he had learned she had taken a coach to Bristol.

"Why Bristol?" he inquired of her.

"I intended to sail for Canada. To begin a new life. To set you free to marry the woman you love."

Love was not what he felt for Claudine. Not as Kate meant love. His feelings for the girl he would have married were base and violent, a commitment and a curse from which there was no escape. Not for the first time he felt himself doomed and was intensely depressed by it. The dip in his spirit came through in his tone.

"Let there be no more talk between us about what might have been. Your new life begins at Honeybridge House."

She had closed her eyes briefly on his words in a kind of thankfulness blended with pain. "I have long thought of it as home," she breathed. "Nothing could ever have changed that."

Shortly afterward on their ramble they came to a meadow where newborn lambs gamboled and she had laughed her sweet, deep laugh in sheer joy at their antics, enchanted when she drew some of them near her, momentarily forgetful of him and all else. He wished some of the laughter and its ensuing happiness would have held in her eyes when she moved once more to his side to continue their strolling, but it was gone like a snuffed-out candle flame, and he realized that in all the time he had known her he had never done or said anything to make her join him in laughter such as she shared with Jassy, Harry, and Jem. It struck him that before Kate had come to Honeybridge House there had been no laughter, no atmosphere of contentment, and he wondered why he had never thought of it before. She had made that house into a home. And he had given her no credit for it. Suddenly he longed to hold that laughing Kate in his arms, but that was one of many facets to her personality that she would share with others and not with him, for too much stood between them and he could not blame her for that. His mercenary purchase of her was a humiliation which must play sorely on her fine pride and spirit of independence, and she had been right when once long ago in the heat of anger she had accused him of treating her as a burden and a nuisance, because his attitude toward her had been far from what it should have been and had set the concrete pattern of their relationship. The greatest barrier of all between them was the final one: the fact that she was not the wife he would have married, nor he the man of her choice.

"Kate—" It was on the point of his tongue to suggest that together they should try to start again, making a fresh beginning, for both of them were caged in the marriage from which there was no escape.

"Yes?" Her light blue eyes, which he had seen change color, breaking to dark sapphire on the crescent of passion, regarded him from across an inestimable distance. There was no way of reaching her. The damage done was irreparable. He changed his mind about what he had been about to say.

"Tomorrow we'll go back to Easthampton."

So he had brought her home. To Kate the sight of the old, flint-walled house which she had thought never to see again, was a poignant moment never to be forgotten, and the rejoicing of Jassy and Jem gave her a welcome that could not be surpassed. Harry was nowhere to be seen. When she was unpacking and hanging away her clothes in the closet leading off Daniel's large bedroom, which she was to share with him, Jassy told her that Harry had drunk himself insensible after Daniel had set out to find her and bring her back.

"Where is Harry now?"

"Today he got up and went off to the yard at the normal hour, but he has taken lodgings with Eliot and Sarah Singleton." There was a pause. "He said he had to get out before Daniel brought you back here."

Kate nodded, understanding. It would have been as intolerable for Harry to go on living under the same roof once her marriage to his brother had been established as it would have been for her if Claudine had come there to live as Daniel's bride.

That night in the wide, carved bed with Daniel slumbering on the pillow beside her, his arm about her, she lay listening to the eternal sound of waves breaking on the shore, and felt herself to be the true mistress of Honeybridge House. It was a good house and she loved it. It had befriended her from the time she had first crossed its threshold and not even Daniel had bidden her be gone from it.

She turned her head and kissed his forehead lovingly as he slept. The words he spoke to her in the darkness were not of love, but of passion, and he did not realize that her complete abandonment came from adoring him and not only from his releasing the dam of her intense sensuality. He had not expected to find her virgin that first night together, but had he loved her he could not have dealt with her more tenderly or ardently. The domain of the bed was hers and there she could keep Claudine at bay even if she was powerless to stop his thoughts dwelling on his lost love at all other times. Never would she forget how distressed he had sounded when he had said that there must be no more talk about what might have been. She had suffered for him in his despair, for all his suffering was her own. It was sheer folly to yearn that he might eventually come to love her with his heart, but it was a yearning that would stay with her however often she counted her blessings and was thankful for all she had. One great blessing was that having discovered that she was his legal wife he had not shirked his responsibilities, but had chased after her and brought her back to fill her rightful place at his side, all his personal preferences put away. On that foundation she would build. On it their relationship could grow strong enough to weather all that might dash against it, even the ceaseless storm of his longing for another woman and her own personal torment over it.

Eliot and Sarah Singleton were the first to be told by Daniel that Kate was his wife. They both drove over at once to Honeybridge House to give Kate their best wishes and bring her a wedding gift, which she accepted warmly, adding it to those presented to her by Jassy and Jem. Although Eliot was in possession of the full facts of when the ceremony had actually taken place, Sarah was not, and she, like everybody else in Easthampton as the word spread, imagined that Daniel and Kate had been married during their short absence from the resort. Several days passed before Kate saw Harry. He came to the house one morning when she was alone in the kitchen making an apple pie.

"So my brother has taken you to be wife to him at last," he said brutally, his mouth tight and thin.

She put down the knife with which she was peeling the withered, winter-stored apples. "Say no more. Let there be no quarrel between us."

"I have one thing of importance to say and one thing only. After that I shall be silent for as long as is necessary, and in the meantime you will remember what I told you and know that it is in my mind too. It is that one day I shall win your love. Daniel doesn't love you and never will. He is besotted by Claudine and there is no other woman for him. He cares nothing for you. I saw his face when Jassy came out with the truth in church and stopped his marriage to Claudine. If he could have escaped the hangman's rope he would have committed murder to be rid of you and regain his freedom."

Her voice was racked on its cry. "Do you think you're telling me anything about Daniel that I don't already know?"

Running footsteps down the passageway brought Jassy to the doorway of the kitchen, the pen to the letter she was writing still in her hand. "What goes on here?" she demanded of her brother. "Are you upsetting Kate?"

Harry gave her a bitter glance. "Still listening at keyholes?" he challenged sarcastically and slammed his way out of the house.

Jassy's cheeks were burning. "The only time I ever eavesdropped in my life was when I returned to the drawing room door that night, intending to say that you could get upstairs unobserved. It was what Harry was saying about Reverend Appledore and a true marriage that made me listen." She tossed her head. "And I'm glad I did."

Kate picked up the knife and went back to peeling the apples, but she was as raw and wounded inside by Harry's words as if the blade had been used upon herself. It was little comfort to her later in the morning when Daniel, jubilant and triumphant, came to tell her first before the others that by the day's post there had been a number of letters from interested business men following an account of the rebuilding of Easthampton which had appeared in the most prominent financial newspaper in the land. Nothing but praise had been given. The redevelopment was launched. Now the time had come to act. The pugilist's venture was not going to end in bankrupt disaster, which many had predicted, but glowed with possibilities for investment.

By next day the interest had become an avalanche. Down from London and the North came business men with shrewd eyes and fat bank accounts. Almost overnight the competition for leases and the securing of property brought the budding resort into national prominence. Daniel reaped the benefit in the contracts that he needed, and at last other men's money began to flow into Easthampton by way of his account, settling his vast debts at a rate that promised a speedy accumulation of profit. Overnight land that he had purchased for almost nothing leaped in value, and several rival hotel companies began to clamor for the site of The Running Hare. Harry proved himself invaluable at this stage, gathering in background information about the companies which doubly strengthened Daniel's bargaining power, and much of his advice was astute and clearly thought out. When eventually the business was settled, Daniel had secured a finger in the pie of profits that the new hotel would make, which meant he could count on a sizable income from that source as well as having the financial gain that would come to him from his own establishment, The Warwyck Hotel. When the tremendous sum for the site changed hands he was able to look again with renewed satisfaction at the hill above the green, knowing it would take less time than he had originally anticipated to start the building of Easthampton House.

In the midst of it all he was training again for two more bouts in the prize ring, and he needed to be restored to favor in the boxing world, for after his defeat by Carey Reid the word had spread that he had passed his peak and was on the decline. Neither he nor Jem doubted that he would win the forthcoming mills, but for the sake of prestige and to regain the support of influential members of The Fancy, whose joint decision could reopen the way to the championship, he had to win in the shortest number of rounds possible and show that he had not lost one vestige of his skill. The training under Jem's instruction was the most rigorous he had ever endured, but he was given no mercy and expected none. They both knew what was at stake. He punched and sparred and ran and skipped until every muscle in his body was tuned and his reflexes had reached a state of flash point. The result was that he won the first bout in eight rounds and the second in six. The Fancy sat up, scarcely able to believe what they either saw for themselves or had reported to them afterward. They were always generous, and their purses flowed in to swell the prize money that Daniel received. One gentleman in addition contributed a hundred guineas to Daniel's share of the gate money, which was always divided equally between the two combatants. As a result bouts that had been arranged for him with notable fighters, which had been withdrawn by their promoters after his knockout, reappeared on the lists once more. It seemed that suddenly everything had taken a turn for the better and nothing could stop his soaring success.

Then, on an April morning, Claudine married Lionel Attwood in the private chapel at Radcliffe Hall. It was the most lavish wedding held in the county for many years. Some of the guests, innocent of the animosity between the speculator of Easthampton and their host at the Hall, stayed in Daniel's own newly completed hotel, with its view of the sea and on the opposite side of the green to the old site of The Running Hare. The inn had been demolished and from foundations already dug and laid was to grow in a splendor of new walls and colonnades and arches under the name of The George IV Hotel, a compliment to the King.

Claudine had hoped that Royalty would be present at her marriage and she was not disappointed. One of His Majesty's sisters attended, but was quite dowdily dressed, a point which met with Claudine's approval, for she did not wish anyone to compete remotely with her on that day of days, and a princess could always be a step ahead of anyone else. Claudine's bridal outfit had been sewn in Paris and the lace veil, which was several yards long, was bordered with tiny pearls and shone with silver thread. If she had not concentrated on her wedding gown and her trousseau she thought she would have gone insane. Hatred of Daniel vied with a craving for him that she could not quell. She had not seen him once since the day she had run from St. Cuthbert's Church, but gossip in her presence had told her that Daniel Warwyck had taken a wife, a young woman who had lived for a time in the same house and was believed to be a distant relative since she had had the same surname. Behind fans it was tittered that undoubtedly he had made an honest woman of this Kate Warwyck, and Claudine, flaming inwardly with jealousy and malevolence, had scarcely known how to restrain herself from screaming at them to stop talking about Daniel Warwyck, whose name she never wanted to hear again.

When the wedding breakfast was over Claudine and Lionel left Radcliffe Hall in a shower of rice and petals. They were bound for Paris by way of a Channel packet from Dover, and they were accompanied as far as the gates and out into the lane by the younger and more active guests, who ran alongside the open landau until the horses gathered speed. The bride and groom waved merrily to those forced to fall behind and come to a breathless halt in the lane. With a laugh still in her throat Claudine turned to settle back in the seat beside Lionel, and then abruptly all gaiety went from her. Approaching from the opposite direction was Daniel, driving a spanking new phaeton with his wife beside him. Claudine could not take her eyes from him. Lionel spoke to her, but she was deaf and blind to everything but the man staring at her as the distance between them lessened rapidly.

Kate watched the whole sequence and everything moved with dream-like slowness, much as colored glass in a child's kaleidoscope changed patterns when rotated and held to the light. She saw how Claudine's gaze was locked with Daniel's, their faces bearing the same expression of hostile yearning, and when the landau and the phaeton drew level with a rush of wheels and spitting gravel Claudine half-raised a hand as if she might have spoken or reached out to him. Then each had gone past and neither looked back.

Kate saw that a nerve was twitching violently in Daniel's temple and his jaw was set. She did not doubt that she had witnessed the silent exchanging of vows of undying love and deep commiseration. Then her own jaw tightened in determination. The heart had a will of its own and could not be coerced, but she would go on hoping as she had always hoped that one day Daniel might come to regard her with a love meant for her alone, and separate from all he felt for Claudine. But there was more against it than the gulf of their names being joined on that marriage certificate, for she could not play-act or be false or pretend to be other than herself with all her faults, and fiercest of all was her pride and private dignity, which made her draw her chill cloak about her like a porcupine thrusting out spines against attack. All that she could count on the credit side was his more tolerant attitude toward her by day, and surely beyond all else there was that oneness they shared when lying heart to heart, that sense of belonging only to each other, with all the world shut out of their own particular Paradise. Once, amused by some wry remark he made, she had laughed softly, which had brought him to laughter and a kind of joyous exultation in which he had cuddled her close and they had rolled in the wide bed like children playing. Out of that laughter had come a fresh discovery in each other, and in the morning he did something which he had never done before, and that was to turn back before leaving the house, take her face between his hands, and kiss her on the lips. She had walked on air for the rest of the day and tried not to be disappointed when the lover-like little incident did not happen a second time.

With a bright spinning of wheels the phaeton carried them round a bend in the lane and Daniel gave a sudden exclamation at the sight of some carts loaded with domestic belongings under roped tarpaulins ahead of them. "Look, Kate! Zounds! Do you see that? The first new residents of the resort of Easthampton are moving in!"

He urged the horses forward and she shared his excitement as they overtook and passed not one short procession but no fewer than five separate family units, each with a wagonette or chaise bearing wife and children, some with dogs that barked noisily as the phaeton went past, others with birds in cages, and cats in baskets. Daniel raised his whip in greeting and Kate waved, both of them unaware of what a dashing pair they made together, and hats were lifted, smiles were returned, and a flutter of hands followed them on their way.

By the time the phaeton bowled into Easthampton, Daniel seemed much recovered from his encounter with the honeymoon carriage and in full control of himself again. The purpose of the drive had been to try out the new phaeton, which was white with gilt on the bodywork, and at the same time he had wanted to point out to her the numerous acres of land, previously waste, which he had purchased for little more than a song and which, if all went well with the first summer season of the new resort, was his guarantee of a fortune, apart from the financial gains that would pour in from other sources.

"We are going to be rich," he said to her with steely satisfaction. Already circumstances had eased at Honeybridge House. He had insisted that she employ a maidservant, the dining room had been restored and refurnished, and the new phaeton was to suit his rising position as the future champion of all England in the prize ring. "You shall be with me tomorrow when I thrust a spade down into the earth to lift out the first clod towards the foundations of Easthampton House. I see no need to wait any longer for work to commence on it." He gave a grunt of annoyance as someone sprang forward to stand in the road ahead with arms outstretched to bring them to a halt. "What the devil—?"

It was Thomas Brown who had darted out of his general stores at the sight of Daniel, and his dirty apron flapped about his short, potbellied figure as he came level with Daniel and looked up at him. "I've had enough from you, Warwyck," he boomed pugnaciously. "You're trying to drive me and honest men like me out of this place where we was born and bred and our fathers and grandfathers afore us."

"What is the trouble now?" Daniel inquired impatiently. Brown had beaten a path to his door both at home and at the yard with his constant complaints.

"That's the trouble." Brown pointed across the laid-out public gardens where daffodils bloomed in a yellow carpet, to one of the new shops on the other side where a rival general stores was being painted and made ready under the watchful eye of the proprietor, previously a stranger to the district, whose family had already arrived and were carrying their possessions into the living quarters. "You and these intruders you're letting in are taking the bread out of the mouths of local folk."

"You have had the monopoly with your shoddy goods for too long," Daniel replied crisply. "If a little healthy competition upsets you there is always the alternative. My price for your property stands as it did when I first made it."

"Yes! After you had frightened out the other shopkeepers and got your grip on this hamlet what is a hamlet no more, no thanks to you. Well, I ain't selling."

"Not yet perhaps. But you will. Since I own the forecourt of your store and the land to the rear as well as the property on either side you will not find another buyer to take it." Daniel flicked the reins and drove on. Brown shook his fist after the shining white phaeton and stumped back into his premises.

Kate felt some concern. Brown was a tenacious little man, who had stuck to his guns over the ownership of his property, and although she had heard enough of his shady dealings to consider Easthampton would be well rid of him she did not think Daniel should underestimate his enemy.

A month later in early May an official opening of the resort was held, symbolized by the cutting of a white satin ribbon stretched across the steps of the Assembly Rooms by Lady Margaret, she and Sir Geoffrey being the guests of honor. Many other distinguished personages were present, and Daniel was pleased to see how naturally and charmingly Kate moved among them, letting none of less importance be overlooked. Moreover he considered she looked more elegant than any other woman in the gathering, the azure silk of her outfit and ribbon-trimmed bonnet suiting her fair coloring and fine complexion.

At the grand luncheon afterward in the Assembly Rooms where crystal and silver gleamed on the white linen covering the long tables, Kate sat beside Mr. Lancelot Barton, Member of Parliament for a constituency in Yorkshire, a grandson of old Hamilton Barton, who had recently died and from whom Daniel had purchased Honeybridge House and most of the land of Easthampton. Mr. Barton and his wife had accepted Daniel's invitation to attend the ceremony with considerable interest, and Mrs. Barton was so taken with the resort that they booked accommodation for later in the season when they planned to return with their little son and daughter. There were many grand speeches and the champagne flowed, but to Kate the highlight of the day was when Daniel suddenly caught her eye and raised his glass of champagne to drink to her alone.

Chapter 15

It was a bright and sunny June morning when Claudine was driven into Easthampton in one of the Attwood carriages. She and Lionel had returned from their honeymoon the day before and at the present time they were barely on speaking terms, not that they had revealed the stress between them to Olivia and Alexander, who had come over to the Grange at once to hear about their travels and express their pleasure at having them home again. Olivia, believing her to be safely ensconced in a state of newly wedded bliss in which faithfulness and mutual devotion flourished, was buoyant and gracious, full of self-assurance and more than ready to give advice on household management and dealing with servants and anything else she thought her younger sister might need to know. Alexander's kiss on her cheek had been chaste enough, but neither of the others had noticed the way he had squeezed her hand and smiled into her eyes, their quarrel of the past having been patched up before her marriage. Comparing him with the fascinating men she had met or exchanged glances with abroad, all of whom would have paid court to her if it had not been for Lionel's obstinate presence, she found his attentions singularly dull. How he could ever have amused her or she could have found pleasure in his advances she did not know. Olivia was more than welcome to him.

"Stop here," she ordered the coachman. The groom at the rear of the carriage sprang down to open the door for her and let down the step. He was a fine-looking young man, for Lionel, as was the custom with many of the aristocracy, matched his servants in height and appearance, particularly grooms and footmen, in order that they should present a uniform appearance when lined up together in the course of their duties.

She had alighted by a gate into the gardens on the site of the old green where people of leisure were promenading and exchanging greetings and conversation as was done in the Steine at Brighton. However, she had not come to stroll there, but to view the resort blossoming in its first season, Olivia having told her it was full of visitors with every hotel room, apartment, and villa fully booked for the whole season.

Twirling her parasol, which cast a lacy pattern over her leghorn hat of straw with its flowing, blue ribbons, Claudine looked about critically and observantly, surprised to see that work had started on the house on the green hill. Daniel's dream was coming true. It seemed destined to be a considerable size, and as far as she could judge it appeared that a curving drive was going to wind down the hillside to meet gates in the lane at the head of the gardens. No house could have a better sea view, and from it Daniel would be able to survey the whole of the resort of his making, including those areas branching east and west where building was still in progress with every indication of more villas and terraces to be erected later.

She could not but give final approval of the resort. The retained trees gave a mellow look to it and the tamarisk hedge softened the stretch of promenade. Nothing stood out as being unsightly or in ill taste, and wooded walks had been preserved in the vicinity of the beach for those who wished to feast their eyes on the foliage of nature as well as the sparkling waves. Everywhere gleaming paintwork and pastel stuccoed walls made a background to the coming and going of carriages, the bobbing of parasols, and the light-footed skipping of children in the charge of nursemaids. A colorful display in the nearest shop window caught her eye and she went across to take a closer look. On shelves were arranged a host of objects that could be purchased as souvenirs of a visit to Easthampton. There were porcelain plates, fans, shell boxes, and glassware, many with tiny, hand-painted scenes of the sands and new buildings of the resort. Next to the shop was the Library, and she entered to cast an eye over the visitors' book, discovering many distinguished names that were known to her. Walking on again she read the concert bills outside the Assembly Rooms, passed through the welcome shadow of their colonnade, and came to The Warwyck Hotel with its uninterrupted view of the sea. On the terrace she sat at a table and ordered a lemonade. From there she could see children enjoying rides on donkeys for hire on the sands. Thomas Brown's bathing machines were doing a busy trade, the shrieks of the bathers resounding clearly as the sturdy dippers seized them and plunged them down under the water. She had noticed that even his general stores were freshly painted to compete with the new shops opened up around his premises.

A lady's voice broke on her quiet contemplation. "Mrs. Attwood—what an unexpected pleasure. When did you get home from abroad?"

It was Lady Margaret who had paused by her table. Claudine displayed delighted surprise, disguising the fact that she had seen in the visitors' book that Sir Geoffrey and his wife were staying at the resort. "Good morning. We arrived home yesterday. Are you alone? Pray join me in some refreshment."

Lady Margaret seated herself in a rustle of cream silk. "Nothing, thank you, my dear. Is this not a delightful resort? Sir Geoffrey and I came several days ago, and I must say I prefer it in every way to Brighton. We have decided to have a summer residence built here, but whether we shall obtain the plot we have chosen is still in the balance. Mr. Harry Warwyck deals with such matters on his brother's behalf and not only does he drive a hard bargain, but there is such competition for the prime sites and we are not alone in our bid for it."

"But surely since Sir Geoffrey is Daniel Warwyck's patron he should be given some preference."

"Oh, he will be." Lady Margaret gave a confident nod. "But Mr. Warwyck only came home yesterday after another fight and my husband is discussing business with him now."

"Did Mr. Warwyck win?"

"Indeed, yes. Quite gloriously according to my husband. It is his sixth successful bout this year." She chatted on again about the resort until Sir Geoffrey came into sight from the direction of Honeybridge House. Then she rose to leave and join him. "Shall you be coming to the ball at the Assembly Rooms this evening? They are most elegant occasions, I do assure you."

"I regret we have a previous engagement."

"What a pity. Mr. Warwyck and his lovely wife are almost always there, which makes it more like a private gathering when they act as host and hostess."

Claudine raised delicate eyebrows. "A pugilist playing host to his betters?"

"Mr. Warwyck is from an old and respected county family, and even if he were not, he would bridge the gap like that gentleman once known as Gentleman Jackson in the prize ring and former Champion of England. You surely know that at first there was some local prejudice against Mr. Warwyck from the local nobility due to their fears as to how Easthampton was to be developed, but since it has already established itself with London society their fears have been dispelled, and much as they might have preferred the place to remain as it was, they are more than ready to receive Mr. and Mrs. Warwyck, who have become much in demand. However"—here she subdued an amused smile—"our good friend is not so easily won over and the tables are quite turned. It is said he refuses invitations daily, and when he accepts it is only at a house that has caused him no offense."

Sir Geoffrey ascended the steps and came to claim his wife's company, but even after he had exchanged courtesies with Claudine there was still some delay through his wife issuing an invitation.

"Since you cannot come to the Assembly ball with us we should be delighted if you could come moonlight sailing tomorrow evening instead. A whole fleet of small boats sets out and it is the prettiest sight with colored lanterns reflected in the water."

Claudine accepted graciously. Left alone she smiled to herself, recalling what had been said about Daniel. How clever of him to break down the social barriers in his own inimitable way. He had cut the ground from under the feet of Alexander and those like him. Revenge was sweet, and Daniel must be grinning to himself daily at Alexander's discomfiture. How neatly it had been executed. How vulgar it made appear Alexander's cowardly attack on him from the carriage at Brighton.

Would Daniel be in the sailing party? It was the expectation that he would be that had prompted her acceptance. Their paths were bound to cross sooner or later and she had never been one to avoid an unpleasant issue. Whether Lionel would accompany her to the evening festivities or not was immaterial to her. His gentleness and aesthetic tastes, which had made such a favorable contrast during their courtship to Daniel's attitude toward her, had become cloying and sickly to her like his own health, which had broken down when he had caught a chill during a boating expedition on a Swiss lake when a squall had blown up. In order not to disturb her with his cough at night he had taken to sleeping in another room wherever they had happened to be staying, and had he not had so keen a sense of duty she sometimes wondered if he would ever have paid her those brief visits which she found so unsatisfactory and frustrating. She was often sharp with him as a result of them, and had been quick to find fault with any plans he had made, such as the sightseeing expeditions he had arranged for her enjoyment. Through her dissatisfaction she had discovered another side to him, for in spite of his general mildness of temperament he could be stubborn at times when driven to the point of exasperation, making her realize then that it was a case of the iron hand in the velvet glove. This at least enabled her to spike him into quarreling with her, an outlet for her pent-up tension, but a cause of distress for his peaceable nature. Everything he did managed to annoy her, often through no fault of his own, but she considered him entirely responsible for their not getting on well together and absolved herself completely from any blame.

Leaving the terrace of the hotel she turned to go back to her carriage along the side of the gardens where she had not walked before, looking into the shops as she went. At the apothecary's her attention was captured by an advertisement for a new cough syrup guaranteed to soothe and cure almost instantaneously. She did not quite believe the extravagant claims, but if it could help Lionel obtain some relief from his cough she thought it worth trying. With the bottle purchased and wrapped in paper she slipped it into her reticule, and half an hour later she was once again in her carriage being driven back to Attwood Grange.

She tossed her reticule and parasol onto her bed for her maid to put away as she removed her hat. Tidying her hair with a comb she forgot completely about the cough syrup, and since Lionel had invited some guests to luncheon she had other things to think about. In the afternoon she was at home to the many callers who wished to see her after her long absence, and she was delighted to have their company. When evening came she and Lionel attended a grand dinner party held in their honor at Radcliffe Hall, and on the way there she told him about the Edenfield's sailing invitation. He hesitated, no doubt remembering the unfortunate episode in Switzerland, but seeing that she appeared eager to go he announced himself agreeable, making only the stipulation that the sea must be calm and the evening mild with no chance of a sudden change in temperature or weather. They were made warmly welcome at the Hall and everyone made a great fuss of them, which pleased Claudine and she preened in her new Parisian gown, knowing she outshone every woman present.

After such a full day and with some lassitude lingering from the recent journey home, she was tired and ready for bed when her maid helped her undress and brushed out her hair. She was almost asleep, her thoughts drifting, when she remembered the cough syrup. For a moment she was tempted to turn over and forget it until the morning, but there sprang into her mind the image of

Lionel racked by the paroxysms of coughing that came upon him. It was always a distressing sight, abhorrent to her in her own radiant good health, and it was as much to put an end to having to view these spasmodic attacks as to a wish to have him cured that had prompted the buying of the physic. With a self-sacrificing sigh she threw back the covers, thrust her feet into pink satin slippers, and reached for her robe to cover her nightgown. The bottle was where she had put it and she frowned over the stupidity of the maid who had not thought to question the weight of the reticule and thus remind her of it. In a flow of rosy satin she went out of her bedroom into the corridor, carefully holding her purchase.

A few candle sconces were kept alight during the night hours and she made her way easily to Lionel's rooms, which were a considerable distance from hers. She heard him coughing as she drew near and wrinkled her nose in some disgust. Fortunately the worst of the attack seemed to be over, but still she had to steel herself to turn the handle of his door and go in.

He was out of bed, clad in a dressing robe, and was taking a second drink of water from a decanter kept at the bedside. At the sound of her entrance he spun about to stare at her in dismayed astonishment, spilling some of the water from the glass, which flung a dark patch on the gray brocade of his robe.

She advanced into the room, holding out the bottle. "Try some of this cough syrup. I bought it for you in Easthampton today—" Her voice trailed off and she came to a standstill, staring in horrified disbelief at the bed. Her husband was not alone. Lying there, one bare arm under his golden-curled head on the pillow, his eyes mocking her, was the young groom from her own carriage.

The bottle fell from her fingers to the floor. Miraculously it did not break, but slowly she drew back as if she feared the seeping syrup from the loosened cork might soil her hems, while her widened, dilated eyes went from the groom to her husband and back again.

Lionel broke the awful silence. "Claudine—"

She uttered a sound that was halfway between a gasp and a

moan. Then she whirled about and ran from the room. Her robe fluttered about her as she sped back down the long corridors and reached the sanctuary of her own quarters. There she turned the key and sank down on her knees, her strength deserting her in the shock she had received. Never should he come near her again. Never. Much that had eluded her before clicked into shape. She recalled Daniel's outrage that she should consider marrying Lionel. He told her she was out of her mind. He had heard or guessed. Perhaps men could detect easier than women that quirk of nature that nobody ever mentioned and which had been whispered to her and others in her convent days by a fellow pupil more knowledgeable than the rest.

Her innocence appalled her. How could she have been so blind, but then how could she have known? Slowly she raised her head, her eyes hardening. Alexander had known. He and Lionel had been at school together and over long years of friendship there could be little hidden from him. Yet deliberately he had encouraged her to marry Lionel where all her other suitors had been belittled and scorned, turned away as not being worthy of her, Alexander always protesting that it was her happiness he had at heart. Her happiness? His lust! He could not endure the thought of her in another man's arms and for that he had knowingly condemned her to one who could give her no joy, no fulfillment, and who husbanded her on sufferance. Throwing her arms over her head she fell into a storm of weeping over her misfortune.

The following day Lionel sought her out in the garden where she was sitting listlessly in the shade of a tree, her hands idle in her lap. Deliberately she turned her face away from him to show that his presence was unwelcome, but he sat down on the white wrought-iron seat beside her and rested an arm along the back of it.

"Since we no longer have any secrets from each other," he said calmly, "it will be as well if we have some discussion."

"There is nothing to discuss," Claudine rasped, her face still averted.

"I disagree. If it is any consolation to you I have dismissed a certain person and sent him away."

"Well compensated, no doubt," she retorted.

He chose to ignore the barbed remark. "I believed when I married you that you loved me. It may surprise you to know that I cherished a sincere affection for you and had hopes that we should settle to an amiable partnership. I greatly enjoyed those hours we spent together with our books and music, which I had expected to continue, but it was not long after our wedding day that you began to show that you found my company boring and at times even distasteful."

She regarded him scornfully. "I do not deny it. I tell you now that I intend to go my own way and you can go yours. We are not the first couple forced to make the best of unhappy circumstances and we shall not be the last."

He coughed, the effort deepening the shadows of fatigue under his eyes, which like his pallor had become permanent since that unfortunate chill, and quickly he put a fine linen handkerchief to his mouth, but when no attack followed he replaced it in his sleeve. "You may do whatever you wish after you have given me a son, provided for his sake you keep scandal at bay."

She drew in her breath sharply. "That side of our marriage is over. Never again—"

"I married you for the sole purpose of having an heir. In that you shall do your duty and when it is fulfilled you can be damned for all I care."

That iron core within him was only too apparent once again. He rose without haste from the seat and strolled back across the lawn toward the house. She watched him go. It made her flesh creep at the thought of the condition he had laid down. She could not bear his touch again and she would not.

Clenching her hands together she swayed in her misery. If only she were with child from their last coming together, but that was most unlikely. Somehow and somewhere she must find a way out of her terrible dilemma.

Like play actors she and Lionel went through the social engagements of the rest of the day together. He was again his customary, courteous self to her at all times, his brutal announcement of his expectations of her having been against his own personal code of good manners, but necessary under the circumstances. Claudine, glancing across at him during a call they made together at the home of a mutual acquaintance and again during a tea party, found it hard to associate his charming elegance with the degradation in which he had indulged the previous night.

When evening came it proved to be as soft and balmy as the day, so that there was no question of the expedition to Easthampton being canceled. At The Warwyck Hotel they were received by the Edenfields in their suite of rooms, where they met the rest of the invited guests and champagne was served. Afterward the Edenfields led the party out of the hotel to cross the promenade and make their way down one of the new flights of wooden steps that made descent to the sands easier than the old seaweed-covered slipways.

It was as pretty a sight as had been foretold. A dozen boats waited at the water's edge adorned with paper lanterns and trailing ribbons, and the boatmen, who had purchased the concession from Daniel to use that part of the beach to take passengers sailing by day as well as by night, were attired in straw hats and striped clothes which gave them a nautical air. Other groups of visiting personages and their ladies had gathered on the sands ready for embarking, and there was much greeting of acquaintances and a deal of merriment, all of which was watched by a large number of local people who had come down onto the shingle to view the spectacle from a respectful distance. The moonlight and pale sands gave luminosity to the scene, but there was added brilliance in the flaming torches that had been thrust into tall iron holders stuck into the sands. In the flickering glow of one of them Claudine suddenly sighted Daniel giving a hand to Kate as they came down the flight of steps, his sister in their wake, and with her a young man whom she recognized as the youngest son of a well-to-do family who lived not far from the Grange. But she gave Jassy and her beau no further attention, her eyes following Daniel and his wife as people turned at their approach to speak and chatter, some to be presented, the gentlemen bowing over Kate's hand. Then Daniel turned his head and Claudine saw that he had sighted her in the midst of the

Edenfields' party. The orange torchlight highlighted one side of his face and cast the other into shadow, but with the reflected glow held in his eyes she thought on a stab of eroticism that he looked like a devil out of Hell bent on ravishment. Then it came to her how she might find a way out of her terrible predicament.

Deliberately and unobtrusively she moved out of the group she was with and sauntered a little distance away, seemingly wishing to contemplate alone the beauty of the sea lapping black and silvery gold. She did not have long to wait before he was within touching distance of her. Slowly she turned her head round to regard him without expression.

"You are not forgiven for the trick you played on me. I never forgive. So do not delude yourself on that score."

"I have never deluded myself in any way concerning you, Claudine. And I must point out that the trick you mentioned was played by Fate."

She knew it was the truth. The expression on his face when his sister had stepped forward to announce the impediment to their marriage was imprinted on her memory, and after the first maddened heat of wrath had subsided she realized that at the time he had been as ignorant of the true state of circumstances as she.

She dropped her lashes to look seaward again. "I see it now as an omen. It was to forewarn me against marriage approached either through headstrong folly or with thoughtless haste."

Her meaning was unmistakable. He made no pretense of not understanding. "My condolences," he said evenly.

She withdrew a step from the water's edge when a wavelet rippled in closer than the rest, and he caught her elbow in his cupped palm.

"I need to talk to—someone," she said urgently, leaning against him.

"You need look no further."

"But not here." Agitatedly she glanced over her shoulder and saw that the ladies in the various parties were being assisted along the wheeled jetties to step into the boats. "Would the cottage where Olivia came to see you still make a suitable meeting place?"

"It would indeed."

"Tonight, then? When the sail is over? I must make a show of returning home before I can leave again."

"I shall wait till dawn if need be."

She made her way back without haste across the sands, bursting into a little laugh and holding out both hands to have them caught in the clasp of the two gentlemen at the forefront of those who had come hurrying to help her, the last lady in the party, to step into one of the three boats reserved for the Edenfields and their guests. Some of the other boats with their full complement of passengers had already put to sea, and boatmen were standing by the bows of the remaining two vessels ready to give them a thrust into deeper water before jumping aboard. Daniel, failing to spot Kate among the passengers waiting to leave, guessed she was in one of the boats nosing out to sea under full sail, and he acknowledged Sir Geoffrey's beckoning invitation that he should join them. Lightly he leaped aboard and took a cushioned seat cleared for him beside Lady Margaret. Claudine, achatter in animated conversation a few seats away, did not as much as glance in his direction. Her husband, on the other hand, joined in with those who gave him greeting.

Kate checked the wave she had been giving him from one of the boats several yards out, and lowered her hand to her lap. He had not seen her, although he had looked for her. She knew why he had been too late to join her, for she had noticed him draw away on the beach to converse with Claudine beyond the range of the flares in the shadows of the rocks by the water's edge. Harry, who was seated beside her, his face masked in rainbow colors from the lanterns swinging above his head, had also spotted the encounter, having been among those waiting on the sands when she and Daniel had arrived.

"There," he said with triumphant satisfaction, putting his head close to hers in order that she alone would hear his low-spoken words. "Of all the boats to choose from Daniel gets aboard the one where Claudine Attwood is a passenger. Did you see how they conversed together on the beach? She's not home five minutes before they are seeking each other out again. It confirms my belief that she only married Attwood on the rebound."

"They are not sitting together," Kate pointed out defensively.

"That means nothing. They can scarcely hobnob under the very nose of her husband. They can consider themselves lucky if nobody else except you and I saw them slide off to talk alone. Gossiping tongues are quick to wag."

"Enough," she said on a flash of anger. "You are committing that very crime yourself."

He laughed good-humoredly and reclined back in his seat, thinking he had made his point and there was no need to pursue it. Recently he had changed his tactics, doing everything he could by carefully chosen words or innuendoes to undermine that ridiculous loyalty that Kate harbored toward his brother, although she could have been deaf for all the outward notice she appeared to take. But he was working on her pride and her spirit of independence. Surely sooner or later she would snap free and go her own way. Then he would make sure it was his way too. She was not happy as Daniel's wife, he was sure of that. He had studied her facial expressions since their first meeting and never missed trying to judge her mood by the variance of color in her eyes, which made him feel he knew Kate as well as anyone could know her, and this conviction inflated his sense of possessiveness toward her. He could tell just by looking at her that there was a void in her life, a total lack of love given and reciprocated that had nothing whatever to do with what took place between his brother and her in the marriage bed. Jealousy, dark and festering, churned again through his veins, and envious hatred of his brother had become such a physical thing that at times it quite thickened his voice and made him wipe away surreptitiously the cold sweat that started at his temples and across his upper lip. Often he thought laconically that he had missed his vocation in life and should have walked the boards, for surely he had mastered better than any actor the ability to smile and converse and bow and radiate geniality when inwardly he went with murder in his heart.

Kate trailed a finger in the water lapping past the boat, watching how the ripples held the liquid flow of the lanterns' reflected color, but her gaze was unfocused and her thoughts dwelled on that image in her mind of Daniel and Claudine standing like lovers together, lost in some deep and intimate conversation. She had become filled with a sense of foreboding more deadly than anything she had ever experienced before and she was desperately afraid. Was she to lose him completely after all? At this late hour when sustained hope had led her to a sweet and private joy with each small victory, each tiny concession, each unguarded, loving touch, was she to discover that she had been living in a fool's paradise and he was as far from her as he had ever been?

A deep sigh racked her. It made her whole body shudder as a child's does when sobbing ceases. Harry noticed and bent toward her with some concern.

"Are you cold?"

It was easier to nod than to enter into any discussion. She let him take one of the folded plaid rugs from a pile put ready for chilly passengers and drape it across her lap. And it was true that she was cold inside from sheer terror that suddenly whatever time had been allotted to her to win some measure of affection from Daniel had run out, and the hourglass was empty. Claudine had come back and merely crooked her finger to have him at her feet again.

Then slowly Kate tilted her chin. She would not be crushed by premonition. Foreboding must be ignored and brushed aside, or else defeat would be inevitable. She had a trump card that Claudine could not match. In that she would put her hope. Therein lay her strength and it would not fail her.

The sail lasted for more than two hours. The flotilla of small boats kept a safe distance from the rocks, but remained fairly close to the shore where the lights of cottages and scattered farmhouses twinkled like new pennies and Easthampton itself resembled the dazzling contents of a jewel box spread out on black velvet under the stars. By chance the boat carrying Kate and Harry was the last to come in to its jetty, and Daniel was waiting on the sands for her. The Edenfields and their party had already departed, their good nights to each other being said beyond the tamarisk hedge where their equipages awaited them.

"Did you enjoy the trip?" Daniel asked Kate when she reached him, but the question was put almost automatically, his eyes preoccupied with some other matter on his mind.

"It was most pleasant," she managed to reply evenly, but was gripped again by an unnerving fear that threatened to paralyze her. It was a relief when Jassy came darting up with her beau in tow to make merry remarks about the expedition and Jem appeared at the head of the steps, whip in hand, to drive them home. Jassy's beau went with them to the curricle, made an appointment to see her again the next day, and then went to find his own equipage, Harry departing at the same time. Kate got in the open carriage to sit beside Jassy, but to her dismay Daniel did not follow her, simply closing the door for them.

"Are you not coming home?" she asked. Sometimes he did make a last round, calling in at The Warwyck Hotel or checking in at the Assembly Rooms or perhaps meeting some companions for a gaming session, but this time she could not shake off the belief that he was bent on some other purpose not known to her.

"Not yet," he replied, signaling to Jem that the passengers were safely installed and ready to depart. He would have stepped back, but Kate put her hand quickly over his on the door, her instincts telling her that at all costs she must not let him go from her on this night of nights or else something terrible and catastrophic might happen to split them asunder for all time.

"Daniel!" There was a note of desperation in her voice.

He looked at her as if seeing her for the first time since Claudine had drawn him to her side. "Yes?"

"Don't leave me!"

He was surprised. "What's the matter?"

She shook her head agitatedly as if she had lost the power to articulate easily. "I particularly wanted to confide in you when this evening was over."

He smiled seriously. Kate was forever concerning herself with the poor and the needy, and it would be nothing that could not wait until morning. Far different was the state of Claudine's distress.

"Your confidence will be welcome tomorrow." He took his hand from under hers.

She drew in her breath sharply, her cheeks coloring. "Is there nothing important enough in all the world to keep you from your plans for this night?"

His eyes narrowed at her. Kate was getting above herself. He would not be questioned and challenged about his affairs. She needed to be taught a lesson.

"No, ma'am," he replied coldly. "I'll be about my own business and not keep you from yours."

Wrathfully he swung away and strode off along the promenade in the direction of The Warwyck Hotel. She did not look after him, but sat very straight and still, lifting her gaze to the troubled eye of Jem, who had turned on the box seat to watch the whole scene, silent as Jassy, who had had to bite her lip to keep from bursting out at Daniel for not doing as Kate wished.

With fierce dignity Kate spoke clearly to Jem. "Let us go home now."

He flicked the whip and the carriage rolled forward. Once behind the bedroom door at Honeybridge House, Kate made no attempt to undress or prepare for bed, but paced the floor of the wide room restlessly, kneading her hands together, her face stricken. This was the night she had intended to tell Daniel that she had had the first indication that she was with child. This was the night she had thought to win him to her at last.

At The Warwyck Hotel, Daniel went straight to the stables. It was customary for him to take a horse for his rounds of inspection from time to time and the groom was quick to bring out the best of the hacks for him. With a clatter of hooves he rode out of the yard and failed to see his brother watching him from the shadows of a doorway. Within seconds Harry had swung himself into the saddle of a horse waiting nearby and proceeded to follow Daniel from a safe distance. When the country road out of Easthampton was reached Harry moved his horse onto the grass verge to make certain that his brother had no suspicion that he was being trailed.

It was well after midnight when Claudine arrived on foot at the cottage. He had been watching for her and stepped out under the lintel, silhouetted against the candlelight within. The pale glow reached out to touch her as she came through the gate and without a word she swept past him into the cottage. When he shot the bolt home in the door and turned she had already cast aside her cloak into a dark heap on the floor.

"You waited as you said you would," she said huskily, her appearance wild and tousled, for she had run part of the way.

"Did you doubt me?"

She shook her head, her eyes glittering at him. It was to be as he had known it would be. If she had truly intended to talk about her troubles upon her arrival that resolution was at an end. In her avid expression he read her need, even though there was another reason beyond the surface one at which he did not guess. With a sudden sharp, animal-like little cry she hurled herself into his arms and their mouths came into attack, each upon the other, matching the hungry savagery of their embracing. For a few minutes their locked shadows swayed on the wall in the flickering candle flame and then, when he would have borne her down into the darkness of the soft hay-bed, she fell before him, tearing him to her. Gradually the wick of the candle burned low.

It was almost dawn when he picked up her cloak from the floor and put it about her shoulders. Already the sky was tinted above the treetops. At the door she peered out warily to make sure the coast was clear. Daniel, preparing to depart himself, moved to the doorway with her. As they looked at each other the memory of the night between them was seared into their faces.

Her lips moved stiffly. "Farewell," she whispered almost inaudibly. Then she gathered up her skirt hems and ran from the cottage, through the open gate and away down the cart track to be lost from sight.

He locked the door and weighed the key thoughtfully in his hand for a moment or two before pocketing it. An odd kind of keepsake. It was as well that the building, already derelict, would continue to crumble away until eventually the roof fell in and the secret of what had taken place there would lie in a rubble of stones.

Claudine reached the Grange and slipped in the side door that she had left unlocked. Removing her shoes, she carried them in her hand as she sped on silent, stockinged feet up one flight of stairs and then another. In the corridors the looped drapes at the windows let in the light of dawn and a few tentative fingers of sunlight were touching the tall chimney pots. With a sigh of relief she reached her bedroom door. With a swirl of her skirts she swung into the room, shut the door soundlessly and sank her head against it, her heart hammering in her breast, her hand still on the brass knob. She was safe in more ways than one.

Abruptly from a part of the room behind her Lionel's voice broke out thickly. "Where have you been until this hour of the morning?"

She spun about, perilously close to panic, and saw him sitting on the four-poster bed in his dressing robe, his face taut and pale. There flashed through her mind the realization that he must have come to her bed at some time in the night and found her absent. Relief that she had not been there mingled with sharp fear of the present situation, but already she had herself under control and she answered with composure.

"I could not sleep. I have been walking in the grounds."

"You lie!" He sprang up from the bed and clasped the nearest post at the foot of it with a violently shaking hand.

She tossed her head. "Why should I lie? The sea trip disagreed with me. Discomfort drove me out into the fresh air."

"For the whole of the night? Your bed has not been slept in at all. You are still wearing the garments of yesterday evening." He stepped from the dais of the bed, his whole attitude menacing. "I'll have the truth from you even if I have to choke it out of you with my own hands!"

He advanced toward her, and although inwardly she quailed, she glared at him defiantly. "What evil suspicion you are harboring in your mind I have no idea," she blazed. "But I say to you that you have no right to accuse me of anything. You are the one who has made a hollow sham of our marriage—"

He seized her by the throat. "Where did you go? Whom did you meet?"

Suddenly she was terribly frightened. There was a wiry strength in his horseman's hands and the pressure he was exerting was closing her windpipe, defeating her frantic efforts to loosen his grip by prizing at his fingers. She could think of only one thing to say that might ease his attack on her, a bluff that extended beyond what had most surely taken place during the night.

"Women who are with child get strange fancies," she gasped. "Some to eat out of season delicacies, others feel trapped by four walls and must seek the freedom of the open air."

He released her so abruptly that she almost fell, but it was to be a long time before she was to discover whether or not her words had made any impact on him, for he was seized by a paroxysm of coughing that rendered him helpless. Concerned only with herself, drawing great drafts of air into her lungs, and with her eyes on her reflection in the nearest looking glass to see how badly bruised was her throat, she did not look in his direction until he began to utter the same dreadful choking noises that he would have wrung from her in another few minutes if an attack had not come upon him. Her eyes widened with horror and revulsion. Blood was running from his mouth and he was swaying on his feet like a reed in the wind. In mute appeal he half-lifted a hand to her, but in the same instant his legs gave way and he collapsed at her feet, face downward, blood staining the carpet.

She stared down at him, filled with a sense of release and exultation. He was dying. Dying. Fate was going to set her free of him. She heard quiet laughter that bordered on a note of hysteria and realized it was her own. For the first time she comprehended the extent of the loathing she had come to feel for him. Suddenly she shuddered. He had reached out a clawing hand and grabbed at her skirts with all the desperation of a drowning man. Mercilessly she snatched her skirts free, and at the same time she heard hurrying footsteps in the corridor approaching her room. Some servant astir must have heard the sound of the fall. Perhaps from the room below. Heaven alone knew what else might have been heard from their raised voices. She must make a show of summoning assistance.

She leaped into action. "Help! Help!" she cried, rushing to the door and flinging it wide. A manservant in his fustian jacket was hovering anxiously. "Quick," she instructed. "Fetch the doctor. Your master has been taken ill. I fear he is dying."

Daniel rode slowly back into Easthampton, but instead of returning to Honeybridge House he turned his horse up the hill to the site of his future home. There he dismounted and wandered with satisfaction through the huge, empty shells of the rooms that would be eventually paneled with silk and set with fireplaces of Carrara marble, while the floors, dusty now with sawdust and shavings, would be agleam with polished wood. On an upper floor he crossed to a window space and rested his weight on the sill to look out over his seaside domain toward the waves tossing sun diamonds in the brightness of the early morning. Below him the work force detailed to building Easthampton House was beginning to arrive. He could see other groups of men gathering to the east and to the west where more new buildings were going up. Painters were already on their ladders at the back of The George IV Hotel, and over all there was that same thriving, industrious look to the resort that he recalled appreciating on his rambles through Brighton at the time when he bid for Kate at the market.

Kate. His eyes grew thoughtful on the image of her. Cool as moonlight, warm as fire, the more she gave of herself the more mysterious she remained. He recalled that he had spoken somewhat harshly to her after the sea trip, but it had irritated him to see her come ashore with Harry, although he had had Claudine too much on his mind to give full attention to the matter. Without doubt his brother was creeping back more and more into Kate's company, and just as an invisible sliver of thorn can stick in the thumb to be a source of discomfort, so had Harry's persistent presence caused him to be sharper with Kate than he would otherwise have been.

He stirred from the sill and made his way downstairs, acknowledging the morning greetings of the workmen as he appeared in their midst. Then he swung himself back in the saddle and rode down through the resort and away along the lane to Honeybridge House. There he left the horse in the stable to be collected by the hotel groom later, and made his way to the outdoor bathhouse near the sparring ring in the orchard. He stripped off his clothes, took a towel, and went down onto the strip of deserted beach by the house. As soon as he reached the water he splashed in until waist-deep. Then he dived under and swam several yards before he reappeared, his dark head bobbing as he struck out strongly through the cool waves.

From one of the windows of the house Kate watched him with love and hurt and anger in her eyes. She had not slept the whole night through and had just bathed herself and changed into a crisp cotton dress to face the day. Never before had Daniel been absent the whole night. Even when gaming he had always returned in the early hours of the morning to tumble into bed beside her smelling of wine and tobacco smoke and excitement, for he was lucky at the tables and invariably won. Some of her most ecstatic moments in his arms had been in those hours of early morning loving, and to her his failure to return at the usual time, his avoidance now of the house and through that his keeping away from her all added weight to her conviction that during the past night he had betrayed her.

Turning away from the window she went downstairs to supervise the breakfast. The little maidservant she had trained was up and going efficiently about her duties. Automatically Kate set dishes to heat and began to prepare the large breakfast that Jem and Daniel always ate with such gusto.

Everything was ready and the table laid in the morning room when she heard the front door burst open as someone entered the house. It was not Daniel, who had come in some time since and had gone straight up to their room, so that she had not yet seen him. Even as she turned from putting down the silver coffeepot on the breakfast table, the arrival's voice boomed out and seemed to fill the hall.

"Daniel!" Harry summoned. The tone of his voice boded no good for anyone, and he sounded drunk. Jem, glancing through the morning newspaper by the window, lowered it abruptly with a rustle of pages and looked across at Kate. Their expressions reflected the consternation of the other. Both of them made for the open double doors at the same time, and they reached the doorway to see Harry standing with feet apart at the bottom of the flight of stairs, while Daniel had come to the head of it, flicking into place the cuffs of the clean shirt over which he had donned his coat.

"What's wrong?" he demanded, starting down the flight. "Is it those new bricks? I thought—"

Harry cut him short. "Is that all you can think of?" he sneered. "This resort of yours? I cannot believe that it really takes second place to Mrs. Attwood."

Daniel came to a halt halfway down the stairs and his face set grimly. In the doorway Kate clutched Jem's arm and quickly he put a gnarled hand over hers in silent reassurance that he was prepared to intervene between the brothers.

Daniel answered slowly and continued down toward the hall, but at a more cautious pace. "For what reason do you come bursting into my house at this unusual hour to drag a lady's name before me?"

"Lady?" Harry echoed derisively. "You don't know the meaning of the word. Kate is a lady as I comprehend it. She's worth a million of those who think themselves better born than she. But you don't understand that." He stuck forth his chin pugnaciously and wagged an aggressive finger at his brother. "You don't care for her and you never did. I've proof enough of that now. So I'm exercising my right to buy her back from you." He dived into his pocket and snatched out a leather drawstring purse which he hurled at Daniel's feet where it spilled out its contents in a shower of gold coins, which bounced away down the stairs and rolled across the hall floor in all directions. "Twenty-one guineas! I didn't have that much when I needed it at the market in Brighton, but there it is now."

"Kate is my wife," Daniel answered dangerously. "She is not for sale."

"Your wife?" Again Harry took malevolent pleasure in repeating his brother's utterance. "What need do you have of a wife when you go a-whoring all night with Claudine Attwood in the cottage near Denwin's Corner?"

Daniel leaped for him with fists lunging. Jem hurled himself forward, but although he seized Daniel by the shoulder and half-hauled him back he was too late to stop one tremendous punch that caught Harry across the side of the face and sent him flying backward to crash against the wall and fall to one knee on the floor. Kate shrieked and rushed to Harry's aid while Jem struggled with all his strength to hold Daniel back from further attack on his brother.

"Hold it! Calm yerself. Leave yer brother be. He's drunk and don't know what he's saying."

Harry reeled to his feet, one hand against the wall to keep his balance, his eyes on Kate, mistaking for sympathy and favor her natural concern for the effects of Daniel's blow, which could have smashed his jaw had not Jem diverted the force of it. "I have been drinking, but I'm not too far gone in my cups to know what I'm saying. I followed Daniel to the cottage and saw the Attwood woman go in to him—"

He stopped short as Kate slapped him hard across his mouth, her eyes blazing. "Go!" she hissed. "Get out of my sight! You Warwyck brothers know no shame and have no scruples when it comes to chasing after what you want. I have come to the end with both of you. Now go."

Stubbornly Harry refused to budge, flinging out an accusing hand in Daniel's direction. "Let him deny it then if what I have told you is not the truth."

Jem could restrain Daniel no longer. He broke free, seized Harry in a terrible scuffle, and hurled him from the house onto the path outside. The gravel cut deep into Harry's hands and scattered under him. Daniel slammed the door on the sight of him with a force that made the whole house vibrate. In bed upstairs

Jassy stirred, rolled over, and went to sleep again, while Jem tactfully withdrew from the hall to take himself off for a walk, leaving
Kate and Daniel alone. Daniel spoke first, making no excuses and
no denial. He would not insult Kate with lies. Enough damage
had been done.

"Tell me that you did not mean what you said about it being
the end," he said.

Her gaze was curiously starry as if she looked at him through a
veil of frozen tears. "I meant it in the sense that the path I follow
in the future will be my own. I consider myself no longer subject
to you, nor will I again to any man."

"But you'll not leave Honeybridge House?" He was privately resolved that he would not allow her to go even if she intended it,
whatever methods he had to use.

"No," she said. "I have too much to keep me busy here for a
long time to come."

He thought it a strange answer and was puzzled by it, but he
had more to say to her. "What can I do to make amends?"

It was as if she looked at him from far, far away. "Nothing,"
she said sadly. "Nothing at all. We have ever been strangers to
each other."

She turned away into the morning room where she opened the
casement doors into the garden and went out into the sunshine,
walking at a slow pace until she reached the orchard. There she
sank down into the flowery grass and leaned back against a tree,
her billowing skirt settling to blend with the buttercups. He
would have liked to have gone to her now, taken her in his arms
and held her in quietude and peace, her head upon his shoulder,
but she had made it plain that he had forfeited all that had been
between them. What had passed with Claudine in that dark and
erotic night had nothing to do with his life with her, but that
would be beyond her comprehension. He and Claudine had held
each other in thrall since the first meeting, and they were still in
bondage to each other, no matter how much each might wish it
were otherwise.

The sound of running footsteps in the lane caught his attention and he went to see who had come banging through the gate. Harry had departed, and it was Hardy who had arrived with some breathlessness.

"You'd best come, sir. There's trouble down on the shore. When the wagons went to get the loads of shingle as usual for the building work Tom Brown barred their way on the slipway, saying they'd take no more of it except over 'is dead body.'"

Daniel frowned as he went from the house with Hardy. There had been trouble with Brown before on the beach. The man protested that removing the shingle daily ever since the building work started had reduced the safety of his bathing machines, making it impossible to draw them up as high out of reach of the tide as before when not in use. During recent rough weather several had been submerged and washed away.

"I'll settle this once and for all," he said, lifting his head as the sound of angry shouts reached them from the direction of the bathing machine site, and he broke into a run, Hardy following him.

In the orchard Kate rose to her feet. The noise of the commotion had reached her and a glimpse through the trees of Daniel and his foreman setting off at full speed told her that something was seriously wrong. Perhaps there had been an accident. She had given aid at many that had varied in severity from cuts and burns and chopped-off fingers to falls from scaffolds and crushed limbs. In most cases she had seen that the patients were properly nursed afterward, frequently dealing with it herself, and with everything on an upward financial swing for Daniel it had become slightly easier to get him to pay out some compensation in the deserving cases.

Darting back toward the house with the intention of picking up the valise of bandages and laudanum and other things often needed in an emergency, she was hailed in her tracks by Jassy from an upper window.

"It looks as if there's going to be some kind of fight near the bathing machines," the girl called, shading her eyes against the sun with her hands. "I can see Daniel's workmen with the wagons waiting to get down the slipway and there's a whole gang blocking their way."

A brawl meant extra bandages. Kate dashed into the house, took down stacks of clean, rolled linen from a cupboard and tossed them into the valise. Gripping it by the handle, she ran from the house and sped along the lane. When she reached the scene a crowd of spectators had already gathered, blocking her view of what was going on. Swiftly she pushed her way through and came out to see that the situation was exactly as Jassy had described. The outraged carters and loaders had attempted to get down the only slipway wide enough to take wagons, but had been thwarted in their aim and kept at bay by Tom Brown and a whole cluster of the roughs and toughs of the resort ranged up with him, all armed with bludgeons of driftwood and solid-looking sticks made lethal with projecting nails. At their feet ammunition waited in the piles of rock and stones that had been collected together. Daniel and Brown were locked in wordy argument across the stretch of seaweedy slipway between them.

"I've told you before, Warwyck," Brown bawled, crimson-faced with temper and shaking a fist. "You have no right to keep taking the shingle from my part of the beach."

"I have every right—and so has any other man to take what nature has provided in the way of building materials along the stretch of shore. Now tell your layabouts and vagabonds to get out of our path and let my men and wagons through."

"You go to the devil!" Brown bent and snatched up a large piece of rock, which he weighed threateningly in his hand.

Daniel breathed deeply and swung from the waist to shout over his shoulder at the employee nearest to him, a youth with a lively, freckled face. "Go back to the yard and tell the carpenters to drop everything else and start building me a fleet of bathing machines. I intend to put our local windbag out of business before the summer is through."

There came shouts of approving laughter from his workmen, which was echoed by the spectators, and some applauded. Daniel's mocking grin at Brown endorsed the taunt and his resolution, a grin that had inflamed to folly many an opponent in the ring, and to Brown it was beyond endurance. He hurled the rock he held, but Daniel dodged instinctively and it smashed home against the shoulder of one of the laborers behind him, sending the fellow falling backward on a high bellow of pain. It was all that was needed to release pandemonium. With shouts his companions attempted to storm the slipway with Daniel at the head of them, the carters urging their horses forward with cracking whips, and those on foot advancing with their shovels and spades, brandishing them like spears. Stones and rocks and lumps of the old sea wall were let fly by Brown's supporters, causing the spectators on the promenade to scatter as they found themselves within range of the flying missiles.

Kate, who had rushed to the fallen man, feared his collarbone was broken, and after doing what she could for him in the way of immediate aid, she darted off to the next victim. It was the freckle-faced youth, who had had no time to obey the order given by his master, having been gashed across the forehead and unable to see for the blood running from it. Kate knelt beside him, swathed the gash in linen and told him she would put some stitches in it for him later. She had to shout to make him hear, for the noise around them was deafening, the horses whinnying with fright, rearing and stamping, and some dogs, attracted by the fracas, were adding their frenzied barking to the shouts and swearing of the opposing forces, which was accompanied by the clang of shovels acting like shields against the barrage, and the thuds and yells as blows went home. The whole situation had become serious beyond measure, and Kate, ignoring any danger to herself, went from one casualty to another.

In the thick of the fight Daniel had had his coat half-torn from his back, finding he had never less than four or five attackers ranged against him, the deadliness of a pugilist's fists known and feared with the certainty that punches coming from one of his repute would smash a man's jaw or splinter his nose or knock him senseless for a week. They used pieces of driftwood against him, one plank with a nail tearing into his forehead and narrowly missing his eye, so that he fought with blood streaming down one side of his face and looked as gruesome a sight as those whose visages had received his knuckles in full, their grunts and groans as they went down adding to the general din. The rules he adhered to in the ring went by the board. His elbows, knees, and boots did almost as much damage as his fists, and seeing a burly brute coming at him with an upraised iron bludgeon he delivered a kick to the groin that doubled the fellow up and sent him crashing down onto the slipway in the path of the first wagon that had broken through. Kate, busy with her ministrations, turned her head in time to see the heavy wheel run over one of the man's legs.

Who he was and which side he was on she did not know or care. Pushing past those engaged in combat, her eyes only on the unfortunate screaming man who needed her help, she made her way down the slipway, but she was never to reach him. A shovel, wielded as a weapon by one of Daniel's own laborers, swung back and crashed against her brow. She did not remember tumbling from the slipway or catching her ribs against a barnacled obstruction that seemed to drive knives into her. All she knew was that blackness was mercifully swallowing up a pain too great to be borne.

Daniel, who had reached the sands at the foot of the slipway, caught the yellow flash of her gown out of the corner of his eye and turned to yell a warning for her to get out of the fray. He was too late. He saw the accidental blow, saw her foot go over the edge of the slipway and watched in disbelieving helplessness as she tilted forward like a rag doll, was tossed against a jutting strut, and went smashing down onto the sloping shingle a few feet below.

"Kate!" Her name burst from his throat in an agonized roar. Knocking aside those who blocked his way, he went charging up the shingle to reach her. Jem, who had come late to the scene, leaped down from the promenade and slithered on the pebbles, making them roll. Some clattered over Kate, and Daniel gave an awful groan at this further affliction, dropping onto his knees beside her. Jem, his weathered face gray beneath his tan, reached out to help turn her over, but Daniel did it himself with tender hands and groaned again at the sight of her chalk-white face with its livid bruises.

Jem spoke in choked tones. "God in Heaven! Is she dead?"

Daniel answered forcefully as if by his own will he could keep life in her "No, no. She can't be. She mustn't be." His eyes were dark and desperate as he lowered his head to press an ear against her chest. At first, failing to hear the heartbeat, he thought she had gone and there welled up before him such an abyss of desolation that he thought his mind must split in the face of it. He could not live without her. Then he caught the faint throb of her heart and was enervated by relief. "She is still alive, thank God," he uttered shakily, taking off his torn coat and covering her with it. "Now get some kind of stretcher, and send someone to fetch the London physician who is staying at The Warwyck Hotel."

He knelt beside Kate, holding her limp hand between his own, oblivious to the rest of the wagons rolling down the slipway with Brown standing defeated and those of his cronies not nursing cut heads or other wounds put to flight. They and others among the laborers who were casualties were soon being attended to, makeshift stretchers being supplied by fishermen for those who needed them, and one of the wagons was taken up the slipway again to provide transport for the injured. Susan Singleton was among those who had appeared to give a helping hand, and it was she who directed that an ancient cabin door once salvaged from a wrecked ship be taken down at once to pick up the prone figure of Kate Warwyck lying on the beach, her tangled gown a splash of brilliant color on the pastel-shaded shingle.

Chapter 16

For a dangerous time Kate hovered in unconsciousness between life and death. Dr. Frampton, the London physician who had come to Easthampton with a view to setting up a junior partner in a local practice, called in a colleague who specialized in such cases, and an operation was performed on the scrubbed kitchen table at Honeybridge House to remove a clot of blood that was causing excessive pressure. It was successful, although some fever resulted, which gave cause for further concern, but eventually Kate, her head in a cap of bandages, her long tresses shorn, came back from the dark depths of oblivion as if awaking from a long sleep, her mind possessed by a nightmare that must have been with her all the time. She had lost Daniel. He had finally rejected her and made his choice. And in his turn he had lost her, for she would not embarrass him or humiliate herself offensively in his eyes by futile attempts to bridge the gap that he had cleaved of his own free will.

All these thoughts came to her on brief waves of semiconsciousness before she finally broke out of the dark shadows that had kept her trapped for such a long time, and thus it was that she did not ask for Daniel or express any wish to see him when her lids lifted and looked at last with clarity and full awareness upon her surroundings and Jassy reading by her bed. The book dropped to the floor as Jassy leaned forward excitedly, seeing that Kate had come back to the world and there were to be no more brief spells of near lucidity that had raised hopes only to dash them again.

"Dear, dear Kate. All will be well now."

Kate smiled weakly. "Have I been ill long?"

"Several weeks."

"What day is it?"

"The last Wednesday in August." Then Jassy saw such a rush of anxiety in Kate's eyes at the length of passed time that she guessed the reason and hastened to reassure her. "You have not lost your baby. The physician suspected your condition immediately and you have received every care. It is fortunate that the accident did not occur at a more developed stage, or who knows what damage might have been done."

"Does everyone know about it?" The question was put cautiously.

"Yes. Daniel's joy has been marred by a desperate worry over you, but now all that is past."

Much was past. But the future held hope and promise of another kind. She slid her hand across the soft cambric of her nightgown under the bedclothes and rested it on her stomach. It would be a son. Already he had proved himself to be stubborn and tenacious, refusing to be shifted by adversity, a true Warwyck. On the thought of what he had already survived, there came other images into her mind of the day she had been struck down. Like magic lantern pictures one passed over another, and she saw again the rearing, neighing horses, the struggling men, and the violent wielding of makeshift weapons.

"That morning at the slipway—what happened?" she questioned restlessly.

"You were struck down accidentally and fell from the slipway to the shingle below."

"How did it all end?"

"Daniel had his fleet of bathing machines constructed in a matter of days, and he set them up where the shingle is on a level with the promenade in front of The Warwyck Hotel."

"But the shore is full of rocks there."

"He had them all blasted out to create the finest stretch of bathing sand. It is that which immediately attracted all the custom away from Brown's machines." Jassy giggled. "The flints held such a variety of colors that Daniel had a fine wall of them built to encircle the gardens on the site of the old green. Somebody asked jokingly if he was making a giant prize ring of the spot, and he promptly decided that the gardens should become known as Ring Park."

Kate was not ready to be told such inconsequential details.

"What of the man whose leg was crushed under the wheel?" she asked fitfully.

Jassy put a cool hand on her forehead to calm her. "There had to be an amputation."

Other thoughts came to trouble her. "What of Harry?"

"He has gone away for good. To London. Through business dealings at Easthampton he had made connections in the capital and has secured a promising position for himself with a firm of land agents. We write to each other. I have kept him informed of your progress." Jassy hesitated, wondering how much she should tell Kate at this point and decided to let wait that Jem, taking matters into his own hands, had stormed out at Harry that he was blind not to see that Kate loved Daniel and had always loved him. As the brothers were no longer on speaking terms, ever since that final day when Harry had hurled the twenty-one guineas at Daniel's feet, no word over the matter had passed between them. Harry, when he had come to say goodbye to her, had asked confirmation as to whether what he had learned from Jem was true.

"I can reveal nothing," Jassy had answered, keeping to the promise she had once made Kate.

"When Kate is recovered," he had said steadily, "I'll come back to demand the truth from her, but otherwise I'll not set foot in Easthampton again."

In the bed Kate uttered a little sigh. "I pray his new life will bring him what was never mine to give." She rolled her head round on the pillow and looked toward the window. She could see a streak of cobalt blue August sky between the curtains drawn against the brilliant sunshine, and the room was held in a shaded, amber glow. It was not the spacious bedroom she had shared with Daniel, but the one believed to have been part of the old nursery suite. "Why am I here?" she asked.

"Dr. Frampton wanted you to have absolute quiet, and this side of the house is away from the sea and the lane. It also has the added advantage of communicating doors to two other rooms where the day and night nurses have been accommodated, because you have been kept under constant surveillance."

"Surely you and Susan Singleton would have been better than professional nurses."

"Oh, these were not the slovenly creatures you are picturing, but two most capable women of impeccable behavior and cleanliness, whom Dr. Frampton employs for attendance on his special patients. Daniel spared no cost in securing the best of care and attention for you." She paused. "He has been like a man demented during your illness. Indeed, a very madness seemed to take him over from the moment he went to the scratch in a prize fight he took part in two weeks ago. Jem said he had never seen anything like it. Daniel beat the only other possible contender for the championship in a matter of five rounds. It's a match that will go down in the annals of boxing."

Kate wanted to say that she was glad that he had won, but tiredness overwhelmed her and and she drifted into a restful sleep. A few minutes later the day nurse came back to the sickroom and in whispers Jassy made her report. Outside on the landing she encountered Jem and hugged him in her exuberance.

"Kate has recovered consciousness! She spoke quite a lot to me. Isn't it wonderful?"

He grinned from ear to ear. "It is. Are ye on yer way to fetch Daniel? He were in the orchard not five minutes ago."

"I will go to him, of course." Her face clouded. "But she didn't ask for him. Not once did she mention his name."

Jem tried not to accept that this held any significance. "Mebbe she didn't ask for anyone, just coming round like that."

"She wanted to know about Harry."

Daniel, who had entered the house by way of the casement doors in the morning room, caught the happy ring of Jassy's voice and guessed immediately the cause. But in the seconds it took him to cross the room and reach the hall he heard clearly the words that Jem and Jassy uttered to each other. Hearing his step, his joyful haste abruptly checked, they looked down in time to see him turn on his heel and go back the way he had come. Harry, he thought in torment. As he always suspected, it was Harry whom she secretly loved, Harry who had made that impregnable, insurmountable barrier between them. In spite of what she had said on that terrible day, it was still Harry whom she harbored in her heart.

Jassy darted to the baluster rail, but he was already gone from sight. "Now Kate is better he is no longer interested," she exclaimed heatedly. "To think I tried to cheer her with some talk of his concern. It was nothing but his conscience that was troubling him. He feared she would die through his folly in aggravating the situation at the slipway into an all-round brawl."

"I don't know," Jem replied in sad bafflement, "but then it seems I don't know nothing about neither of 'em no more."

A few miles away at Attwood Grange another invalid was struggling toward recovery. It took the form with Lionel of departure for Italy where once again the only hope for him lay with the Italian sun. The Grange was to be closed up again as soon as he and his wife had left, and already some of the rooms were swathed in dust sheets and the valuable silver put in storage in a safe place. Claudine, dressed in traveling clothes, took a final glance in her dressing-table looking glass, tucked away a stray curl, and made her way to the stairs. She had made the coming change of abode and climate as well as her condition an excuse for a whole new wardrobe of clothes, and she overtook the giant caterpillar of her brass-cornered trunks and boxes being carried out to the waiting equipages at the door.

She was thankful to be leaving the Grange behind, for it had become like a prison, all social life having ground abruptly to a halt when news of Lionel's collapse had spread, everyone naturally supposing that she would want to remain ceaselessly at his sickbed and later, as he slowly made progress, to be by his wheeled basket chair. Only Alexander had seen through the expression of patient hope and gentle bravery that she presented to those who came to the house to make considerate inquiries after the sick man, and as an escape from boredom she had seen a way to strike Alexander down for having encouraged her into the obnoxious marriage in the first place. It had proved ridiculously easy to get him more securely on the hook than he had ever been. Farewells had been said to him and to Olivia, but an unsigned note passed into his hand had ensured that he return to the house again. He was waiting for her in the library.

He turned from the window as she entered and crossed swiftly to close the door after her. "My darling." He took her into his arms and as she tilted her head aside he kissed her on the cheek and on the throat before once more seeking her lips, but she eased herself away from him, ever tantalizing, never fulfilling her unspoken promises.

"Please, Alexander," she said in deceptively soft tones. "I have something to say and we have little time. Lionel will be helped down to the carriage very shortly."

Eagerly he questioned her. "Have you changed your mind about going with him?" He did not know how he would be able to endure her absence. It had been hard enough when she had gone abroad after the wedding, and although Lionel had issued an invitation for him to visit with Olivia at the Attwood villa on the Adriatic coast, he had become used to seeing Claudine nearly every day again on some pretext or another, and would miss her beyond measure.

She dashed his hope with her next words. "No, not at all. Italy is a country I have always wanted to see, but from what the doctors told me yesterday it will not be a place of long sojourn."

It was as he had feared, and he felt a genuine distress, for he had known Lionel a long time and never once had he wished for his demise; on the contrary, quite apart from the bonds of Lionel's friendship and neighborliness on which he set high store, he wanted Claudine's husband to thrive. The prospect of her as a young, rich widow was not to his liking. He sought to cement their relationship once and for all.

"When the worst happens—if it must happen—then I shall become your adviser and guide, standing between you and all who will seek to take advantage of you." His arm went about her narrow shoulders in a protective manner. "In the future you need look to no one but me."

"But I'll not be alone."

He was puzzled. "What do you mean?"

She kept her lashes lowered to hide the gloating jubilance in her eyes. "I am going to have a child. An heir—pray God—for Lionel."

Under her lashes she watched the way the color blotched in his face. If she had needed convincing about his motives in approving her marriage to Lionel all last doubts would have been banished. With difficulty Alexander found his voice.

"I'll be like a father to the infant."

"And like a husband to me?" she saw, as she had intended, that he took her provocative query to be a declaration of hitherto unspoken affection combined with the promise of submission as soon as she was free. His expression became one of triumph and passion.

"Claudine," he exclaimed eagerly and would have embraced her ardently, but she whirled like a top from him and faced him from some little distance away.

"I shall have no scruples about taking a married man as a lover," she said deliberately and with emphasis, "since I have already crossed that barrier." Her thin eyebrows raised at him. "Have I shocked you, dear brother-in-law? You look ashen."

It seemed as if he might choke. Her meaning was clear. "Then the child is not Lionel's?"

She put her head to one side and pursed her mouth in a little smile. "Did I say that?"

He charged across at her, provoked beyond endurance, and seized her wrists, jerking her to him. "Who is the man? I demand that you reveal his name!"

"You are hurting me," she protested, losing patience. "Let go at once. I can hear that Lionel is being brought downstairs. Release me, I tell you."

He obeyed, letting his own shaking hands fall to his sides. Claudine sped across to the library doors, opened them, and swept through. Through the doorway he saw her go to the foot of the flight with every show of fussing concern and solicitude for the invalid coming slowly downstairs, half-leaning, half-carried by two menservants. Pity and compassion swept through Alexander at the skeletal condition of the still handsome man who was pinning his hopes in vain upon the Italian sun, and he would have stayed where he was in the library, afraid that he might give away his feelings, but Claudine was already announcing his presence to Lionel.

"Alexander has come to see us into our carriage. Is that not considerate of him?"

Lionel's beautiful smile lit his thin features as Alexander came forward. "What a kind friend you are. We shall be looking forward to seeing you and Olivia at the villa. Be sure and bring all the latest news of the county with you."

"I will do that."

Alexander followed as Lionel was assisted out of the house and down the steps to the carriage. Claudine, going before her husband, gave constant instructions that he was not to be hurried, must be given time on each broad step, and be allowed respite to get his breath. Alexander thought cynically that had he not known otherwise, even he would have been tempted to think she had become the most devoted of wives. She insisted on Lionel being seated in the carriage first and then, pausing before entering, she turned her cold, vixenish smile on Alexander.

"Yes, please do as Lionel says and bring us all the latest gossip. Perhaps Easthampton will see a few more scenes such as that affair over the taking of shingle from the bathing-machine site. That Daniel Warwyck is full of surprises. I declare there is no way of knowing what that old enemy of yours will do next." Her smile widened to display her even little teeth and her eyes mocked him mercilessly. "Is there?"

With that she stepped lightly into the carriage to sit down opposite Lionel, while the groom flicked up the step and shut the door before leaping up into his place with his fellow groom at the rear. Alexander, unable to take his eyes from Claudine in sick fury at what she had revealed to him, stepped forward.

"*Bon voyage*," he said hoarsely. He tore his gaze from her and reached up to shake Lionel's hand through the open window. "I wish you a speedy return to health. Take the greatest care."

"I will indeed. Farewell, my friend."

Claudine fluttered her white-gloved hand. "Farewell, brother-in-law." Through the glass she continued to hold his maddened glare, her green eyes glinting with malicious amusement, until the carriage took the curve of the drive and she was lost to his sight. He continued to stand there while the rest of the carriages in the entourage bearing servants and baggage rolled past him with a rumble of wheels and a scattering of gravel to go down the drive and out through the gates. Not until the last one vanished into the lane beyond did he manage to gather his outraged wits together and signal for his horse to be brought forward. It was a source of bitter regret to him that when he had thrust Daniel Warwyck from the barouche at Brighton he had not caused him to crack his skull and so put an end to his pursuit of Claudine there and then. But he would make sure that the pugilist paid in full for pleasures already taken and would never have the advantage of Claudine's widowhood when it came. Somewhere and somehow he would see that the scoundrel was wiped from the face of the earth.

In the carriage Claudine settled herself comfortably against the soft upholstery. Since Lionel's collapse there had been a truce be-

tween them. Whether he remembered clutching at her skirts in
appeal for aid she did not know, but she doubted it. He had been
extremely ill, and it was sheer willpower more than any temporary
recovery of strength that had made the doctors decide that he
should make the journey to his villa in view of undeniable evidence that miracles did sometimes happen. It was one of these
same doctors, consulted by Claudine, who confirmed that she was
indeed in the first months of pregnancy, but assured Lionel that
as she was strong and young and in perfect health there was no
reason why she should not make the journey with him.

"That is as well," Lionel had replied in her hearing, "because I
have no intention of traveling without my wife's company."

Glancing across at him Claudine noticed that he was craning
his neck for a last glimpse of the rooftops of Attwood Grange
above the treetops, his face racked and tears in his eyes. She realized for the first time that he was as much aware as any of those
attendant upon him that his chances of seeing his birthplace
again were very slim indeed. Then he drew back in his seat as the
last chimney pots were lost from his sight, and he proceeded to
watch the passing countryside, the slopes of the hills where he
had hunted since first old enough to ride to hounds, the river and
streams he knew from boyhood, and the farmhouses and cottages
of his tenants, many of whom had lived and worked for generation after generation on the Attwood land. Only when the boundaries of the estate were left behind and the outskirts of Merrelton
drew near did he look across and address Claudine for the first
time since the journey had started.

"I hope you will not find life at the villa too tedious. There is a
terrace that faces a private bay, and it is there under the shade of
an awning that I spent much of my convalescence last time. You
will be able to take walks in the garden, but carriage rides must be
avoided as soon as we are safely arrived, for the roads are rough
and stony. I have a fine library in the villa where you should find
plenty to interest you, and there's entertainment when local musi-
cians come to the gate and play with quite remarkable touch and
talent. Otherwise there is little to do. There are a number of

noble Italian and British families who have residences in the district, but until I am recovered in health I cannot allow you to accept any hospitality that cannot immediately be returned."

She did not want to start quarreling with him again, but she was appalled at the restrictions being placed upon her. "While you are recovering at the villa I plan to take expeditions to Rome and Florence and Venice. There is no need for me to disappear from the public eye for a long while yet."

"Why?" he snapped at her. "Are you less advanced in your condition than you would have me believe?"

He almost caught her off guard, but outwardly she retained her composure, her mind busy with the realization that she had not lulled his suspicions about the night she had been absent from the Grange.

"Not at all," she replied coolly, "but the garments that have been made for me to wear as the months go by have been most skillfully cut to enable me to keep secret from the casual observer that I am in the family way."

He answered her in quiet, level tones, his snapped outburst over, the strength of sustaining it beyond him. "You may wear what you like, but dates and nine months' gestation cannot be coerced. For that reason you shall not at any time leave the villa grounds, which have a high wall around them and a lodge-keeper at each locked gate. I'll not risk some tale of a miscarriage being brought to me from Rome or any other place where you may have planned to visit an abortionist and rid yourself of an uninvited burden."

She was truly affronted and angry. "Such a thought never entered my head. I want this baby I am carrying."

"Nevertheless the conditions of your being constantly at the villa remain the same. I am under no delusion about the present state of my health and what my chances of survival might be, but"—here his wearied voice strengthened stubbornly—"I intend to live long enough to see the child born. I know exactly when we were last together and if there was no conception that night you will appear to go four or five weeks beyond your time." An irrevocable threat entered into his words. "I tell you that no bastard shall inherit from me."

"Your insults are insufferable," she cried. "I will not endure them. Stop the carriage at once. I shall return to the Grange and you can go alone to Italy—"

"Leave me now and you will be penniless with nothing but the clothes on your back."

She gaped at him incredulously. "Are you out of your mind? I have my own fortune, which gives me no need of yours."

"You are mistaken. As my wife all that you owned became mine upon our marriage, and although I was willing to let you do what you wished with your own fortune all the time you proved a dutiful partner, I would have to withdraw the privilege in the face of your desertion." The unpleasantness of the scene was telling on him, and taking a brandy flask from his pocket he carefully unscrewed the top and poured a measure into it, which he downed before continuing what he had to say. "In the same way, should you fail to give birth at the allotted time and thus prove you have carried another man's child, I would bequeath nothing to you beyond a small annual income to keep you in some gentility until you married again, and then the allowance would stop." He saw he had rendered her speechless. Never before had he seen her so utterly at a loss, and he continued to address her in the same mild tones, although there was an icy cut to them. "But since you insist the child is mine we have no need to look so bleakly on your future. Nobody will be happier than I if you bear me a healthy son."

She nodded, managing to look disdainful of all suspicion, but she knew herself to be defeated. She who could get whatever she wanted from men like Daniel and Alexander had met her match in one whom she had considered malleable and weak. He alone had mastered her. All she could do was to hope for an early or premature birth of the child she knew to be Daniel's.

Chapter 17

It was snowing slightly, blowing in flurries from the sea, when Daniel stood surveying Easthampton House in all its pristine glory. It was finished. A graceful building of complete simplicity, its beauty in its lines and lack of ornament, enhancing the splendid Ionic portico and tall windows. He was reminded of a sea pearl, smoothly fashioned and the more exquisite for it, the very color of the creamy stucco given an underwater tint by some curious trick of light from the sea, which would be increased when the oaks and beeches and chestnuts to the north, east, and west of the house put on their lush foliage when spring came. To the glorious front of the house open lawns sloped from the forecourt to the gates below, because he had wanted not so much as a rosebush to impede in any way the view of the spread-out resort and the sea beyond. It had all set him neck-deep in debt, but the amazing popularity of the resort in its first summer had set him high on the pinnacle of financial success to which there appeared to be no foreseeable end.

Around him on the forecourt his footprints in the powdery snow crossed and crisscrossed each other, showing how he had passed to one end of it and then the other to study the house to his complete satisfaction. After a final scrutiny of the portico he went up its steps to re-enter the brass-knockered door, whipping off his cloak and shaking the snowflakes from it as he entered. Warmth met him after the chill outside, for servants had moved into their quarters that morning and fires had been lit, banishing the last traces of new paint with the fragrance of apple wood. The hall was lighted through the high ceiling by a circular glazed lantern which flooded the elegant central staircase with sunshine on brighter days, but on this cold afternoon, with a covering of snow on the glass, all was bathed in a soft, gray glow. He tossed his cloak and hat onto the nearest chair and then paused at the open double doors of the long and finely proportioned drawing room where Kate, who had been viewing the house inside while he had been stomping happily around outside, had finished her tour and was sitting on one of the chairs in profile to him, looking into the fire, one elbow resting on the curved arm, her hand drooping at a graceful angle from the wrist in a frill of blue silk cuff. She was at the end of her eighth month, and one of the reasons he had bullied and chivied and driven the labor force on the house to get it completed in record time was that he had wanted it ready for when his child would be born.

As he approached her, his feet making no sound on the Aubusson carpet, some of his happiness ebbed and the old sadness crept in on him as chill as the day outside. Kate had never moved out of the bedroom where she had been nursed back to health, leaving him to sleep alone, and it seemed to him sometimes that by day and night he wore loneliness like a cloak. He hoped that when they moved into the new house on the morrow they might make a fresh beginning and put the past behind them. Not that Kate ever uttered one word or gave a glance of reproach. Her attitude toward him was calm and good-natured with nothing to put stress and strain on the household at Honeybridge House, and at times he was tempted to wonder if she had forgotten during her illness exactly what it was that had split them asunder seemingly beyond recall, but then he knew that was not the case. On the odd occasion when some reference was made to the brawl on the slipway her remarks showed clearly enough that there was no lapse in her memory and all that had led up to her receiving the blow on her forehead had come back to her with her recovery. She was still as determined as ever to ensure what she considered to be the rights of his workmen, and where once his clashes with her had irritated him, he now welcomed them, enjoying her spit and fire, taking inward pride in her level argument and logic and common sense. Because he loved her. He believed now that he had loved her almost from the start, the first unconscious stirring taking root without his ever being aware of it.

Strangely, it was not the heart-stunning shock of thinking she had been killed during the brawl that had brought him to his senses, but what had occurred less than half an hour before it. When Harry had tossed the twenty-one guineas at him and he had looked down at the coins dancing about his feet it was as if he had come face to face with his own fate. Had he not won his prize fights and had such a sum in his purse, Kate would never have been his. It thundered home how much she had come to mean to him, she who was beyond price. Then seconds later Harry was tearing down with bitter words and all too truthful accusations the whole structure of his marriage to her. Like flotsam before the tide the broken pieces of it had floated away, leaving them man and wife in name only, she yearning after his brother, he beside himself with love for her.

"Well, Kate," he said inquiringly, setting a hand on the back of her chair, "what do you think of the house now that all is ready?"

She turned her head toward him with a little start, a smile breaking on her mouth. "It is as beautiful as you said it would be. The sea blues and greens with the ivory walls give it a cool and somewhat mysterious atmosphere. It's like looking through clear water at a sea bed, but it is sunshot water, because the gilt on the cornices and the pale gold damask panels and the rich carpets counteract any feeling of coldness that might have resulted." She glanced about her and nodded, giving the final seal of approval. "It is fit to house the King of England, to say nothing of the next champion of the prize ring."

He chuckled confidently. "This is only February, and I do not intend to wait until I have won the championship in May before taking up residence. Tomorrow we shall move in."

She looked at him blankly and rose from the chair, the advanced stage of her pregnancy making her slow and awkward in her movements. "I can't leave Honeybridge House. I'm going to have the baby there."

Had her expression not been so serious he might have laughed, thinking she was making some teasing joke, but as it was he saw that she was in earnest. "What are you saying?" he demanded. "I do not understand you. The whole point in getting the house completed before the scheduled time was that you should be brought to bed within its walls."

Her gaze was very wide and clear. "I have never once said that I wished our child to be born anywhere else but at Honeybridge. It is home to me. I love every brick and stone of it, and I feel safe there. Since the day you made your pledge on it I have always known that it is my haven and none can ever turn me out of its doors."

He was both aghast and baffled. "Pledge! What pledge? And are you implying that security would be denied you here?"

She was amazed that he did not immediately remember the occasion to which she had referred. "When I came to Honeybridge to nurse Jassy you gave your word that I might stay there for as long as it suited me. That promise enabled me to strike roots, and although I left once of my own free will you took me back there, and I knew that unless I wanted it I need never leave its portals ever again."

He seized her by the arms. "I have never heard such foolishness. Easthampton House is *our* house, *our* new home. You are my wife and will be mistress here till the end of our days."

She closed her eyes sharply and tightly to drive away an image of herself alone within these echoing, elegant walls, he having left long since at the return of Claudine's siren call. He, mistaking the reason for her shut lids, thought he had handled her too roughly and released her arms to take her face on either side with gentle fingertips. His voice lowered to a subdued and coaxing note.

"You are near your time and have taken a quaint notion into your head. You will be safer in this house than anywhere. I know you will feel quite differently about it when all your possessions have been installed—"

She thrust up her hands with the palms together on a sensation of panic and then shot them wide to dash his touch from her. "This is a palace. I don't belong in such surroundings. I need a home. This grand and glorious edifice has no heart."

He was hurt beyond measure, and out of the pain with all the longing that lay behind it his wrath erupted with all the sudden violence of a volcano. "It is you who have no heart. That was given away long ago and left us the poorer for it. I tell you that our child shall be born in this house. It is his inheritance." He, like Kate, had never doubted that she would have a son.

She had gone deathly pale, but in the flash of her eyes was the bright steel of her implacable will which had carried her through so much in the past. "I'll bear him under the stars and a hedgerow before I let him utter his first cry under this roof where love is doomed to be a stranger." She caught up from the sofa nearby the fur-lined cloak he had given her at Christmastime and wrapped it about her, its softness rippling.

It had been on the tip of his tongue to demand caustically of her whose fault it might be that love was lost, thus laying all the blame at her door, but in all fairness he was obliged to check the outburst, knowing his own errors had been many. Nevertheless there was no excuse for her flagrant defiance of his wishes and he would have his way. He gave his ultimatum.

"You will move into this house tomorrow or else you can stay at Honeybridge forever."

She was adjusting the hood of her cloak and the fur framed the stark paleness of her face. Only her eyes held color, a blue deeper and darker than he had ever seen there before, awash with a depth of emotion that was beyond definition.

"Then I choose Honeybridge," she said in a voice that did not quaver, but was barely above a whisper. "Easthampton House was never built for me or for this child I carry or for any other children we might have had. I had hoped that when it was completed I would find some niche in it where I could feel that I belonged, but I looked in vain. There is no place here for me."

To her relief he let her go in silence. He did not rampage after her or try to hold her back physically or prolong in any way their final parting. If it had been possible she would have loved him all the more for it, but her mind, heart, and very soul had long been a single passionate flame of love for him that flared at a peak that defied her own comprehension.

Through the window he saw her go down the steps of the portico, and a manservant, who had been sweeping each one clear of snow, went running to hail from the stables the carriage that had brought them to the house together. The terrible truth was that she had been right in sensing that he had had no thought of her in his head when he had first conceived the idea of building himself a grand house on the hill. It had been Claudine at whom he had wanted to flaunt it, Claudine whom he had expected to entice within its walls, Claudine whom he had expected to stalk its floors with her proud chin high while she held sway over all social gatherings there. But gradually his plans for it had lost the flamboyance that would have made the right setting for Claudine's redheaded witchery, everything changing to take on instead the serene beauty that was Kate's, the house's simplicity echoing her quiet grace, its colors a reflection of her eyes and hair, and its mystery and coolness and deep warmth all compliments to her personality. She had seen it and not recognized herself because there was no lamp to light that was strong enough to banish the shadows of Harry and Claudine.

On the seventh day of March in the early hours Kate was delivered of a strong and healthy male child. Daniel, who had waited in his grand and lonely house until sent for, came wildly galloping through the pinkish dawn and the noisy twitter of stirring birds. Jassy, who had chosen out of loyalty to stay on at Honeybridge with Kate, much as she would have preferred to lady it at the new mansion, met him in the hall. He knew well enough that had there been any choice Jem would have preferred to remain in residence at Honeybridge with them, but with the championship bout drawing near and training at its peak his old trainer did not care to let him out of his sight.

"How is Kate?" he asked Jassy at once, not completely trusting the word of the servant sent to fetch him, who had said there was no cause for any alarm.

"Somewhat exhausted by a long and difficult labor, but otherwise she and the baby are well."

He waited to hear no more, darting on up the stairs, and when he reached Kate's bedroom he had to hold onto the brass knob of it for several moments to draw breath from his ride and stop himself from bursting in. Thus, to Kate, lying tired and tranquil, the babe in the crook of her arm, it appeared that he entered at a casual and uninterested pace, and she dropped her gaze quickly to their sleeping son, afraid to see enmity in his eyes, for they had not seen or spoken to each other since the day she had left him at Easthampton House. His hand, cool from the early morning air outside, took up hers and he placed a light kiss upon her fingers.

"I thank God that you and the child are both safe and well," he said quietly. Words such as any devoted husband might have made, except that with him she knew them to be spoken out of courtesy.

"Is Richard James not handsome?" she breathed, her eyes still on the infant. They had decided on the names long since, Richard having been her father's name and James was after Jem, a natural choice for godfather.

"He is indeed." Daniel looked down with an overwhelming, choking pride at the little pink, wrinkled face under a crown of hair as dark as his own. Tentatively he reached out a loving fingertip and touched the soft cheek. Pain that Kate should have kept him at a distance at the time of birth, not asking him to be near, twisted like a knife in him and she had made her present distaste at his presence plain by the way she was deliberately concentrating her attention away from him. Who would have thought her capable of such cruelty? Kate the gentle, Kate the kindly, Kate the generous, who out of the perfection of their shared physical passion had produced the son whom she intended to keep at Honeybridge away from his charge. But that he would not allow. Kate might choose to deny him herself, but he would have his son. When the boy was weaned he would take him away to Easthampton House, but it was not the time to tell Kate that now. Let her have her hour. His was to come. He could not live the rest of his life without either of them.

"I can see you are wearied by all you have been through," he said, "and I must leave you to rest, but not before I have given you a birth gift, which I hope will please you." He took from his pocket a string of pearls, which he looped about her neck. Before she could utter a word of thanks he had gone from the room.

She looked down at them lying against the beribboned bosom of her nightgown, and gathering them up in her palm she pressed them to her lips while the babe she cradled, the bed she lay in, and the room itself were lost to her sight in the cascading overflow of her tears.

Four weeks later Eliot Singleton baptized Richard James in the church that stood within sight and sound of churning shingle under the splashing waves. Jem and Sir Geoffrey stood as godfathers while Jassy, who had carried her nephew into church, undertook the role of godmother. Daniel, who had called in regularly at Honeybridge to see his son, had driven Kate to the church in his curricle and was at her side throughout the service. Afterward on the neutral territory of The Warwyck Hotel a cake was cut and wine drunk to the baby's health by the small group of those who had attended the christening.

Eliot, prompted by Sarah, took the opportunity to draw Daniel aside when he turned from conversation with Lady Margaret. "I have known you long enough to speak frankly, Daniel," he said without preamble, "and it is a cause of deep distress to those who have come to know you well that all is not as it should be between you and Kate. It is neither natural nor normal that you should reside in one house and your wife in another. If you have quarreled let me act as go-between and bring you together again."

Daniel took a mouthful of wine from the glass he held. "Nothing can bring us together. The gulf has widened beyond all chance of bridging it."

Eliot shook his head. "That is something I refuse to believe. Remember that to forgive is divine."

"It is not a question of forgiveness." Daniel replaced his emptied glass on a waiter's tray and took a full one in its place. "I think both Kate and I could manage that if there was nothing else in our path."

"But what could there be of any importance to compare with the unity of your marriage?"

"Nothing, when you put it like that. But sadly some marriages are doomed before they start." With that final remark Daniel drifted away. Not for Eliot's ears or anyone else's the stated fact that his estranged wife had ever been in love with his brother. Or that he had been caught in the net of another woman's spell, which held him enmeshed in spite of his love for Kate.

The following day Jem called on Kate at Honeybridge House. "Ye said yesterday at the hotel that there was something ye wanted to see me about, ma'am."

She nodded, not sitting down as she bade him, but pacing a step or two restlessly before swinging round to face him. "It's only a matter of days until the championship bout is held at Chichester. I want to see Daniel fight."

Jem was taken aback. "Ye know that's not possible."

"I'd make sure he did not see me. Not like last time. But I want to be there."

Jem thrust himself up from the chair abruptly, showing that he was not prepared to discuss it with her. "I don't like to refuse ye, but I must for Daniel's sake. Ye'll get no help from me."

"Jem! Please." She caught at his arm in appeal.

He shook his head firmly. "Ye couldn't sit with the common herd and there'd be no means of smuggling ye to the ringside. Added to that I'd not risk Daniel catching a glimpse of ye as he did before, 'cos ye know what happened then. No, ma'am. Ye must put all thought of going anywhere near the mill right out of yer head. It'll be no place for ye. Ye want Daniel to win, don't ye?"

"You know I do," she replied fervently. Then seeing by his expression that it would be useless to try further persuasion she let him go without saying any more. But the idea of attending the fight remained with her. She turned over in her mind how she might manage it, forming her own plan.

On the afternoon before the championship bout she joined the crowd lining the route out of Easthampton that Daniel was to take. She had not been at the house when he had called earlier in the day, but fortunately Jassy had been at home to give him their good wishes, and he had gone into the nursery to see Richard in his crib.

All around her excitement was high. Local people and the season's early visitors alike were caught up by the prospect of having a new British champion rise out of their midst, and the betting on the result of the forthcoming bout was fast and furious. Some of it was going on behind Kate in a new tavern which had been opened on the premises formerly owned by Thomas Brown, who had been overtaken by ill health in the autumn and forced to retire. Some said it was no more than a fine excuse to save his face over slowly being squeezed out of business, but others less kindly disposed toward Daniel said he had been driven out through the trouble over the bathing machines and the shingle. But whatever the truth might be, Brown had left the resort and gone to live with his sister in the country.

"Here he comes!" The shout went up as Daniel's carriage was seen leaving the forecourt of Easthampton House, and the sun flashed on the spinning wheels and the polished paintwork as it took the drive that looped like a ribbon to the open gates below.

Had Daniel been royalty he could not have had a better send-off. People waved and applauded while he acknowledged it all with an unusual modesty, in spite of his customary wide grin and confident air. To Kate's eyes as he went flashing past he looked almost shy. He is touched by such good wishes from his resort, she thought. There was much in Daniel that was vulnerable, a deepness to the heart that few suspected.

With everyone else she waved him out of sight, Jem at his side.

Then the crowd began to disperse and as she moved away someone spoke her name.

"Kate."

With a start she looked up into a familiar face that she had not
seen for several months. "Harry!" she exclaimed. "What a surprise. How well you look."

He did look well and also older with a new presence to him, a
poise and a sophistication that had not been there before. His
clothes were the latest in fashion and of good quality, well cut
with the unmistakable stamp of a London tailor. Only his smile
held the same boyish charm, but it enhanced the face of a man
experienced and knowledgeable.

"And you, Kate? Jassy wrote that you had recovered from the
accident and again to tell me that I have a nephew."

"I have never been in better health and Richard is thriving.
What brings you to Easthampton?"

They had fallen into step and before he replied to her question
he invited her to drink chocolate with him at The George IV
Hotel where he had stayed overnight. Once they were settled at a
table in a bow window with a view of the sea he explained.

"Firstly I came to see you," he said, but in such calm and ordinary tones that any fear she might have had of yet another
distressing scene between them was lulled. "Secondly, I am en
route to Chichester where I intend to see that brother of mine become Champion of England."

"Does he know?"

He gave a shake of the head. "Daniel and I have not been in
touch since that black day last August and that is how it will
remain, but nothing could keep me from the fight." At that point
the chocolate was served and as she poured it into the gilt-rimmed
cups he continued: "I am told that you and he are parted."

Her face took on a hollow look. "It is the truth, but I'm still his
wife, so do not—"

He interrupted her. "I have not come back to Easthampton to
cause you any more unhappiness. There is just something I must
ask you. Jem said he thought you had always been fonder of him
than any of us realized. Is that so?"

The strained expression on her features deepened. "It is, but Daniel would never have welcomed that knowledge and it would have been a burden to him. That is why I never wanted him to discover how I felt."

"Is that the reason why you never told me? You were afraid I would blurt it out." When she nodded he smiled wryly. "None knew better than you my headstrong ways in rage and jealousy. To me it has always been that Daniel has had everything that I have always wanted." With the shadow of regret darkening his eyes he regarded her across the table. "To you he has always come first, and I was too blind with love to see it."

"But you have made a new life for yourself in London," she said quickly, wanting to stave off any protestations of continued love on his part. "You look most prosperous and all must be going well."

"It is, I'm glad to say." Again a smile curled the corners of his mouth with a certain wryness. "Since I cannot have you I must compensate myself with a financial success to equal Daniel's. It drives me on and there is no reason why in the future I should not meet him at the same level. Heaven alone knows why, but I seem to have a gift for making people want to buy what I have to sell, and I have been lucky in purchasing for myself some apparently worthless land in London which I sold at a handsome profit some two months later. I learned much of such dealings in Easthampton." His hand paused in stirring the chocolate in his cup. "Today, from you I have learned most of all."

She knew he had at last come to an acceptance of the fact that he could fight everything to get her except her love for Daniel. That had defeated him. They talked on for a while longer and then he went with her to Honeybridge where Jassy welcomed him with a hug and the joyful laughter of surprise. Kate left them talking together and went upstairs to see to the baby. When she came down again Harry broke off his conversation with Jassy.

"I hear you intend to leave for Chichester before dawn tomorrow and attend the championship bout in borrowed male attire," he stated incredulously, not without a twinkle of amusement.

Kate looked accusingly at Jassy, but the laughter rippled in her voice. "You told him." Then, still on a note of mischief at her own audacity, she explained her reasons to Harry. "I want to see Daniel win and I dare not go in any other way. Jassy told me once of a maid in this house who sometimes went to prize fights in her brother's clothes."

Laughing himself, Harry shook his head at the preposterous notion. "You will look enchanting but unconvincing, my dear Kate. I have a better idea. I shall escort you to Chichester myself and I promise you that you shall see the fight without having to resort to such subterfuges as male disguise. A closed carriage at a well-secured vantage point will allow you to view without being viewed in turn."

"That's much better," Jassy said with relief. "I have been worrying about Kate alone in the enormous crowd that will collect. But what about accommodation?"

"Kate shall have my room and I'll bed down on somebody's floor. Chichester will be full of acquaintances known to me from pugilistic circles."

Thus it was settled, and Kate departed with him shortly afterward, Richard being left in Jassy's charge. When they drew near the ancient city the traffic on the road became congested and Kate was reminded of the day she followed the mill from Harley Heath to the Lewes vicinity. Once in the city the crush became worse, but Kate did not mind the constant holdups in the narrow streets, for there was much to look at in the decorations, which ranged from special shop window displays to private windows draped in bunting and banners bidding welcome to Daniel Warwyck and the present champion, Ned Barley, whose boast was that he was invincible. The inns appeared to be crammed with customers, some spilling outside, and from the carriage seat beside Harry, who was concentrating on getting the horses through to the hotel of their destination, Kate watched the surging panorama going on all around them. Once she thought she saw a man she recognized in the crowded doorway of The Fox and Hounds Inn, but she had looked on him for no more than an instant before he had pushed himself in through the door and out of her sight.

Then a street band caught her attention, making her smile at its cheerful din, and it was not until later that she realized she had been left with an odd disquiet as if something at the back of her memory had been stirred, but whatever it was she could not recall. Perhaps the man had been one of the few who had chosen to be obstreperous when she had personally served the tea and coffee to the laborers at the yard, but it was strange that it had caused a chill to lie at the pit of her stomach.

Harry's room was booked at The Dolphin where they found the hallway jammed with new arrivals from stagecoaches and other vehicles clamoring for accommodation, all refusing to accept that everything in the whole city had been booked long in advance. Kate was shown up to the room while Harry went out to seek someone of his acquaintance who would have floor space under a roof or in a stable loft to share with him.

Everywhere the streets, which branched out from the stone market cross in the four points of the compass, were alive with people and equipages as far as the eye could see. If such a crowd had assembled on the eve of the bout, whatever would it be like on the morrow?

Harry returned at the dining hour with the information that everything was organized, both to getting her a good view of the mill next day and obtaining a bed for himself that night.

"My luck was in," he said, going downstairs with her to the paneled dining room. "I met the great Tom Cribb himself, who hailed me, wanting to know where my brother was to be found. I had already heard that Daniel was staying at The Fox and Hounds in South Street, and then old Tom, who knows all the talk and gossip of the boxing world, asked me where I intended laying my head since I was no longer Daniel's bottle holder. When I explained that I was among those hundreds of The Fancy without a place to sleep he insisted I make use of one of the extra truckle beds being put up for his company in his rooms at The Swan. Naturally I accepted with gratitude."

They came into the dining room where they were shown at once to a table, and as soon as they had seated themselves Harry continued to give her other news he had gathered up, but she was mulling over the information that Daniel was staying at The Fox and Hounds, wondering why it should have relit a candle of unease within her. Then she recalled that the man she had vaguely recognized had been going into that very inn. There could be no connection, and yet—?

"You are not listening to me," Harry broke in gently over the menu. "I asked if you would like me to order for you."

"Please, do," she replied. His consideration left her free to search her memory again as to where she had seen that man in the street before.

Ned Barley arrived to stay at The Dolphin before they had finished dinner. Roaring cheers outside had announced his coming into the city, Daniel having enjoyed a similar ovation at an earlier hour, and when the present champion actually stepped into the hotel many diners leaped up from the tables to go to the doorway and applaud him. It was then, through some clearance of space, that Kate spotted Alexander Radcliffe with a party of gentlemen at a table at the far end of the long room. Thoughtfully she spooned her strawberry syllabub. Radcliffe was an old enemy of Daniel's. He would not be here to cheer Daniel on the morrow, but only in the hope of seeing him lose. Yet he had not joined the show of enthusiasm provided by Barley's supporters, merely giving a single glance over his shoulder at the commotion. Perhaps he had only come along to watch impersonally what was expected to be the best fight ever seen.

After dinner, the evening being fine and mild, she and Harry went for a walk as far as the Canal where reflected stars floated on the dark water. To her it was as it had been in the days of their friendship before his passion for her had erupted and changed everything, and she was content in his company, but how it was for him she could only guess. Many times she felt his eyes on her face as if he could not look enough upon her, knowing that such a time for them would never come again. He did not seem to mind her lapses into silence, but as he saw her back into the hotel she felt she owed him an explanation, and told him about the man she had seen.

"I find myself associating him with something evil that happened," she said. They had reached her door under the dark beamed ceiling of the corridor. "Something like—like"—it came to her—"fire. That's it. The fire at Honeybridge House." Her eyes became full of fear. "Now I know where I've seen that man before. He was one of the two attackers who tried to come in through the window. I injured one and the other—the man I saw today—must have been among those who escaped. He has come to Chichester to do Daniel some harm. Perhaps at Radcliffe's instructions! Daniel was convinced Radcliffe was responsible for all that happened last time. You must go to Daniel at once and warn him."

He took the matter somewhat less seriously, but he sought to quieten her. "It is almost ten o'clock and Daniel will have been safely in bed long since. You know Jem's rules about early nights before a fight, and especially so in view of what Daniel must go through tomorrow."

She refused to listen. "You must go to The Fox and Hounds at once or else I'll go myself. Radcliffe failed to bring Daniel down last time, but who can say that he is not going to try some other trick intended this time to ruin his chance of winning the championship? If Daniel fails to beat Ned Barley this time there'll be no second chance."

He gave in, not looking forward to blundering in on his brother, who would be less than pleased to see him at any time, to say nothing of being woken up from essentially needed sleep. "I will go. Do not worry any more. Daniel shall be warned."

"Thank you," she whispered tremulously, lowering her head and pressing her fingertips against her closed eyes.

He hesitated a few moments longer before departing. "Do you love him so much?" he questioned in a cracked voice.

She raised her face again. "With all my heart. From the moment I first saw him in the market place at Brighton. He is more to me than life itself."

In a poignant silence he nodded once and then again. After that he went away down the crimson-carpeted stairs and she entered her room, anxiety still not lifted from her mind. Until the fight was over and Daniel had won she would know no peace of mind.

At The Fox and Hounds two shadows moved stealthily in the courtyard at the rear of the inn. They had climbed over the flint wall and both were careful to avoid the bright patches of lamplight thrown down by the open kitchen windows from which came a noisy clatter of crockery, the clash of cutlery on trays, and the sizzling of joints on spits and other cooking foods. Having scouted out the area earlier in the day both kept clear of the litter of crates and empty bottles, the drained kegs and finished barrels. Directly above an outhouse roof was the latticed window on the first floor that opened into an alcove, which was secluded from a corridor and gave access to the suite of two rooms to the right of it. It was the two windows of these adjoining rooms that held the men's attention, for the first one was still lighted where the other leading out of it was in darkness.

"It's an hour since Warwyck's light went out," one muttered to the other. "'E should be asleep by now, and if 'e ain't it won't make no difference. Come on."

The speaker was given a foothold on the linked hands of the other and the litheness of much experience clambered soundlessly onto the outhouse roof. He reached down a hand and helped to haul his companion up after him, and then with ease he was able to open the latticed window above it, having first made sure that there was no one near. It was a deal easier to enter than Honeybridge House. From below on the lower floor in the tap-rooms and parlors there rose the muzzled buzz of many voices, guffaws and shouts, and somewhere there was drunken singing.

"All clear," he whispered to his fellow felon, who climbed in after him. After pressing an ear to the door to make sure there was no conversation within or any other sound to indicate that Jem Pierce was not alone, he breathed heavily through his wide nostrils. "Right. Get outta sight. 'Ere goes." He drew a knife from his belt and held it behind him while the other man followed suit with a heavy cudgel and stepped back into the corner of the alcove. Then he rapped quietly on the door with his knuckles.

Jem was sitting at the table reading a newspaper by lamplight. Although he made sure Daniel went to bed extra early on the eve of a fight, he himself always found it difficult to get to sleep on such occasions. Excitement, nerves, and a constant churning over in his mind of the tactics his fighter should use made it impossible for him to retire until long after his usual hour. At the sound of the tap on the door he lowered the newspaper with a frown, having left instructions at the desk that on no account was Daniel to be disturbed and all callers and would-be well-wishers were to be kept at bay. He rose from the table and went to the door, but did not open it.

"Who's there?" he questioned, keeping his voice low in order not to waken the sleeper in the adjoining room.

"Urgent message for Mr. Pierce from Mr. Jackson."

Jem put his hand on the key to unlock the door. Gentleman Jackson was to be Commander-in-Chief of the championship bout, and since he had called on Daniel that evening before going on to The Dolphin to greet Barley it could only be some unexpected development of some seriousness that necessitated a message that could not wait until morning. No one knew better than Jackson the importance of getting a good night's sleep before a bout and he would not willingly risk the waking of Daniel through the delivery of a note. But past experience put Jem on his guard. There was always the chance that it was a hoax being used by some member of the press anxious to gain a foothold for an interview on the eve of the mill, or even some enthusiastic member of The Fancy who had slipped past the vigilance downstairs to get a private word with the pugilist on whom he intended to wager his money.

It was this sense of caution that made Jem stand behind the door as he clicked the key, ready to put a shoulder against any unwanted invasion, but the man standing in the alcove, which was dimly lit by rays from a candle sconce in the main corridor, merely handed out a folded sheet of paper. Jem widened the aperture, reaching out his hand. It was then that the intruders acted. The knife flashed toward Jem's heart, but the angle at which he stood by the door deflected both aim and blow. Nevertheless it slashed home and as he staggered, the other attacker was on him like a spring-heeled jack, bearing him backward so that he fell bleeding across the bed, which creaked and swayed, but still prevented any thump of his falling body on the floor to alert anyone in the room below. The scuffle, brief though it was, was heard by Harry as he reached the head of the stairs, having got past those on duty below only by producing papers to prove his identity as Daniel's brother. With Kate's premonition of danger coming suddenly alive in his mind he swung up his cane, which he had bought for his protection in the London streets, and pressure on a section of the silver knob of the cane caused a sharp blade to snap out at the end of it.

At a run he reached the door, which had been closed again. Throwing it wide he burst upon the scene of Jem lying with eyes closed and blood pouring from him as the two intruders were cautiously opening the communicating door into the darkness of the adjoining room.

"Daniel!" Harry roared with all the force of his lungs and charged forward. Neither of the intruders panicked, the profession of thuggery they followed having toughened them to be ready for any emergency, and the man with the knife turned to defend himself against Harry while the other plunged on into the bedroom to carry out the assignment for which they were to be handsomely paid.

Daniel, roused from sleep by Harry's shout with an alertness that sprang from the pitch of his training, sat bolt upright in bed in time to see figures silhouetted against lamplight in the framework of the opened doorway, and one detached itself to rush toward him with a cudgel upraised. In the same instant his primed reflexes hurled him to one side of the bed to avoid the descending blow aimed to break his legs. In a tangle of sheet and blankets his bare feet smacked down on the floorboards and his body showed pale in the dimness as he dodged another whirl of the cudgel, and the attacked became the attacker. The cudgel dropped to the floor from nerveless fingers as a punch to the ribs winded its owner, only to be followed by the smashing of jawbone. Daniel did not wait to see him fall, but dashed through into the bedroom where Harry, whose length of sword-stick had given him an advantage over the knife, had succeeded in cornering his prey.

"Drop the knife," Harry ordered, his blade point at the man's throat.

The knife dropped with a clatter. Daniel had turned to Jem, snatching linen from the bed to stem the awful flow. "He's still breathing," he exclaimed hoarsely. "I'll get help." Seizing Jem's dressing robe from a chair as he rushed by, he thrust his arms into it and sashed it about him as he ran to the head of the stairs and leaned over the balusters. "Help! Murder!"

A waiter appeared with startled face upturned. "What, sir?"

"I fear murder has been committed. Summon a doctor immediately and send assistance to deal with the captives." Not waiting to hear the cry of alarm being raised by the waiter he dashed back toward his quarters in time to see that Harry's prey had given him the slip and was making for the opened corridor window. With the technique of the throwing fall used so often in the ring, Daniel flung himself forward and brought the man crashing down. He was briefly aware of a stab of pain through his shoulder as they hit the floor, but he thought no more of it as he regained his feet and saw that the runaway lay sprawled in unconsciousness, completely stunned by the fall. Already people were thundering up the stairs, and leaving the felon to them he ran back into the room where Harry was holding his upper arm, his face drained white, a red stain about his cut sleeve.

"He had another knife concealed on him," he said, "and threw it as he made a bid for escape."

"You'll live," Daniel replied with brotherly bluntness, "but whether Jem will is another matter." Together they leaned over him and Daniel grabbed wads of fresh linen to press against the wound.

A crowd was gathering in the corridor and people came pushing in through the door, some to gape, others to deal with the unconscious man discovered on the floor of the adjoining room, and the landlord, who was a burly fellow, had difficulty in elbowing his way to the bedside. He showed his dismay at the sight of Jem and did not notice at first that Harry had also been knifed.

"A doctor 'as been sent for, sir," he said to Daniel. " 'E only lives across the street and'll be 'ere any second."

"Good," Daniel replied. "In the meantime clear the room of these people, get the two villains round to their senses, rope them up, and send for a magistrate."

As the landlord made to obey his instructions the doctor arrived, a path cleared for him all the way up the staircase and into the room. He was a young man, fresh come to his practice in Chichester, but he had been several months with a senior doctor in Portsmouth and had had good training in dealing with the knife wounds of seamen. His manner of speaking about Jem's injury still held nuances of that nautical experience. "A long slash, but clean," he muttered, going about his business with him, "and no important blood vessel severed. The patient has lost a lot of gore, but he looks to be a tough old walrus." Seeing Jem's one good eye flicker open, he smiled down at him. "It will take more than the stab of a knife to sign you off, my friend."

Jem was too weak to reply, but a corner of his mouth twitched as if he sought to confirm the doctor's statement.

When he had been stitched and bound up, given a dose of laudanum to diminish the pain and induce sleep it was Harry's turn to have his wound dressed. It was superficial but painful, and when the doctor left he sat very white and still in a chair. Daniel poured him a brandy and another for himself. Since almost all Jem's rules for the eve of a fight had been broken within the space of one short hour there was no point in keeping a small measure of brandy at bay. He handed Harry a glass and leaned his weight against the edge of the table as he took a swallow of his own.

"Now," he said, giving his brother a quiet grin, "tell me exactly where the devil you sprang from."

He listened attentively to all that Harry had to say. Then they talked more freely than they had done for a long time, and some part of what had been good in their relationship in the past came back to them. It was inevitable that Kate should figure in much that was said.

"I must get back to her," Harry said with effort, for he was fighting off a physical listlessness caused by his wound. "She was worried enough when I left, and some exaggerated tale may reach her at The Dolphin, because you can be sure every taproom in Chichester is already buzzing with what has occurred."

"You must spend the night here," Daniel insisted. "You can share my bed. I'll write to Kate and tell her briefly what has happened and reassure her that Jem is going to pull through."

Gratefully Harry stumbled off to bed while Daniel sat down at the bureau in Jem's room where they had been talking. When the letter was written he dashed sand on it, sealed it, and jerked the bellpull for a servant to deliver it without a moment's delay.

Kate, receiving the letter, read it through many times. At its conclusion he had invited her to sit with the distinguished guests who would have seats near the umpires, saying that he retracted all he had said in the past when he had forbidden her ever to come near a fight of his again. He added that he saw only honor in her presence and so would all else there when they heard that it was she alone who had saved him from suffering broken limbs and perhaps even losing his life.

The May morning dawned clear and blue with enough soft clouds about to reduce too sharp a sun brilliance in the fighters' eyes. A local woman, clean and neat in her person, had come to nurse Jem, who lay weak and still, yet was fully aware that it was the day he had long looked forward to with all his hopes since he had first given a sparring lesson to a tousle-headed young boy in a stableyard far away in Devonshire. When it was time to leave, Daniel took the hand of his trainer.

"I shall miss you today, Jem, but I will remember all you have said, all you have taught me, and I shall not fail you. Tom Cribb will second me in your place in the ring, but it is your voice I shall hear. Wish me luck, old friend."

Jem nodded, his disappointment at not being able to be at the bout so overwhelming that the tears ran down the side of his face. "Ned Barley is said to be the finest fighter the prize ring has ever had. Better than Mendoza or Tom Cribb in his heyday or any of the other big names. Beat him and ye'll have proved yourself the greatest of 'em all. Go then and conquer. Good luck go with you."

Daniel pressed his trainer's hand between both his own, conveying his thanks for the good wishes and all that had been done by Jem to bring him to this day of days. Picking up his hat, he put it on as he left the room, a tall and dashing figure dramatically dressed in dark blue, his snowy, high-collared shirt setting off the sky brightness of his neckerchief, his own prize-ring color.

Before he reached the hallway he was met by the magistrate's clerk with a letter for him. He read that both criminals had confessed to being paid to incapacitate him with broken limbs or fingers, but it had been made clear to them when given the villainous task that should it come to murder there would be no disappointment on the part of the person who had instigated the crime. The felon who had organized the attack would reveal nothing more, but his accomplice, anxious to save his own skin, had mentioned the name of a certain personage, a gentleman of repute, which had been let slip in his hearing. As a result a Mr. Alexander Radcliffe, presently staying at The Dolphin, had been questioned for two hours, but allowed to go again, there being no charge due to lack of evidence.

Daniel tucked away the letter. Radcliffe had had a narrow escape. He thought it would be a long time—if ever—before his old enemy risked setting some plot in action against him again. With a smile as much to himself as to those who applauded him in the hallway he passed by them and out into the bright day to be met with a great burst of cheering from the crowd waiting to see him. Flags waved and banners fluttered. Sir Geoffrey's stylish silver-gray barouche and four awaited him, with the two postillions liveried to match, and he stepped into it to further cheering.

The barouche followed a set route through the town, giving everybody a chance to see the challenger and afterward Ned Barley, who would follow in his backer's carriage a few minutes later. When Daniel passed The Dolphin he looked toward it although knowing that Kate, escorted by Harry and Sir Geoffrey at his request, would have already left to be at the ringside before his arrival. From every window of it faces were beaming down on him as had happened all along the route, many women waving scarves and handkerchiefs in his own color, and a billowing banner bore his name in sky-blue letters.

The site of the ring was some three miles distant with access to it supplied by a drawbridge across the Canal. The boards of it rattled under the wheels as the barouche carried Daniel into the heart of the great scene to roars of approbation as people leaped to their feet at his approach. Thousands had gathered there and more were arriving every minute in a constant river of humanity and equipages and horses. Wagons loaned by local farmers had been arranged in a wide circle, a stand of tiered benches had been put up, and the rest of the grass slopes were covered by a sea of people. In the middle was the ring itself, constructed of deal planks and built six feet off the ground with rounded posts and three rows of wooden rails. The usual roped area kept a clearance between the ring and the spectators while the umpires' specially erected platform was built high with other chairs set at a lower level to accommodate the backers and other distinguished guests. Already in her place was Kate and he was truly glad to see her there, authority given to the exceptional presence of a lady at the ringside by both Sir Geoffrey and Mr. Jackson, who stood by her chair. As soon as Daniel had alighted from the barouche he took off his hat, held it to his heart, and bowed deeply to her. Briefly their eyes held before he was surrounded by a number of well-wishers, but it had been long enough for a curious current of understanding to pass between them.

Kate pressed the white-gloved palms of her suddenly trembling hands together and she swallowed nervously. He knows, she thought frantically. Her innermost feelings were no longer hidden from him. It was not hard to guess the culprit. Her gaze shot toward Harry, who had his arm in a sling and was among those clustered around Daniel. How could he have been so cruel as to betray her? It only showed how right she had been to keep her love secret through so much heartache, so much despair. Would Daniel mock her in his new knowledge? Or would he use it in an attempt to bend her to his will? Yet there had been no steeliness in his eyes when he had looked at her, no show of triumph, only an intensely private quietness close to a homecoming.

Over the entire site more cheering was rising in waves. Ned Barley, the champion, had arrived with his backer in an emerald-green phaeton, the coachman in a coat of the same shade and everything en suite. He himself was attired in white with the vivid green of his neckerchief showing like a flag, and he was waving exuberantly to the crowd, first on one side and then on the other. He was a big, handsome man, a favorite with every rank of The Fancy from the humblest to the swells, for although he was a braggart and a blatant exhibitionist he always fought a clean fight, and in that he was well matched with Daniel.

At the ringside the two of them greeted each other. "You're a brave man aiming to put your mitts up at me," Ned jested good-humoredly. "I expect to make mincemeat of you."

"Is that so?" Daniel replied with a grin. "Well, one cannot become a champion without some punishment in the process."

Ned chuckled at the riposte, taking no offense, and together they turned with friendliness toward the ring, Daniel throwing his hat in first and Ned following suit. A coin was tossed and Ned won, choosing the corner with his back to the sun. Then a ladder was propped against the ringside by each of the opposite corners and both men climbed up and entered the ring at the same time, Ned bending between the rails, and Daniel swinging himself lithely over the top one. Kate, watching him, wondered if she was the only one to notice a flicker of surprise stab into his face as his arm took his weight. It was as if he had felt a totally unexpected twinge of pain, but it had gone as quickly as it had come and his confidence looked unassailable as he began to strip off.

Ned had just sighted her, but he was told who she was, and having earlier heard the tale, much embroidered along the way, of

how she had intervened in saving her husband's life, he promptly
showed his respect by bowing to her as Daniel had done earlier. As
before, it turned thousands of pairs of eyes on her and she acknowledged the champion's bow as she had her husband's, with
an inclining of the head.

The formality of the combatants removing their neckerchiefs
was observed, the seconds of each taking the respective colors to
the same post and tying them there in a soft swirling in the
breeze of sky-blue and emerald-green silk. It did not take either
man long to remove his polished boots and strip down to knee-
length milling breeches, canvas shoes were laced up, and then
both men were ready, each at the peak of health and spirits, their
eyes sparkling and animated at the prospect before them, giving a
hard choice to those placing last-minute bets. They shook hands
firmly. The seconds retired to their respective corners and for a
fraction of time a hush descended as all present seemed to hold
their breath. The great moment had come.

Like a clap of thunder thousands regained the use of their
throats as the two combatants opened the bout with individual
caution but no delay, Daniel stopping neatly a hit from Ned before endeavoring to plant a heavy punch, which was parried. Then
Ned got in lightly on Daniel's jaw, but immediately afterward was
caught in turn to the left and right of the head. The crowd roared
appreciation. Several former champions and other pugilists of
note among the spectators leaned forward eagerly, knowing by all
the signs that they were about to witness a mill the like of which
might never come again.

To Kate it was to prove three hours of pride and nightmare.
She knew nothing of the science of boxing, but even she could see
that here were two fighters unlike others in their unique skill and
the harlequin swiftness of their feet. In the punches that smashed
home they were as fierce as lions, their punishment of each other
merciless, but when one slipped or fell accidentally the other
sprang away and no tricks were played. Gradually her conviction
grew that Daniel was fighting with a handicap, the twinge of pain
she had observed earlier having grown into an agony that fre-

quently made him go white to the lips when he bored in with a right-hander on the mark, all his force behind it, or brought Ned to a fall with some other blow from the same fist. She noticed that when he was floored he never placed any weight on that hand or arm to rise up again, and that his seconds were equally aware of it, Tom Cribb paying attention to it between rounds and there was the gilding of brandy in the bottle put to his lips.

Round after round went by, some ending with the combatants crashing down together, others through individual floorings of intense ferocity. The blood was running freely, both of them stained across chest and arms, Daniel with a closed eye, and Ned with cheekbone exposed, but still the fight went on. Both men were exhausted, Ned swaying on his feet and Daniel having to shake his head at times to clear it, but their mutual onslaught continued, the thud of hits landed being heard all over the ring.

To Daniel it was as if his entire body had become a single paean of pain. What damage he had done to his shoulder when tackling the escaping felon the previous evening he had no idea, but what had been no more than a slight stiffness upon waking had become a raging torment that consumed every nerve and fiber of him as though he were upon a rack. Only one thing was clear to him, and that was he had already aggravated the injury to a point where this was his last fight and he would never enter a ring again.

Smash, smash, smash. Again his fists went home, his left still operating like the kick of a horse, his right weaker, but landing a punch on Ned's throat that sent him down like a shot. Another round was over.

The cold sponge being applied to his face by his bottle holder did nothing to quench the white-hot pain that was searing through him with such force that he found it difficult to breathe. Tom was giving him urgent instructions in his ear.

"You must finish him in this round. He's groggy and he's ready for it. Do you hear me, Daniel? It must be now or never."

Now or never. That had a ring of old Jem to it. Lurching up

from his second's knee, raw brandy still stinging his throat, Daniel advanced to the scratch with fists ready to meet with one supreme last effort an adversary equally primed to the kill.

It was, perhaps, the greatest round of them all, the courage of both combatants making up for a lack of speed and pitch of technique through a physical exhaustion that few other men could have survived on their feet. The climax came suddenly. After some severe infighting Ned planted a heavy facer. Daniel staggered, recovered himself, and then charged forward as though propelled by energy created by the pain he could no longer endure. He let fly with his left, caught Ned under the ribs, and finished him with a tremendous hit under the eye. Ned went flying backward, crashed through the rails, which splintered like matchsticks before his weight, and landed on the grass below where he rolled over and lay still. The fight was over.

The whole crowd leaped to its feet. The cheering and shouting reached a crescendo rarely heard before, and hats were thrown up in the air, many never to be found again. The whips leaped into action, moving forward on foot and horseback to keep back the enthusiastic spectators from swarming up to the ring. Daniel was aware of Tom and others clapping him on the back while the referee made his announcement.

"Gentlemen! I give you the new Champion of England, Daniel Warwyck!"

Tom threw a robe around him and Daniel raised his left arm in victory, his right hanging limply at his side. And he was looking for Kate.

"Daniel! Daniel! Congratulations."

There she was among those gathered on the grass just below the ring, rejoicing at his triumph, her eyes aglitter with tears she could not keep back at all he had been through with such dauntless courage and the present battered, bloodstained picture he presented, the condition of his battle-worn knuckles worse than they had ever seen before. As he came to the rails to lean over and speak to her, she ran forward, her bonnet falling from her head and dangling by its ribbons tied at her throat as she looked up at him. He thought she never looked more beautiful, with her hair left in soft disarray, tendrils wispy against her face.

"Wait for me. I will come down to you in a moment." Then he turned to inquire after Ned, and learned, that he was recovering consciousness and had suffered no broken bones in the fall. It was good news. He had never fought a braver man. Seeing the victor's colors being brought to him, he held out his hand to receive them and the blue and green silk squares were laid across his palm.

Kate was watching him, her own hands still raised against her breast and clasped in the emotional tension of all that had taken place. But when she thought with a joyous hope that he was going to look toward her again she saw his attention caught sharply and with impact by somebody else beyond her and away at the edge of the crowd. With a sudden terrible sinking of the heart she slowly looked over her shoulder and followed the direction of his gaze.

An elegant carriage with the hood down was drawn up by the bridge. How long it had been there was impossible to tell, but in it was a familiar figure clothed in deepest black, whom neither of them had seen for a long time. Her hair shone flame-bright against her crêpe-lined bonnet brim and the widow's veil that floated from it. Claudine had come home.

Daniel took a long, deep breath at the sight of her. Her provocative smile, full of unmistakable promise, was directed at him, and as if to emphasize she had come back to him with a new freedom she rose to her feet in the carriage, challenging him as once she had challenged him at their first meeting. She was waiting to receive the colors of victory. This time there would be no rejection of them.

But this time there would be no offering of them. His colors were for the woman he truly loved. The colors were for Kate. He stepped between the rails and went down the ladder where the whips kept back those who would have crowded upon him.

Kate stood quite still, her head high, courageous and loving, not knowing that victory was already hers in more ways than one.

Daniel knew he would never be quite free of Claudine's spell. The old, dark magic had still been there, the sexual allure ancient as time had still communicated itself to him across the distance of the crowded field, but Kate had taught him how to love and she alone was the woman he wanted to be with for the rest of his life.

Scarcely able to believe that it was happening, Kate saw him holding out the colors to her as he approached. She took them from him with the fingertips of both hands and pressed them to her lips, her gaze locked with his, letting him deep within her heart.

"I'll treasure the colors always," she whispered.

He put out his arm and drew her against him. "As I shall treasure you, my darling Kate." Careless of the crowd's continued exuberance, heedless of the shouts, the stares, the cheers, and the ceaseless buffeting in waves against the bastion of whips, his arm tightened about her and he bent his head to kiss her warm, responsive mouth with such love that to her they could have been entirely alone in that huge meadow instead of in a tiny section walled in on all sides by surging humanity.

Claudine observed them coldly from her distant carriage for a few moments and then she resumed her seat, drawing the widow's veil back over her face. Daniel had never loved her. He had taken her out of his hatred for her, thinking to stem his passion even as she had used him for her own purpose. Any foolish hopes she might have cherished that the narrow gulf between hatred and love had been bridged were dashed away. He would never know that a daughter had been born to her, for she had chosen to leave the infant in a convent where she would be well looked after and when older would probably take the veil unless that newborn mass of red-gold hair, so like her own, denoted a similar fiery character, in which case the nuns might do better to secure an early marriage for their charge instead. Claudine had no qualms about relegating all responsibility, having no maternal instincts, and she considered that the baby had served its purpose. By an odd twist of fate Lionel, although he had lived until the day of the child's birth, had been too ill to comprehend anything for several weeks beforehand; thus he had never known whether or not he had fathered the child. That was her secret. Let others think the babe had been stillborn. She had sold the villa in Italy and would never go there again. As Lionel's widow she had his fortune and hers to satisfy her every whim for the rest of her days.

Her coachman was having some difficulty in getting back across the bridge and they were proceeding at a snail's pace when some-one, making his way across on foot, drew level with her and raised his hat.

"Mrs. Attwood. Good day to you."

She turned her head sharply and saw it was Daniel's brother. He looked exceedingly well dressed, but had his arm in a sling. "Mr. Warwyck," she said in acknowledgment, but distantly. She had never spoken to him before this occasion although she had seen him often enough.

"Are you returning to Attwood Grange?" he inquired conver-sationally, keeping up with the carriage.

Her eyes were hard as agates beneath her veil. "No. I have changed my mind about opening it up again. It never meant as much to me as it did to my late husband. I am on my way back to London."

"May I accompany you? I would appreciate a ride. It will be impossible to get any sort of transport from Chichester."

Her tone was icy. "Could not your brother supply you with a carriage?"

"I borrowed one of his to bring his wife to Chichester and they will need it to transport a wounded invalid back home."

It sounded as if he had a tale to tell and her own company al-ways bored her. She had nearly gone insane in Italy. Alexander had changed his mind about visiting her, which was not surpris-ing, and Olivia in her letters had shown no disappointment, hav-ing news to tell that at last she was in the family way. But why should she grant a favor to Daniel's kin? It was her last chance to retaliate against the name of Warwyck, petty though she knew it to be.

"Then look elsewhere for your transport, sir. I should not wish to be seen in the company of anyone connected with a common pugilist."

At that point the coachman spotted a break ahead and with a snap of his whip took advantage of it, jerking Claudine's haughty profile away from Harry's sight, leaving him glaring after her for a few moments before he fell in again with those of the crowd jostling along in the wake of the elegant wheels. Shortly afterward he happened to overtake her, her carriage caught in a jam of other vehicles, and was near enough to hear her utter a vexed and hopeless little laugh.

But it was not the delay that had caused that odd sound to come from a widow in deepest mourning. Reaction to Daniel's final and utter rejection had set in and she was trembling so much that her veil was shivering. Her pride was devastated and her self-respect had suffered a mortal blow. She had thought to bring him running and he had shown her that she had lost him beyond recall. A void stretched before her that she did not know how to fill, but fill it she would with other men, other passions, other pleasures. She would never look back, never risk being humbled again, and take as she had always taken.

The laugh broke from her once more. It was the only way she could stop from weeping at the loss of the only man who would ever mean anything to her. How easily and insidiously hatred could turn to an all-consuming love.

Two days later Daniel drove Kate and Jem back to Easthampton, keeping an easy pace not to make an uncomfortable ride for his old trainer, who lay propped against pillows, blankets over him. It seemed providential to Daniel that Harry had left behind at Chichester the plain carriage that was normally little used, because it was enabling them to return to the resort without being recognized, and it was no time to find the road blocked with cheering crowds when Jem had to be hastened into bed with all speed.

He took a fork when they drew near the outskirts of Easthampton and when he would have taken another to lead him to Honeybridge House Kate spoke from where she sat beside Jem.

"You're taking the wrong road."

"But—" He twisted in the driver's seat to look back at her and then knew by the way she was looking at him what her meaning was.

"Let's go home," she said softly, her eyes smiling, "home to Easthampton House."

He returned her smile, holding her gaze lingeringly, wanting to kiss that wonderful mouth of hers, wanting to touch and love and gather her to himself, but that would come a little later.

"Home it is," he said. The whip cracked out above the horses' heads, and forgetting momentarily the invalid in the carriage he sent them galloping with manes and tails flying until Kate cried out for him to slow down.

At the steps of Easthampton House servants came running to carry Jem indoors, and hand in hand Daniel and Kate followed. On the threshold he drew her to him and kissed her, intending a kiss of welcome, but such was his love for her that once his mouth was on hers he could not bring himself to leave it. Thus were they sighted from the lane and the shout went up.

"Warwyck is home!"

It seemed as if the whole resort heard it. Within minutes a huge crowd had gathered from all directions and was streaming through the gates and up the drive, waving streamers and banners and flags, cheering and shouting. Somewhere in the midst of it a band was thumping drums and blowing bugles. Still the people came until a sea of them was spread down the entire slope of the hillock and out across the green to the shore. Kate would have left Daniel to the acclamation but neither he nor the crowd would let her go, and at his side she stood smiling and waving until neither of them could wave any more, and at last they turned into the house. With the coming of darkness bonfires were lit on the beach, a procession with flares followed the lanes like a bright and flickering snake, and the celebrations continued until dawn.

During the weeks that followed, laurels of every kind were heaped upon Daniel as the new champion. He attended innumerable banquets, benefits, and receptions held in his honor, and received a silver vase, entitled the Championship Cup, of elegant proportions and massive weight. In addition he saw the best doctors in London, but the injury to his shoulder, slight enough when it had occurred, had been aggravated beyond measure by his treatment of it during the championship bout, and there was no chance of his ever being able to fight again.

At a benefit at Fives Court he announced his retirement from the prize ring. Jem had recovered sufficiently to be able to accompany him, and thus was there at the close of Daniel's pugilistic career as he had been at its birth. Never had a bigger crowd of The Fancy gathered at Fives Court. When Daniel stepped up on the stage the ovation delayed by several minutes the special presentation. At last Mr. Jackson was able to make himself heard, and Daniel received from him on behalf of The Fancy a magnificent belt in the sky-blue and emerald colors of the late fight, its clasp a pair of fists worked in gold and bearing an inscription. There was more applause when he buckled it on, and then Mr. Jackson concluded what he had to say.

"There is one thing more that is to round off a career in the ring that will go down in the annals of boxing history. As you know, His Majesty King George IV was a keen follower of the ring in his days as Prince of Wales and later as the Prince Regent, and he still holds the greatest respect for the profession. He was my own personal backer during my days as a fighter and I was among those pugilists commanded to form a guard of honor at Westminster Abbey at his coronation. Today I received a communication from the Palace telling me to present Daniel there a week from tomorrow. His Majesty wishes him to go through the whole fight by describing every punch and blow to him. Members of The Fancy—I give you a Champion of England without equal: Mr. Daniel Warwyck."

The whole vast assemblage stood in thunderous homage to Daniel, and a considerable time elapsed before the applause subsided to allow him to speak.

"Gentlemen, I thank you for your kindness to me today and throughout my time in the ring. May your prize purses, which launch every beginner and sustain the glorious science of self-defense in this country of ours, never fail you."

He went down from the stage. All present rose again from their seats to applaud as he made his way across the court. His back was clapped and there were shouts that the ring would never see his like again. With Jem, who was unashamedly wiping his eye with a handkerchief, being much moved by the whole event, he went out to a waiting carriage. Together they returned to Easthampton.

Kate came running across the hall of Easthampton House to meet them and she flung herself joyfully into Daniel's arms, her own locking themselves about his neck. Jem, seeing how ardently they kissed, shook his head with a smile and went on into the drawing room where the lamps were lit and the windows stood open to the starry night. As usual Jassy was out with her beau, chaperoned by the young man's older sister, and Jem realized that there would be only three of them again at table when he sat down with Daniel and Kate to a late supper. The three of them. It wasn't right. Neither of them was aware of it but he had become an intruder. Jassy, caught up in her own social whirl and rarely to be seen around the house, had no such misgivings about her position there, but that was because she was expecting to be betrothed soon and was already looking forward to a home of her own.

He sat down heavily in a wing chair, thankful to rest after the long journey that had been made in a few hours, and looked about him at the beautiful sea-green room. It was not that the elegance of the mansion overwhelmed him, for Kate's moving into it had changed it from a showplace into a home, the whole house becoming imbued with her own warmth and happiness as if she had made it come alive with love. In fact, that was it. She and Daniel were so lost in love that for a while they needed no one else. It was more like living with a bride and groom than a couple wed for nigh on three years. He would have to go.

Over the supper table there was so much animated talk between Daniel and Kate about his farewell to the prize ring that day and the forthcoming visit to the Palace that it was not until the meal was almost over that Jem managed to broach the subject.

"Ye know, it weren't only ye, Daniel, who retired from the ring today. It were my retirement too, and I'd like to mill my way now into old age with a place of my own."

They both looked at him in consternation and startled dismay. "You can't leave us," Kate exclaimed. "You're one of the family. You belong here."

"It's out of the question," Daniel stated as if that put an end to it.

Jem gave his head a shake. "Forgive me for correcting ye, Mrs. Warwyck, but I don't belong. Ye and Dan have each other and yer baby son. God will that ye'll have many more children to fill the rooms under this roof. I'm asking ye to rent me Honeybridge House. It don't look right to see it shut up and since ye, ma'am, won't let it be sold I'd be glad to live out the rest of my days there." His eye twinkled. "It ain't too far for young Richard to walk down to see me when he's old enough, and I reckon I'll still be able to teach one more young 'un how to put up his mitts and learn him the patter and the flash."

Thus the matter was settled. That night before getting into bed Kate stood at the open window and looked out on the moonbathed resort and the opal waves beyond, an aura of reflected light about her loosened hair, the mild sea breeze billowing her robe.

"I'm glad Honeybridge House is to be lived in again," she said softly.

Daniel came and put an arm about her waist before raising her chin gently with his fingertips to look down into her face. "You are not homesick for it, are you?"

She smiled. "No, my love. I'm with you and never wish to be anywhere else."

His smile answered hers and when she laid her face against his chest his arm held her closer. Over her head he looked down at the resort where lights still twinkled in profusion. He and Kate had come through much tribulation before discovering how much each loved the other and all was well, but he did not suppose that the years ahead would be devoid of troubles and difficulties not only for the two of them, but for the resort as well. What was more, the shadow of Claudine would never be entirely banished. But Kate in her wisdom knew that well enough and was the stronger for it. Kate's love was his haven as once Honeybridge House had been hers. Kate, the beloved, was his citadel. Kate.